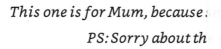

This one is for Mum, because

PS: Sorry about th

CW00520537

Thanks and acknowledgements

A huge thank you to my girlfriend for not only creating the book cover but for keeping me going when real life kept getting in the way of getting this finished, for your honest criticism and encouragement, but most of all just for being there with me. I love you very much.

Special thanks to my good friend, Alma, proud Texan, test reader extraordinaire and geek confidante.

Finally, I would like to thank all of you writers of books, films and TV shows for all the inspiration, learning and pleasure you've all given me over the years. You all helped write this book as much as I did.

I always love to hear from my readers so you can find me here at thekingpin@hotmail.co.uk if you want to say hi

REVENANT DAYS

By Ian King

ONE

The numerals on the cheap digital clock beside the bed glowed a dim, red 6.30am and the radio alarm began playing for the briefest of seconds before a hand appeared from under the duvet and decisively silenced it. Daniel Cross sat up and groaned as he met the morning. Shafts of dawn sunlight speared through gaps in the ill-fitting curtains and he squinted and cursed half-heartedly as he swung his legs from the narrow bed and padded naked to the bathroom.

The small bathroom had no windows and he cursed again with more feeling as the flick of a switch sent a brighter light stabbing into his eyes. Cross ran the tap and sluiced cold water across his face, palms rasping across a three-day growth of stubble. He was a big man, tall and broad of shoulder, his long arms cabled with muscle and his hands calloused and scarred. Cross stared into the mirror and appraised his bluntly handsome face.

Shit, he thought. *For someone who was dead this time last week, you don't look half bad.* His gaze travelled down to his chest, through the lightly tangled salt and pepper hair to his mysterious new scars. They covered the upper left of his chest in fluid, looping swirls. They weren't the vicious and jagged slashes left by a knife fight, though Cross wore some of those too, but scars with a hint of artistry, a hidden pattern. To the right of these, just above the clavicle, was the round, puckered scar that people of certain backgrounds would quickly recognise as a bullet wound.

Cross smiled grimly as he ran his fingers across the raised, baby-pink skin of his latest scars. *You're still kicking, sunshine. You're still kicking.* He turned on the shower and climbed into the tiny cubicle before the water began to warm, ignoring the cold and the hazy, unsettling memories it tried to awake. They scratched at the edges of his mind like prying fingers of ice trying to show him things he wasn't ready to remember just yet.

He washed quickly and efficiently and stepped out of the shower to roughly towel himself dry. Cross took a final glance in the mirror as he passed, rubbing a "that'll do fine" hand over his short-cropped hair and moved back into the cramped bedroom to get dressed.

A crisp white shirt, light grey suit and smart but functional black shoes. When you looked like Daniel Cross it always helped to at least dress respectably. He patted himself down for the obligatory keys, wallet and weapons check and then walked outside into the bright and busy London morning. It felt good to finally be out and he raised his face to the sun, enjoying the warmth on his skin that further banished the hidden, frigid memories that kept *scratch-scratch-scratching* at his brain. He'd been holed up in his tiny safe-house apartment for over a week now, resting, healing and planning and he'd been going stir-crazy. Enough was enough. Now it was time to get to work.

If all went well then someone was about to have a very fucking bad day.

Cross was, to put it bluntly, a criminal. He'd served his country through a number of grubby little wars and left the army with little more than a finely developed sense of cynicism, a shitty pension and a tiny piece of shrapnel still lodged firmly under his right arse cheek that ached when it rained. His very own rectal barometer.

He'd never got the hang of civvy-street and a normal life, and to his credit he really had tried. At least for a month or two anyway. When all was said and done though there were a lot of easier and quicker ways to make a living than enduring the water-torture drudgery of a nine-to-five. Add to that the fact that Cross had always enjoyed getting in a good fight now and again and life on the wrong side of the law suited him just fine thank-you-very-much.

Cross wasn't surprised that a fair number of villains were ex-military. Depending on which path you took during your service, military training might as well have been designed to turn you into a criminal. You learned when and how to fight, how to stay under the radar and disappear before popping up again under a different name and wearing a different face.

That pull to violence you were taught to resist was encouraged until snatching away a human life became as easy, and about as meaningful, as snatching your keys off the kitchen table, while during active duty the normal rules and all those little civilities that defined the social contract were thrown out of the window. For a soldier at war what was 'normal' became a very different animal.

Sure, there were plenty of soldiers who finished their tours and wanted nothing more than to get back to that sane standard of normal life at home, only to find they no longer fit the standard mould, or that they were particularly sane. Cross had known too many veterans who ended up putting a gun in their mouths after a few years of recurring nightmares, doomed relationships and hitting the bottle.

He'd ended up sharing a few beers with an old fella from the 22nd one night who told him: "There's no such thing as a soldier coming home without a scratch, Danny. Most of our scars just aren't on show." Cross agreed with him, mostly. Some soldiers might make it back, but they never really came home.

Of course, there were the soldiers like him on the other side of the coin. Those who found that they missed the rush, the savage glee that came with the chaos of violence, and paradoxically, the strange freedom that came with living within a very narrow set of parameters. At the sharp end of things it was as simple as it gets: kill or be killed and all the red-tape and meaningless minutiae the civilised world told you was important and shoved down your throat every day meant nothing anymore. A normal life just couldn't cut it after that so what the bloody hell were you supposed to do?

Ok, you could join up with one of the private military companies that the yanks loved so much but that was a little too close to being back in the ranks for a lot of square-bashers. The money was good and the dress-code better than army-greens but there was still a bit too much 'yes sir, no sir' involved, and in the current political climate you'd just end up shipped back out to the sand and taking pot-shots at Ali Baba again anyway.

Mercenary work was an option but that meant getting on the radar of too many intelligence agencies who never gave you a moment's peace, plus the fact that you'd spend half your time in some West African toilet of a country dodging machetes and Ebola, so no thank-you. No, being a villain was definitely the way to go.

If Cross had learned anything since leaving the military it was that when your tours were over and you came back home you found the people you'd supposedly been protecting, and especially those people who'd paid your pitiful wages and sent you to some shit-house to get shot at, didn't really give a fuck about you trying to get your life back to normal, so too bloody right he was going to look after himself first.

Cross worked as a free agent, claiming no allegiance to any of the dozens of crews operating out of London, a choice he made almost as soon as he left the army. Why swap one dickhead barking orders at you for another dickhead barking orders at you? Such a choice had its ups and downs of course and despite what proved to be a natural talent for navigating the murky, leech infested waters of gangland, Cross still managed to piss off exactly the wrong sort of people now and again, not that it worried him overmuch. Occupational hazard and all that.

In the main he managed to keep the right people sweet and to grease the right palms at the right times. He knew when it was better to ask for permission and when it was easier to ask for forgiveness, when to run, when to fight and when to keep his mouth shut and his head well down. Cross had a simple code that had served him well: Just don't fuck people about.

What you saw was what you got and what he said was what he meant. If Cross said he was going to do something for you, or to you, then he did it. Simple enough perhaps but still rarer than rocking horse shit in his chosen trade.

Cross always found a dark comedy in the fact that other criminals appeared to put so much stock in him being reliable and trustworthy. Being *honest*. He grinned as he thought of some of the toe-rags he'd dealt with over the years. Men and women who'd sell their first born with a smile for the right price lauding him for being someone they could count on, all because he'd done what they paid him to do and didn't fuck them over in the process like it was some almost unattainable virtue.

Cross wouldn't piss on any of them if they were on fire, but they paid well enough.

He headed towards Canning Town tube station to move further into the city and wipe the shit of East London off his shoes. He'd never liked it round here, even when he was growing up, and being forced to hole-up in a dingy, two-room flat above a bookies for a week had been torture. Cross had preferred getting shot at in Basra to this place. At least the weather was better.

Despite being just a stone's throw from the regenerated, fashionable and *"How bloody much for a pint?"* Docklands area, Canning Town remained (in Cross's scholarly opinion) a shithouse. He stopped at the entrance to the station and lit a cigarette as he leant against a wall and watched the grey-faced commuter horde scuttling past. He shifted as the still healing scars on his chest pulled tight and took stock of what he knew.

Not a fucking lot.

His memory of the night he died was hazy at best. There'd been a fight, he was certain of that much, and he was willing to admit that he'd probably lost that particular scuffle seeing as he ended up dead. The rest was just fragmented images and feelings. Cross remembered being tied to some sort of table with his body tightly bound and his head strapped down so he couldn't move a muscle.

The bastards, whoever they were, had even *Clockwork Orange'd* him and clamped his eyelids open. He remembered piercing lights shining on his face, shadows moving through the glare and serious eyes above surgical masks as they carved stinging patterns into his chest. He could almost swear he'd heard singing or chanting too, but that was bloody ridiculous. A stinging pain on the inside of his arm as they injected him with something and then everything slowed down. His vision dimmed, and suddenly he could feel his heartbeat reverberate through his body, felt it slow and stutter and then...stop.

He remembered falling. Not physically but like he was falling out of his body, his mind, as if the very core of him had somehow been torn loose and set adrift. Down and down and down through an endless dark and into a biting, malicious cold. Then he remembered the vast chorus of despairing screams and knew that one of those voices had been his. Cross shook himself free of his spider-web thoughts and lit another cigarette, glancing at the sun as if to reassure himself it was still there.

After that it was all blank. Cross didn't even remember getting away, if indeed he'd even managed to escape or had just been let go. One minute he'd been the unwilling star of what looked like some sort of surgical sacrifice and the next he was naked and bloody in an east London alleyway. He snorted a laugh. The poor cabbie he'd flagged down had certainly taken some convincing to take him back to his small safe-house in

Canning Town. Cross actually lived in the suburbs in a nice, unassuming two-bed terrace but if he'd gone back there he might as well have just put a bullet in his head and finished the job for them, whoever they were.

So he thought. *Here's what I do know: Sometime last week I was carved up like a Christmas fucking turkey, and they killed me while they were doing it. As if they weren't already taking the piss. I don't know the who or the why of it and I certainly don't know how I'm back here again, but someone does, and I'll bloody well find out what's going on if I have to kick down every fucking door and bust every head in London wide open.*

As plans went it was admittedly short on detail but sometimes it was best to keep things simple. Procrastination wasn't his style. Set a goal and go straight for it, resolving the details and removing the obstacles as you went, however you needed to do it. Cross believed in momentum and purpose, decisiveness and immediacy. If you moved quickly enough and hit hard enough then most of the time they never even knew you were coming.

He flicked his cigarette to the floor and walked into the station. It was still rush hour but Cross had never had a problem with crowds. Crowds were something for other people to deal with and everyone always seemed to find the room to move out of his way. Cross didn't even have to barge his way down the heaving stairs to the ticket barriers. He moved in his own space as people melted from the path of the big, grim-faced man who looked like someone had stuffed a particularly bad-tempered grizzly into a suit.

Cross headed west-bound and into the city proper. He was hungry, and he needed a bacon sandwich and information, in that order. Luckily, he knew just where he could get both. He stayed on the DLR until Bank station and then switched to the Central line for a short hop to Chancery lane and Mario's cafe. Cross had no idea where the name had come from as it had never been and probably never would be owned by someone named Mario, but then the name of a greasy spoon cafe could be anything as long as they served up a decent cuppa and a fry-up.

Mario's was actually owned by one Augustus Grantham, an ex-fence who, almost like something out of an old noir detective story, had finally gone straight when he met the love of his life. Well, more or less straight. A crook was always a crook to some degree and Cross knew that Gus made a point of keeping up with the tall-tales and escapades of his former colleagues, particularly when he could turn a profit from it.

He'd received a few lucrative tips from Gus over the years and they'd built up a wary kind of friendship, the sort characterised by favours done and favours returned with neither one having screwed the other over just yet. It wasn't much as friendships went, but in this business sometimes that was as good as it got.

As was his habit, Cross stopped across the road from the cafe and checked the place out through the wide and surprisingly clean windows while he had another cigarette. Marios was breakfast-time busy with what looked like the usual crowd.

A smattering of Financial Times types, who were too old-school for an iced Frappucino from Starbucks, had mugs of proper English tea while they checked the pink broadsheets. A few students sat in a group with their collective noses buried in iPads and MacBooks while the ubiquitous group of builders each demolished a large fried breakfast before heading onto site.

It was too early for most of London's slags and scumbags to be up and about and Cross was confident he could have his little chat with Gus on the quiet, so he crossed the road and entered the cafe, choosing an empty table in one of the back corners which gave him a clear view of both the interior of the cafe and the street outside.

He sat quietly and waited, ostensibly studying the menu on the table while his eyes surreptitiously scanned the busy room. Kate, the woman who'd changed Gus from the man who took everything from bent stereos to pilfered master-pieces off your hands to the man who fried your first coronary for you bustled about behind the counter, wiping down the surfaces for probably the hundredth time already that morning. She was a small, plain woman. Pretty enough in her own way but with a tired look that said she'd already worked far too hard for far too long with no end in sight anytime soon. Cross had always liked Kate. The feeling wasn't mutual.

Gus appeared from the kitchen with a mug of tea and a plate in his hand and he waddled towards one of the builders to deliver his cholesterol-rich bounty. Gus was a big man and Cross reckoned he'd probably been pretty tasty in a fight when he was younger but now he was just fat. His bald head gleamed with sweat from the heat of the kitchen and he caught Cross's eyes as he paused to wipe some of the excess away from his forehead with the tea towel that dangled from his apron.

His eyes widened and he stood in the middle of the room with the tea towel frozen half way to his face. Cross raised a hand in greeting and let the slightest hint of a smile curl one corner of his mouth. Gus managed to nod back and then motioned for Cross to wait while he walked back to the counter and conferred with Kate. The look she shot towards Cross was just as surprised but far less welcoming. While the two exchanged hushed and heated whispers, Cross slipped his gun from the back of his trousers and held it under the table.

The fat ex-fence walked back to Cross and squeezed his bulk into the chair opposite. He nodded another greeting. "Morning, Dan. Got a bacon roll and a cuppa on the way for ya." He was a study in nonchalance and Cross grinned. You could never let people see you were rattled in this life, particularly those you might count as friends. "Lovely, cheers, Gus. How've you been?"

Gus shrugged. "Can't complain," he said. "Better than you by all accounts, aren't you supposed to be dead?" Cross laughed. "Apparently I got better." Gus snorted a laugh of his own, some of the tension leaving his eyes. Kate arrived with the promised bacon roll and cuppa and gave Cross an icy nod as she put them down in front of him. Cross smiled his thanks and Kate left without a word, squeezing Gus's shoulder as she walked past. Upon reaching the counter she surveyed the room to make sure her actual, paying customers were all settled and then walked out to the kitchen.

Gus looked slightly embarrassed. "Sorry about that, mate she's…" Cross waved the apology away. "Forget about it, I doubt many people would be too pleased to have a dead bloke walk into their place." Gus leaned forward with his elbows on the table while Cross took a big bite of his bacon roll and then spoke through the mouthful. "So, what do you know?"

"Me? Why would I know anything?"

"Yes, you. We both know you still keep your ears to the ground and your fingers in the pies. Let's face it, you're probably about the closest thing I have to someone I can actually trust." Cross grimaced and then took another bite. "Fuck knows I don't like saying it but I could use some help here." Gus shook his head and resignation warred with a tightly controlled fear in his eyes. "Sorry, Dan, I can't help you this time."

Cross's eyes went suddenly flat. "I've always liked you, Augustus but I'm more than happy to put a bullet in that belly of yours if I have to." He nodded downwards as he spoke and Gus moved his gaze towards Cross's hidden hand beneath the table. Gus knew that this wasn't an idle threat. Once Cross had decided on a course of action he'd follow it through without thought of consequence. When he was in that mind-set you were either with him or an unfortunate obstacle that had to be removed.

Cross was basically a decent enough bloke but there was something almost elemental about him. If he needed to he'd burn through you and yours like you weren't even there, leaving nothing but ashes in his wake and forgetting you'd even existed before they cooled. Gus stiffened in his seat and placed both hands flat on the table. He closed his eyes and sighed. "Bullet in the gut sounds good," he said. Both men were silent for a few, tense seconds and then Cross shrugged, clicking the safety on the gun and stowing it back in his trousers.

He took a swig of tea as Gus whooshed a sigh of relief and slumped backwards in his chair. Cross put the tea down and then put both his hands on the table where Gus could see them. "That bad is it?" he asked. Gus nodded soberly. "Yep. Don't take this the wrong way but I don't even wanna be seen talking to you right now, son."

"Can you stretch to a clue?"

Gus pointed upwards. "Shit floats; you wanna look to the top of the pile."

Cross snorted in sour amusement. "Of course I do."

Cross stood up and Gus stood with him. "Cheers for the breakfast mate. I'll see you later. Maybe." Cross clapped Gus on the shoulder and then walked from the cafe without a back-ward glance. The fat man stood for a few seconds and bowed his head slightly. He really did want to help Cross but there were some people you just didn't fuck about with. Daniel might have killed him, but he'd have done it quickly, which is more than he could have expected from the alleged perpetra-tors of Daniels' attempted murder. He shook himself and then moved back to the kitchen.

"Sorry, Kate, I know you don't..." Gus stopped as he walked into the kitchen to find Lincoln Barnes waiting for him. Barnes was a tall, well-built black man in his late twen-ties, wearing an expensive tailored suit with that noncha-lance and disdain that made it look like he had a team of as-sistants who spent hours dressing him every day. Lincoln also wore a pair of supple black leather gloves, an odd wardrobe choice for the time of year, unless you knew Lincoln which meant you knew exactly why he always wore them.

He was known for being as competent and reliable as he was ruthless, which came as no surprise seeing who he worked for. Gus wrung his suddenly nervous and sweating hands on his towel. "Uh, h-hello Linc," he stammered. "What can I do for you?"

Lincoln smiled widely. "Come on, Gus, I know you're not as stupid as you look."

"I didn't tell him anything, I swear!"

"Of course you didn't, that's because you don't know anything. I bet you've heard enough rumours to have given him something though haven't you?

"Look, I... hang on, where's Kate?

Lincoln flicked his eyes towards the large chest freezer next to him. "She's...chilling."

"You fucking bastard!" Gus lurched forward, reaching for a dirty knife that lay on the work surface to his right. He was brought up short by the small but deadly looking pistol that was suddenly in Lincoln's hand and pointing at his face. The fat ex-fence who was seconds away from being a fat ex-everything dropped the tea towel and rubbed a hand across his tear-filled eyes. His voice was quiet and resigned as he spoke. "Just tell me one thing; is any of it true? Did those mad bastards actually try it?"

Lincoln looked slightly pained. "Yes, they did. Against my advice I might add. We're not entirely sure it worked, although we think he brought something back with him." Gus grinned savagely at this. "And I bet that's pissing them right off isn't it? I hope Danny kills every fucking one of you!"

Lincoln shrugged. "Maybe he will, Augustus. You won't be there to see it though." There was a polite cough as the silenced pistol spat fire and the bullet tore through Gus's left eye and ripped into his brain. The fat man fell, dead before he hit the tiles on the kitchen floor.

Despite the ever-present gloves he wore, Lincoln still took a few sections of paper towel from a roll on the counter and thoroughly wiped down any surfaces he might have touched before carefully picking up the ejected shell casing from the floor and putting it in his pocket. He used the paper towels to open the back door and wipe down the handles before he walked from the kitchen without a backward glance, leaving the bodies of the closest people Cross had to friends going cold behind him.

This whole affair really was an insane mess, and in his opinion, both dangerous and completely unnecessary. But what the bosses wanted the bosses got and his job was to facilitate their desires as best he could. While they respected him enough to at least listen to his advice there was nothing to say they had to act on it. Lincoln thought he'd seen it all as he clawed his way free of the council estates and up through the ranks of one of the biggest and most ruthless gangs in London, but this? This was madness on an entirely new scale, and if he was honest with himself he had to admit he was actually scared.

He walked a few streets down from Mario's and beeped the locks of his Audi open before smoothly getting in and closing the door to shut out the smells and sounds of the London streets. Lincoln clicked on the stereo, closed his eyes and listened to Al Greens' gentle wail, stealing some time just for himself for a few, blissful minutes. He turned the stereo off, took out his phone and punched in a number that was quickly answered.

"The cafe is closed," he said and then listened for a few seconds before replying. "No, he didn't get anything useful apart from a free breakfast. I'll keep an eye on him and make sure he doesn't cause too much mischief until we're ready." Lincoln hung up the phone and started the engine, quietly pleased as always with its subtle, confident rumble.

He'd let Cross walk free from the café. The time wasn't right to pick him up just yet and he certainly wouldn't be doing that on his own. He pressed a hand to his side to feel the tenderness of healing ribs. Cross had thrown a wicked knee into him when they'd picked him up that night and even for six of them he'd been a handful.

Cross was a simple enough creature. Not that Lincoln underestimated him, he was too smart to do that, but he knew the man well enough. Cross would go to one of a few sources that he could bully the information he needed out of, and once he had that he'd be looking to kill certain people as pain-fully as possible. *Not this time, old friend. This is a different game to the one we usually play. Just how different remains to be seen.*

Lincoln Barnes had the unsettling feeling that with this particular change to the rules there wouldn't be many of them walking away from the field after the dust had settled and the blood had dried.

TWO

Miles Harrington settled back into the deep leather chair and placed his mobile phone on the small teak table next to him. He glanced distastefully at it as he picked up his cup of earl grey before raising the cup to his face and inhaling with evident pleasure. He crossed his long legs, ensured there were no errant creases in the trousers of his immaculate suit and then took a sip of the strong tea before relaxing with a contented sigh.

"Well?"

Miles glanced over to the next chair in the study. Marcus Harrington was almost a mirror image. Both twins shared the same slim and elegant build and dignified patrician features. Both reclined in deep, leather chairs as they enjoyed their first cup of earl grey, and both of them were utterly insane.

"Well what?"

Marcus raised his eyebrows, the only sign of his slight irritation and abandoned his tea in favour of his pipe. He took his time to fill the bowl and then to tamp down and aerate the tobacco before lighting it, enjoying the ritual as always. After a few long and luxurious puffs it was alight to his satisfaction and he turned his attention back to his twin.

"I assume that was Barnes with an update?" Miles smiled as he caught the sweet scent of the tobacco and then grimaced. "How can that stuff smell so fine and taste so foul?" It was a rhetorical question which Marcus duly ignored, content to smoke his pipe and wait.

Miles put his cup down and shifted in his seat to face his older brother. Marcus may only have been older by a matter of minutes, but tradition was a stern mistress to the Harringtons and first-born was first-born. The twins lived and worked together as equals but, in truth, it was equality as defined by Napoleon, that vicious and traitorous Orwellian swine.

"Yes, that was Barnes. He's tidied up a potential loose end and he's following Cross as per your orders." Miles wrinkled his nose in distaste. "As predicted, Cross is hunting for information. He went to see that odious little fence, Augustus, who can't have told him much."

Marcus raised his eyebrows. "Don't dismiss him so lightly brother-mine. Augustus has always been a sly one and I'm sure he's heard a few rumours by now. At the very least he might have given Cross a name." He smiled. "Or perhaps two."

Miles took another sip of tea and delicately snorted a laugh. "Even if he has I don't think we have anything to worry about. He's on his own and the word is out that he's ours. I'm sure Cross will kick down a few doors and crack a few skulls but he won't find out anything we don't want him to, at least until we're ready to pick him up again." He threw an enquiring glance towards his twin. "And when will that be exactly? I still don't understand why we've let him run loose for so long, or how Cross got away in the first place. He was *dead* for Christ's sake."

Marcus sighed and took another long puff on his pipe. "We can't make a move until *he* tells us, and we're not due for contact for a while yet." Marcus grimaced. "If I'd known dealing with these...creatures was so restrictive I might not have bothered." Miles laughed, pleased as always to see his twin annoyed. "But think of the benefits, Marcus!" he crowed. "Think of the potential, the power we could have!"

The elder twin looked down his nose at his little brother. "We already have power, Miles. A wise man should know when enough is enough or you're just a slave to avarice." Miles looked genuinely puzzled. "It will never be enough, brother. You know that. This thing we've done, think of all that we've already learned! Think of all that we thought we knew, blown away like so much dust in a single night!"

Miles leaned forward, patrician dignity forgotten as he gesticulated in a rare display of excitement. It could almost have been mistaken for actual emotion, unless you knew Miles Harrington. "What we've done could change everything! What we've done is...beautiful!" Marcus raised a hand to cut off his twins' tirade. "What we've done didn't fucking work, Miles! That's why we're waiting on *them* to tell us what went wrong, and I hope to Christ they have a better idea than we do."

The younger Harrington leant back in his chair, a contented smile on his face. "All will be well, Marcus. We have Cross in hand and I'm sure our partners over there are dealing with their end of things. You never could stand being kept in the dark." Marcus barked a harsh laugh at this. "On the contrary, it's what I do know that's bothering me. I was rather hoping the next world would be a trifle more orderly than this one."

Now it was Miles' turn to laugh. "I find it oddly comforting that chaos and chance are still present on the other side. I always imagined the afterlife being frightfully dull." Marcus pulled a face. "Yes, I can see how that would appeal to you." The elder Harrington mentally shook himself and placed the comforting pipe on the small table next to him. "In any case, it's too late to worry now, and certainly too late to back out. We'll just have to hope our new partners know what they're doing."

Miles laughed again. His brother did have an unfortunate tendency to fret over the details. "I'm sure they do brother," he smirked "One assumes they've had millennia of practice at this sort of thing." Marcus nodded, conceding the point. Slapping his hands on his thighs he stood and motioned for his brother to follow him. "Well," he said, "we still have other business to attend to so we'd best be off, have Mr Callan bring the car round front will you?"

The younger Harrington nodded and began to walk out

of the luxuriously appointed study. He stopped in the doorway and looked quizzically back at Marcus. "Where are we going?" Marcus smiled fondly at his twin. "Some of our girls in King's Cross aren't putting the effort in so I think a quiet word is in order, and I know how much you enjoy educating them." Miles clapped his hands, looking for all the world like a delighted child. He patted his breast pocket to feel the slim weight of the straight razor nestling there and walked jauntily from the room, whistling a merry tune as he went.

Elsewhere.....

The ancient study was much like the Harrington's and yet somehow *other*. The chairs and desk, the bookshelves filled with large leather-bound tomes, even the deep carpet all invoked a feeling of antediluvian age. The room seemed to groan under some imperceptible and indefinable weight as though it lay at the bottom of countless fathoms. The eastern wall of the study was dominated by several large windows and every now and again a flurry of what could have been snow, or possibly ash, batted softly against them. It was dark outside, a stygian gloom that could have hidden whole suns in its depths and inside the study it was spitefully cold.

Malleus, sat behind the large desk in a leather chair, was a perfect fit for the frigid room. Even in his rage he was cold. His whole being was comprised of rigid control and glacial implacability, of sharp angles and reptilian thoughts. His soul, if he could be said to possess such a thing, was the lifeless, obsidian tundra that lay outside.

Malleus was naked. His skin was a pale white, his muscles and bone structure flawlessly constructed; as well they should be as Malleus had sculpted them himself. He reached forward with long fingers to flip open the beautifully crafted cigar box on the desk. He took one from the box and raised it to his face, breathing deeply of the scent and allowing the merest hint of an emotionless smile to curl his perfect lips. It was only then that he deigned to acknowledge the two other occupants of the room.

"Well", he drawled in deceptively smooth tones, "would someone care to tell me just what the *fuck* happened?" The objects of his ire were like hammers to his scalpel. Roughly formed, almost blocky in shape and with barely discernible features on their square faces. Somehow, they still contrived to look nervous as they looked at each other, both hoping the other would speak first. The demon lords' eyes glowed a sudden red and the cigar in his pianists' hand flared into life. "Do not try my patience further." He warned.

One of his subordinates plucked up the courage to finally answer. "I, we, well we're, er, not really sure master." Compared to the silken tones of Malleus their voices rasped like corpse-cloth being dragged across a dusty floor. Malleus raised a despairing hand to his eyes. "I would love to say it was prescience that allowed me to see that one coming," he said, "unfortunately it's lamentable experience. More prosaic perhaps, but just as useful."

He raised a long-fingered hand to forestall any response and continued on. "Our human counterparts did their job, we all felt the conduits arrival did we not? Kelthezar was in place to receive him and yet what should have been a simple transaction was, as the humans say, fucked into a cocked hat."

He rose from behind the desk and paced in front of his increasingly nervous underlings. "I realise we undertook this experiment with limited resources and under clandestine circumstances, we all know what would happen if *he* got wind of it." He clasped his hands behind his back as he continued to stalk the room. "This deal with the humans, who have given even me a few tips on how to win 'bastard of the year' I might add, could have changed everything. This could have finally shifted the balance in our favour. We could have set that sanctimonious bastards' entire universe burning down around him."

Malleus stopped in front of his two servants and placed

a gentle hand on their shoulders. "And yet the most you can tell me is that you're not really sure? Come now gentleman, we all have to do a little better than this don't we?" The hapless underlings nodded eagerly and one of them spoke again. "We know that Kelthezar is nowhere to be found and that the..." he stopped and looked nervously at his companion who nodded him on. "Well, we know the hostage is missing as well, master"

"WHAT?!" It wasn't so much a shout as it was an explosion of raw energy as Malleus, for the first time in perhaps ten thousand years, lost his temper. His servants were flung back across the room to crash into the wall and the desk behind him shattered into a thousand pieces as the grimoires lining the bookshelves smouldered and withered in the heat of his fury. Malleus trembled as he controlled his rage and the smouldering room trembled with him. Such displays were unwise, bound as they were to draw attention from the denizens of this darkest place. Or even worse, from *him.*

His servants picked themselves up, one pulling a long and jagged fragment of the desk from his stomach as he stood. Not a flicker of pain showed on his half-formed face as he did so. Malleus sighed and gestured with one long fingered hand. The broken and burning pieces of the desk spun through the air, flames winking out as the desk rebuilt itself behind him. A glance at the bookshelves doused their flames but he left the leather-bound books charred and blackened as a pertinent reminder of the dangers of losing control.

The desk sat behind him once more, pristine and perfect. The leather chair had escaped destruction during his outburst and he righted it with a thought and sat down. He frowned as he realised something was still missing and a flick of his elegant fingers made the cigar box appear again, an exact replica, down to the smallest imperfections hidden within the wood. His servants glanced at each other and then bowed their blunt heads in a show of respect.

Across the many worlds within creations boundaries,

behind the glorious cacophony of the cosmos, some things remained constant. One of these immutable laws was that there was power and then there was *power*. The raw destructive energy released by his rage might have looked impressive, yet it was a small thing, an easy thing. Malleus held the power to shape and mould the world around him and this was a thing that a mere handful of beings in all of creation were capable of. For Malleus and these few others, the universe itself would bend to their will; the cosmos would shape itself to their design. That was *power*, the only kind that really mattered. One of the servants, braver or perhaps just foolhardier than his companion, spoke again.

"Master, had we been able to remain closer to the conduit perhaps we could have done something, but..."

Malleus held up a hand to stop any further explanation. The last vestiges of his anger bled away as he acknowledged the hopelessness of their position and relented somewhat. "This was always going to be a difficult task. We needed all of our strength at the point of arrival to exert control and that was the one thing we were unable to provide. Had we done so we would have certainly been discovered." He drew on his cigar and sent a plume of blue smoke towards the shrouded ceiling, staring into it for long moments as though divining its secrets.

"If it was the hostage then you would have been powerless against him in any case. I take it his guards are nowhere to be found? The braver servant nodded assent. "We searched for them, master but could find no sign and assumed them destroyed." Malleus smiled wryly at this. "Or they're hiding out on the most backwater world they could find after such a monumental fuck-up. I imagine the loss of the hostage is causing something of a stir?"

Now the other servant joined the conversation. "Indeed master." He bobbed his blocky head. "It appears that any other, er, irregularities are being overlooked at the moment, perhaps we can use that to our advantage?" Malleus raised his pale eyebrows in faint surprise at his servants' unexpected perceptivity and rose smoothly to his feet as his decision was made.

He gestured to the braver underling. "You, make the necessary arrangements for a visitation. I'll need to confer with our...allies." This last was said with a sneer and the two servants curled their mouths in a hideous approximation of a smile. Malleus gestured towards the clever servant. "And you, contact some of those idiot disciples with your own visitation. Do we have any of the blessed we can call on?"

The clever servant nodded. "Aye master, though I must warn you the closest we have are the Cobleys." Malleus looked quizzically at his underling who bent his unformed face into a grimace. "That unfortunate business with the Bishops' daughters, master."

Malleus sighed. Now he remembered who the Cobleys were. Still, sometimes you just had to make do with the tools at hand. "Very well, contact the Cobleys and their coven. They can augment the Harringtons more conventional forces should the need arise." He smiled suddenly. "I'm sure the Harringtons will get on just swimmingly with Mr and Mrs Cobley." The smile disappeared as he pointed a stern finger. "Just make sure they're aware of the strict parameters in place," he warned, "if I see another one of their unsanctioned massacres or torture orgies I'll bring them here and give them a place in my own menagerie for an eternity or two."

Both servants nodded and moved to leave the room. They pulled up short as Malleus spoke again, wrapping them in his power to hold them still. "Be cautious, gentlemen. I cannot impress the need for secrecy on you enough. If *he* gets wind of what I'm planning then we'll be drowning in a river of blood and excrement with the souls of the Bishop's daughters until the end of time." He relaxed his mental grip and both servants bowed again before scurrying from the room to begin their appointed tasks.

Malleus sat down and leaned back in his chair. He sent

another blue haze of smoke towards the ceiling. *Well, Mr. Cross,* he thought to himself, *the game is truly afoot now, and I wonder just how far you'll be prepared to go to remain in play?*

THREE

Cross was walking west towards Holborn, a curious mortal mirror to Malleus as he smoked while lost in thought, remembering what Gus had told him. *Look to the top of the pile eh?* That was a short enough list at least. The trouble was that it was a short list of really big bastards. Cross mentally shrugged. Whoever was responsible they were obviously overdue a fucking good hiding, and Cross had never been one to walk away from an unsettled score, whatever the odds.

Whoever it was had enough muscle to have him kidnapped and Cross was well aware that this on its own would have been no mean feat. To be sure of success they'd have needed five, possibly six men and not just any toe-rags with a skinhead and some biceps either. A crew that far up the totempole would have the resources to find out everything they needed to know about him. They would have known his military record and skill-set so they would have made sure they had some proper hard-men on the payroll for that job, and as this obviously wasn't amateur hour, Cross was certain they would have done their due diligence before doing...whatever the fuck it was they were doing.

Which was what exactly? What sort of scheme had surgical murder and resurrection as its opening gambit? And why go to all that trouble and expense and then just let him walk? Cross stopped suddenly as the thought, far too late now, finally slammed into his brain. *Because they obviously haven't finished with you yet, dickhead. Christ, how could you be so fucking stupid?* If they weren't finished with him then they were certainly watching him, and if they were watching him then that meant...

Cross sighed and lit another cigarette as he leant against a nearby wall, suddenly drained of energy. *Gus. Sorry, big man, I really am.* He mentally shook himself. He'd settle the score for Gus and Kate along with his own. He owed them that much at least. Cross realised that he couldn't fly blind anymore. He needed to find out just what had happened and why, and most importantly, who it was he needed to kill. The trouble was that the people connected enough to know anything were too useful to just setup for a bullet, so who could he turn to?

Cross grinned suddenly. *Of course,* he thought, *I'll go and have a word with the Meat-Packer!* He started walking west again with renewed purpose and the promise of mayhem shining in his eyes. Cross was about to really fuck up someone's day and that always bought a smile to his face. In a little over ten minutes he was winding through the twisting backstreets of Soho, already hearing the muted, bass-drum thump that marked where his new quarry laired. He checked his watch to see it was still a little before 9am. Last night must have been a good one if they were still going now.

He turned into an alleyway and stopped before the gaudy neon sign of his destination. The legend above the door read: 'Ma-Ma's'. The single door framed by blacked out windows opened and two ladies stumbled out as though propelled by the sudden blast of music, dressed to the nines and laughing as they staggered away arm in arm. Cross shook his head and opened the door to step inside. Ma-Ma's was comprised of a single, narrow room with a long bar on the left-hand side and gloomy, secluded booths to the right. The air smelled of perfume, sweat and cigarette smoke. The smoking ban in force across the UK was more of a guideline in a lot of these underground bars. In areas of London like Soho, people never let something as trivial as the law interfere with having a good time.

A small dance floor and DJ stand nestled at the back of the cramped space, the former playing host to a few bodies gyrating drunkenly or stumbling in an exhausted, chemical stupor to the deep trance music being played by the platinum blonde on the decks.

Cross scanned the room in a fraction of a second, noting distances, obstructions and possible threats, dismissing most out of hand and marking the small handful that might cause him a problem. This was a purely instinctive action by now, drummed into him by years of training and some very hard-earned scars and Cross never walked in anywhere without both assessing the possible dangers and knowing the quickest way out in case things suddenly went sideways.

A few heads turned to mark his entrance, but no-one except the barmaid paid him any particular attention. He shook his head again. Fucking tranny heaven. Ah well, who dares wins and all that. Cross moved to the bar, sliding in between the two other customers perched on bar stools. He ignored them as he smiled at the barmaid who was really far too muscular to be wearing *that* dress. The hint of a five 'o' clock shadow on 'her' face didn't help much either.

"Morning, ladies!" Cross still wore his winning smile as he nodded at the transvestites flanking him. He turned to the muscular barmaid. "I'll have a beer, and let Tony know that Daniel Cross is here to see him." The 'barmaid' was stone faced as he opened a bottle of beer and slid it towards Cross. "I don't know any Tony. I think you've come to the wrong place, friend." Cross sighed. "Ok mate, we'll play it your way. Let *Antonia* know that Daniel Cross is here to see him, there's a good girl."

The transvestites to either side slid from their bar stools and stood glaring at Cross who simply smiled and took a swig of his beer. The barmaid narrowed his eyes and folded his thick arms. "Antonia isn't seeing anyone."

Cross shrugged. "He'll see me. Just tell him I'm here." One of the other transvestites, the brunette in the green dress behind him spoke. "Crystal, you want us to get rid of him?" Cross burst into laughter. "Crystal?! Yeah, you look delicate, mate! Look, just get Tony down here and stop fucking me about. I'll be out of your wigs and we'll all be happy". Crystal put both hands flat on the bar and leaned towards Cross. "I said Antonia isn't seeing anyone, so I suggest you drink your beer and fuck off before you get hurt!"

Cross sighed to himself. *It's always gotta be the hard way with some people.* There was a sickening crunch as he back-handed the bottle into Crystal's face, shattering the cheek-bone and nose and sending him crashing to the floor. Cross rammed his right elbow back into the mouth of the brunette behind him even as he swung the bottle towards the other transvestite who was still too shocked by the sudden violence to move. This time the bottle broke on impact, gouging deep into the man's rouged cheek and eliciting a panicked, stran-gled wail as he sank to his knees, pressing a hand to his ruined face.

Cross spun to see the brunette, face a mask of blood and rage, climbing unsteadily to his feet. Cross kicked him solidly in the head and put him down again, the wig slipping from his scalp as he fell. He checked his third assailant and left him crying on the floor, confident he was out of the game as blood dripped through his fingers from the jagged gash in his face. The music had stopped and Cross smiled at the small sea of shocked faces in front of him. He leant over the bar to check on the unconscious Crystal. "Oops." he said.

Cross turned to face the room again and smartly clapped his hands. "Well it looks like Crystal was delicate after all. Now, is anyone going to do the smart thing and get Tony for me?" The small crowd was motionless until a slim, elegantly dressed figure appeared silhouetted in a doorway to the left of the podium.

Cross smiled in satisfaction to see Tony make an ap-pearance. Cracking skulls wasn't the subtlest way to get some-one's attention, but it usually did the job. Tony spoke into the shocked silence; voice a perfectly smoky husk as he stood with hands on slim hips, smoothing down an already smooth classic black dress.

"I thought you were dead?" he purred. "I've been throwing this party since I heard the news." Cross grinned in reply. "Put those claws away, Tony. A five-minute chat and I'll just be a bad memory again." Tony turned towards the DJ. "Get this cleared up would you? Get them a few streets away before you call the ambulance and I'm sure I don't need to tell you that nothing happened here, right?" The DJ nodded, not taking murderous eyes from Cross as he moved towards the moans and whimpers still coming from the bar.

Tony raised his voice to address the small and now silent crowd. "We're closing up until tonight ladies and gentlemen. I'm very sorry you had to witness this grotesque display and I can assure you it won't happen again." He looked pointedly at Cross as he spoke.

Cross ignored him, already moving towards the small door at the back of the dance floor that led upstairs to the office, completely disregarding the angry crowd he moved through. The suddenly sober patrons of Ma-Ma's began to file towards the front door, a few of them stopping to help the DJ pick up the still unconscious Crystal and the other injured customers, both shocked and bleeding as they staggered towards the exit.

Cross knew their shock would give way to fury soon enough, it always did when you were on the wrong end of a kicking, but he knew none of them would say anything to the police, for Tony's sake rather than fear of him. Cross knew their type and was unimpressed. Wannabe hard-men, mini-skirts and mascara notwithstanding, who'd been brutally educated that they weren't anywhere near as dangerous as they thought they were. He'd added 3 more enemies to his long list but no-one of any consequence. As he played the gent and ushered Tony through the door in front of him he forgot about them altogether.

Tony was furious. His whole body radiated the emotion and Cross could see it in every step he took, in the swing of his arms and the suddenly jerky sashay of his hips. Cross smiled to himself. *Good*, he thought. *Always nice to start with them off-balance.* There were only a dozen steps to the upstairs office, but Tony's anger was too great to be held in even for the few seconds it would have taken them to reach the top.

He whirled round to face Cross and jabbed a finger into his face. "What the fuck was that about?!" Tony rushed on without allowing Cross to answer. "And his face! You fucking ruined his face! How dare you come into my place, *my place*, and do that!" Cross simply stared, one corner of his mouth curling into the slightest of smiles, a smile that let a promise of further violence shine coldly in his eyes. He didn't reply. He didn't have to.

Cross saw the slight twitch in Tony's jaw as his anger was pushed aside. He'd have never admitted it was fear that doused the fire of his rage, and he was controlled enough not to let it reach his eyes, but they both knew. Tony waved a dismissive hand and proceeded up the stairs again. "Whatever. Let's have a drink and get this over with shall we?" They walked into the small office, Tony taking the larger leather chair behind the desk as he motioned Cross to sit in the single remaining chair on the opposite side.

The office was a spartan and simple affair, a world away from Tony's projected world of haute couture and glamour, or at least what Tony thought was glamorous. The desk was cheap and simply made, screaming bargain flat-pack from every stark line and easily inflicted scratch on the plywood surface. The top of the desk contained a laptop, cables trailing untidily down the side to the floor, a brimming ashtray and a lamp, also obviously a bargain buy.

As much as Tony's lifestyle choice mystified Cross he had to admit he looked the part. Tall and slim but curving just enough in all the right places and blessed with razor sharp cheekbones, naturally tanned skin and slightly accented eyes and full lips. *You'd never bloody know* thought Cross. *At least until you came across his cock and bollocks anyway.* He inwardly winced at his poor phrasing and pushed the thought aside as he continued to study the man in front of him, known disparagingly in some circles as the "Meat-Packer".

Tony wasn't a hardcore villain by any stretch, contenting himself with running a few grands worth of class B's and illegal scrips from the club every week, but Cross had heard enough not to take him lightly, La Perla's and fake tits or not. London gangland was basically a boy's club with all the attendant tall tales and gossip that implied, even if they'd stripe you up with a razor for suggesting all those hard-men loved to natter like fishwives. Once you'd been in the game for a while, rumour and innuendo, sometimes mixed in with a rare few facts, started to swirl around you, almost with a life of their own. Villains trailed hearsay and scandal behind them, mostly started by enemies, some by grudging admirers and others started by the villains themselves.

Cross remembered a few such tales about Tony, most of which, unsurprisingly given his lifestyle choices and the limited imaginations of the bigoted denizens of gangland, centred around bizarre sexual practices of course. One such tale stood out however.

A few years ago, Tony had a particular favourite who worked for him at the club. The young lad had fled from some miserable northern shit-hole, mistakenly thinking as so many do that life in London would be better than whatever they'd left behind. By all accounts the young lad was beautiful.

Tony kept him away from the illegal side of his business and had him working behind the bar, or more often than not, just holding court with him at the club so he could be seen with this beautiful young thing at his side. Tony was head over heels in love with the boy, so the story went. He certainly loved him enough to lavish him with expensive gifts, to let him move into the expensive flat in Hoxton and give him the keys to the BMW.

In a shocking twist which surprised absolutely no-one apart from Tony, the beautiful young lad was caught entwined in Tony's silk sheets with a Brazilian model he'd met at London fashion week.

They found the body a week later in Hackney marshes, face down and bloated in the mud on the banks of the river Lea. The talk around the campfires said that even without the decomposition and the local wildlife that had taken a nibble the boy would have been hard to identify. Tony had made sure his beautiful, treacherous boy wasn't beautiful anymore. Cross smiled to himself. *Hell hath no fury indeed.*

His reverie was broken by the squeal of poorly made hinges as Tony opened a cupboard under the desk and retrieved a bottle of whiskey and two glasses. Tony tilted the bottle towards him in silent enquiry and Cross nodded. Both men remained silent as the glasses were two-finger filled and Tony slid one across the desk. Cross picked it up and inhaled the smoky aroma with obvious relish. He tipped his glass to Tony and took a sip, letting the whiskey fill his mouth and start its silken burn across his tongue and down his throat, luxuriating in the taste and sensation. A good whiskey, Cross always maintained, should be felt as much as tasted.

Tony took a sip himself and despite the recent carnage Cross had caused in his club he smiled, although his pleasure came more from knowing that what he drank cost an obscene amount of money. He put his glass down and leant back in his chair, one hand moving to trail lightly through his thick, blonde hair. "Let me guess", he said, "You want to know if I know anything about your recent…misfortune?" Tony's relaxed façade showed the slightest of cracks as the light touch on his hair almost became a tug. Cross stayed silent and took another sip of his whiskey.

"You realise the position you're putting me in don't you?" Tony laughed bitterly as he answered his own question. "Of-course you do, you just don't give a shit." Cross just stared across the desk, content to sip his whiskey and let Tony work his way towards the only possible conclusion to their meeting. Tony lost his elegant drawl, his carefully cultivated purr made suddenly cheap and ugly by his frustration and fear. "For

Christ's sake! You don't realise who's behind all this!"

Now Cross laughed. "Why the bloody hell do you think I'm here?"

"They'll kill me!"

"And you think I won't?"

The question was delivered without a hint of menace, more a statement of fact than a question and was all the more terrifying for it. Tony paled and finished his whiskey in two quick swallows before immediately pouring another. Cross held his own glass out and Tony refilled it with a hand that showed just the slightest tremor. It was enough for Cross to notice and he smiled in satisfaction. *Gotcha.*

Cross decided to play nice. He often did when he knew he'd already won. "Look, Tony, there's no reason this has to get ugly. We've never had a problem before so no reason to start now." Tony raised his eyebrows and Cross nodded, conceding the unspoken point. "Fair enough, the bottle in your mates' face was unfortunate but what's done is done. If Crystal or whatever his bloody name is had just done as he was told then your girls wouldn't be on their way to hospital."

Tony started to reply and Cross waved him to silence. "I said forget about it. You tell me what you know and I'll do you the favour of sneaking out of the back door and keeping my mouth shut. Deal?" Tony wilted in his chair, not so much relaxing as deflating. "Deal," he sighed. Cross grinned. "Good lad! Now, what the bloody hell is going on?" Tony sighed. "Honest answer? I don't know, not for certain anyway."

Cross frowned and Tony hurried to placate him. "Look, you know what it's like. Everything you hear is mostly Chinese whispers or outright lies, and believe me there've been a lot of whispers going around about you lately."

"Such as?"

Tony ignored the question. "Let's start with the one fact I do know, shall we?"

"Go on then." Cross settled back in his chair and took another sip of the excellent whiskey. Tony followed suit before he spoke again. "One thing I do know is that Lincoln Barnes arranged your pick-up, and if he was involved..." Cross broke in: "Then it was the Harringtons."

He shook his head. "Cheeky fuckers." Cross put his glass down, the whiskey forgotten in his confusion and mounting anger. "Why though? We've never had a run-in before. Fuck me; I've even done a few jobs for them and Linc in the past and never ballsed any of them up. Ok, I never had much time for the pair of stuck-up ponces but I can't think of anything I've done that's worth killing me over."

Tony snorted a laugh, still managing to make it sound effeminate. "I'm sure they hold you in equally high regard." Cross grinned in reply. "Fair point. Still, killing me is taking the piss, whatever the reason." He stopped and looked enquiringly at Tony. "Which is what exactly?" He waved Tony's imminent protestations of ignorance away. "I know, I know, you don't know anything concrete but what's the chatter?"

Tony shook his head. "Believe me; the squealers have been getting their moneys' worth out of this little caper. I've heard everything from black magic to an elaborate sex game between you and Miles Harrington. Apparently, you two have been fucking each other blind for years." Tony laughed at Cross's raised eyebrows. "Calm down, honey. If it's any consolation people are putting more credence in the black magic story."

Cross shrugged, not really caring what the rank and file of scumbags thought about him. He had a name now, a target. He finally had a solid lead and, with that, the chance to get some payback. "The Harringtons eh? Probably way past time something sharp happened to those tossers anyway." Tony looked aghast. "You can't be thinking of going up against the Harringtons? They'll kill you!"

Cross shrugged again, unconcerned. "They already tried that, and it didn't stick. Nobody's untouchable, Tony." Tony shook his head, almost admiringly despite himself. Cross would do it too, or at least make the attempt. He'd fail; obviously, the only thing to worry about was how much damage he could do before he went down.

By "damage" of course, Tony meant what damage Cross could do to him if, *when*, the Harringtons put the pliers to him before he died. Tony knew how tough Cross was and he was sure that he'd cause the Harringtons some serious headaches before they put him down, but Cross ending up in a shallow grave was a forgone conclusion. All that mattered now was making sure he didn't end up sharing it. Cross saw the decision being made almost before Tony knew what he was planning himself. A fleeting rush of micro-expressions across Tony's face, the dilation of his pupils and the subtle stiffening of posture all but screamed his intentions.

Cross had spent far too much of his life with people trying to kill him and he was acutely attuned to impending acts of violence, especially where they concerned him. He set his feet to the floor, spreading them ever so slightly as he shifted forward on the pretext of setting his glass down. He appeared to relax back into his seat but an imperceptible shift in weight left him coiled and ready to move. Tony smiled at him, picked up the bottle and placed it back in the cupboard under the desk.

Cross was moving even before Tony's hand reappeared holding a gun. For a big man, for any man in fact, Cross was fast. The gun had barely cleared the desk and was still pointing down as Cross whiplashed forward, his huge hand crushing Tony's in an iron grip and savagely twisting. The wet snap of bone was clearly audible and Tony managed a brief squeal of pain before the rigid fingers of Cross's other hand speared into his throat.

Tony's head folded forward with the force of the blow as Cross brutally crushed his windpipe. He flopped and gasped for air like a landed fish as he fought to breathe through his mangled windpipe. Cross ignored the strangled gasps and plucked the gun from Tony's writhing grip. He slipped the magazine out to find it was fully loaded with hollow points.

Very expensive and *very* nasty. Cross looked down at the dying Tony and shook his head in reproach. *Vicious cow*. Trust Tony to fork out for hollow points, the haute couture of handgun ammo. *Nothing but the best eh, mate?*

While London wasn't quite the Wild-West yet it was a lot easier to get hold of guns than most people thought. What did limit the use of firearms, at least semi and full automatics, was the outrageous cost of ammunition. It wasn't uncommon to pay as much for a full clip as you had for the gun itself so only the larger crews were usually tooled up past pickaxe handles and the odd sawn-off. With this in mind, Cross pocketed the clip. He now had a few people on his list that would look a lot better with a fist-sized hole blown through their chests.

Cross finished his whiskey and then wiped down the glass and anything else he might have touched. Tony lay still and quiet, that singular and final stillness a body only displays when all life has fled. The big man looked across the desk at the wreckage that used to be a human being and felt nothing past a quiet sense of satisfaction for a job well done. Cross walked from the room without a backward glance and headed back downstairs to the bar. Still empty. *Good.*

Tony was going to be found at some point but Cross reckoned he had a good few hours before he had to worry about that, and seeing as he was about to go up against the Harrington brothers he'd either be on the run or dead by this time tomorrow anyway so why worry at all?

Cross stayed true to his word and left via the back entrance into a small, piss-reeking alleyway and walked slowly back towards the street, waiting a minute or two before a group of people walked past that was big enough for him to move out behind and blend in with. *So, what next?* Taking on the Harringtons was no easy task but Cross had always believed that with proper planning, the judicious application of violence where appropriate and a big enough pair of balls there wasn't much that couldn't be done.

What he needed now was somewhere to hole up out of the way, not only to plan his next moves but the fact that he'd been to two places and left three bodies behind him since getting out of bed this morning was sure to start raising a few eyebrows amongst the constabulary. He checked his watch to see it was just after 10am. Cross had the feeling it was going to be a long day. Moving away from Soho and onto the Strand he ducked off the main road to wend his way through a selection of side streets and back alleys before reaching his destination.

One thing London wasn't short of was cheap hotels, B&B's and rooms you could rent by the hour. Coppers and villains both knew that these places were often the go-to bolt holes for the discerning man on the run, so they'd be the first places they started checking. The sheer amount of them scattered across London meant it would take them a while, but they only needed to get lucky the once and it would all be over.

The famous Savoy hotel was nearby on the Strand, but just across the road from that was the Strand Palace. Not quite the five-star opulence of the Savoy but more than nice enough to be well out of the usual bracket of hidey-holes. Besides, Cross was under no illusions that he'd fit in with the Savoy crowd and it was best to keep a low profile as much as he could.

He moved into the foyer of the palace and walked easily across to the counter with a winning smile in place for the receptionists. Cross always had a few hooky credit cards that he knew were good for a grand or so and he booked a room under the name of Derek Baron, a dentist from Shepherds Bush if memory served. It cost him an outrageous premium for the early check-in which Cross paid with a smile, like he always did when spending other people's money.

The room was crisp and clean and Cross opened the window the scant inches that were allowed before kicking off his shoes and settling onto the bed, ignoring the "No Smoking" signs and lighting up a cigarette. So, he thought, *it's me against the Harringtons and all their muscle, not the least of which is Lincoln Barnes.* Cross had a lot of respect for Lincoln. Christ, he actually quite liked the bloke, or at least he used to.

If Tony had been telling the truth then the odds were it was Lincoln following him, not likely the twins would leave that to one of their lower ranked bully-boys, which meant it was probably Lincoln who'd pulled the trigger on Gus and Kate. While he might not have seen it happen he knew they were dead. Cross had killed them both the minute he walked in there.

Cross would settle that score and settle it hard. First thing to do was make sure he could slip past Lincoln, if he hadn't already, or even better, take him out all-together. Not only would that allow him to move unhindered, but it would send a clear message to the Harringtons that Cross was onto them, and that he was coming for them.

There was little point in subterfuge. Both Cross and the Harringtons knew where they stood and what was coming. Now it was time to cause them some hurt and let the fuckers sweat for a while. As much as Cross might have respected Lincoln he'd make sure he put him down dirty for Gus and Kate and his fists twitched at the prospect. Still, even if he took out Barnes, the Harringtons had plenty of other goons to call on, everything from ex-council estate to ex-military.

One-on-one? Easy. Cross was confident he could take out any of them without too much trouble, but they wouldn't be using Queensbury rules for this game and they were bound to come at him mob-handed at some point. He silently cursed. *Fuck it*; he might actually need some help, no matter how much he didn't like to admit it. Sure, he was owed a few favours here and there, some pretty substantial ones among them, but taking on the Harringtons? Favours only stretched so far.

There were a few other crews out there who could match them, even a few who could burn their whole operation down without breaking much of a sweat but Cross didn't want to go down that route unless he really had to. Not only were outfits like the Russians or the Triads notoriously volatile but getting them involved really would be making a deal with the devil.

"You've got no idea how apt that phrase is, sunshine!"

Cross bolted from the bed, gun drawn and tracking the room before he realised the voice had sounded in his head. "Jesus Christ!"

"Not quite. He's a friend of a friend though." Cross sensed the amusement in the reply and the voice spoke again. *"You're setting the bed on fire by the way."*

Cross looked down to see his cigarette smouldering on the pristine white duvet and he hastily retrieved it without relinquishing his hold on the gun. Cross was quite understandably terrified. He'd seen and done a lot of awful things in his life, things that would have unhinged the strongest of people and he fearfully wondered if this latest escapade might have finally pushed him over the edge.

During his tours overseas he'd seen it all. Friends eviscerated by roadside IED's, their entrails wrapping round his boots as he stumbled to his knees in their shit and blood and screamed their names, his own voice unheard through the ringing in his ears. He'd seen heads exploding from a sniper's bullet just a few feet away, fragments of bone stinging his face while the coppery tang of blood sprayed across his tongue. Cross had walked through the wreckage of torched villages, breathing in the ash of roasted women and children, tears choking him as much as the ash as he stared at the piles of tiny bones.

Cross suffered his share of sleepless nights, and nightmares when he did manage to sleep, but he'd always taken a grim pride in the fact that none of the things he'd seen and done, none of the ruinous damage he'd suffered and inflicted on others had broken him. Voices in his head?! Perhaps he'd finally found his limit after all? Suddenly, Cross felt his fear subside. No, it wasn't subsiding. He could still feel it squirming inside his gut, but it was being nullified somehow, as if he was suddenly just an observer in his own head.

The voice sounded again, smooth and reassuring. *"Calm down, son. You haven't lost the plot just yet. I've turned the tap off on some of your adrenal responses for now; it was getting a bit loud in here with you yelling. Now, go to the bathroom and look in the mirror and I'll explain what's going on."* The disembodied voice paused and then returned but slightly hesitant this time. *"Just try not to freak out when you look in the mirror ok?"*

Cross moved to the bathroom like an automaton, that calming sense of numbness flooding through him like he was submerged in a sea of Prozac. He flicked on the light and kept his gaze to the floor until he stood square against the sink and firmly braced his hands against it. Then he raised his head to see someone else staring back from the mirror.

"Fuck me," he said quietly. The stranger's reflection smiled and waved. The face was handsome and fine-boned with lustrous white-blonde hair and a curious but still pleasing androgyny. The thought that the recently departed Tony would have killed for hair like that popped into Cross's head.

The stranger in the mirror laughed. *"I bet he would have done too! Don't lose any sleep over that wanker; he had what was coming to him. Nice job of that by the way."* Cross was still wrapped in that unnatural calm as he asked: "And you are?" The stranger smiled showing perfectly white teeth. *"I'm Andariel. I'm an angel."*

"Come again?"

"An angel. Harps and wings and all that bollocks?"

"Really? All you lot sound like you come from the East End then?"

The figure in the mirror, Andariel, shook his head. *"Nah, more like Kensington I guess. I just thought you'd be more comfortable if I used your usual thingamy, er, vernacular."*

"I'd rather you didn't, it's like having Dick Van Dyke doing his Mary Poppins thing in my head."

Andariel laughed, the sound full of good humour. Whoever

or whatever he was, he seemed to be enjoying himself immensely. *"Fair enough, it's your mind after all. Is this a more palatable accent?"* Cross grimaced, still disconcerted not to see his reflection follow suit in the mirror. *Now he sounds like he's reading the news*, he thought. The image of Andariel frowned in reproach. *"I heard that."* The angel in the mirror sniffed delicately. *"No pleasing some people."*

Cross shakily lit another cigarette. "Ok then," he said. "If I haven't gone mental in the last ten minutes and I really have an angel in my head then do you mind explaining just what the fucking hell is going on?!"

Andariel looked appraisingly at him. *"I'll explain what I can but it's a lot to take in and you might be better off discussing it with someone who's actually human."* He paused. *"Well, more or less."* Cross started to reply but Andariel held up a silencing hand. *"First off, I'm going to relax my hold on your adrenal responses and give you all your faculties back. I think you can handle it."*

Feeling began to seep slowly back into Cross's awareness, not all of it welcome. He ruthlessly crushed a rising sense of what he feared might be panic, no way he was going to lose it in front of a talking reflection. He breathed slowly and deeply, willing himself to be calm and in control. Andariel smiled and shook his head. *"Very good,"* he said. *"Never underestimate the power of the human ego when it comes to pretending everything's tickety-boo. Ok then, I'll try and keep this as simple as possible. A few days ago, you died."*

Cross barked a laugh. "Yeah, I noticed that."

"Died and went to Hell to be more specific."

"Figures. I never thought I'd be going to Disneyland when I popped my clogs, I haven't exactly been an altar boy."

"Yeah, I noticed that."

"Funny."

Andariel stopped smiling, his look changing to one of sympathy. *"You can't remember much, and trust me, that's for the best. You can remember enough though yes?"* Cross grimaced and forced himself to concentrate, to finally search out the memories that he'd kept hidden and locked away in a far corner of his mind. "It's more feeling than remembering. Dark and cold, no, more than just cold. Like the cold was inside me, like it *was* me." The big man stopped suddenly, embarrassed at letting his emotional guard down and waxing poetic to a talking reflection in a bathroom mirror.

Andariel smiled again but sadly this time. *"Yes, that sounds about right. That cold you felt? That's despair. Eternal and unending despair and you were only in the, well, arrivals lounge I suppose you could call it. You were yanked back out before you got to the really bad bits."*

"Yanked back out?"

Andariel paused as he thought how best to frame his reply. *"Getting you in and out quick was the whole point. You were never meant to stay there, this time at least."* The angel sighed. *"This is harder to explain than I thought. Basically, you were sent there as a vessel. You were supposed to drop in and pick up a particularly nasty piece of work called Kelthezar and then when you came back it would have been him in the driving seat and not you. I guess you could call it a sort of psychic bungee jump."*

Cross thought for a second. "You mean I was going to be possessed? Like in the Exorcist?"

"Bingo! Those scars on your chest near your heart? Sigils of binding and limitation. Full-blown possession is a tricky business; beings like us have a tendency to make human bodies explode a bit if they're not properly prepared."

"Ok, I think I'm with you so far. Does this sort of thing happen a lot then?

Andariel looked suddenly grave. *"Not like this it doesn't. This is a new idea and I'm not surprised it was Malleus that came up with it."*

"Malleus?"

"A demon. Not one of the rank and file either. Malleus is one of the elite. Think of him as an assistant vice-president of Hell or something."

Cross snorted in disdain. "Cunt."

Andariel laughed. *"Yes, that sums him up perfectly."* The angel became serious again. *"Malleus isn't to be underestimated though; he's very powerful and extremely dangerous. If he'd actually managed to pull this off..."*

"And the Harringtons are working with him? How'd that happen?"

There was a mental shrug inside Cross's head, a curious feeling like his brain had hiccupped. *"I don't know how they established contact, but I'd assume it was Malleus who got the ball rolling and approached them with the proposal. It's a... complicated process for you humans to talk to anyone on our side."*

Cross thought for a second. "You said this was a new idea? What do you mean?"

Andariel grimaced. *"This part is really hard to explain. If a 'normal' possession occurs then it makes a lot of noise, for want of a better term. There are rules, checks and balances in place to make sure this sort of thing doesn't happen without the proper authorisation, and they apply to both sides. Angels and demons running around the mortal realms gets a lot of celestial knickers in a twist, so we try and avoid it when we can.*

What Malleus is attempting appears to be completely undetectable. If he could perfect the technique then he could move hundreds, possibly thousands of demons to the many worlds without anyone knowing. The damage he could cause before he was stopped would be catastrophic, if we could stop him at all by then."

The angel paused to reflect for a second. *"It's all about balance really, the great plan that is. A supernova here, a black hole there, this galaxy intersecting just so with that one, this culture meeting that one at precisely the right time and so on. It really is quite impressive when you stop and think about it. Malleus wants to kick the scales over and set them on fire just to see what happens."*

A sudden thought occurred to Cross. "Hold on, you said "many worlds", plural. So it's not just earth then?" Andariel laughed again. *"Good Lord no! I like you humans but you do have an unfortunate tendency to disappear up your own arses some-*

times. There are billions of worlds out there, all of them teeming with all manner of life. Say what you like about God, but he doesn't do anything by halves."

"So he really created the lot then? That wasn't all just Sunday school rubbish for the kids?"

"Well as usual you lot made a complete pigs-ear of understanding it all and passing the message on. I swear, the dissemination of religious teaching has been the biggest game of Chinese whispers in creation. You're inventive little buggers though, I'll give you that. We all love that virgin birth story in heaven, and that water into wine one? Genius!"

The angel winked conspiratorially. *"We actually appropriated that idea; meetings are a lot more fun now."* Cross laughed, finding he was warming to his celestial hitchhiker. Andariel looked at him appraisingly. *"I must say I'm surprised at how well you're dealing with all this. You've been murdered and sent to Hell, and then returned with an angel in your head who's just taught you more secrets of the cosmos in the last 5 minutes than every religious icon, leader or charlatan has known since the dawn of time. Bravo!"*

Cross just shrugged. "No point making a fuss about it is there? Granted, it's a lot to take in but trust me, you don't go through the things I have and not end up believing in something, even if you'd never admit it to yourself, let alone anyone else." Cross lit another cigarette and perched on the edge of the bath. "I don't remember much from the few times I got dragged into church but isn't God supposed to be..." He looked into the distance and then clicked his fingers as the elusive word came to him. "Omnipotent, that's the one! If he's in charge of the whole circus then how come this Malleus dickhead can pull one over on him in the first place?"

Andariel's reflection slowly clapped as a smile spread across his face. He nodded approvingly at Cross. *"Well done. That's the rub isn't it? The way I understand it is God put it all together and hammered out the basic rules but then it's all down to us, or rather you to just get on with it and see what happens. Om-*

nipotence was another one of your human conceits actually. You lot could have been a planet sized PR department for him."

"The way you understand it? Are you telling me you lot don't actually know what he's doing then?"

"*Christ no!*" The angel was genuinely amused by the concept. "*What on earth gave you that idea? We're just the worker bees, Daniel. We were given our instructions a few thousand millennia ago and then just left to manage it all as best we could.*"

"So where is he then?"

Andariel shrugged in the mirror. "*Buggered if we know. Off creating another cosmos? Waging a tireless crusade against an alien deity? Gone fishing? None of us up there really have a clue, apart from possibly Michael and he isn't saying anything. Stuck up bastard. Lucifer might know and he's a lot chattier than most of the upper echelons are but, as you can imagine, we don't really move in the same circles.*"

"The Devil is...chatty?"

"*Oh yes. Funny too if you catch him in the right mood. Buttons can tell you all about him, he talks to Lucifer more than I do.*"

"Buttons?"

Andariel waved the question away. "*You'll meet him later, but we're getting ahead of ourselves a bit here. Now, obviously I'm not about to properly possess you, I'm supposed to be one of the good guys after all, but I don't imagine you want me stuck in your head any more than I want to be here.*" He looked at Cross apologetically. "*It's a little cramped to be honest. No offence.*"

"None taken. So, what do you suggest then?"

"*We need to get me a body. Anything recently dead will do, I'm not fussy.*"

Cross digested this request with admirable equanimity. "I don't think I've ever stolen a body before, but I'm pretty sure I know a bloke who can help us." He pulled a face. "He's a pervorted little shit but beggars can't be choosers and I'm sure there isn't much that shocks you anyway."

"*And who is this paragon we're going to see?*"

"Chandra Krishnan. Doctor Chandra Krishnan if you please.

He's a tit surgeon at some Harley Street clinic but he consults over at the university college hospital as well. If I twist his arm just right he can get us into the mortuary there and we can see what's on offer."

"Splendid! Once I'm properly attired we'll go and see Buttons. He can help explain things a bit better than I can and I think we're going to need his sort of help before this is all over." Andariel was suddenly grim faced. *"Understand something, Daniel. You're not only up against a few gangsters here. Without wanting to sound too melodramatic the forces of Hell itself are going to be after you. Probably my lot too once they get wind of it, and then it really will be a nightmare."*

"They're not gonna swoop in like the cavalry and save the day then I take it?"

Andariel laughed but the sound had a bitter sting to it. *"Not bloody likely. You're already Hell-bound so as far as they're concerned you're as good as batting for the other side, and I'm not exactly flavour of the epoch either."*

"Fuck 'em then."

"That's pretty much what I said to them."

Cross laughed and pushed himself from the edge of the bath. "Ok, genie. Get back in your bottle and let's go and steal you a corpse" He stopped suddenly and shook his head. "I can't believe I just said that."

The laughter of an angel in his head followed him as he left the room.

FOUR

Doctor Chandra Krishnan knelt in front of his secret shrine, filled with a sense of awe as he stared at them. Their perfection filled his soul even as it stole his breath. So different yet still with such symmetry that it had to be by design. If Chandra Krishnan needed a reason to believe in a higher power then it was here in this room. Chandra Krishnan, as he did every day, knelt in supplication before his secret and hidden God.

Doctor Krishnan bowed his head and then slowly, reverently closed the cupboard doors that hid his shrine from prying eyes. His God was for him and him alone. As always, he was stricken with a sense of loss as the doors closed and he sighed, already feeling the essence of the divine leaving him again. He heaved his portly frame from the floor, grunting with the effort and began to dress, struggling to press his erection into his trousers.

He was in his fifties now and yet his round face held an almost cherubic cast that often caused people to think he was still in his thirties. He was a precise and tidy man in all aspects of his life, as befitted one of the best plastic surgeons in London. Unfailingly polite and respectful to both neighbours and colleagues he still shunned company and attended the various professional and social functions he was invited to only rarely, and even then leaving as soon as decency allowed. Doctor Krishnan was a very private man who needed only his God to sustain him.

Consequently, the knocking at his front door was a most unwelcome interruption. No, it was more a hammering and Doctor Krishnan had a sinking feeling he knew exactly who it was banging on his door in such an uncouth manner. He decided to stay quiet and hope the unwelcome interloper, whoever it was, gave up and went away. This faint hope was shattered by the shout coming through his door.

"Chandra! Open the bloody door!" The banging resumed, and Chandra's heart sank as he recognised the muffled voice, which continued its tirade. "Come on you old nonce, I know you're in there!"

Doctor Krishnan hung his head and sighed, knowing that he had no choice. Cross would keep making a scene with this dreadful racket and soon the neighbours would be popping their heads from their doors like Meerkats to see what was going on.

He raised his voice as he walked down the stairs towards the door. "Please, Daniel! I'm coming. Just cease that infernal ruckus!" Chandra opened the door to see a grinning Cross leaning on the door frame like he was an old friend who the Doctor would be delighted to see again. Cross walked in without waiting to be invited in and sauntered towards the kitchen as he spoke over his shoulder. "Hey, doc! I need a small favour and I'm dying for a cuppa, is the kettle on?" Chandra looked quickly out of the open door, relieved to see none of his neighbours' curtains twitching. He gently closed the door and steeled himself. If Daniel was after a favour it certainly wouldn't be small. The Doctor sighed and followed his unwelcome guest to the kitchen.

Cross was fiddling with the espresso maker with a bemused expression on his face and Chandra hurried forward to shoo him away before he broke anything. "Daniel!" he barked and then quickly modulated his tone as he smiled ingratiatingly. "Please, sit down and I will bring you some tea." Cross grinned at him. "Cheers, doc, I could murder a brew. It's been one of those mornings."

Cross moved away from the espresso machine and sprawled in a chair at the large oak table which dominated the kitchen. He lit a cigarette. "Do you mind?" He asked through a wreath of smoke. Doctor Krishnan bit down on his annoyance as the vile smell of smoke filled his spotless kitchen. "Not at all, Daniel. I shall furnish you with an ashtray." The doctor bustled about the kitchen, depositing a saucer in front of Cross to double as an ashtray and then started to brew the tea. Both men were silent. Cross was perfectly relaxed as he sat and smoked while Chandra's every movement betrayed how discomfited he was.

Daniel *knew*. Daniel had seen the secret, hidden and most perfect God. Daniel hadn't told but how could anyone keep something so sublime a secret forever? Chandra cursed the day they'd met, cursed his own sense of decency and the oath that bound him. It had been almost a year ago when Doctor Krishnan returned home late one evening from his Harley street clinic and seen the slumped figure at the end of his road crawling inch by torturous inch and leaving a trail of blood behind him. Whatever his faults and his more…esoteric predilections the doctor took his work seriously.

The Hippocratic Oath wasn't merely a rote jumble of words to him, it actually meant something. He firmly believed he was put on this earth to help people, to save people and so he'd rushed over to offer what assistance he could.

Chandra's first thought had been to call an ambulance as a single glance showed him how much blood the big man had lost, even before he saw the huge, gaping wound that ran down the outside of his left thigh. Cross had batted the phone from his hand and then grabbed his wrist, still frighteningly strong in even in such a weakened and perilous state. "No ambulance." he gasped. "No police." Against his better judgement (and now much to his continuing regret) the portly doctor had acquiesced, dragging the injured man the short distance to his door and manhandling him down the hall and into the kitchen, which was no easy task. The large oak table where Cross now sat insolently smoking was where Chandra Krishnan had saved his life.

The wound to Daniel's leg had arrived courtesy of a

very angry member of a Triad gang apparently. Chandra didn't know the details and had no desire to know anything about that frightening side of life in London. The gash ran across the meat of Cross's thigh and he'd been fortunate that the large blade had missed his femoral artery, though in his darker moments Chandra privately wished that might have been otherwise.

Doctor Krishnan had stitched and patched the now unconscious man up as best he could and then left him to recuperate while he took some much-needed rest himself, secure in the knowledge that his mysterious patient would be out cold for some time. The doctor had jerked awake in his chair after an hour or so of fitful sleep and was disconcerted to see the blood-soaked kitchen table was now empty.

Confusion quickly turned to panic as he heard a muffled thump and the creaking of floorboards above him. The rotund surgeon had leapt from his chair and ran upstairs as fast as he could. He knew he was too late even before he heard the sound of cupboard doors opening.

What he hadn't expected was Cross's uproarious laughter at what he found. Cross had been completely unapologetic that he'd invaded the privacy of the man who'd just saved his life and all of Chandra's self-righteous anger and indignant spluttering paled in the face of what Cross found lurking in his bedroom cupboard. Since that night the hapless doctor had been a worm on a hook. He'd spent the first few months in an almost constant state of terror, petrified that Cross would divulge his secret and profane his worship but, true to his word, Cross stayed silent.

The big rogue had, in all honesty, been quite restrained in the favours he'd requested and had always been polite enough to ask rather than demand, though both men knew such politeness was a facade. His requests were usually for no questions asked medical attention, but on a few occasions it had been medication or equipment that Cross had required, some of which was obtained at great personal risk and expense.

For Cross's continuing silence it was a small price to pay. As Chandra came to realise a state of constant fear can only be maintained for so long. After a while either a breaking point is reached or you become accustomed, or perhaps just inured, to the new status-quo. Doctor Krishnan chose the latter and his life had returned, more or less, to normal.

Chandra finished making the tea, finding comfort in the familiar motions of the ritual and then pouring Cross a steaming cup of Darjeeling before settling opposite his unwelcome guest.

Chandra was pleased to see that Cross didn't desecrate the brew with milk. At least the man wasn't a total barbarian. The two men sipped their tea and both sighed in appreciation. Cross raised his cup. "Good cuppa that, doc." Chandra smiled, putting down his own cup and looking over at Cross above steepled, pudgy fingers. "Thank you, Daniel. What may I do for you this morning?"

Cross looked slightly uncomfortable and Doctor Krishnan began to feel a sense of foreboding. "Bit of an odd one this, doc. I need to get into the mortuary and borrow a corpse."

"Excuse me?"

"Well, I say 'borrow', I can't make any promises you'll get it back." He held up his hands to forestall the doctor's inevitable complaints. "Any stiff will do, as long as it's in good working order."

"Apart from being dead you mean?"

Cross laughed. "Don't be a smart-arse. I mean as long as it's not missing any useful bits like legs or a head or whatever." Cross took another sip of his tea and smiled encouragingly across the table. "C'mon, doc. This is easy. All you need to do is let me in and I'll sort out the rest." Chandra wrung his hands. Cross had never asked to enter either the hospital or clinic grounds before, all their dealings had been concluded either here or by a brief meeting and handover at a park or train station and he was more than a little perturbed at this sudden change and escalation in their arrangement.

A dead body?! What on earth did he need that for? Cross had been watching the emotions chase each other across Chandra's chubby face. "Trust me, doc," he said, "You're better off not knowing. I'll be in and out before you can blink and I'm very good at getting in and out of places without being seen." Cross grinned. "If it's any consolation then it's highly unlikely you'll be seeing me again once we get it done."

Chandra took a large gulp of the too hot tea and cursed as he burnt his mouth. He put the cup down; looking sourly at it like it had betrayed him in his hour of need. "Very well," he sighed, "it's not like I have much choice is it?" Cross laughed at this. "That's the spirit!" The doctor blew on his tea before taking another, more cautious sip. "Getting you in there shouldn't be too problematic, and finding a cadaver that meets your requirements even less so, but how on earth do you propose to get out again? A man dragging a corpse onto the street will hardly be inconspicuous."

Cross shrugged. "Leave that to me, I've got it all in hand. You just get me in the room and I'll be done and dusted in five minutes." He stopped suddenly and cocked his head as though listening to something. "Ok, more like ten minutes." Chandra was far from happy with Cross's blasé attitude but he knew he had no choice. He simply couldn't risk his perfect, hidden God, his *life* being exposed and as affable as Cross often appeared the doctor knew he would tear his world apart without a second thought and without feeling the slightest twinge of guilt.

"Very well, Daniel. I assume that you can wait until tonight? I have a consultation scheduled for today that I simply cannot miss." Cross winked at him. "More new recruits for upstairs eh?" Doctor Krishnan tried to hide his anger at hearing such blasphemy. "Never you mind, Daniel! The mortuary will be down to a skeleton crew, if you will pardon the term, for the night-shift and the dead of night surely suits this kind of..." "Undertaking?" laughed Cross. The doctor winced. "Quite.

Shall we say 10pm? The shifts will have just changed so the staff will be occupied with the handover and we should be able to enter undetected." Chandra looked quizzically over the table. "And where may I reach you should I need to between now and then?" Cross spread his arms expansively. "I'll be waiting right here for your call, doc."

The doctor began to sputter his protests until Cross rose smoothly from his chair and leaned across the table to tower over him. "Non-negotiable. Don't worry, I'm not going anywhere near your bedroom again. I'll put my feet up and watch telly; you won't even know I've been here." Chandra was a study in abject misery. For such a private person to have an unwanted guest alone in their home, their sanctum? It was torturous. He knew that arguing was futile and would only serve to irritate Cross, something he'd be wise to avoid. If there was one thing the big man excelled at it was backing people into a corner and leaving them no choice but to do what he wanted.

Cross softened his glare and moved away from the table to take up a less threatening position leaning on one of the kitchen counters. "Doc, for what it's worth I give you my word I won't interfere with any of your...interests while I'm here. The worst thing I'll do is probably mess your kitchen up a bit when I make some lunch." Chandra looked up from his clutching, sweaty hands and looked pleadingly across the room.

Cross sighed. "Whatever else I've done I've never lied to you have I?" Chandra was forced to admit that was true enough and he nodded. "Very well, Daniel. My home is yours, please make yourself comfortable and I shall see you tonight." Chandra stood and began to clear the teapot and cups from the table. Cross watched him in silence and lit another cigarette. As the doctor made to leave the room, Cross moved to stop him at the door with an outstretched arm. "I know I probably don't need to say this but if anyone but you comes calling here later we both know what will happen, don't we?"

The rotund little man nodded despondently and then took a deep breath and squared his shoulders before staring up to look Cross in the eye. "I can assure you your threats aren't necessary, Daniel. I said I would help you and help you I shall. An even and honourable trade, yes?" Cross grinned and slapped him on the back. "I think we're both a long way from honourable, doc, but I appreciate the sentiment." He moved his big arm from the doorway. "Have a good day, doctor Krishnan and I'll see you tonight."

Cross sat at the kitchen table again, listening to Chandra clattering around in the hallway before hearing the door close and footsteps recede down the path. He moved from the kitchen, down the hall and entered the small sitting room to the right of the front door. Cross peered through the net curtains and watched the doctor trudge to his car like a condemned man and drive away. *"Are we really going to sit here all day?"* asked Andariel. Cross snorted. "Like fuck we are. I'm pretty sure he's scared enough to do as he's told but why take the chance?"

"Good. I could see some of what was going on inside his head. You know his first thought was you sodomising the corpse? Mucky little pup." Cross pulled a face. "I knew a couple of blokes in the Navy that used to swear by it. Never saw the attraction myself though." He shrugged. "Each to their own I guess."

Cross thought for a second. "Can you do that then? See what people are thinking I mean?" He felt Andariel's mental shrug. *"Some of us can. I get little flashes now and again."* The angel laughed. *"Most of the time I'm happier not knowing what you lot are thinking about."*

Cross clapped his hands together. "Right," he said. "Let's get cracking."

"Cracking into what exactly?" Andariel asked.

"Getting you out of my head and into your own body of course."

"Now?"

"Yes, now. The longer we hang about the more chance we have of getting caught and killed." He stopped and thought for a second. "Again."

"Don't we need the doctor's help for that?"

"Help? He'd be a bloody liability. I know Chandra and he's got about as much spine as a Pot Noodle. The doc would be sweating and stuttering as soon as we walked in. We might as well wear a neon sign saying we shouldn't be there."

"So what was the point of this little visit?"

Cross laughed. "Well you can never go wrong with a free cuppa. No, the real point is misdirection. I trust that fat little fucker about as far as I could throw him. We don't move in the same circles so it's not like he's about to call the Harringtons and grass me up, but he could still say the wrong thing to the wrong person and word gets round quick." Cross lit another cigarette as he moved towards the front door. "If that happens then anyone looking for me will be looking here or lying in wait at the hospital tonight, so we do it now when no-one's expecting it."

"Clever. I'm impressed, Daniel."

Cross shrugged and opened the door, eyes flicking up and down the street to make sure it was clear before he stepped out. "Never be where they expect you to be." Andariel was quizzical. *"I assume you have some way of getting us inside the mortuary then?"*

Cross reached into his jacket pocket to pull out a slim, black leather wallet. He flipped it open in front of his face to reveal a police warrant card and badge, assuming Andariel could see through his eyes. The warrant card showed a photo of Cross, though he was clean-shaven, and his name read "James Spencer".

The badge was the silver coat of arms that marked the holder as a Detective Inspector in the Metropolitan Police, based out of New Scotland Yard.

"I have a bloke in Whitechapel makes these sorts of things for me." explained Cross. "None of your cheap rubbish either. He's a miserable old prick but he's one of the best forgers I've ever worked with." Cross stopped suddenly. "Hold on a minute." He fished around inside another pocket and removed a pair of the headphones that came with a mobile phone. He slipped one bud into his left ear and left the cable and mic dangling before replacing the other end into his jacket pocket.

"There." He said. "Now I look like I'm on the phone rather than a nutter walking down the road and talking to myself."

"I take it you've used plenty of fake ID's in your time then? Do we have a backup plan in case someone is feeling particularly officious and calls this Scotland Yard to check your credentials?" Cross was unconcerned. "The trick to blagging your way in someplace is looking bored really. You're supposed to be there, it's your job and you've done it so many times the whole thing is commonplace, if not an outright bloody nuisance. As long as you look bored and don't really take the piss with whatever you're asking for then you're usually ok."

"And when it isn't ok?"

Cross laughed. "That's when you knock someone out and run for it. I'm a copper asking to look at some stiffs to see if any of them match a description from an active case, that's all. Nothing out of the ordinary in that request and odds are they'll point us towards the freezers and leave us to it."

Cross thought for a second. "How's this going to work anyway? You taking over a corpse I mean? I don't have to do a ritual or chant or anything do I?"

The angel in his head laughed. *"No, nothing like that. Just touch the body and we're done. I'll be up and about in a few minutes and we can just walk out."* Cross grunted. "Good. In and out quick and then we can get on with pissing on the Harrington's chips." A thought suddenly occurred to him. "Hang on, I had to have those scar things cut into me right?" Andariel knew what the question was before it was asked.

"Sigils of binding. Don't worry, I won't explode over you half way down the road. I'm reanimating a corpse rather than a full-blown possession so it works a bit differently. It's a lot easier moving in when the tenant has already left. It's your souls that cause all the problems you see."

"Not really. I thought souls and the like were just made up anyway."

"Oh no, they're quite real. As well as being a vast resource of energy the soul acts as a kind of signature."

"Signature?"

The angel sighed. *"I don't really want to start a metaphysical lecture but each species has its own unique soul and signature. When you die and your souls move to the afterlife then your signature helps determine where you go."*

"Heaven or Hell?"

"More than that, it determines which *Heaven or Hell you go to."*

Cross was shocked at this. "You mean there are more than one?!"

Andariel snorted in disgust. "Of course there bloody are. There you humans go, thinking you're unique snowflakes again!"

Cross laughed. "Alright, don't get your knickers in a twist. I only found out *you* existed an hour ago and I've had a lot to take in since then. You have to admit that multiple Heavens and Hells might be a bit of a bombshell?"

The angel appeared contrite. *"Yes, you're right. It's been that way since the dawn of time for me but I should remember this might be a little fantastical for you."*

"A little? Bloody hell, I was an atheist until this morning!"

The angel laughed at that. *"We decided to keep each afterlife separate although there is some overlap with the more advanced species who are already coexisting in the mortal realms."*

"So if two species have interacted with each other during their existence you push their afterlives together and knock the wall through?"

"It's a little more complicated than that but basically yes."

"The whole thing sounds bloody complicated to me, mate."

"At the last count we had a little over 978 trillion sentient races in creations' boundaries, 'complicated' doesn't even come close."

Cross's mind boggled, almost rebelled at the sheer scale of what the angel was telling him. He'd seen a short movie once that attempted to show the size of the known universe by showing the earth and then panning out and out and out. Every time you thought that just *had* to be it the scene moved farther and farther out. It was hard to wrap your mind around that, let alone billions of races filling that vast space, a heavenly host watching over it all and, somewhere out there, the God who created the whole thing.

It was all so much to take in but, more importantly, largely academic. Cross had to focus on living through the day first. He'd ponder the mysteries of the cosmos tomorrow if he was still breathing. He grinned suddenly. If he wasn't then he'd be experiencing some of those mysteries first hand anyway. Cross brought his mind back to some of the more pressing issues.

"So, without the soul in there you won't be blowing up, but what about this 'noise' you were talking about? Won't you taking over a dead body start the alarm bells ringing?"

"No, it's the transition from our side to yours that makes all the racket. I'm already in the physical realms and under the radar so we don't have to worry."

"Can you hear it when it happens?"

"Hear what?"

"The noise you keep talking about."

The angel sighed. *"Like I said it's not a 'noise' as such. That's just the easiest way to explain it. You don't have the same senses as we do. If I told you it was more like the smell of a dream or the touch of a colour you'd be none the wiser would you?"*

Cross shrugged. "Fair enough, let's just stick with 'noise' then."

Andariel laughed and then stopped as he thought of something himself. Cross must have been getting used to having Andariel in his head as he too felt the question before it was asked. "Yes," he said. "They'll have clothes there. Whatever the poor bastards were wearing when they get wheeled in gets bagged and tagged so we'll be able to kit you out with something rather than trying to sneak you out in the buff."

"Just as well." said Andariel. *"I know how you humans get when you see some genitals on display."* The angel sighed. *"I've*

*never understood how you're perfectly happy with drone strikes
blowing up a village or chopping someone's head off on the internet,
but show some of you a pair of tits and the sky starts falling."*

"Never had a problem with a pair of tits myself." said Cross
with a grin. Andariel wryly chuckled. *"You're a credit to your
species, Daniel".* Cross and his invisible companion were in
Hammersmith and Fulham, not far from the poetically named
Ravenscourt park, so called after Thomas Corbett bought the
estate of Paddenswick in the 1800's and renamed it "Ravenscourt" after the ravens displayed on his coat of arms.

London was full of parks like this, calming oases and
tranquil expanses nestled amongst the bustling streets, offering a much-needed respite from the grey stone, steel and glass
buildings that were prevalent across the city. Their verdant
calm stood in stark and glorious contrast to their surroundings and, if he had a bit more time and half of London and the
afterlife weren't trying to kill him, Cross would have sat by
the lake and enjoyed the brief peace it offered.

He'd always liked visiting the various parks around the
city. If you sat in just the right place you could faintly hear
the noise of the city as a muted hum and know that while the
cacophony of commerce and modern life still hurtled through
the streets it was far enough away, if even for just a few, brief
moments, not to touch you anymore.

There was an underground station nearby but Cross was
buggered if he was going to sit in a sweaty metal tube halfway
across London, so he walked to the main road, stuck his arm
out into the traffic and hailed a cab. The university college
hospital was at least a half hour drive away, probably more
with London traffic being what it was, and Cross sat back in
the cab, stretched his legs out and allowed himself to relax for
a few minutes. He felt the presence of Andariel retreat inside
his head, the angel sensing that he needed to be truly alone
for a while. Cross had hit the ground running this morning and
hadn't stopped. This was the first time he'd been able to take a
deep breath and let it all sink in.

Gus and Kate. The loss hurt him more than he cared to admit, and the fact that he'd been instrumental in their murder was an even deeper cut. Cross was under no illusions that they were still alive. He knew how the Harringtons operated. As soon as Cross had visited the café he'd shown that the ex-fence might be useful to him and the twins would have ordered Gus's execution without hesitation. Poor, kind, tired Kate had just been in the wrong place at the wrong time, an innocent dragged into this twisted maelstrom the twins had birthed with their insane scheme.

The deaths of the closest people Cross had to friends was yet more red in the Harringtons' ledger and those deaths would be answered, whatever it took. What was the saying? 'Before you embark on a journey of revenge, dig two graves.' *Bollocks*, thought Cross. He'd fill a cemetery with a smile before this was all over. Cross allowed his anger to rise, to simmer and seethe within him, enjoying the savage rush the emotion brought as he always did. Then he crushed it down again, compacted and froze it to a diamond-hard core, enjoying the feeling of ruthless control even more than the warming burn of rage.

Cross had long ago mastered his anger along with his fears. Years of training had been further honed in the chaotic crucible of warfare. Every scar was a lesson, every defeat and triumph taught you more about yourself and what you were capable of doing or enduring. Death was never more than a shadow away and pain was merely information, targeting data, a measure of how much longer you could keep up the fight.

He'd soon learned there was no profit in fear and doubt and remorse, only in resolution. Once your mind was set right there was merely what needed to be done. Pain. Rage. Fear. They were tools, no more and no less. Once you accepted pain as a constant and death an inevitability then they were just adjuncts to your will and determination.

He breathed deeply and cleared his mind, emptying it

of the anger and pain to focus on the mission at hand. Cross felt his churning emotions quiet within him, as if his soul was a turbulent sea and he'd just frozen the surface, turning the chaos to crystalline clarity.

Now there was only his mission, a perfectly straight and razor-sharp line with him at one end and the broken bodies of the Harringtons at the other. Even after years of training most people were unable to master themselves to this degree and this pinpoint, laser focus had kept Cross alive while those around him dropped in welters of blood and screams or curled into whimpering balls of defeat.

"You're a surprising man, my friend." Andariel's voice was thoughtful, and unless Cross was imagining things, carried an undercurrent of respect. The Angel chuckled. *"I don't look down on you humans like some of my brethren. Even after a few thousand years of study you people can still surprise us."* Cross grunted. "And horrify you I suppose?" He felt that curious mental hiccup again as the angel shrugged inside his mind. *"Yes, but not for the reasons you might think."* Andariel felt Cross's silent question. *"You're thinking Hitler and John Wayne Gacey and the like aren't you?"* Andariel chuckled again but almost sadly this time. *"One thing you learn after a few hundred millennia of watching life evolve on a billion worlds is that what you call 'evil' doesn't change. It can't, and so it's doomed to stay stunted and shrivelled while creation grows around it. The only truly horrifying thing about evil is its predictable banality."*

Cross snorted. "Tell that to some poor woman getting raped and watching her kids get murdered and see how far you get."

"Well we're 'bigger picture' sorts up in Heaven. We have to take the long view, weigh up the averages and what have you."

"Like auditors?"

"Now that's just rude."

Cross laughed, his good humour restored. He glanced out of the window to see the hospital just up ahead and told the driver to stop so he could walk the last hundred meters or so and scope the place out. He paid the fare and gave a generous tip (with someone else's money of course) and then lit a cigarette as he stood behind a parked van and studied the entrance. *Ok then,* he smiled to himself. *Let's go steal ourselves a body.*

FIVE

The university college hospital was located slap-bang on Euston road and just a stone's throw away from both the main Euston station and Euston square underground. Traffic, both foot and vehicle based was very heavy which suited Cross perfectly. He scanned the crowds around him and then, satisfied he didn't recognise anyone, strode purposefully towards the main entrance. Before he entered he flipped open his fake ID and hung the small wallet over his breast pocket so the silver badge was clearly displayed.

He stopped to let a man pushing a frail old woman on a wheelchair go through the automatic doors before him. The man thanked him, and upon noticing his ID, gave him a respectful nod. Cross mimicked the gesture to the reception staff as he walked briskly past, taking the first corridor on the left. *"I take it you know where you're going then?"* asked Andariel.

Cross grinned. "No idea. It's more important to look like you know where you're going though. Most people are what I like to call 'stupid and lazy'. Have a badge or something official showing and walk with a purpose and most people just ignore you. Too much hassle even asking questions half the time."

As Cross suspected he soon came across one of those 'You Are Here' maps stuck to a wall and he quickly scanned it. Obviously, he'd gone the wrong way and he muttered a few choice words as Andariel silently laughed inside his mind. He found the mortuary and swiftly mapped a route to it that wouldn't take him back past the reception before setting off again with a purposeful stride.

Cross nodded and sometimes smiled at doctors, nurses and patients alike. While not a duplicitous man by nature he'd always enjoyed deceptions like this and he was honest enough to admit that it was at least partly a carry-over from childhood. In that part of his brain where he was still ten years old this sort of subterfuge always made him think he was James Bond.

Cross continued through the maze of identical corridors and down several flights of stairs, wondering why they always seemed to build mortuaries in basements. He finally found the mortuary and as he suspected there was a camera there. Also as he suspected, considering the budget issues every hospital suffered with, it was a cheap model and only pointing down towards the door as a cost-effective and cursory effort at security.

CCTV was something you had to get used to working around when you operated in London, what with Englands' capital having more surveillance than anywhere else in the world. Like any villain worth his salt Cross knew his cameras. Even the good ones had blind spots, leaving unmonitored areas referred to as "dead ground". Cross kept to the right-hand side as he moved down the corridor, angling his head and shoulders slightly to the left to keep his face hidden. They might get a partial look at his face, but he'd have to be really unlucky to have anyone recognise him if they ever checked the footage.

He slowed as he approached the doors and checked the walls for information signs or notice boards. He found what he was looking for to the left of the doors and ran his finger down the list of names until he found a Doctor who was marked down as being out for the day. Cross rang the buzzer and waited as he composed a suitably bored expression on his face. After almost a minute he rang again, twice in quick succession this time.

The door was opened by a scrawny looking young man

in scrubs. A few strands of ginger hair poked out from beneath the hygienic hairnet he wore, and he looked even more bored than Cross pretended to. Cross took the wallet from his top pocket and held it up in front of the orderlies' face. The orderly glanced once at the ID and then his apathetic gaze moved back to Cross. His eyebrows lifted ever so slightly as if even that was a Herculean effort.

"Can I help you?" His voice was halfway between weary sigh and whine and clearly showed that the last thing he wanted to do was actually help anyone. Cross took an instant dislike to him. The downside of subterfuge was that it was usually bad form to give someone a smack in the mouth. He nodded once at the orderly and put the fake ID back in his pocket. "DI Spencer. Doctor Keswick is expecting me."

"Keswick isn't here."

Cross knew Doctor Keswick wasn't there, which was why he'd asked for him. He affected a slight look of confusion. "Really? I spoke to him last night about a possible murder enquiry and he thought he had an unidentified male that might fit a description we've been given."

The request was nonsense of course. It was highly unlikely the yard would send a DI on a goose chase like this, but most people would jump at the chance to be involved in a murder enquiry and Cross found that giving his marks a good story to tell down the pub usually made people a bit more inclined to help. Most of the time anyway.

The orderly stayed silent as he leaned on the doorframe and studied Cross with disinterested eyes. Cross carried on. "Doctor Keswick said I should come down this morning and I could try and ID our guy."

"Keswick isn't here."

Cross supressed the urge to slam the little fuckers' head into the wall and just go in and take a body. "I understand that, sir. Is he due back soon?" The orderly perked up a little at being called 'sir'. "'Fraid not, he's not due back in until tomorrow and Doctor Welling is at some meeting or other. She won't be here until this afternoon." Doctor Welling, whoever that was, not being there either was a stroke of luck and it was about bloody time he had some.

Cross cursed in feigned irritation. "Bugger it. I've got court this afternoon and this case is already going as cold as your punters in there." Cross rasped a hand across his stubble and pretended to think for a second. "Any chance you can help me out? I just need to make a visual ID and I'll be out of your way."

Cross tried to reassure the orderly he wouldn't have to do any actual work. "If it is our guy then I'll come back when Doctor Welling is around to sort out the paperwork." The orderly mulled it over, obviously enjoying this little experience of being in charge. "I dunno," he whined, "I'm not supposed to let anyone in when the Doctors aren't around." He smiled suddenly, a sickly grin that exposed crooked teeth. "Then again you are a copper so what's the harm?"

The orderly stepped back and motioned for Cross to follow him as he moved deeper into the mortuary. His rubber soled shoes squeaked over the tiled floor as he led Cross towards the rows of large, coffin-like drawers situated on the rear wall. Cross glanced to his left as he heard the splatter of water to see another orderly hosing down one of the metal examination tables, cursing quietly as the hosepipe caught on a trolley full of medical equipment and rattled the various saws and scalpels. The sudden jangling of metal seemed overly loud in the subdued quiet of the large room.

His reluctant guide rounded a corner and then stopped and gestured towards the bottom row of drawers. "We've got four on ice at the moment, A through to D." He stopped and screwed up his face as he thought for a second. "I think two have already been ID'd but I'm buggered if I can remember which ones." He shrugged and grinned his sickly grin again. "The toe-tags will tell you though. You ok to get on with it? I'll be in the office if you need anything." His expression clearly showed he'd be most disappointed if Cross did actually need anything.

Cross nodded at him. "I'll be ok from here, sir. It's not the first time I've done this after all." He smiled at the orderly. "I'll let you know when I'm done, I should only be a few minutes and then I can get out of your way." The orderly lazily waved a hand and moved towards the office without looking back, his disruptive visitor already being forgotten.

Cross opened the first drawer, grunting at the weight of the body it held. He pulled the covering sheet back to reveal a grossly fat corpse, the skin grey and waxy looking. Andariel delicately snorted inside his head. *Not a chance!*

Cross grinned. "I thought you said any of them would do?" He looked at the tag and the accompanying paperwork. "Suspected coronary. On the Bakerloo line of all places. I bet everyone was cursing this poor bastard for holding them up on their way home from work."

Not the most dignified of ends.

"Are any of them? Doesn't matter who, how or why we go, we all end up with a stupid look on our face and our trousers full of shit when we die." The angel's tone was wry as Cross pushed the drawer shut and moved to the next one. *Very philosophical, Daniel.* Cross shrugged. "Well we all spend a fair bit of time thinking about death, especially in my line of work. I guess it's not something you lot have to worry about is it?"

We can be destroyed which I suppose is similar, and it's certainly something we try and avoid, but death? I don't think you can die without really being alive first and I'm not sure we qualify.

Cross paused with the next drawer half open. "That's pretty sad when you think about it."

Not really, said Andariel. *Don't forget we don't have the same emotions as you humans. We couldn't. Not and stay halfway sane for longer than a few hundred years anyway.* Cross was about to reply as he pulled the sheet back on the next cadaver but was interrupted by Andariel's pleased exclamation. *This one will be perfect, Daniel!*

Cross looked down at the body. "Are you sure?"

"Of course, it's in excellent condition. Relatively speaking."
"But it's.."
Andariel laughed in genuine amusement. *"A woman? I'm not a man, Daniel, that's just a gender you automatically assigned me. I don't even have a gender as such. Try to remember I'm not actually human."* Cross shrugged. "Fair enough, it's your body your ladyship."
"Very funny."

Cross looked down at the pale corpse. "Ok then, what do I have to do?"
"Place one hand on her head and the other on her heart and just wait. I'll come round after the transfer. It should only take a minute or two." Cross lost his smile. "You want me to put my hand on her…?"

The angel sounded exasperated. *"For the love of God, just put your hand on her left tit! I promise she won't mind."* Cross gingerly did as he was told, closing his eyes and thinking of anything but how the cold yet still soft flesh felt under his hand and fighting the disgusting but automatic desire to squeeze.

He stood that way for what seemed an eternity and then opened his eyes to see Andariel grinning up at him. The newly clothed angel glanced down to Cross's hand still grasping her left breast. "Shouldn't you at least buy me a drink first?" Cross whipped his hand away like it was scalded. "Fuck off!" Andariel's silvery laugh echoed around the room and she swung her legs off of the gurney and stood up.

She looked herself up and down with obvious pleasure and then winked at Cross. "I do have good boobs though don't I?" Cross grimaced. "I think I preferred having you in my head to be honest." He looked away as Andariel began to stretch and bend, testing the flexibility of her new body and causing all manner of alarming jiggling to occur. "I'll go and find you some clothes. Keep the noise down, the last thing we need is one of the orderlies seeing you doing bloody star-jumps in the buff." He quickly turned and disappeared around the corner.
Andariel was ecstatic. It had been hundreds of years since

she'd worn flesh and she'd forgotten what a sublime feeling it was. She focused her will and smiled as she felt her heart start beating again, feeling the warmth suffuse her as her sluggish blood began to flow, her skin losing its grey pallor and blushing pink. Closing her eyes, she concentrated and began to travel through her new body, pleased to find it was disease free and that the cause of death had just been due to an unfortunate clot in her femoral artery.

As a precaution she thinned her blood slightly. While a reoccurrence couldn't kill her it would be both debilitating and extremely painful. Andariel smiled and rubbed her left thigh as a ghostly memory of the pain scratched across her nerve endings. She'd forgotten all of these interesting quirks and foibles of the human form and it felt wonderful to, well, *feel* again. Andariel looked up as Cross returned with a handful of clear, plastic bags and a slightly apologetic expression on his face.

"Looks like she died at home, all she's got is a skimpy nightshirt in here." He deposited the bags down onto the recently vacated gurney. "I grabbed whatever I could find so hopefully there's something in here that fits." Andariel began to rummage through the bags and had soon selected a pair of jeans, a grey vest and a pair of military style boots. She completed her outfit with a thin black jacket and then faced Cross, holding her arms out to invite comment.

Cross nodded approvingly. "Looks good." he conceded. Cross had to admit the angel did indeed look good. Her new body was slim and athletic and her long, red hair framed a pretty face with a charming brush of freckles across the pale skin of her nose and cheeks. She smiled at Cross and he decided she was actually a lot more than just pretty. He sighed inwardly. This was going to take some getting used to.

While Andariel fussed and cooed over her new body, Cross looked towards the office to see the irritating orderly sitting with his back to them and reading the paper. Annoying little shit he may have been but Cross had to admit that lazy people made life so much easier sometimes. A glance around the corner revealed the path to the door was clear and Cross couldn't see the second orderly anywhere in sight so he judged it safe enough to make a sharp exit.

"Oi, Lady Lazarus, time to go." he said. Andariel looked over and rolled her eyes. "A biblical reference, how cute." She grinned suddenly, overcome with the exuberance of life on the physical plane again. The angel actually giggled and Cross smiled and shook his head good naturedly at the sound.

Andariel's new body was petite and Cross towered over her. He ushered her in front of him as they exited the mortuary, keeping his back to the camera and shielding her from view with his bulk. As they moved back up through the corridors he put the fake warrant badge back in his pocket. DI Spencer wasn't needed anymore; they were just a couple of normal people doing normal people things.

The big man started as the angel took his arm. "What're you doing?" Andariel shrugged and smiled up at him. "This looks more natural." Cross started to reply but she cut him off. "Trust me," she said, "we can't both be striding through London grim-faced and looking like we want to maim someone, even though that's exactly what we're going to be doing." She slapped Cross lightly on the chest. "People will remember a great lump like you walking round with a face like a smacked arse."

She grinned mischievously up at him. "Now you're just a grumpy looking bloke with a pretty girl on his arm. All people will be thinking about is how you managed to punch so far above your weight."

Cross fought back a smile. "Face like a smacked arse?" Andariel looked crestfallen. "Please tell me I got that saying right?" she pleaded. "I like that one!" Now Cross did laugh. "Yeah you got that one right." He looked curiously at her. "I know you're not actually a woman but, if you don't mind me saying, you already seem a bit…"

Andariel finished the thought for him. "Girly?"

"Well, yeah."

The angel shrugged. "Yeah that'll happen. As much as I'm in control of this body it's still 'hers'. I've got her hormones and her brain to contend with now. My thoughts have to run through her neural pathways, so I've got a couple of decades worth of her habits and thought processes to deal with, I'm bound to pick up a few mannerisms and quirks of hers along the way."

"And that's normal is it? I mean, I assume you've done this before?"

"A few times, yeah. Not for a while though so it'll take a bit of getting used to again."

Cross looked curiously at her. "When was the last time you were down here?" Andariel thought for a second. "The 12th century was the last time. Michael wanted some of us to keep an eye on Genghis Khan seeing as he was causing such a fuss down here what with murdering tens of thousands and the whole 'enemy of God' thing, so I joined his horde for a while. I was a man then, of course."

She looked appraisingly at Cross. "When all is said and done I think I prefer being a woman really. The whole penis arrangement is a bit unwieldy."

Cross shook his head. "So, you were part of the Mongol horde that conquered Asia and most of Europe and the thing that sticks in your mind is that it's a bit awkward having a dick?" Andariel laughed. "Not quite. The thing that sticks in my mind is getting my head cut off." She winked at him. "That's a bloody shock to the system, I can tell you that."

"Did he do it?" asked Cross. "Genghis I mean?" The angel looked a little shamefaced as she replied. "No, it was during the sacking of Kiev." She brightened up a little as she thought back and remembered the wonderful chaos of battle. "Good little fight that was!" Cross refused to be side-tracked. "So who cut your head off?" Andariel snorted in disgust. "A bloody Russian farmer with a scythe, if you can believe that?"

Cross laughed and Andariel slapped him on the chest

again. "Don't you start; I'm still living that one down." She shook her head. "Lose concentration for a second, get decapitated a bit and you're a laughing stock!"

They reached the exit and stepped outside. Cross immediately lit a cigarette and inhaled deeply. "Christ, that's better." He looked down at the angel on his arm. "So where are we off to then?"

"To see Buttons, I told you that earlier."

Cross sighed. "Yes, I know that. I mean, where is he?" Andariel shrugged. "Haven't a clue really. I know he's in London though." Cross made a show of looking around. "Any chance you can narrow it down a bit?" Andariel chuckled. "Of course, I'm winding you up. Get me a map and I'll be able to track him down." Cross thought for a second and then moved off, tugging the angel along with him. "Easy enough" he said. "Euston station is full of tourists so there'll be somewhere selling maps round there."

They moved off through the crowds and bustle of London, just another faceless couple on the city streets. Cross smiled to himself. *If only they knew.* They soon found one of the myriad stalls selling traditional tourist tat such as flags, toy double-decker buses and the plastic police helmets shaped a bit like a tit. Cross grabbed a map from a rack and opened it up. A single glance at the proprietor silenced any complaint he was about to make.

Andariel ran her fingers across the map and then delicately tapped a single digit down. "There he is!" Cross peered over her shoulder to see she was pointing at a church in Islington; St. Mary's to be exact. He grinned to see it sat between Highbury and Angel and pointed this out to her. "That's a good sign I take it?" The angel shook her head. "You lot and your bloody signs" she sighed. Cross laughed, he was already starting to enjoy yanking her chain. He stopped as a thought occurred to him. "Hold on" he said, "This trick with the map, can you find anyone with it?"

Andariel knew exactly what he was thinking. "I won't

be able to find the Harringtons, Daniel. Malleus would have shielded them from any sort of mystical hanky-panky like this. There are other methods we could use but I'm not doing that unless things get desperate." She looked up and smiled at his disappointed face. "You look like a kid who just dropped his ice cream."

Cross shrugged. "I was looking forward to you doing a bit of hocus-pocus." He held up a placating hand. "Don't get me wrong, the map thing is pretty good, I guess I was just expecting it all to be a bit flashier."

The angel snorted in disdain. "Yeah because fanfares of trumpets and flaming swords wouldn't get noticed. Besides, I'm an angel, not Wonder Woman."

"Well she has a better outfit for a start."

Andariel jabbed him in the ribs and put the map back. "Shall we just get a move on? Christ knows what the other side are getting up to while you're standing here trying to be clever." Seeing as they were outside of Euston Station anyway, Cross decided to suffer the underground. Islington was only a ten-minute journey and he could just about stomach travelling on the tube for that long.

"What are these other methods then?" asked Cross. Andariel looked puzzled. "Eh?"

"You said there were other ways to find people but only if things got desperate, and let's face it, there's an argument to be made for that already. What other ways are there?"

Andariel grimaced, obviously not happy about sharing such information. "There are a small handful of beings across the worlds that can see or hear or sense things happening from miles away, sometimes things that haven't even happened yet."

Cross looked at her quizzically. "You mean psychics?" he scoffed. "Auntie Joan has a message from beyond the grave and all that rubbish?"

The angel looked gloomy. "Most of them are charlatans and just general arseholes," she admitted. "Some of them though…" She shuddered just to think about it. Cross noticed the shiver and was surprised at how discomforted she was. "You mean it's actually real?" He stopped and thought for a second. "I should really stop being surprised by stuff like this by now."

Andariel was still walking arm-in-arm with the big man and she gripped his arm tighter for a second. "It shouldn't be," she sighed. "Even we don't know how they can do it and the boss never said anything about them to us either. As far as we can tell people like that just shouldn't exist, if they even *are* people." Andariel paused for a second as she thought how to explain it best. "You have to understand the nature of the cosmos really. For these…beings to do what they can means they're somehow tied into the fabric of creation itself. They're not just skating over the surface like the rest of us; they're inside the blood and bones of the universe. She shuddered again. "Even we're not built like that. Their potential is…appalling."

Cross nodded to himself. "So, either the boss knows and just chose to keep you lot in the dark, in which case he's a bit of a dick, or they're an aberration, something he didn't plan on, which should be impossible. I can see why you don't like either option."

"Exactly. Luckily, they're extremely rare and even then most of them have no idea just what they could be capable of. One or two of them are extremely dangerous though and there's a fair few of us on both sides that want to go back to the old way of dealing with them.

"Which was?

"Burning them alive usually did the trick."

"Ouch."

Andariel shrugged. "If it aint broke…"

They made their way through the busy station, Andariel looking around with unabashed delight at the heaving crowds and brightly lit shops and drawing in deep breaths as she smelled the air. Suddenly she grabbed Cross's arm and pulled him to a halt. Cross was instantly scanning the crowds and nearly dropped into a fighting stance until he saw the look of almost stupefied pleasure on her face.

Andariel sniffed the air again in wonder. "Oh my God, what is that divine smell?" she asked. Cross looked around and saw the nearest food stall.

"Er, looks like Cornish Pasties to me."

"I've got to have one!"

"We're stopping for savoury products? Really?"

"Oh be quiet, some of us haven't eaten for eight hundred odd years and even then it was mostly goat."

Cross sighed and got out his wallet to hand over a ten-pound note. "Go on then, get me one while you're at it." Andariel took the money and clapped her hands in glee as she rushed off to the pasty stall. She didn't wait until she got back to Cross before taking a giant bite out of hers and covering herself in crumbs and chunks of thick pastry.

Andariel handed the remaining pasty over to Cross and took another bite, closing her eyes in ecstasy as she struggled to move her jaw enough to actually chew the huge amount of food in her mouth.

Cross laughed and took a bite of his own. It was piping hot, and he had to admit, pretty bloody good. Andariel was fanning her hand in front of her mouth and sucking in air as she tried to cool herself down. She tried to speak to Cross but he couldn't make out a word of it round the mouthful of meat and pastry she was devouring. "That good eh?" he asked. Andariel held up a grease smeared thumb and grinned at him. He laughed again and took another bite.

For all that he was in the middle of an utterly insane shit-storm and highly unlikely to survive the day, Cross realised he was enjoying himself and he knew that a big part of this was down to the crumb-flecked angel in front of him. Not only wasn't he going up against the Harringtons and Christ knew what else alone anymore, which was a big plus in itself, but Andariels' easy going nature and sense of humour was infectious. He smiled inwardly. Damned if he didn't like her.

She'd wolfed down her pasty in record time and was licking her fingers clean. Cross held his out which was still mostly intact. "You want to finish mine off?" he asked. "I've already had breakfast." Andariel snatched it away from him and immediately began to tuck in. "You're a good man, Cross," she mumbled through a full mouth "if it was up to me this would get you into heaven straight away."

She finished the second pasty in record time and then licked her fingers before wiping her greasy hands on her jeans. "That's better," she said "I feel ready for anything now!" Cross snorted. "You'll certainly be ready to use the toilet in an hour or two." Andariel grimaced. "I'd forgotten about that. Still, things have moved on a bit since the last time I had bodily functions to worry about."

She grinned at him. "I'm looking forward to it actually!" The angel hooked her arm through his again. "Ok then, let's go find Buttons and we can really start kicking the spokes out of the Harringtons' wheels."

"And bludgeoning them to death a bit," said Cross. "Don't forget the bludgeoning."

They moved towards the escalator that would take them to the platform and deep underneath London towards the mysterious Buttons. Andariel chattered away, still looking at the most mundane things with wide eyes and a huge smile. "I'm quite excited about travelling on this 'London Underground'". Cross glanced down at her and shook his head. "Trust me; you'll get over that soon enough."

SIX

Her name was Tamsin Lowe, but everyone called her Tammy. Well everyone apart from *them* anyway. They called her 'Miss Lowe', an obviously false veneer of politeness and deference that did nothing to mask their utter contempt for her. Tammy looked around the small yet beautifully decorated room she was being held in and marvelled again at the unfairness of it all. Despite what first impressions and appearances might say, Tammy knew she wasn't a bad person. In the main she was kind and generous (apart from when she needed a fix) and the other girls in the Kings Cross stable all liked her.

She held them while they cried and helped patch them up when some piece of shit punter had knocked them around. Tammy cared about her friends, in truth they were more of a family than she'd ever known, and she took some small comfort from the knowledge that these feelings were reciprocated.

Tammy and the other girls had all carved out what small measures of happiness and comfort they could take from a world that, at best, seemed to show them utter indifference, if not outright hostility. It wasn't much but at least it was something.

The girls were all variations on the same sad and sordid story. All the girls had suffered under alcoholic mothers, heavy-handed fathers or sneaky uncles slipping furtive, sweaty hands up their nightdresses. Girls like Tammy didn't leave home; they ran to the uncaring streets, vainly hoping that things could be better.

Strings of failed or abusive relationships usually followed as they tried desperately, futilely, to live like normal people did, not realising they were already too damaged, tragically locked into Sisyphean cycles of abuse and self-loathing. No jobs, no prospects, no money. No chance.

Girls like Tammy were buffeted and broken by life, scoured and hollowed out until all that was left for them was the bottle or needle. A short, brutal and pointless existence made all the more tragic by the fact that they could never crawl far enough into those bottles to truly forget how pointless and painful it all was.

Then there were people like the Harringtons. Born into wealth and comfort, the world around them full of open doors and open arms. A life of ease and elegance with every chance offered and every opportunity theirs to explore. They had so much, they could *do* so much and yet it was never enough.

Their wealth and power were used to garner more of the same and Tammy and her sad and broken friends were exploited and abused without remorse or pity. She wasn't a person to them, she was just a commodity.

Tammy looked around the room and sighed. Why should people like that have so much and she so little? Maybe they had so much *because* they were like that? Maybe it was only the callous and amoral that truly prospered? Perhaps that was the natural order of things? From what Tammy had seen, from what she'd *lived* that certainly seemed to be the case.

She shuddered as she thought back to the awful scene at Kings Cross that morning when the Harringtons had arrived, full of reptilian smiles and cheerful malice, to "educate" them.

Tammy and the other five girls of the Kings Cross stable were kept in a spartan flat which sat next to the main overground line from Kings Cross station. Two minders stayed in the flat with them, ostensibly for the girls' protection but everyone there was well aware of their real purpose and they certainly didn't move too quickly when one of the punters started smacking them around.

The minders were there to make sure the girls didn't leave or, now and again, ferry one out to a client who wanted a home visit. Men visited the flat on almost a twenty-four-hour basis and the girls often serviced a dozen men each in a single day. It wasn't prostitution; it was slavery, plain and simple. A visit from the twins was never a good thing and always ended in pain and degradation for one or more of the girls, particularly if Marcus gave his twisted little brother free reign.

Today it had been poor Jenny's turn. Tammy wasn't sure which was more horrifying: Miles' clearly visible erection as he cut her or the look of amusement in Marcus's eyes as he looked on with a fond smile. Miles took his time and cut slowly and carefully, obviously relishing every cry and drop of blood. He didn't mark her face or body, disfiguring the merchandise was bad for business after all, and neither did he hurt her enough to stop her working but he made sure that her pain would last for days.

Miles cut her time and time again. Each incision a tiny line that was invisible at first and then slowly bloomed crimson as the flesh split open. He cut across each joint of her knuckles, twenty small cuts that would reopen every time she moved her fingers and cause her pain for days on end. He slowly carved a shallow and stinging wound across the backs of her knees to ensure that either sitting or standing would cause her pain. Finally, he cut his name into the soles of her feet which made him laugh like a child.

As he cut her he constantly looked around the room at Tammy and the other girls to make sure they were watching and appreciating his twisted artistry. Tammy knew their looks of fear were every bit as exciting to him as poor Jenny's pain.

"You, come with me." Marcus's command was softly spoken and Tammy had raised her tired, frightened eyes to see his finger pointing at her, and a ball of cold dread twisted in her gut.

Neither of the twins had spoken to her on the drive

back and she watched as the busy city streets gave way to a motorway and then the quiet roads of a picturesque village. Tammy shivered. The sun shone brightly outside but the air-conditioned car was cold. They drove through guarded gates and down a long and winding gravel drive to come to a halt outside a huge house. Tammy barely felt the painful grip on her arm as the driver pulled her from the car and hustled her through the large, double doors and inside before almost throwing her into the small room.

Now Tammy was here, wherever here was and still nobody had spoken to her. She assumed she'd been brought here to pleasure the men; at least that's what she hoped. Perhaps Miles still ached from the restraint he'd been forced to show with Jenny? She was terrified at the thought of becoming a plaything for that madman and his straight razor. Hers was the sickening terror of the truly helpless. She knew the twins could do whatever they wanted to her and no-one would come to save her. No-one would care. No-one would even realise she was gone.

Tammy felt sick and cold but couldn't tell if it was just the fear or the craving for another fix. She'd already shot up this morning, her 'breakfast' fix, but that had been hours ago and her body would soon be demanding more, causing her to sweat and shake and retch until she appeased it with a flood of opiates. Addicts like Tammy didn't use drugs to feel good anymore; they had to use them just to feel normal again for a little while.

She jumped as the door opened and her fear subsided slightly as she saw it was Marcus and not Miles that smiled coldly in the doorway. Tammy tried to return the smile, but the burgeoning pain of her withdrawals and her despair turned it into a sickly grimace. Marcus fought down a shudder. *What a despicable creature* he thought. Marcus, like many people born into wealth, just couldn't understand what was wrong with people like Tammy, letting the world dictate its terms to them rather than taking the world by the throat and demanding it work to *their* rules.

People like Marcus believed that life could be bent to their will with just hard work and determination. People who had never had to do a days' work in their lives often did. He hid his disgust behind his false smile and motioned her towards him. "Miss Lowe," he purred "If you would be so kind as to come with me please?" Tammy stood up from the chair on shaking legs, smoothing her lank hair and wiping the cold sweat from her forehead in a vain attempt to look alluring for him rather than merely sick and bedraggled.

Marcus led her from the small room and through a series of winding hallways. Tammy looked around at the art adorning the walls and the sculptures on small tables that dotted the halls at irregular intervals. It was all meaningless to her apart from the fact that it was obviously expensive, evidence of a life of ease and plenty forever out of her reach. They passed many doors as they moved through the hallways, all of them closed. Tammy was lost. She couldn't believe any house could be this big. Finally, they came to a doorway at the end of this latest corridor and Marcus opened it to reveal a set of spiral stairs.

She followed him up, her wasted muscles protesting the climb with every step and she was grateful when they reached the top. Her fear returned as she saw the doorway and her sluggish thoughts began to race as she wondered what was on the other side. Marcus turned and smiled at her again as he opened the door and she sighed with relief to see the room was empty, thanking an absent and uncaring God that Miles was nowhere to be seen. Marcus stepped aside and ushered her into the barren room.

Had Tammy been thinking clearly, she would have wondered why she was being taken to an empty room. At least, the room was almost empty. A small and battered copper bowl sat on the dusty floor and she looked at it in confusion. Miles, hidden behind the door, stepped forward, and with practised ease, smoothly ran his razor across her throat. Tammy felt no pain, which was often the way with razor cuts. It felt cold, like an icicle had been stroked gently across her neck and then the cold was submerged in the rush of warm blood as her severed carotid artery jetted blood across the room.

Miles grabbed a handful of her greasy hair and knotted it round his fist as she fell choking to her knees to guide the already faltering flow of blood into the bowl. He smiled at the sound it made as it pattered against the copper surface and breathed deeply of its beguiling, metallic scent. Marcus entered the room and closed the door, hardly sparing a glance for the carnage in front of him. He checked his watch and hoped this wouldn't take too long.

Tammy's eyes began to dim and the last thing she saw was her own blood brimming at the top of the bowl and then pouring over the sides onto the dusty floorboards. The darkness took her then and she began to fall, almost feeling a sense of relief that her painful mockery of a life was over. This momentary sense of calm turned to panic as she realised she wasn't alone. Another shared the darkness with her, a coldly burning presence that shoved her aside as it climbed towards the dwindling spot of light so far above.

Tammy fell through the dark toward a sea of screams and her voice joined that unholy, despairing chorus. Death was to be no release and Tammy knew with dread certainty that a million more lifetimes of pain and degradation awaited her below. As Tamsin Lowe fell to her underserved damnation she knew that her screams would never end.

Malleus opened stolen eyes and climbed to his feet in his new flesh. He turned to see the twins who both nodded grudgingly in respect. Malleus raised a hand to the corpses ruined neck and the torn flesh and vocal chords knitted back together in seconds. He delicately cleared his throat and then turned and spat blood into the bowl behind him. Malleus closed his eyes again and felt for the link that bound him below, ensuring that he wasn't bleeding too much power into the mortal realms.

The demon was here but not here. His flesh, his 'self' still resided in the cold, dark tundra of Hell. This was just a projection of his consciousness, but even this pale reflection of him had enough power to animate the corpse and carry his voice across the vast and haunted gulf between the worlds. Communicating like this was a delicate process, one that required finesse and unwavering control. Too little power and the stolen body would falter and the link between worlds would be severed, while pouring too much power through would cause the vessel to disintegrate or alert *them* to his presence.

He cursed inwardly. *Damn these rules and restrictions! Damn his sanctimonious, vengeful father and his favoured children and thrice-damn his so-called master and his hunter!* Malleus calmed himself and opened his eyes to look upon the twins. What wonderful specimens of the human race they were! Callous and cruel and completely oblivious to the true ramifications of their precipitous actions, and blind to the inevitability of their own extinction and torment.

They knew! Heaven and Hell, paradise and damnation were no longer just mythical, abstract concepts for the Harringtons. They were reality and the twins knew their actions, their *lives* were rushing them headlong into the pit and yet they pushed blindly onward.

Or perhaps they weren't blind after all? Over the millennia Malleus had tutored, seduced and cajoled the very worst of humanity and sometimes even he had been surprised at the spectacular results they achieved.

They were so small and frail, so brief, their lives sparking and then guttering out like mayflies and yet they still possessed the most towering arrogance. According to humanity, the vastness of creation, the whole of eternity, circled round the singularity of their importance.

This delusional arrogance, coupled with their almost unbridled lust for power, meant the Harringtons were probably fully aware of where their twisted and malefic path led them and they simply didn't care. Perhaps their arrogance and

Ian King

madness were so great they believed they could somehow cheat him? Could cheat the laws of creation itself?

Even if all they planned came to pass and they strode through the ashes of a burned and broken cosmos while the creator wept and wailed in chains, even then Malleus would ensure they suffered for eternity. It was what he did. It was what he *was*. By the void but he loved humans sometimes.

With thoughts of their eventual and delicious torment running through his mind his smile to the twins was completely unfeigned. "Good morning, gentlemen." he purred. He glanced down at his temporary vessel and smiled wryly. "Couldn't you have found me something to wear that was a little less raddled?" The demon lowered his head and sniffed delicately. "And it smells."

Marcus huffed with impatience. "I'm sorry our former employee doesn't meet your exacting standards but I'm sure you can appreciate the obstacles involved in procuring an athlete or captain of industry to have their throats cut at such short notice?" Malleus laughed. "Always so serious, Marcus!" he chided. "You're taking all the fun out of this little enterprise of ours."

Miles joined in the laughter. "I'm always telling him the same thing. What's the point in plotting to overthrow God himself if you can't have fun with it?" Marcus snorted in disdain. "One of us has to resist acting like a giddy schoolgirl at the thought of setting the universe on fire, Miles, particularly considering how 'this little enterprise of ours' is working out so far." Miles grimaced at yet another rebuke from his dour sibling while Malleus waved away his concern.

"We have had something of a setback," he admitted, "but it's nothing we can't resolve, Marcus. Steps are being taken as we speak, and we'll soon have Mr. Cross in damnations chains again. We will soon be free to pave the way for more of my brethren to cross over and then the fun can really begin." The demon flicked a stray hair from his face, a perversely human gesture and Marcus felt a creeping horror steal over him as he looked at what just minutes ago had been a young woman. The knowledge that something ancient and cold now stared at him through those dead eyes was unnerving.

He fought back his momentary unease and arched an eyebrow. "And these steps are?" Malleus paced around the small room, clenching his fingers and rolling his neck as he felt the pilfered flesh begin to settle and seep into him. He shuddered at the feeling, this forced and unwelcome intimacy with the base mortal world. How he hated wearing such frail, filthy skin!

He ceased his pacing and faced the twins. "My subordinates are contacting some of our...representatives here on earth and they will be arriving shortly to assist you." The demon grinned, showing blood stained teeth. "Mr and Mrs Cobley are very committed to the cause I can assure you."

Marcus and Miles exchanged a look. "And Mr and Mrs Cobley are?" asked Miles. Malleus shrugged. "I suppose you would call them 'Satanists' or some such." Malleus sniffed. "I never cared much for the word myself."

"Satanists? Really?" Marcus was obviously decidedly unimpressed. Malleus sighed. "Don't get hung up on the term," he advised. "We refer to them as the 'blessed' and they've been imbued with some rather special talents."

Malleus clasped his hands behind his back and began to pace the small room again as he lectured the twins, like an obscene Poirot in a gallery scene. "As you're aware we can't operate on the mortal realms ourselves, so we defer certain tasks to our agents. Heaven, Hell and all the places in between employ these clandestine methods to play our great game." He stopped pacing and cocked his head as he thought for a second. "I believe you'd refer to it as a 'loophole'."

Miles was curious, his stunted emotions stirred as always by thoughts of power. "They're still human then?" he asked. "These 'blessed' of yours?" Malleus smiled at him, well aware of what piqued the mortals' interest. "Human enough for our purposes," he smirked. "The process is simple enough and relatively painless. If you're of a mind to join their ranks I'm sure we can come to some arrangement." Miles began to speak but Marcus cut him off. "No, thank you," he said firmly, ignoring Miles' furious look. "Let's just stick to the task at hand, shall we?"

Malleus smiled inwardly at the twins' fractious display. Even among his supposed allies he couldn't help but foment ill-feeling and discord. It was his very lifeblood. "Very well," he said. "I assume you've been keeping an eye on our truculent lab rat?" Marcus nodded. "Of course. As expected he's trawling the streets for information. Knowing Cross, he'll be looking to find out what happened to him so he can indulge that barbarian nature of his and kill someone."

"That someone being you I take it?" laughed Malleus. Marcus shrugged, unconcerned by the potential threat. "Cross won't get within a hundred feet of us unless we want him to. Barnes has been tailing him all morning and tidying up any loose ends Cross might create as he blunders through London."

"Ah, Lincoln Barnes," said Malleus with a slight smile. "An interesting man."

"Barnes? Really?" The twins shared a puzzled look and Malleus cocked his head curiously. "You can't see it can you?" he asked. "See what?"

"Most of you humans lack control, you lack the will to control yourselves and until you master that you will never truly control the world around you. Barnes? You can feel the willpower and control almost smoking off of him." He shook his head. "Remarkable really, considering how limited you people are."

The twins remained unconvinced. "I'm sure Barnes will be pleased to learn you're a member of his fan club," sneered Miles. "What I'd like to know is just what went wrong. Would you care to shed any light on our current predicament?" Malleus pulled a disgusted face, partly at having to explain himself to these pitiful creatures and partly at how blinkered they were. How could they stand being so blind? How could they be content to move through life so crippled?

They were fools to discount a man like Barnes. They had no idea just how rare a man they had in their thrall and squandered his unique talents on petty thefts and thuggery. If the twins were fools to discount Barnes, then they were doubly so to ignore a man like Daniel Cross. Cross may seem bluff and rough around the edges, but Malleus had instantly seen through that façade to the real man beneath, a man of fierce intelligence and ruthless will. Those qualities were why Malleus had chosen Cross as the conduit in the first place. A possessed body was a tool, a weapon and it always paid to ensure you used the sharpest of blades.

The demon wondered if Andariel had made himself known to Cross and, if so, how much he might have told him. He highly doubted the angel would have possessed him, they were laughably squeamish about such things, but Andariel had always been unpredictable, which was one of the reasons he had ended up abandoned and chained in the pit.

The angel escaping his bonds and hijacking the conduit was a definite problem and a serious one, but it was a problem that could be contained, a problem that could be solved and Malleus was confident they could get their scheme back on track if they moved quickly and decisively enough.

He *hated* having to rush things, but time was of the essence. The longer he stayed here, the more noise they made in the mortal realms the higher the chance of the other side, or even worse, *him* finding out became. Malleus shuddered to think what would happen if Lucifer found out just what he was up to. His cold rage flared. The Morningstar, first amongst the host of heaven and now absolute ruler of Hell, power and will incarnate and yet still a slave to the creator and the dreary, constricting status-quo imposed upon creation. How he hated him!

The demon pushed these thoughts aside and faced the twins again. "For the last few thousand millennia, Heaven and Hell have been in a state of...truce shall we say? The war amongst the host almost tore the fabric of reality to shreds."

Malleus stopped and smiled as he remembered the screaming chaos of the war that had lasted for a thousand years and more. If he closed his eyes he could still feel the fiery essence of dying angels exploding over him, could still feel their agony and terror as he put his pathetic brothers to the sword.

He sighed wistfully. "It was a wonderful time." Malleus began to pace again, enjoying the precise and measured *click-click* sound the high heeled boots that this body wore made upon the dusty, wooden floor.

"Since then we've been in what you could call a 'cold war'. The ruling body of Heaven and the current master of Hell seem content to let this carry on indefinitely. I, however, am not and there are even some among my former brethren in Heaven who feel the same way, though they lack the courage to do anything about it." He carried on pacing as he spoke uninterrupted, both twins enthralled by the unfolding tale.

"Michael and his angels believe their sole purpose is to ensure creation continues to run to plan, even in the apparent absence of its creator." Malleus sneered in disdain. "The mighty Archangels have become little more than caretakers, keeping the cosmos neat and tidy and tick-tick-ticking along. And Lucifer?" The demon shook his head. "The being that almost toppled God from his throne now sits brooding on his own as he hoards your tarnished souls. Better to rule in Hell indeed!" he spat.

Marcus and Miles exchanged a nervous glance, feeling the temperature in the small room suddenly drop by a few degrees as Malleus let his anger seep out. The demon lord mentally shook himself and controlled his fury until the room began to warm again. "One of my opposites, although a far lesser being than I, is an angel called 'Andariel' and he chafes under the strictures of Archangel Michael's rule." The demon smiled suddenly, his good humour restored. "Andariel and some few others within the host have certainly helped to keep things interesting over the last few eons. To continue with the cold war analogy Andariel and his little troop of malcontents have been involved in a number of border skirmishes and clandestine operations across the realms, often against the express orders of the heavenly host. I suppose you could call him something of a renegade."

Malleus stopped suddenly and pressed a hand to his stomach as it gave an alarming and painful twinge. "What on earth is happening to this body?" he demanded. Marcus looked slightly shamefaced. "Ah, she was a heroin addict; you're probably going into withdrawals."

"Oh this is absurd!" Malleus forced himself to ignore the discomfort and carry on. "We recently caught Andariel on the outskirts of Hell, no doubt sneaking around on one of his ridiculous spying or sabotage escapades and he's been our guest ever since." Malleus smirked. "It appears that Michael had finally reached the end of his tether with his rebellious underling as he seemed quite content to leave the little bastard to our tender mercies."

Marcus nodded in understanding. "But he's not your guest any longer I take it?" Malleus looked aggrieved. "No, he's not. Unfortunately, Andariel has now taken up residency in the mind of Daniel Cross." The demon almost smiled. "I have to admit I didn't see that one coming. It's almost nice to know I can still be surprised."

Marcus was less enthusiastic. "So Cross has been possessed by an angel?" he demanded. "We're dealing with one of the heavenly host rather than a two-bit crook and you're just bothering to tell us this now?"

Malleus levelled a cold stare towards him. "Careful," he warned, and Marcus paled at the quiet rebuke. "It's highly unlikely Andariel will have possessed him," he assured them. "Angels are sadly burdened by outmoded concepts such as 'honour' and 'free will' and other ludicrous conceits. He's still fighting the good fight, albeit while ignoring his own partyline and in his own childish way. He wouldn't have taken over a host against their will."

"So what's the worst that could happen?" asked Miles.

The demon shrugged. "If Andariel makes himself known, and assuming finding out he has a renegade angel in his brain doesn't send Cross insane, the worst Andariel can do is feed him information, possibly direct him towards someone who could help, although they're are unlikely to become directly involved."

"And these people are?"

"I have my agents and the angels have theirs but there are others out there who could prove problematic. They've refused to pick a side for the last few thousand years however, so I doubt they'll start now" He raised a hand as Miles began to speak again. "I already have people in place watching them and I assure you they will take whatever actions are necessary."

Marcus nodded, content to let the subject rest for now rather than antagonise the demon further. "Very well", he said. "So how do you suggest we remove Cross's new playmate and get things back on track?"

"That's simple enough. If he's half as good as I think he is he'll have found out you were behind his abduction, or perhaps Andariel has told him if he's chosen to reveal himself. You know him, what do you think he'll do next?"

"He'll come here to try and kill us and burn our house down."

Malleus laughed. "Exactly! You have to admire his singleness of purpose really." Miles looked confused. "Are you suggesting we let him?"

"Why waste time chasing him all over London if he'll be happy to come to you?" asked Malleus. "You have enough men here to secure the grounds and the blessed will also be at your disposal should Andariel or anyone else prove troublesome. I assume you can make the necessary arrangements in time?"

Marcus glanced over at his twin. "Miles, can I leave the surgical team to you?"

"Of course, brother. I assume the drawing room in the east wing will be suitable?"

Marcus nodded his assent. "Thank you, Miles." He started to

speak but was interrupted by a discrete *chirp* from his mobile phone. "Excuse me for a second" he sighed. He listened for a moment. "Send him up," he said. He looked at Malleus. "Barnes is here. If we're about to stake ourselves out as bait I'd like his input." Malleus smiled. "Very wise." In less than a minute the door opened, and Lincoln Barnes entered the room.

If the blood-spattered floor and the dishevelled whore that smiled redly at him in blood-drenched clothes unnerved Barnes then not a flicker of it showed on his face. He simply nodded respectfully to the three occupants of the charnel room, closed the door behind him and waited. "Ah, Lincoln," said Marcus, "we'd like your advice on our next move regarding Mr. Cross." He stopped and then motioned to Malleus. "I assume no introductions are required?"

Lincoln shook his head. "Of course not." He nodded again to Malleus who returned the gesture. Lincoln faced the twins again. "What are you proposing?"

Miles stepped forward. "Malleus believes, and we concur, that as Cross will almost certainly be coming here to enact his childish revenge fantasies we might as well save ourselves a lot of effort and just let him come to us."

He smiled condescendingly at his employee. "We would, of course, value your opinion." Lincoln ignored the sneering look on the younger Harringtons' thin face and concentrated on the question. He was used to the twins looking down on him and saw no value in wasting his time and energy getting angry about it.

The twins looked down on everyone. Growing up in the poorer boroughs of London, even in the 21st century, Lincoln had been a victim of bigotry and racism for most of his life, although in most cases only the once before he dealt with it decisively or sometimes permanently. At least the twins weren't bigoted as such. They despised everyone who wasn't them, which was equality of a sort.

Lincoln returned to the matter at hand. "I agree," he said, "We know the ground, and more importantly, we can control it. A suggestion though, if I may?" The twins nodded their assent and Lincoln continued. "Cross is ex-military which is dangerous enough. What's worse is he's *smart* ex-military and he'll sniff out an obvious trap from a mile away. How averse are we to taking a few casualties, gentlemen?" The two humans and the demon looked at each other and shrugged. Malleus looked at Lincoln in mock reproach. "I'm surprised you even had to ask."

"Good. We need to let him think he's fought his way here and won through on his own. He's a soldier, so let's give him a war to fight." Malleus slowly nodded in appreciation. "Good," he echoed, "very good." The demon took the floor and returned to his measured *click-click* pacing of the room. "We throw a few obstacles in his way and he'll be too busy enjoying himself killing people to wonder if perhaps getting here was a little *too* easy." He looked over at Lincoln. "I take it you still have eyes on him?"

"Of course. He stopped at an address in Hammersmith, the residence of Doctor Chandra Singh, a known associate, and then met someone at the university college hospital, a young woman. We don't know who she is, but we can't keep up with every snitch and hooker Cross might consort with. Mr. Joslin is still tailing him now and I've got Chapman and Thomas ready to go mobile when Joslin checks in. The last we saw, Cross and the girl were headed east on the underground. Probably going to Islington unless he's leaving the city, which seems unlikely."

Malleus stopped his pacing and his eyes flashed as he stared at Lincoln. "Islington?" he barked. "This girl he met at the hospital, did we just see him leave with her or did we see her going in?" Lincoln was puzzled by the demons' sudden interest. He was under no illusions that he could accurately read this creatures' emotional state but the posture of the body it inhabited suggested Malleus was far from relaxed anymore. Something was obviously wrong. "As far as I know we just saw them leave together. We were watching him rather than looking out for anyone else. Is there a problem?"

The demon looked at him through narrowed eyes. "There could be," he admitted. "It could be coincidence but one of the other entities I spoke of is said to reside in Islington and I'd rather not take any chances at this point."

Marcus looked at him quizzically. "I thought these others were unlikely to get involved?" The demon snorted in disgust. "This one might. He *has* picked a side and he loves his work." Malleus clapped his hands. "I'll take my leave now, gentleman. Let me deal with our potential problem in Islington while you concentrate on Cross. Mr and Mrs Cobley should be here within the hour, along with their coven. They've been informed they are to follow your instructions, but I must warn you they can be a trifle enthusiastic, so I'd suggest you didn't use them for anything requiring too subtle a hand."

He moved away from the humans to the centre of the small room. "I shall remain on the other side when the transaction takes place to ensure there aren't any further problems from my end. All being well this will all be over by tonight," he stopped and smiled, "or perhaps I should say it will all begin tonight?" The demon laughed at his own joke and the body of Tamsin Lowe crumpled to the floor as the demon's laughter echoed through the room.

Malleus opened his own eyes once again and sighed in relief to see the familiar surroundings of his private study. It was good to be home. Earth was such a grubby little place. He leant forward on the desk and peered over steepled fingers as he considered this latest development.

The girl. It all hinged on the girl. She could, as Barnes had suggested, simply be an associate of Cross's. He was well aware how these human criminals liked to surround themselves with a network of informants and flunkies. But if not... *Would Andariel have done it? Would he have exposed himself to such a degree?* Inhabiting a body of his own would certainly grant him more power and reanimating a corpse was far less risky than a full-blown possession but it *was* still a risk.

If anything, the host of heaven were even bigger sticklers for the farcical rules regarding meddling in the mortal realms, and if Andariel made too much noise Michael would have him back in golden shackles in an instant. A far more comfortable prison than the last to be sure but a prison all the same.

Then there was the Islington conundrum to consider. Do nothing or take action? Both carried risks, but what was the more dangerous option? Malleus decided the greater risk was to do nothing at all. This entire enterprise was a huge gamble so why balk at taking a further chance? He smiled as he remembered an old human saying he was fond of: *If you're going to be a bear then you might as well be a grizzly.*

Besides, Buttons had been a thorn in his side for far too long and having the little bastard dismembered would be immensely satisfying, not least for the angst it would cause his master to lose his favourite pet. The demon closed his eyes and sent his silent order of execution out into the void.

SEVEN

The church of St. Mary in Islington had stood on what would become the centre point between Angel and Highbury Corner since the 13th century. Rebuilt in the 15th, 18th and 20th centuries the church had worn a few faces during the course of its long history. Reverend Buttons had worn even more.

His first name and his first face were almost lost to both time and memory, but he remembered all of the people he had been since he was chosen and taken and changed so long ago. When the Elizabethan dramatist, John Webster, had married his heavily pregnant second wife under special license and amidst such scandal in 1606, Buttons had performed the ceremony, almost laughing himself silly at the parochial and hypocritical outrage on display from some quarters of the parish.

Buttons had worn a different face and used a different name when Charles Wesley and George Whitefield were expelled from the pulpit in 1739, accused of having "all the spirit of the devil" in them. Considering Buttons' true vocation this had made him laugh even harder. In 1759 he watched as Phillip Quaque, son of King Birempong Cudjo of Fante, was baptised, the first black man to be ordained as a priest in the Church of England.

More names and more faces followed. Samuel Ajayi Crowther, William Hagger Barlow and John Whatley Hopkins to name just a few. The list went ever on. It didn't matter which face he wore or which world he journeyed through; eventually Buttons always returned to his haven at the church of St. Mary.

In 1940 he watched in horror as a German bomb destroyed his beloved sanctuary, and though nobody would ever know it, Buttons was instrumental in ensuring the appeal by the Reverend Hugh Gough for the church to be rebuilt was successful, despite the objections of the bishop. Buttons could be very persuasive. The current incarnation of St. Mary's was a beautiful building, the huge worship area surrounded by large windows to bathe the room in sunlight and decorated with two superb murals by the renowned church artist, Brian Thomas.

Reverend Buttons tutted quietly as he inspected the mural on the east wall and found a large splatter of blood across the bottom-left corner. It was already drying and he scratched forlornly at it before turning to survey the church and see what other damage had been done. Aside from a broken pew it appeared the mess really wasn't that bad. The bodies and the blood, barring the unfortunate redecoration of the mural, would be easy enough to remove and he started dragging the first of the corpses towards the vestry.

He was a small man, but he lifted the dead-weight of his unfortunate assailants easily enough, humming a hymn as he worked and adroitly avoiding getting any blood on his shoes. He'd already had to get changed once this morning.

He was just beginning to mop up the first of the puddles of blood when a knock sounded at the door. Buttons sighed inwardly. *It never rains but it pours.* His mind quested outwards to see who his visitors were, and he gave a delighted laugh as he moved swiftly to the door. He pulled it open to see a large man arm-in-arm with a pretty redheaded young lady. The man was stone-faced, but the young woman was grinning as she disengaged her arm to rush forward and hug the small churchman.

The two of them embraced and then held each other at arms-length to inspect the other's latest body. Andariel was laughing as she looked at him. "Couldn't you have found anything bigger?" she teased. Buttons joined in the laughter.

"I'm being inconspicuous!" He looked at her critically. "You certainly stand out". He wagged a finger at her in mock reproach. "You always go for the pretty ones. You're getting predictable in your old-age!" Andariel stuck out her tongue. "Oh hush. Nothing in the rules says you can't do the Lords' work while looking fabulous." She stopped and thought for second. "There isn't anything that says that is there!?"

Buttons laughed again. "You're asking me?" Andariel looked at her old friend. The last time she'd seen him he'd been wearing the body of a large, muscular man in his early thirties. Now his body appeared around fifty years of age with close-cropped grey hair. His black shirt hung on his slight frame, the stark, white clerical collar he wore sitting loosely around his thin neck. She smiled as she looked at his eyes. Whatever body he wore the eyes were always the same and their good-humoured sparkle was always a comforting sight.

The small man smiled at Cross and held out his hand. "Hello there. Our mutual friend here is frightfully lacking in manners I'm afraid. I'm Buttons. And you are?" Cross shook his hand. "Daniel Cross, er, pleased to meet you reverend." Buttons caught the look of confusion on his face and smiled. "Not quite what you were expecting eh?"

The small man looked pointedly at Andariel. "See?" he smirked. "Inconspicuous!" The angel rolled her eyes at him and then sniffed the air as the scent of blood came to her. "What have you been up to?" she asked. The diminutive churchman shrugged. "It's been a busy morning." He narrowed his eyes and levelled a finger at her. "I suspect you might have something to do with it actually. You turning up today is a little too coincidental for my taste."

He motioned them through the door and then followed them in, closing and locking it behind them. Andariel and Cross took in the blood-soaked room without comment as Buttons moved the mop and bucket out of the way and then led them towards the vestry. He opened the door to display the five, bloodied and broken corpses inside. "Any idea why these idiots tried to kill me this morning?" he asked. Cross looked into the room and his eyes widened in surprise.

He looked from the battered bodies to the small man beside him and then back again. At least one of the corpses was missing a vital piece of its anatomy and Cross saw one of the wayward limbs sticking out from the bottom of the grisly pile. He looked at Buttons and raised his eyebrows a fraction. There was obviously a lot more to him than was apparent at first glance.

Buttons noticed the look and made a disgusted face. "Messy I know," he apologised. "I was pressed for time though." Andariel looked over the mound of corpses and found the dismembered limb Cross had just seen. She grinned and nudged Buttons with an elbow. "Did you really beat one of them to death with their own arm?" she laughed.

Buttons shrugged. "I thought that might dampen their enthusiasm, but I think they were more scared of whoever sent them than they were of me, and that doesn't bode well." He closed the door and led them through the back of the church to a small kitchen, pointing them towards a table and chairs that had clearly seen better days. The little man bustled about the kitchen preparing tea and biscuits and hummed happily as he worked. He was genuinely pleased to see Andariel. It had been at least a hundred or so years since their last meeting, he forgot just which plane it had been on now, and he had often wondered what his angelic friend was up to.

For a being like Buttons, normal human relationships were problematic to say the least. He supposed it must be easier for the angels (and certainly easier for demons) but he'd begun his life as a normal man, and despite the profound changes he'd undergone, the many worlds he'd visited and the myriad different species and creatures he'd dealt with over the long centuries, he still felt a pull towards human beings.

He had allowed himself to grow close to people too many times over the millennia, and if he let it the pain of their loss could still be crippling. The changes his master had wrought upon him enabled him to compartmentalise his mind and emotions to a large degree, but he could never deny them completely without losing the last vestiges of his own humanity, something to which he fiercely clung to.

Andariel was remarkably human in her character, showing much more emotion than most of her pious and dour brethren and being able to have a friend who he wouldn't have to watch age and die while he changed his name and face again and again, a friend who he could have a relationship with that wasn't based on lies was a vital anchor in his long life.

He poured his guests a tea, placing an old-fashioned tea-cosy over the pot then adjusting it *just so* before he was satisfied and motioned for them to help themselves to a biscuit. Cross didn't need telling twice and dunked a Hob-Nob into his cup with obvious enthusiasm. He demolished it in short order and took a large gulp of the piping hot tea, closing his eyes in satisfaction and raising the cup slightly towards Buttons. "Thanks reverend, you're a life-saver."

Buttons smiled at him. "My pleasure, Daniel. You can never go wrong with a good cuppa." Cross grinned and took another biscuit. "A man after my own heart." Andariel snorted in good natured derision. "You two are easily pleased." Buttons laughed and took a Hob-Nob from the plate. "It really is good to see you my friend. I'm going to take a guess this isn't a purely social visit though?"

He carefully placed a hand in his jacket pocket and produced a small knife. "Particularly considering one of my earlier guests was carrying this." He passed the knife across the table and Andariel wrinkled her nose as she hefted the weight and looked down the edge of the blade. "Ooh, nasty! I haven't seen one of these in a while."

Cross leant forward to look at the knife the angel was turning in her slim hands. "What's that then?" he asked. Andariel handed it over and Cross cursed softly as he touched it. The weapon was bitterly cold. He looked at it closely and saw a sinuous pattern flowing beneath the metal of the blade.

The pattern within the blade constantly changed, and even though the same pattern was never displayed twice each of them looked *wrong* somehow.

He quickly put it down and wiped his fingers on his trousers. Andariel went to pick it up again and then decided to leave it where it was. "It's called a *Kraal*," she explained. "They're very rare, which isn't a bad thing believe me. The world they came from was an awful place. The creatures that lived there were even more destructive than you lot, and that's saying something."

Cross ignored the jab. The fact that a considerable percentage of humanity were arseholes wasn't his fault after all. "You used the past-tense. I take it that place didn't have a happy ending then?"

Buttons barked a sharp laugh. "You could say that. A lot of people still think flame-grilling the entire planet with a giant solar-flare was a bit over the top." Cross raised his eyebrows at the angel sipping her tea across the table from him. "Did you do that?"

Andariel shrugged. "I might have had some input," she admitted. Andariel looked at the two men staring at her. "What?! They were coming up with much worse things than the *Kraal*. If they'd stayed confined to their own planet we would have just let them get on with it, but the nasty little bastards were starting to exterminate other worlds for sport and we can't have things like that," she pointed to the eerie knife on the table "and worse loose across the cosmos."

Buttons looked over at Cross. "We weren't pointing fingers were we, Daniel?"
"Wouldn't dream of it."
"Oh shut up the pair of you. Have you ever tried to orchestrate a targeted solar flare? No, you haven't and it's bloody hard work let me tell you." The angel crossed her arms and pointedly looked away. Cross took another Hob-Nob. "Has she always been this touchy?" he asked. Buttons grinned at him. "You don't know the half of it my friend."

Cross quickly changed the subject before Andariel could launch into another rant. "So this *Kraal* thing, what's so bad about it?" the angel looked first at the knife and then at Buttons. "Do you want to explain it?" she asked. "You've always been better at explaining stuff to mortals." Buttons nodded and gingerly touched the hilt of the knife with a single finger so it span slowly round on the surface of the table. Cross was sure he could hear a menacing hiss as the ill-aspected blade moved.

"The *Kraal* were a particularly nasty species indigenous to the planet our hard-working friend here barbequed a few hundred millennia ago. I suppose the closest analogy to a creature in this world would be a form of scorpion. The world in question had an extremely harsh environment and it was a miracle any forms of life evolved there, let alone sentient beings, so it's not surprising a few people thought arbitrary extermination was a little harsh." He held up a hand as Andariel started to protest. "That's not a criticism my friend," he assured her. "I'm just stating a fact. I'm actually inclined to agree with you." Buttons looked at Cross. "It's no mystery they turned out like they did considering how brutal life was there. It was like an entire planet of rabid dogs and there's only one thing you can do with a rabid dog. More tea?"

Cross was slightly taken aback by the sudden shift in conversation from alien worlds to another cuppa, but he'd never turned his nose up at a second cup of tea and he wasn't about to start now. "Er, yeah that'd be good, thanks." Conversation halted while the little vicar poured everyone a second cup and refreshed the dwindling pile of biscuits on the chipped plate.

Buttons sat down and took another Hob-Nob before continuing. "The *Kraal* was extremely venomous and even more aggressive. The sentient race of that world were called the *Arimaskai* and they discovered a rather ingenious way to weaponize them." He stopped and dunked another biscuit into his tea as he thought of how best to explain the process to Cross. "You know how these 3D printer things are becoming all the rage now, yes?"

Cross shrugged his big shoulders. "Stuff like that goes over my head a bit," he admitted, "but I get the general idea." Buttons nodded in satisfaction. "Ok then. Essentially a 3D printer is turning data into a physical object. The process the *Arimaskai* used turned a physical object into data, for want of a better term, but kept the essential *anima* of the creature alive and then allowed them to mould it into a different shape." Cross leant back from the table slightly. "So that thing is still alive?"

Buttons shrugged. "More or less." He grinned at Cross. "And it's really rather angry!" The small man put his cup of tea down and leant across the table. He nodded towards the dreadful weapon sitting next to the plate of Hob-Nobs. "A *Kraal* can kill pretty much anything, they're deadly in any form, and it's a weapon that really *wants* to kill you."

Cross looked at the small but obviously lethal weapon in front of him. It was wrong on so many levels. It looked wrong, it's shifting patterns making his eyes itch and his stomach turn and it *felt* wrong, particularly now he knew how it had been made.

The big man almost thought he could feel the weapons' deadly intent and desire to harm. On the other hand, Cross was a soldier and he knew the practical benefits of such a weapon, particularly considering what they might be up against. He mentally shrugged. When all was said and done ancient, murderous blades from another world were actually the least of their problems today.

Buttons looked over at his friend and smiled. "So," he said. "I assume you can shed some light on what's actually going on? I'm taking a wild guess that you're in the middle of it?" Andariel returned the smile. "Well, you know me; I never could leave well enough alone." She cleared her throat and leant forward, placing her elbows on the table. "Ok, firstly, what's wrong with me turning up on your doorstep like this?" The small churchman looked confused. "Think about it," prompted the angel. "Think about what you do." Buttons' eyes widened as he realised what Andariel meant. "I didn't feel a thing!" he gasped. "How did you get to earth and into that body and I didn't feel it?"

Andariel nodded grimly. "Exactly." She pointed towards Cross. "Actually it was our big friend here who bought me over." Buttons looked enquiringly at Cross who just shrugged. "Don't look at me", he said. "It wasn't my idea." The Angel laughed and then began to explain the days' events and the insane scheme of Malleus and the twins. Buttons listened in silence and then shook his head with a disgusted look on his face. "Malleus," he spat. "I don't know why the boss has never given me the go-ahead to put an end to that fucking snake!" He grimaced and looked over to Cross. "Sorry, please excuse my language." Cross smiled. "Don't mind me, reverend. You fill your boots."

Buttons stood up and began to pace the small kitchen, obviously agitated. "This is bad. This is very bad indeed. The fact that I'm only just hearing this from you means that the boss hasn't caught wind of it yet, so Malleus is free to do as he pleases, for now at least." Andariel nodded. "That's one of the reasons we came to see you. I was hoping you could get a message to him. If we can give Lucifer the heads up, then he'll come down on Malleus like a celestial ton of bricks and it'll all be over." Cross looked back and forth between the renegade angel and the small vicar. "Hold on a second! Are you telling me you work for the Devil!?"

Buttons stopped his pacing and smiled over at Cross. "I do as a matter of fact." Cross just looked at them for a few seconds and then reached into his jacket pocket for his cigarettes. "Ok then," he said. "Firstly, does anyone mind if I smoke?"

Both Andariel and Buttons waved their assent and Cross lit a cigarette with obvious relief. "Christ, I needed this. Now secondly, would either of you care to explain why I'm having tea and biscuits with a vicar who works for Satan and his best friend who just happens to be an angel?"

Andariel and Buttons both laughed and Buttons moved back to the table and sat down. "Don't worry, Daniel," he reassured him. "It's really not as bad as it might sound." The little man looked suddenly sad. "At least, doing what I do isn't so bad. How I got there however…"

Buttons looked away for a few seconds as he cast his mind back through the centuries. "I was born over 800 years ago in a small hamlet in what's now Sussex. Nothing remains of it now, not even an entry in the history books, and perhaps that's for the best?"

He reached across to Cross's cigarettes on the table. "May I?" he enquired. Cross wordlessly nodded and handed the small man a cigarette and then lit it for him, already spellbound by his story. This man, or whatever he was now, had been alive for hundreds of years and Cross couldn't begin to imagine the things he might have seen and done.

Buttons grimaced as he inhaled. "I haven't smoked for nearly a hundred years," he explained, "this body isn't used to it." He coughed lightly and then smiled. "Still good though." He took another drag, longer this time and then continued with his tale. "My family, like all the families in the hamlet, were poor. We worked from sunrise to sundown and still we often went hungry but, in the main, we were happy enough.

"England looked completely different then of course. Vast swathes of dense forest covered the land and our tiny home was tucked away, deep within the trees. We went unnoticed by the rest of the world and that suited us just fine." Buttons ground his cigarette out and sighed. "The rest of England was in chaos. The Vikings had sacked Lindisfarne and began their ceaseless raids, further and further inland and more ferocious each time. People were terrified. They were a heathen scourge, a punishment from God and a kind of madness gripped the land, but for us? Hidden away in the deep forest? We were safe, or so we thought."

He stopped and picked up the teapot, grimacing as he shook it and realised it was empty. Andariel took it from him. "Here," she said softly. "Let me do that." She laid a hand on his shoulder and squeezed as she moved past him to the sink and Buttons smiled his thanks.

"They found you then?" asked Cross. "A raiding party?" Buttons shook his head. "No, deserters from Alfred's army. Some of our own." Cross nodded in understanding. He'd seen soldiers lose it and go feral before when a small bunch of lads went AWOL after a spectacularly fucked up deployment in the Congo.

He hadn't blamed them for wanting to run, to disappear, but what they did to some of the locals as they fled? After seeing that, Cross and his recovery team, and even the accompanying military police, had ignored the "bring them back alive" part of their orders.

Buttons sat silently, staring into space as he thought back across the painful centuries. "What happened?" asked Cross, gently.

"I was out hunting, so I was far enough away not to hear the screams, but I did see the smoke. By the time I got back it was too late. Most of the bodies were too badly burned but I saw enough to know the women had been..."

The little man looked at Cross. "I was betrothed. We were going to be married the next spring. She was..." Buttons shook his head. "She suffered the same as my mother and my sisters. My father? My father had been nailed to the door of our cottage, so he could watch it all before they burned it down." Cross said nothing. What was there to say?

"It took me a long time, years, but eventually I found them all." Buttons looked down at the table. "Many people had to die just for me to find them all, and when I finally did? They received tenfold the pain my family had suffered."

Still, Cross remained silent. He offered no absolution, that wasn't his to give, and he offered no judgement. Who was to say he wouldn't have done the same? Buttons raised his head and looked at him. "I'm not ashamed that I killed them, put them in front of me and I'd kill them all again. But by the end?" Now the little man looked ashamed. "By the end I had begun to enjoy it."

Andariel had finished making the tea and poured them all another cup before she sat down. Cross and Buttons thanked her and she shrugged. "No problem. Looks like we've eaten all your biscuits though. Sorry."

Buttons laughed and took a sip of the piping hot tea. He looked at Andariel in surprise. "Not bad," he said. "Have you been practising?" The angel just smiled and shrugged her way out of her jacket. It was getting hot in the small kitchen. Buttons winked at Cross. "Another few decades and she might even get the hang of it." Cross laughed, pleased to see the little man's good spirits returning. He'd already decided that he liked him, agent of the Devil or not. After a few sips of tea, Buttons continued.

"After the last one died I was lost. All I knew by then was how to hunt men and inflict pain. I was little more than an animal, and like an animal, I returned to the forest. To do what I don't know." Cross had a good idea what Buttons had planned all those centuries ago but said nothing. He was sure Buttons knew too.

"Anyway," sighed the little man. "That's when I met him".

"Lucifer?" asked Cross and Buttons nodded. "I'd wandered back home, to what was left of it at least. I'd buried the dead and the forest had already begun to reclaim the few ruined buildings that remained."

He smiled sadly. "It was peaceful, even beautiful after a fashion. He was sitting on the trunk of a fallen tree as though he was waiting for me, which of course he was. "'Sit with me a while' he said, and I asked him why. I remember his smile was sad, so sad. 'For I am no stranger to pain' he said, and so I sat, and we talked and, well, that's when he offered me a job."

"A job?" Cross had clearly not expected the tale to end with such a prosaic statement and Buttons chuckled. "Well there's a little more to it than that but it would take far too long to explain. Believe me; you haven't experienced red-tape until you've made a deal with the Devil." Andariel barked a laugh. "Ha! You want to try dealing with my lot!" Buttons and Cross both laughed and the sombre mood mercifully lifted.

"So what do you do exactly?" asked Cross. Buttons looked at Andariel. "I assume you've explained the basics about possession and the like?" Andariel nodded her assent. "A bit of a crash course but he's quicker than he looks so I think he understood it." Cross grinned at her. "Cheeky cow."

Cross lit another cigarette and offered the pack to Buttons. After a moment's hesitation the small man took another one and lit it before he spoke again. "Lucifer really isn't what you'd expect," he began, "he's actually very easy going once you get to know him." Andariel nodded in agreement. "Yeah, I always thought he was alright, despite the rebellion." She shrugged. "He always seemed to be smiling. Not like he knew something we didn't, it was more like he took a genuine pleasure just from being here and being a part of it all which is a lot more than I can say for some of the other nob-jockeys up there." She looked surprised and Cross laughed. "Nob-jockeys?" Andariel grinned and tapped the side of her head. "That must have been one of hers that slipped out, I like it though!"

Buttons blew out a long plume of smoke. "No-one really knows what started the war in heaven," he explained. "Lucifer isn't saying anything and God is in the wind so all we're left to go on is the propaganda being spewed out by the more strident agitators on both sides. The bottom line is that Lucifer doesn't want another war, at least not from what I can see, and he seems quite content to divide his time between keeping Hell ticking over and wandering the cosmos."

He grinned conspiratorially. "Ok, he might give things a little nudge or a kick here and there to poke a stick in God's spokes, but he seems to be more interested in just seeing what creation has to offer and how it's all unfolding nowadays."

Cross caught on quickly enough. "So he doesn't want to

upset the apple-cart and let his mob run around down here being a pain in the arse but it would be bad form for him to be seen reining them in. Can't have him doing the Lords' work what with him being the great adversary and all."

Buttons nodded in appreciation. "Exactly," he said in an admiring tone. "When one of the more unruly demons breaks ranks and crosses to the mortal realms without permission then I get sent to sort things out before they cause too much damage and rattle too many cages. I either send them packing back to Hell or resolve the problem in a more permanent fashion." He sniffed and flicked ash onto the empty plate in front of him. "Most of the time I choose the latter option, the demons I deal with are the worst kind of scum. The universe is better off without them."

Cross grinned. "So you're like an enforcer then?" Buttons understood the reference and waggled a hand in a *maybe* motion. "There's a little more to it than that but, yes, that's essentially the job description." Andariel laughed. "So modest my friend," she teased. She looked at Cross and then nodded towards the small reverend. "Buttons here is a bit of a legend. Some of the upper echelons on both sides know, or at least suspect, what he is and who he works for, but the rank and file don't. To them he's a rumour, a nightmare." Buttons was self-depreciating. "Just doing my job."

"So how did you two meet?" asked Cross. Andariel chuckled and picked up the tale. "It was around, what? Five hundred years or so ago?" Buttons cast his mind back and nodded. "Give or take a decade," he smiled. Andariel gestured animatedly as she spoke. "I was wandering the borders between Heaven and Hell, basically seeing what mischief I could get up to really." She winked at Cross. "I've always had a bit of a hard-on for Malleus and his little coterie of sycophants so if I can catch one of them out and put the boot in then I count that as a good day." Cross laughed at the petite, bloodthirsty angel across the table. "Anyway," she continued, "as luck would have it I caught one of Malleus's stooges out in the open, whipped out the old flaming sword," she looked over at Cross, "we do actually use those by the way, and then got to work."

Andariel stopped and grimaced as she remembered what happened next. "My eyes were bigger than my belly as it turned out and the fight wasn't going as well as I planned." Her eyes flashed defiantly as she looked at them. "I would have had him eventually though!" Cross and Buttons wisely said nothing and the angel carried on. "I was flat on my back, and to be honest, things really weren't looking too clever for me," she jerked a thumb towards Buttons, "and that's when he turned up."

She shook her head and laughed. "Frightened the fucking life out of me! One second there's a demon cackling over me about to stick an axe in my face and the next there were body parts, entrails and all sorts flying about the place. I wiped the blood from my eyes and there he was, just standing there calm as you please in that bloody awful mask of his."

"Mask?" asked Cross. Buttons looked almost embarrassed. "It's a bit of an affectation really," he admitted, "but it seems to have the desired effect when I'm on the clock." He reached into his pocket and removed a plain, canvas mask. It was devoid of any features save for a pair of bone-carved buttons for eyes sewn into the stained, rough material. The small churchman slipped it on and Cross recoiled. The little man suddenly loomed larger in the room, the blank face radiating power and menace. Cross could feel the bone 'eyes' boring into him, through him and he shivered. "Fuck me," he breathed. Buttons quickly took the mask off and laughed at their expressions. "See? It does the trick!"

"Doesn't it just?" Cross looked closely at him, hardly able to reconcile the fact that this small, jovial man who'd just made him a cup of tea was actually the Devil's secret weapon. He breathed a sigh of relief as Buttons put the dreadful mask back in his pocket. "Was that your idea or his?" he asked. "Mine," said Buttons with a smile. "The boss seems to like it though. Demons have a terribly high opinion of themselves as the scourge of creation and I think seeing them shitting a brick before I kill them appeals to his sense of humour."

Buttons stood and began to clear away the cups and plate. He filled the sink and began to wash up, speaking over his shoulder as he did so. "I assume our next order of business is putting a stop to Malleus's latest power-grab then?" Cross nodded. "Seeing as how Malleus and those Harrington twats decided to kill me and tried to have me possessed by a demon I think it's only fair we royally fuck up their day, don't you?"

Buttons grinned over his shoulder. "I'd say that was a perfect way to restore some karmic balance to the universe. I'd suggest we make ourselves scarce though, they're obviously watching this place, probably you two as well so we should try and disappear for a while." He put the first of the washed crockery onto the draining board and Cross walked over, grabbed a tea-towel and began to dry it.

He looked over to Andariel still sitting at the table. "You comfy there while we do all the work?" he teased. Andariel had a troubled expression on her face. "Not really, no". She clutched her stomach and looked at Buttons. "I think I need to use your toilet." Cross burst into laughter and Buttons pointed to a door at the other end of the kitchen. "Through there and second door on your left," he said.

Andariel quickly got up and walked out of the room, putting her middle finger up to Cross as she barged past him which made the big man laugh even harder. "Two Cornish pasties in about five minutes flat," he explained. "I knew they'd come back to haunt her!" Buttons joined in the laughter and handed Cross the last cup to be dried. Once this small job was done the two men sat back at the table and had another cigarette while they waited.

They sat and smoked in companionable silence for a few minutes until a thought occurred to Cross. "Those stiffs back in the vestry, were they demons?"

Buttons shook his head, a disgusted look on his face. "Just normal humans," he said. "Even if one of them had a *Kraal* it's still bloody insulting really. I would have expected a few of the blessed if not a full-blown demon at least."

"The blessed?"

Buttons leant forward as he began to explain. "Mortals who have proven particularly useful or amusing are sometimes augmented by their patron demon. The more powerful the demon the more powerful the blessed become. I know for a fact that Malleus has a few of them scattered around the realms so either he's getting desperate sending regular humans after me or he's really not giving me enough credit."

Cross thought for a second. "So are you like one of the blessed then?" Buttons made a face. "In a way I suppose I am," he admitted. "However, my talents were given to me by Lucifer himself rather than a mere demon so the changes I underwent were a lot more profound."

"But you're still human though?" asked Cross and Buttons smiled sadly. "I like to think I am, but I've lost as much as I've gained, and how much humanity can you lose and still think of yourself as human?" Cross snorted. "Trust me," he said, "you've got a lot more humanity than some of the people I deal with on a daily basis." He held out his hand. "For what it's worth, reverend, I'm glad we met, and not just because we're about to go hunting demons." Buttons smiled again, this time in genuine pleasure and took Cross's proffered hand. "That's actually worth a lot, Daniel. Thank you".

Cross grinned. "No charge". The big man faced Buttons with a curious look. "So how does it all work then? Moving between heaven or hell and our world I mean. Are they both..." Cross stopped, at a loss how to even frame the question. Buttons stepped in. "Are they both real and physical places or is heaven a realm purely of the spirit? He asked and Cross nodded. "Yeah, it's a little hard to wrap my head around."

Buttons laughed. "It took me a few decades to do that so I wouldn't worry. I'm not sure my explanation will make it any clearer for you, but I'll do my best." Buttons stopped and thought for a while as he considered the best way to answer

Cross's question. It wouldn't be easy. The human languages didn't even have words for some of the concepts Cross wanted explained.

"Well, to start with the cosmos as you know it and heaven and hell are all physical, or I suppose it's more accurate to say they all have their own physicality. They're also all in the same place geographically speaking, although not geography as you understand it." Buttons frowned, wondering whether this was making any sense at all and was heartened to see Cross nodding sagely.

"So they're all physical places, but not really, and they're all in the same place, but not really." Cross grinned. "How am I doing so far?" The demon hunter laughed. "I told you it would be hard to explain. Ok, how about this? Think of it all as a radio."

"All of what?"

"Everything. Both sides of creation."

"Heaven, Hell and the universe are like a giant radio?"

Buttons smiled. "Stay with me. Inside the radio, for the purposes of this explanation at least, are all the radio stations, each of them on a different frequency. They're all there but you can only hear the one you're tuned into."

Cross laughed. "Bloody hell, I think that actually makes sense. So I'm tuned to the frequency of my universe and Angels and Demons are all tuned to a different one?"

"Sort of." Said Buttons. "It's closer to say you *are* one frequency and Angels and Demons are another. The difference is that celestial beings can change their frequency and move from one plane to the next."

"So the 'noise' they make as they move is like static?"

The small demon hunter laughed and clapped his hands. "I suppose it is, do you know I never thought of it like that?"

They were interrupted by the return of Andariel, a sickened look on her pale face. "That was horrific!" she gasped. "Don't ever let me eat those things again." The two men laughed as she slumped into a chair next to Cross. He smiled over at her and reached into his jacket pocket. "You're actually sweating," he said. "Here, use this." He handed her a clean handkerchief and the angel wanly smiled her thanks. She mopped her brow and then went to hand the handkerchief back to Cross who told her to keep it. "So," she said as she stuffed the handkerchief into a pocket in her jeans, "where are we off to then?"

Cross checked his watch and saw that it was coming up to midday. He looked at his two companions. "Well I'm starving so how about we have our little council of war over a pub lunch?" he suggested. Buttons smiled. "An excellent idea, I could murder a pint actually and I know just the place."

"Walking distance?" asked Cross and Buttons shook his head. "Not unless you're really into walking." Cross smiled nastily. "Good," he said, "we'll kill two birds with one stone then." Andariel had a puzzled look on her face. "What are you talking about?" Cross, still smiling, lit another cigarette. He checked the packet to see there were only a few left and made a mental note to stock up again as soon as possible. Whatever else might happen today he wasn't going to run out of cigarettes as well.

"We know we're being followed so we need to take care of that little problem and I'm buggered if I'm going to piss about with trains and cabs all day." He took a long drag on his cigarette and then continued. "If Lincoln is half as good as I think he is I'm betting he's running a mobile and a foot team to follow us and the mobile mob will have a car, so we'll kill them, take their car and Bob's your uncle!"

"Bob's my what now?" asked Andariel and Buttons laughed. "It's a figure of speech," he explained. "It basically means 'job done and everything is alright'" The Angel nodded as she digested the information and Cross smiled as he watched her silently mouth: "Bob's your uncle" to commit it to memory. Cross held out a hand and waggled his fingers. "I'm hoping one of you two can do some of your mumbo-jumbo and find out exactly where our stalkers are?"

Buttons and Andariel exchanged a glance and then Buttons closed his eyes for a few seconds. "Done," he said as he opened them again. "Dark green VW just on the corner. I can only feel two of them so I guess whoever's on foot is hanging back."

Cross stood up to leave by the back door but Andariel waved him away. "I'll take care of this," she said in a tone that brooked no argument. "They're probably still wondering who I am so it'll be easier for me to get over there without spooking them too much if they see me." She sniffed. "Besides, I'm the only person here who hasn't got to kill anyone today."

EIGHT

Kenny Chapman shifted in the drivers' seat, wincing as he felt his sweating back peel away from the leather of the chair. It was hot in the car and he was bored and uncomfortable. He couldn't run the air-con without risking draining the battery and the bastard steering wheel kept jabbing him in the knees every time he tried to find a comfortable position. It had only been an hour, but it already felt like they'd been sitting here for bloody ages.

Kenny was disappointed with how much sitting around and doing nothing seemed to be involved in a life of crime. As a young man he'd greedily envisioned the girls and drugs and money, the prestige and respect and fear his criminal status would afford him.

There had been some of that to be sure, but in reality, the life of a gangster seemed to entail short, sharp periods of excitement, fear and violence and much longer periods of essentially doing fuck all. Kenny Chapman wasn't the sharpest knife in the drawer but even he was beginning to realise that perhaps the life of an outlaw wasn't quite as glamorous and exciting as it appeared in the movies. He glanced over at the young lad dozing next to him and cursed under his breath. Kenny would be the first to admit he wasn't exactly a human dynamo, but Kai Thomas elevated laziness to an art form.

Kenny jabbed Kai in the ribs. "Wake the fuck up!" Kai jerked awake and glared at his partner as he rubbed his side. "Fuck off, Ken." Kai smeared a hand across his face and sat up straighter in his seat. He peered into the wing mirror at the church behind him and sighed. "Well look at that," he drawled, "there's still fuck all happening." He cracked the window open a bit further and then lit a cigarette. "How long do we have to stay here anyway?"

Kenny shrugged, following Kai's example and lighting a cigarette of his own. "Until Linc tells us we can go," he said. "Waste of fucking time," muttered Kai and Kenny laughed at him. "Keeping you from all your important work are we?" Kai blew smoke out of the window. "Keeping *us* from an afternoon in a beer garden."

Kenny was forced to concede the point. It was a beautiful day with clear blue skies and warm sunshine, with just enough of a breeze to stop it feeling too hot. At least it would be if you weren't stuck in a fucking car watching a church. He sighed and decided to throw Kai a bone. No point in winding the little prick up too much if he was going to be stuck with him all day. "I'll call Linc in a bit and give him an update. They haven't moved for over an hour so maybe they're settled in for the day. Linc might send someone to relieve us as there's fuck all going on. I think Joslin is still out there trailing them on foot so maybe he can take over?"

Kai refused to be mollified. The siren song of a cold pint was all he could hear. "What's the big deal about Cross all of a sudden anyway?" he asked. "I haven't heard about anything he's done to piss the twins off so why are we gunning for him?" Kenny pulled a face. "Fucked if I know. Linc says keep an eye on him so we keep an eye on him, end of story. Not like they're about to explain themselves to us is it?" The younger crook's face darkened. "Hired fucking help is all we are," he complained. "It's not like we don't put good money on the table for the pair of cunts and Linc's starting to think his shit don't stink either."

Kenny laughed derisively. "And you're gonna tell him that are you?" he mocked. Kai shook his head and grinned, slightly shamefaced. "Not fucking likely! I'll just keep moaning to you about it." Kenny smiled, almost in spite of himself. Kai might be a lazy little shit with a daft name, but he'd worked with worse. The two men were silent for a time. Neither was the greatest conversationalist and they both sat wrapped in the 'could have, should have, would have' thoughts of those who felt terminally short-changed by their lot in life. They both jumped as the rear door opened and twisted in their seats to see the petite redhead they'd been following grinning at them from the back of the car.

Kai managed a brief: "What the fu.." before Andariels' hands shot forward to grasp them both by the throat. A sharp and savage twist was followed by the wet stereophonic 'snap' of their necks breaking in unison and Kenny and Kai were quickly and efficiently shuffled off of the mortal coil, ending their squalid lives as dazed and confused as when they'd begun. Andariel smiled at her handiwork. *Just like riding a bike* she thought.

Her smile faded as she belatedly considered the logistics of the situation. She couldn't leave them here, nor could she just dump the bodies on the pavement and it suddenly dawned on her that she had no idea how to drive a car either. *Bollocks.*

A movement to her right caught her eye and she looked over to see Cross lean in through the drivers' side window and smile at her. "I take it you haven't got your license?" The angel huffed in impatience and began to drag Kenny's body into the back to free up the driving seat.

Kenny wasn't a small man and Cross noted the ease with which she moved the dead weight. Andariel was obviously a lot stronger than she looked. "Of course I can't bloody drive," she said. "I was on horseback the last time I came down here." Cross slid into the drivers' seat and grinned at her in the rearview mirror. "Well if we rob a stagecoach later you'll be the first person I call."

Andariel wrinkled her nose at him. "Can we just get on with it?" She jabbed the body next to her. "I think this one shit himself." Cross started up the car and drove round the block to the back of the church. There was a small, walled courtyard at the rear of St. Mary's and Buttons was already standing beside the open gates. Cross drove through and Buttons shut the gates behind him. Cross got out of the car and looked across the roof of the VW at Buttons. "Can we stick these with the rest?" he asked. Buttons shrugged. "Might as well. Two more bodies aren't going to make a difference; the carpet in the vestry is already ruined."

Buttons took Kai's body from the front while Andariel dragged the unfortunate Kenny from the back seat and across the courtyard towards the back door of the church. "What are we going to do about all the stiffs anyway?" asked Cross. "I take it we're not just leaving them here for a cleaner to find?" They'd reached the vestry by this point and Buttons hooked the door open with his foot and then heaved Kai's body on top of the pile. "Good lord, no!" he said. "Mrs Crompton would have a fit, the poor dear. Here, give me that." He took Kenny's body from Andariel and added it to the charnel mound in the vestry. He looked at it critically. "It really is starting to smell bad isn't it?"

Cross cast a professional eye over the bloody pile and sighed inwardly. That was a lot of bodies. Buttons stood next to him. "I assume you've had to dispose of a few corpses in your time?" he asked. Cross nodded. "I've done my fair share," he said, "and a proper pain in the arse it is too." Buttons returned the nod. "Oh yes. Even one is bad enough but have yourself a little massacre and it's a nightmare. Did you ever try feeding them to pigs?"

"Pigs are good. You still need to pull the teeth and fingernails first though, unless picking through pig shit afterwards is your thing. Burning is harder than it looks too."
"Surprising just how much bone gets left behind isn't it?"

Andariel looked at them smugly. "That's why we use weapons forged in the hearts of stars," she crowed. "They don't even leave ash behind when you're done." Cross raised an eyebrow at her. "Bring a couple of spare flaming swords did you?" he asked.

"Well, no but.."

"Ok, moving on then."

The angel muttered to herself while Buttons chuckled. "Dumping them out at sea is always good."

"Yeah but sorting out the boat is a headache and you still end up having to drive to the coast or a quarry with a dead body in the boot of your car. More trouble than it's worth really."

"True," conceded the small churchman, "Plus you have to weigh them down enough to stop them floating to the surface in a few days."

"Chicken wire."

"Excuse me?"

Cross grinned at the slight vicar. "Wrap the body in chicken wire when you dump it. When they start to bloat the wire cuts into them and releases the gas. Stops them floating back up."

Buttons nodded his head in admiration. "Now that is a good idea." Then he laughed as he remembered something. "I found a particularly voracious microbe living on the bark of a tree on one world I worked on. You could grind the bark into a powder, sprinkle it over a body and the little buggers would chew through a corpse in minutes, bones and all."

Cross's professional curiosity was piqued. "Yeah? Now that does sound handy." Buttons grimaced. "It might sound good on paper but it was a devil to handle safely outdoors." Andariel smirked at him. "Came a cropper did you?"

Buttons looked slightly embarrassed. "Well the wind changed suddenly and next thing I knew my foot was being eaten away." Andariel burst into laughter at this and both Cross and Buttons joined in.

"It's not funny!" he admonished even as he laughed with them. "I had to cut my own bloody leg off at the knee to stop them spreading!" This just made them all laugh harder. Buttons was the first to control himself and he briskly clapped his hands together.

"Well we're pressed for time and chopping them up and putting them in bin bags won't be fun for any of us. I don't make a habit of this but I'd say this qualifies as a special occasion." The small man began to roll up his sleeves. Cross looked at him curiously. "What are you going to do?" he asked, and Buttons grinned at him. "There are a few places in the universe where the fabric that holds it all together is a bit…thin I suppose you could say. If you find one of those places you can move across time and space in the blink of an eye."

Cross remembered an article he'd read, or perhaps it had just been a Sci-Fi movie he'd watched once. "Like a wormhole?"

"Exactly. They're extremely rare which is just as well, or the universe would probably unravel, but there are some of us that can create our own when the need arises."

Andariel looked aghast. "He lets you do that?!"

"Lucifer? Of course, it was his idea in the first place. There's no point him sending me on a job to another arm of the Milky Way and it takes me five hundred years to arrive is there?" He waved away her concerns. "Yes, yes I'm well aware of the risks and I only do it when I have to. I'm not opening up rifts in the space-time continuum to pop to the shops or anything."

Cross was grinning from ear to ear. "You're really going to open up a portal to another world? Right now? Here in the vestry?" Buttons laughed. "Yes, I am." Andariel was less than impressed. "You're like a pair of bloody kids! You can't go poking holes in creation and dumping bodies on random planets whenever you feel like it!"

"Oh, don't be such an old woman! The planet I use doesn't even have a proper name, let alone a sentient race."

"So you've done this a few times then?"

"Let's just say more than once but less than a lot and leave it at that shall we?"

Andariel folded her arms and just stared at him. Buttons snorted in good natured derision. "I know you're basically hard-wired to take offense at anyone playing fast and loose with the weave of creation, but you don't usually worry about following the party-line too closely do you?"

"This is different!"

"How?"

"Because...because it just is ok?"

"You can take the angel out of heaven..."

"Oh shut up and get it over with"

Buttons laughed and then clapped his hands and cleared his throat. "Ok then, I'll have some quiet please. This takes a fair bit of concentration and believe me when I say you really don't want me making a balls-up of things."

"Just how dangerous is it?" asked Cross with a hint of trepidation in his voice. Buttons shrugged. "Worst case scenario is I let it get beyond my control and the two planets end up colliding, but that hardly ever happens."

"Doesn't sound like such a good idea now does it?" crowed Andariel. Cross just grinned at her. "You're crazier than a bag full of cats if you think I'm going to miss this." The angel started to retort but Cross silenced her by putting a finger to her lips. "Shhh!" he admonished, "the man said he needs quiet!" Andariel knocked his hand away and glared at the two men. "Fine," she huffed and then stepped back, pulling Cross into the doorway of the vestry with her. "Stay well clear of it then, I don't want you going arse over tit through the hole and have to fish you back out from the other side of the galaxy."

Buttons stood with his hands clasped in front of him and his head bowed as though he was at prayer. He splayed his fingers and then slowly, as though pushing against a vast weight, began to move his hands apart. Cross saw the slight tremor in his arms and shoulders as he forced his hands further and further apart and shook his head in wonder as he watched the little man push against the weight of the universe itself to force a doorway open. He jumped slightly as the mound of broken bodies in the centre of the vestry sagged and Cross realised that Buttons was opening the wormhole directly underneath them.

The mound sagged further as the bodies on the bottom

of the pile began to fall through the rift. He heard a splash and smiled as he realised that Buttons was still dumping the bodies out at sea, just not a sea on planet earth. As the hole between worlds widened the rest of the bodies quickly fell through and Cross laughed in pure delight as he felt a salt-scented breeze wash over him.

He couldn't pass up an opportunity like this and moved forward to get a better look. The breeze tugged at his jacket as he stood on the edge of the portal and looked down onto a turbulent sea. Cross estimated the distance at around ten feet below him, close enough to feel the spray and he laughed again as a wave broke beneath and sent droplets of water across his face.

It was darker on whatever world lay below him, Cross assumed it was either dawn or dusk, and the electric light spilling through the rift from the overhead bulb in the vestry gave the sea beneath him an eerie look, further exacerbated by the sight of several corpses drifting away and slowly sinking beneath the waves. Cross found it difficult to look at the edges of the wormhole, almost painful in fact. They were too... sharp. Too *real*. The forces at play were immense. The fabric of creation, the 'weave' as they'd called it, was being violated at the quantum level and Cross knew that titanic energies were being held at bay within the confines of the vestry, all by the indomitable willpower of the slender demon hunter. The sheer scale of it made his brain hurt. It was absolutely terrifying, and he was loving every second of it.

Buttons and Andariel joined him at the edge of the portal, the angel clearly both curious and impressed despite her reservations. "So where exactly is this place?" asked Andariel. "It's in the Lyra constellation, over a thousand light years from Earth." Buttons sounded quite pleased with himself and Cross laughed. "I'd say the odds of the Police finding this lot just dropped a fair bit then." Buttons smiled. "I told you this was a good way to dump a body."

"Reverend, this is amazing, it really is. If it does all end up going pear-shaped today then I can't say I didn't go out on a high." Cross looked the small man in the eye. "Thank you for this." Buttons laid a hand on his arm. "You're welcome, my friend. Let's do our best to all stay alive today though shall we?"

Buttons turned to Andariel. "This place, Kepler-62e I think the boffins call it, is over half again the size of earth and it's basically a huge ocean. No life past the microbial level as far as I can see so the impact of a few corpses ending up there now and again should be fairly minimal." Andariel nodded, still not entirely mollified but willing to concede that Buttons hadn't simply picked a planet at random. The little man grinned at her. "I have to be careful with the coordinates of the rift of course, I don't want to go opening it under the surface and flooding a perfectly good planet Earth now do I?"

The Angel grimaced. "Yes, yes," she huffed "Very funny. Can we stop pissing about with the laws of creation for five minutes and get back to the task at hand?" Buttons guided them away from the edge of the rift and began to close it. "Once it's open it isn't too difficult to keep it stable," he said. Cross caught the strain in his voice and shook his head in admiration as the little man once again shouldered the weight of a galaxy for a few seconds. The reverend carried on, his voice distracted as he concentrated on the task at hand. "Closing one of these things is usually the hardest part. The universe doesn't like people poking holes in it and it always wants to snap back into place."

"That's not a good thing I take it?" asked Cross. The portal was almost closed now and Buttons smiled over at him, sweat beading on his brow. "Well letting the portal close uncontrolled would cause a bit of a bang."
"How much is a bit?"
"Equivalent to about a thousand Krakatoa's going off at once. Give or take."
The small man shuddered as the portal finally closed and whooshed a sigh of relief. He stretched his back and then

125

smiled over at them. "And done!" he said. "Now, shall we go and get that pint?"

NINE

The demon visited Mr and Mrs Cobley while they were shopping at Homebase in Battersea. Mrs Cobley had been complaining about how drab and tired their small conservatory looked for months now and Mr Cobley had finally relented and agreed to redecorate. Mrs Cobley wanted the room to feel cosy and so only a "warm" colour would do, whatever that meant. Mr Cobley was casting a critical eye over yet another colour chart and trying to differentiate between the muted oranges that were 'Autumn Fern' and 'Jungle Ginger' when the printed colours began to swirl and run together on the laminated board.

Mr Cobley brightened considerably. A visitation usually meant their master had a task for them which would certainly take precedence over an interminable weekend of painting and decorating. He looked over to Mrs Cobley who was examining her own colour chart, that one consisting of indistinguishable shades of yellow.

His wife was a small, plump woman who favoured smart but comfortable pantsuits and large sunglasses like her heroine, US senator and former first lady, Hilary Rodham Clinton. Mrs Cobleys' fiercely lacquered and imposing hairstyle added at least another three inches to her height but even this didn't put her on a level with her much taller spouses chin.

Mr Cobley was tall and whip-thin and his usual attire was more the comfortable trousers and brown cardigans of the retired school teacher. Some of the more uncharitable people of their acquaintance sometimes used the words 'gangly' and 'cadaverous' when describing Mr Cobley and while this may have been uncharitable it was also unfortunately true.

The cadaverous Mr Cobley smiled over at his plump and power-dressed wife. "Sweetheart? I think I've found the perfect colour for us." Mrs Cobley marched over to her husband and broke into a smile as she realised what was happening. It was busy in Homebase and yet neither of them worried about the visitation being observed by any of the other customers.

None of the stunted 'normal' humans scurrying around them had the wherewithal to discern what was happening under their very noses. The Cobleys, strange as it may seem at first glance, ranked amongst the most powerful of the servants of Hell and so the talents imbued upon them by their infernal master were many and varied.

Once such talent they possessed was the ability to distinguish time in separate streams and, to some extent, exist between them. They could see time march stolidly past as everyone else did but their shrivelled souls were also attuned to the haunted gulf that lurked outside of time. The Cobleys' perceptions constantly flickered between normal time and the strange hyper-reality that existed between seconds.

The unaltered human mind couldn't perceive any of this and so all appeared perfectly normal on aisle seven. The demon manifesting itself in the orange colour chart was placed perfectly between one second and the next, out of sight and out of time. The Cobleys fully shifted their perception to the strange half-life that lay between *now* and *then* so they could talk to their demonic patrons' messenger undisturbed.

The colours of the chart flowed together to create the semblance of a blocky, half-formed face and Mrs Cobley briefly wondered how that particular blend of orange would look on her conservatory walls. The amorphous face shifted as the demon spoke. "Humans, attend! Our master has need of you." Mr Cobley grimaced. Demons had never mastered the art of small-talk. They were always so bloody rude. It was like talking to Germans.

Mr Cobley knew he might as well try and ice-skate up-hill but he was determined to keep trying to instil some rudimentary manners into the fractious and uncouth denizens of Hell.

"Good afternoon, Mok," he smiled. "And how are you today?" The demon was silent for a few seconds. "I'm Jok," he finally said. "Mok is elsewhere."

Mrs Cobley affectionately slapped her husband on the arm. "Mr Cobley is terrible with names and faces!" she laughed to Jok. "He does try though, bless him." She smiled at the demon lurking in the colour chart. "So, what does Malleus want us to do, dear?"

Jok was silent for a time. Talking to humans, particularly these humans, was always so strange. "You are to go here immediately," he said and the Cobleys winced as the demon seared a location into their minds. Imparting knowledge this way was inarguably efficient, but it was also decidedly uncomfortable. "Upon arrival you will meet with a human by the name of Barnes. He will give you and your coven further instruction."

The Cobleys looked at each other and then back at the orange-hued demonic apparition in front of them. "A human? A normal man in charge of us?" Mr Cobley was obviously less than impressed. Jok carried on: "These are your orders from the master and you will follow them or be cast into the deepest bowels of the pit to suffer for all eternity." Mr Cobley sighed inwardly. A simple 'yes' would have sufficed. He silently added 'melodrama' to the demonic list of shortcomings.

Mrs Cobley wasn't unduly worried by the lamentable lack of manners on display. If she'd wanted her contacts in the afterlife to mind their p's and q's she would have worked for the other side. Poor Mr Cobley was such a stickler though! She recognised the beautiful village that Jok had just put into her mind and felt a frisson of excitement. Mrs Cobley, her mind as much on climbing the social ladder and having a nice place in the country as it was on serving the glory of Hell and bringing about the downfall of a feeble, geriatric God, had always had her eye on moving out of London and into a nice cottage with a proper garden, although the chances of her and Mr Cobley ever affording that were slim at best.

Being a demon lords' right-hand on the mortal plane definitely had its perks but unfortunately it didn't pay very much. She smiled at the demon again. "Don't you worry, dear, we'll head over there and see your Mr Barnes straight away. Do you know why the master wants us there so urgently?" The demon began to fade and his voice echoed in their minds as the Cobleys stepped back into normal time. "You are to help us hasten the end," intoned the rough voice. "The end of all things."

Mr Cobley hung the colour chart back onto its hooks in front of the shelves full of paint tins and smiled at his wife. "Well now," he said and Mrs Cobley beamed at him and patted his hand excitedly. "I know, dear! Do you really think this could be it?!"

"What? Armageddon?" he asked and Mrs Cobley giggled and nodded as he uttered that lovely, lovely word. Mr Cobley put his arm around her and planted an affectionate kiss on her cheek. He adored seeing her excited like this. "I certainly hope so my dove," he said. "It's about bloody time!" They walked from the store to their sensible saloon car, chattering animatedly about what they would find at their destination and what their role in their master's plans might be.

It took Mrs Cobley a few seconds to realise that Mr Cobley was driving towards home rather than going to pick up the motorway to head out of the city.

"Where are you going, dear?" Mr Cobley patted her leg. "Just a quick stop at home." He paused for a second as a transit van, doubtless being driven by some working-class oik, suddenly pulled out of a side road just in front of him and *tut-tutted* at the display of inconsiderate driving.

"We still have a guest to attend to and I think it will be better to start our new task without any distractions don't you?" Mrs Cobley nodded her agreement and smiled. He was always thinking ahead was her Mr Cobley! "Quite right you are, dear. I'll put the kettle on and we can have a nice cup of tea as well."

It was only a ten-minute drive back to their three-story town house in Stockwell, Mr Cobley, as always, opting for the route that ran alongside the green expanse of Clapham common. Both of them smiled as they drove past Long Pond and Cock Pond on the common, knowing what secrets those small bodies of water held in their graveyard silts.

They were soon past the common and driving through the grey streets of Stockwell where their smiles faded. Neither of them liked the place much anymore. Oh it was wonderfully convenient for access into and out of the city, and a long time ago now it seemed, it had once been a nice place to live.

Now of course it was full of foreigners. Most of the decent people had long since moved away, replaced by large families of *ethnics*. On the other hand, most of their new neighbours were an insular lot with no interest in getting to know the Cobleys or, more importantly, in their comings and goings.

As usual they spent some minutes trying to find a parking space along the crowded road. *If we are about to help kick-start the apocalypse and begin the genocide of the human race* thought Mr Cobley sourly *I might actually get to park outside my own bloody house for once!* As they walked through the door, Mrs Cobley headed straight to the ground floor kitchen. "I'll put the kettle on, dear," she called over her shoulder. "You go and deal with our guest."

Mr Cobley smiled his thanks and then began his slow walk up the three flights of winding stairs to the converted bedroom at the top of the house. He huffed his way up the narrow stairs and winced as he reached the halfway point. His knees had been giving him terrible trouble lately. He unlocked the large, heavy door at the top of the stairs and entered their Satanic chapel, breathing deeply of the charnel air and smiling.

The room reeked of fear, of blood and shit and desperation. It was beautiful. The Cobleys had put a lot of work into this room and they were very proud of it indeed. Floors, ceiling, walls and windows had all been fully soundproofed by Mr Cobley himself and he'd also installed the manacles on the wall as well as those on the hand-carved altar.

The altar really was a marvellous construction. Mr Cobley had planed, carved and polished the large section of African Blackwood himself. African Blackwood, sometimes known as Mozambique Ebony, was uniquely attuned to the magics of death which was exceedingly rare for living wood. Most altars, both those used for dark works and the simpering worship of the Christians, were made from stone but African Blackwood was a natural conduit between the mortal realms and the other side.

Mrs Cobley had done an excellent job of painting the walls with the jagged sigils and runes of demonic script. They covered the walls from floor to ceiling and funnelled the fetid energies the Cobleys created in their chapel directly to their master. For the best results these sigils should be drawn in the blood of new-born innocence and Mr Cobley shook his head as he remembered what an arduous and perilous task it had been to source the necessary…materials. He beamed with pride as he looked around the room at his industrious wife's handiwork. It had been worth all the effort.

The sacrificial altar dominated the eastern wall of the room, perfectly placed to catch the rays from the setting sun that shone through the small, cell-like windows high on the western wall. Conventional wisdom held that evil thrived in the darkness, in the night, and to an extent this was true. In reality, the darkness was more the domain of secrets than what mortals called 'evil' and the night and its secrets were ruled by a different mistress.

The real power, the true witching hour was found at dusk when the light itself slowly surrendered to the dark. The offerings the Cobleys made to their master died as the sun died with them.

Their latest sacrificial plaything stared at him with wild eyes from her prone position on the cold, black wood of the altar. Mr Cobley sighed inwardly. He hated to rush things like this, but needs must when the devil drives, as they say.

He moved closer and smiled as he gazed down at the young girl's torn and ravaged body. She really was exquisite. Both of the Cobleys had enjoyed her body over the last few days. Both had tasted of her flesh and blood and tears and gloried in her muffled screams and whimpers. The spells Mrs Cobley chanted as Mr Cobley worked on her with the stone-bladed knife slowly flayed her soul even as he agonisingly flayed her skin. Mr Cobleys' smile widened as he ran a delicate, loving finger over the crimson patterns carved into her desecrated body.

There was little left of her mind by now. She had been reduced to a ragged core of animalistic pain and terror, her so-called humanity stripped away to reveal the true, feral self that lay hidden underneath, and she made no sound as she tracked his movements with wide eyes. The girl didn't cry. She had no tears left. Mr Cobley sighed again as he picked up the knife and gently stroked her matted hair. "Sorry about this, little one. You deserve so much more from me than this." As he spoke he pushed the sacrificial knife between her ribs, driving it up and into her chest with the ease of long practice. The young girl stiffened as the knife found her heart and sliced cleanly through the right ventricle wall. Her eyes closed as she finally, blissfully died.

Mrs Cobley came into the room and handed him a cup of tea. She looked down at the altar. "It's a shame isn't it, dear? I know how you hate to leave a job half done." She squeezed his arm and smiled at him. "Still, we mustn't fret! I'm sure the master will have us busy as bees from now on!" Mr Cobley

Ian King

sipped at his tea. Mrs Cobley had made it nice and strong, just the way he liked it and he closed his eyes in pleasure. "Yes," he mused. "I must say I'm very curious as to what's going on. All of this is most unusual."

"I know! It's exciting isn't it, dear?"

"I can't say I'm thrilled about this Barnes character, whoever he is. What is Malleus thinking putting one of the cattle in charge? And why are we only just finding out what's going on now? It's obviously something important so why weren't we involved from the beginning?"

"I'm sure the master knows what he's about, dear. Besides, if he doesn't then we still have our other...option."

Mr Cobley brightened at this, even as part of him quailed at her reminder of the dangerous game they played. Still, if you wanted power then you had to take risks, and as his dear wife had just reminded him, Heaven and Hell weren't the only powers out there. They would continue to play the loyal servants of Malleus for now, to bow and scrape and cower as he demanded, but when the time was right...

Bless her dear heart. She always knew how to cheer him up. "You're right! Sorry, I was bleating a bit there wasn't I?" He placed his half-finished cup of tea on the blood-soaked altar and clapped his hands together smartly. "Well then," he said. "We don't know how long this might take so can you pack us a weekend bag while I attend to this please?" He motioned towards the scarred and broken corpse manacled to their altar. Mrs Cobley smiled and went on tip-toes to peck him on the cheek. "Of course, dear. You leave it to me."

Mrs Cobley bustled off downstairs, humming happily to herself and leaving Mr Cobley with the scoured shell of the thing that used to be a young girl. He gazed down at her for a few seconds before slowly, almost reverently caressing her cooling flesh. He dipped his finger into the wound in her chest and then sucked his finger clean of her dead blood, smiling as he felt himself stiffen. Mr Cobley took a final opportunity to stroke and squeeze the cold but still pliable flesh before he laid his hands palm down on her body, his left hand over her breasts and his right on the torn and burned flesh of her thighs. He closed his eyes and concentrated.

The flesh beneath his hands darkened and wrinkled, the discolouration slowly spreading across the rest of the young girls' corpse. Her lips deflated, pulling back from her broken teeth in a rictus grin. Her small breasts wrinkled and sagged and the bones of her chest, shoulders and hips were thrown into stark contrast as Mr Cobley evaporated all the fluids in her body. The entire process took less than a minute and he straightened and opened his eyes to gaze down at the frail and desiccated form below him.

There he thought, pleased with his handiwork. *That should stop any odd smells causing the neighbours to complain. Not that they have any right to make a fuss with that foul muck they cook up every night!* He left the satanic chapel and closed and locked the door before heading downstairs to help Mrs Cobley pack. Mr Cobley loved his wife dearly, but he knew how forgetful she could be when she was excited.

He winced as he slowly descended the stairs. He really should see someone about these bloody knees of his soon. Mr Cobley grinned suddenly. If he could manage to get a Doctor's appointment before the end of the universe that is.

TEN

Miles Harrington stood staring at the crumpled body of Tamsin Lowe in the small and dusty attic room of the mansion. His flat eyes crawled over her from top to toe as he searched for some spark, some feeling of…something. He found nothing, he felt nothing.

Miles drew no distinction between the living and the dead. Both were equally as inconsequential to him, both committed that most cardinal sin of being *dull*. Miles moved alone through a world of two-dimensional beings. He was the only real thing in a world of cardboard cut-out scenery, of shadow-play and puppets. Miles supposed he should feel lonely and perhaps he would have done could he have felt anything at all. There was no sound in Miles' world, no colour or light until he created it through the artistry of pain.

He looked at Tamsin again and shook his head. She would never appreciate what he had done for her. At the moment of her death, while she gasped and choked as her blood gushed from her throat she was vibrant and alive. For those briefest of seconds she had actually meant something. Her dull greys had bloomed into glorious colour and she *glowed*. For those few, precious moments Miles had made her truly real. He had made her beautiful. Miles knew the truth. The world around him was a sham, a pale facsimile that only truly lived and breathed, was only truly real, when *he* made it so.

Miles knew the truth. With each death he forced life into this lifeless world and if he could just kill enough? Why then the world would finally be as it was intended to be. Colours and sounds and feelings in a glorious, cacophonous and eternal cascade. Miles wondered if this would bring him real happiness and then realised that he wouldn't be able to recognise the emotion anyway, whatever it was.

The thought didn't depress him. He smiled as he thought of all the death to come. They would watch creation burn around them, burn and drown in ashes and blood and the sweetness of tears. A billion worlds and countless creatures would be filled with his light and glow brightly, fiercely as he changed them and made them real.

Miles smiled wider at the thought of the chaos and pain they would unleash and wondered if this was what anticipation or perhaps even pleasure felt like? He supposed it must be. His reverie was broken as the door opened behind him and he turned to see Lincoln Barnes and two other men standing in the doorway. Miles assumed they were two more of the faceless crew that worked for him and Marcus and instantly forgot about them. Just more puppets, as was Lincoln of course, but at least he could be an *interesting* little wooden boy.

Lincoln nodded towards the younger Harrington, masking an almost instinctive revulsion with deference. Lincoln had known many men who seemed without conscience or feeling, indeed he knew the value of being able to supress his emotions and operate solely on expediency and cold resolve.

But Miles? Miles wasn't simply a man with no feelings, that would make him just a common psychopath and Lincoln didn't believe that diagnosis adequately explained Miles Harrington. Miles was a cipher, an absence, a blank spot that looked like a man as he ghosted almost silently through the world; with the only sounds he made being the whispering snickers of his precious razor.

"I'm sorry to disturb you, Miles. Marcus has requested we dispose of Miss Lowe. If you don't mind?"

Miles took a final look at the useless and broken thing on the floor beside him and then smiled his dead-eyed smile at the three men. "Of course not. She serves no further purpose." He brushed his hands briskly together. "Are we prepared for the arrival of these Cobley people and their ridiculous coven?"

Lincoln motioned to the two men behind him and stepped into the room, standing to one side of the door to allow them access to Tamsin's body. "We are. I believe they're already on their way. I was going to give them their instructions in the eastern conservatory if you have no objections?"

Miles waved the question away, bored as always by the minutiae. "Whatever you think is best. Do you anticipate any trouble from them? Seeing as they are these 'blessed' or whatever Malleus calls them?" Lincoln gave a slight shrug. "I don't care what they are. They'll follow their instructions to the letter or I'll deal with them accordingly."

"Mr Barnes you are a delight at times. I was curious to see these 'blessed' for myself but now I really want to witness this meeting."

"Of course, sir. I'll contact you as soon as they arrive."

"Very good, Barnes. Well, don't let me keep you."

Lincoln nodded and then left the room behind the two men burdened with Tamsin's corpse and shut the door. Miles stood alone in the centre of the empty room and stared into space, thinking of nothing at all.

Lincoln oversaw the loading of Tamsin's body into a nondescript transit van and went over the disposal protocols a final time with his two subordinates. Satisfied they knew what was required of them he waved them away and then returned to the mansion. Marcus was in his study, undoubtedly obsessively poring over his accounts as usual and Lincoln saw no reason to disturb him. If the elder Harrington wanted him he'd soon make it known. Miles was still upstairs doing God only knew what and Lincoln was quite happy to leave the twisted creature alone with his reptilian thoughts.

He moved into the large kitchen and was pleased to find it empty. Lincoln put the kettle on and dragged a stool close to the worktop so he could sit down. A few minutes alone just to clear his mind and prepare for what was to come. After all, it appeared it was going to be a very busy day so no-one could begrudge him a cup of tea and a brief moment of peace before the universe came crashing down. Lincoln mechanically made the tea while his mind was far away, flitting between the future and the past, wondering what was to come and how the bloody hell this whole mess had begun.

What the hell are we doing? He thought as he stirred a second sugar into his tea. *What the hell am I doing, more to the point?* Lincoln wanted no part in this grandly insane scheme. There, he'd said it, at least to himself. Lincoln Barnes had spent his life training, moulding and honing himself into a man that the world would be forced to respect. Into the sort of man *he* could respect and be proud of when he stared into the mirror. He'd fought his way up from nothing, from being '*just another nigger*' from a poverty-stricken council estate, to a man whose name rang through the streets of his city.

Lincoln wanted to carve his name into the world, not burn the whole thing down. That was the true insanity of the demon's plan, the plan the twins had so happily embraced. Oh, the rhetoric sounded grand enough. Putting the universe to the sword and battering down the walls of Heaven and blah, blah, blah. But then what? What point in being the lord of all you surveyed when all you saw was ashes? Lincoln shook his head. And what chance was there that Malleus would share his desolate throne with the twins? Lincoln smiled sourly. A snowball in Hell's chance.

He could see why Miles had embraced the plan with what seemed like, for him at least, childlike enthusiasm, but Marcus? Marcus had always been the steady hand and the level head and Lincoln knew he was too intelligent not to have considered all the possible outcomes, both of victory and defeat. Lincoln sighed inwardly. Miles embracing slaughter and suffering on a, well, biblical scale wasn't the most horrifying thing, or even particularly surprising. No, this time it was Marcus that worried him. Lincoln harboured a creeping suspicion that Marcus was doing all this just because he was bored, and that was truly terrifying.

Lincoln finished his tea just as his mobile phone chirruped politely in his jacket pocket. He placed the empty cup in the sink and took out his phone. *Here we go.* Lincoln answered the call and listened for a moment. "Of course," he said "We're expecting them. Escort them through the gardens to the conservatory; I'll wait for them there."

He put the phone back in his pocket and moved through the huge house towards the conservatory to greet the Cobleys. Halfway through the twisting corridors he remembered that the deranged lunatic in the attic had wanted to be present for this first meeting and pulled his phone out again to call Miles.

As it turned out, Miles was already in the conservatory, obviously eager to see the favoured mortal servants of Malleus and how Lincoln would handle the situation. Lincoln entered the conservatory to find Miles sprawled elegantly in one of the many chairs in the large room. The conservatory was hexagonal in shape, boasting floor to ceiling windows that afforded a spectacular view of the landscaped gardens. The large back doors were open and the warm summer sun and the scent of flowers from the gardens flooded the room. Lincoln shook his head at the incongruity of it all. This was hardly the setting he'd picture when about to meet a demons' warlocks or whatever it was they called themselves.

He heard voices along the path and looked over to see a middle-aged couple arm in arm, the woman dressed like a plump parody of a business woman and the man like a paedophile school teacher, the woman chattering excitedly as they looked about the huge garden. They were followed by four others, a younger bunch but just as motley and ridiculous looking as the two so-called 'blessed'.

The group behind them, the 'coven', were a jarringly mismatched crew. At the forefront of the group was a huge, muscular skinhead, festooned with crudely drawn tattoos and staring around him with a belligerent eye. He was followed by a slim, bespectacled Asian teenager, what looked like a teenage girl fresh from a council estate, complete with a tracksuit and the tightly scraped back hair known disparagingly as the 'Croydon facelift' and a grossly overweight woman whose round face was so hidden in folds of fat that her age was impossible to determine as she sweated and waddled her way through the sun-drenched garden.

The Devil may have all the best tunes, thought Lincoln, *but the hired help definitely has room for improvement.* The thin, gangly man and the plump woman, Mr and Mrs Cobley he presumed, headed towards him while their cut-price coven hung back and curiously eyed their surroundings. The woman smiled at him while the man's gaunt face remained impassive, with just the tiniest hint of a sneer.

"Hello, dear! You must be Mr Barnes I take it?" The woman held out her hand and Lincoln politely, if somewhat bemusedly, shook it. "I am," Lincoln nodded towards the odd couple. "Lincoln Barnes, a pleasure to meet you Mrs Cobley." He stepped back and motioned the group into the conservatory. "Please, come in and make yourself comfortable." The Cobleys and their coven filed into the conservatory, Mrs Cobley animatedly chatting to her husband as she cooed over the tasteful and expensive furnishings.

Mrs Cobley spied the languid form of Miles Harrington who sat by the adjoining door to the house with a faint smile on his face. She laughed and fluttered her hand in front of her face. "Ooh! I didn't see you there, fair gave me a fright!" She selected the chair next to him and perched there demurely. Lincoln nodded towards Miles and addressed the group. "This is Miles Harrington, one of our employers." He caught the brief look of anger on Mr Cobleys' face at this and smiled to himself. He'd chosen his words carefully and provoked just the reaction he'd expected. Mr Cobley could prove to be a problem and it would be better to nip things in the bud straight away.

Mrs Cobley, however, was like a garrulous steamroller. "Such a beautiful place you have, Mr Harrington! Those gardens of yours are spectacular! I adore the arrangements and they're all proper seasonal flowers too. The Purple Sensation and the Goldfinch Ramblers go together so beautifully." She giggled. "I'd never have put those two together in a million years! Who'd have thought it eh?"

Miles sat staring at her with a bemused expression on her face and Mrs Cobley gushed on. "Oh, but I expect you have people to do all that sort of thing, a busy man like you! Still, you should be very proud, such a wonderful home!" To say that both Miles and Lincoln were taken aback by the Cobleys would have been an understatement. While neither of them had known quite what to expect from the chosen mortal servants of Malleus it certainly wasn't this.

Miles' expression turned to one of amusement as Mrs Cobley babbled on, enjoying the absurdity of it all. Lincoln, however, looked at the Cobleys through narrowed eyes, suspecting their humble and humdrum personas were a façade designed to mask who and what they really were.

Lincoln decided to push them a little and see how easily those facades could crumble. It was a risk, a big risk. Lincoln had no idea just what these bizarre servants of Hell were capable of and it was quite possible they could simply kill him out of hand if he antagonised them too much. It was indeed a risk, but a calculated one. Malleus himself had given Lincoln operational control and he was reasonably certain their loyalty to, or at least their fear of Malleus would stay their hand and he needed to get a sense of how they were likely to act over the next few hours.

Powerful they may be but if they were incapable of exerting any self-control then they'd be worse than useless, the Cobleys would be a danger to the whole enterprise and highly likely to get them all killed.

"Mrs Cobley, please. We have more pressing matters to attend to than the gardens, don't you agree?" Lincoln injected just a touch of feigned exasperation into his tone and he smiled inwardly as he saw her face stiffen and her eyes flash. It was a fleeting moment, less than a second, but it was enough. *There you are*, he thought to himself.

Mr Cobley went to speak and Lincoln held up a hand to silence him, the insulting gesture calculated to push them that little bit further. Miles abandoned his languid pose and sat forward in his chair, an eager expression on his face. He could taste the tension in the air, and as always, the prospect of violence and blood began to stir his stunted passions.

Lincoln ignored the younger Harrington and locked eyes with Mr Cobley. "Let's all be clear on one thing," he said in a calm, quiet voice. "Until this particular task is done you work for *me*, is that understood? You don't have to like it, in fact I couldn't care less what your feelings on the matter are, you just have to do as you're told."

Lincoln saw the shocked look on the faces of the coven, all save the big skinhead who glared at him furiously, shifting his bulk as though about to launch himself from the chair. Lincoln stared at him impassively for a few seconds and then switched his gaze back to Mr Cobley. "Rein your boy in, Mr Cobley," he warned. "Look at me and tell him what a bad idea it would be."

Mr Cobley looked at Lincoln. His complete confidence and apparent lack of fear was, he had to admit, impressive. Mr Cobley shifted his perceptions to gaze upon Lincoln, to gaze *into* him, with different eyes. Mr Cobleys' own eyes widened just a fraction at what he found and he nodded once to Lincoln with a thoughtful expression on his face. He turned to face the infuriated skinhead. "I'd do as he says, Terry, for your own good."

Terry looked at Mr Cobley, his face a mixture of disbelief and anger. Lincoln had known dozens of Terrys' type over the years and wasn't impressed. The only thing bully-boys like Terry had going for them was their size and the only way they knew how to deal with any given situation was to hit it until it went away. Still, Terry could come in handy, if only to act as a punching bag to keep Cross busy for a few seconds. Sometimes, a few seconds was all it took.

Lincoln looked over the others and shook his head. Christ knows what he was going to do with this lot. He sent one of the men inside with instructions to make their guests tea and then motioned those who were still standing to sit down. They arrayed themselves around him on the various chairs while Lincoln remained in the centre of the room. He smiled at them warmly, the very picture of the genial host.

"Ladies, gentlemen, thank you all for coming on such short notice. Now, before we begin in earnest, exactly how much do you know about why you're here?"

Mr Cobley grimaced. "Not a great deal, Mr Barnes, we were simply told to come here and avail ourselves to you immediately." The peremptory summons obviously still rankled Mr Cobley and Lincoln smiled at him ruefully. "Yes, they can be a bit brusque can't they?" There was no need to ask who 'they' were.

Mr Cobley nodded in agreement. "Yes, they usually are. Then again, I suppose one shouldn't expect the usual human niceties from beings that aren't actually human. Our messenger did allude to this particular task being of great import however." He motioned towards Mrs Cobley. "I don't say this due to an excess of ego but they wouldn't have asked Mrs Cobley and I here if it wasn't something vital."

Lincoln inclined his head towards the Cobleys, acknowledging this small reminder of their power and status within the twisted little court of Malleus. "I quite agree, Mr Cobley, and rest assured you are all a vital part of this enterprise."

"Which is what exactly?" asked Mrs Cobley. They were interrupted by two of the men coming in from the kitchen bearing trays of tea, all of which were gratefully accepted apart from Terry who simply stared at the man offering the cup and then looked out of the window in obviously feigned indifference. Lincoln ignored the petulant display and carried on:

"I assume you're both well aware of the problems your master faces in travelling to the mortal realms? In person I mean."

Mr Cobley nodded. "Quite. Finding a way to resolve that

issue has been a priority for all of us for some time now." Mr Cobley stopped and looked at Lincoln in surprise. "Do you mean to tell me the master has finally found a way?" Lincoln returned the nod. "Yes, we believe he has. This first attempt hasn't gone strictly to plan but it appears the theory is sound." Lincoln went on to explain the situation in more detail and the Cobleys and their coven listened with rapt attention.

"So we need to find this Daniel Cross, bring him here and send his soul back to Hell?" asked Mr Cobley. "That should be simple enough."

"Perhaps not," argued Lincoln. "Malleus believes there may be other interested parties assisting Cross by now, though who or what they are he hasn't made clear. We can handle Cross with little difficulty but these other...entities require a more specialised set of skills, which is where you and Mrs Cobley come in."

"What exactly do you need us to do for you, dear?" asked Mrs Cobley.

"Cross will be coming to us, that much is certain, and he's smart enough to know it's a trap but he's determined enough to exact his revenge to come here anyway, and he's certainly skilled enough to cause us significant problems when he does arrive if we're not prepared, and that's without any additional help he may have garnered along the way. We can handle Cross, but we'll need you to nullify any other threats."

"And you have no idea who or what these other threats might be?"

"Malleus seemed to become quite agitated when Cross headed towards Islington, though he didn't care to tell us why."

Mr and Mrs Cobley exchanged a black look. "Buttons," said Mr Cobley and made the word sound like a curse. Lincoln looked at him curiously. "Buttons? Can you elaborate please?"

"Buttons is a whisper, a myth," explained Mr Cobley. "For hundreds of years there has been talk of a hunter of great power, a being who can banish or even destroy demons when they enter the mortal realms. We're not sure who or what he is, or if he even exists but it's been rumoured that he makes his home in London, in Islington to be precise."

He looked at Mrs Cobley. "Perhaps there's more to these rumours than we know?"

"That's not even the worst-case scenario, dear," interjected Mrs Cobley. "This girl he has in tow is still a mystery and we'd be stupid not to assume that she's of obvious value or Cross wouldn't have her tagging along." She paused and took a sip of her tea. "We know she appeared at the hospital which seems an odd meeting place don't you think? No, I think we should prepare ourselves for the possibility that Cross went to the hospital to find a vessel for his stowaway."

"You believe the angel has taken human form then?" asked Lincoln and Mrs Cobley gave a slight shrug.

"The creature would certainly be more effective with a physical body of its own, though its powers would thankfully still be curtailed. If this Cross is as capable as you say then he'll know how high the odds are stacked against him, wouldn't he try and even things up as much as possible?"

Lincoln agreed. He'd do exactly the same in Cross's position. He looked at the Cobleys and revised his opinion of them. They were already proving their worth. Lincoln still thought the rest of the coven were little more than a distraction but even cannon fodder could be useful if used correctly. "So, our worst-case scenario has Cross on his way here with an angel and this mysterious 'Buttons' as backup, both of whom I can assume will prove to be problematic?"

Mr Cobley nodded soberly. "Even with the constraints of a mortal body the angel will still be far more powerful than a normal human, and Buttons?" Mr Cobley spread his hands in a 'who knows?' gesture. "As I said, Buttons is a myth but if even half of the tales are true then he or she or it will be extremely dangerous."

"Too powerful for you to handle?" asked Lincoln. He wasn't goading them further and his tone was clinical and matter of fact. He had to know if he had the resources he needed to deal with this problem and Mr and Mrs Cobley knew it was a fair question under the circumstances.

"We can certainly handle the angel in its current form," said Mr Cobley and Mrs Cobley nodded her agreement. Lincoln looked at them both closely and could see nothing that suggested false bravado, just a quiet confidence in their abilities. "Buttons, if indeed that entity is involved, which is a big 'if', is an unknown quantity."

The tall, thin man paused for a second and then spoke again. "Mr Barnes, please understand that I don't say this to impress or self-aggrandize but Malleus has bestowed many talents upon us over our decades of faithful service. We stand among the most powerful of the blessed; indeed, we are likely among the most powerful mortal beings on this planet." He stopped and smiled fondly at his plump wife. "We are also a very good team and I assure you we are confident we can deal with whatever may be coming our way."

Lincoln was actually mildly impressed with the Cobleys, and despite having seen no evidence of the many 'talents' they spoke of certainly felt a lot more confident they would prove effective. Lincoln began to believe they might actually pull this off, though he still wasn't sure if that was a good thing or not. He looked over to Miles who lounged in his chair and stared into the distance. Lincoln had seen him briefly stir as he began to push the Cobleys, obviously eager to see bloodshed erupt but now he had lost interest and retreated into that desolate space within his mind.

"Miles? Do you or Marcus have any questions for our guests before we begin in earnest?"

Miles waved the question away, still not deigning to look at his underling or the mismatched group that filled the conservatory. "No, I'm sure you're quite capable of handling the little details yourself, Barnes. I have to go and talk to those uppity surgeons to prepare for Cross's arrival."

The slender lunatic and would-be destroyer of worlds rose smoothly to his feet and walked from the conservatory without a backward glance. Lincoln watched him go and then offered a wry smile to the Cobleys. Lincoln had been somewhat harsh with them at first, but for a good reason and behind the disguise of pedestrian domesticity they wore, Lincoln believed they were astute enough to know why he had spoken so brusquely. The Cobleys, it appeared, possessed both power *and* control which meant they could be very dangerous indeed.

"Our employer could also learn the value of common niceties; you can see why he gets on so well with our partners on the other side."

Mrs Cobley laughed and Mr Cobley smiled in response. "Think nothing of it. What we're trying to accomplish here is far too important to worry about social graces or bruised egos." Mr Cobley put his empty teacup down on the small table in front of him and then leant forward with his hands on his bony knees, looking like some sort of predatory insect. "Shall we get down to business then, Mr Barnes?"

Lincoln nodded and began to outline exactly what he needed the Cobleys and their coven to do for him.

ELEVEN

Cross, Andariel and Buttons sat outside a pub overlooking the river Thames. Cross had driven their stolen car, which Andariel complained still smelled slightly of shit from the unfortunate Kenny Chapman, south of the river Thames, that almost mythical domain where taxi drivers, but obviously not angels, feared to tread. They parked the stolen car in a secluded alley near the pub. It was lunchtime, but as it was the middle of the week the place wasn't particularly busy, and they'd had no trouble claiming a table commanding a good view of the wide river.

The sun shone brightly overhead and dappled the surface of the Thames as Cross watched the boats go by and sipped his ale while they waited for their food. The few other patrons had cast a curious glance their way as they placed their orders and sat down, and Cross was forced to admit they probably weren't the most inconspicuous trio.

Andariel took a large and distinctly unladylike swig of her pint and smacked her lips in appreciation. "This is good! What is it?"

"This is Timothy Taylor's 'Landlord' and, yes, it's very good," replied Cross as he raised his glass to his oddly matched companions. Andariel and Buttons returned the toast, the angel taking another huge gulp before she set her glass down. Cross grinned at her. "Don't you go getting half-cut, I imagine it's been a while since you've had a drink?"

Andariel nodded. "Best part of a millennia, but don't worry," She grabbed her glass and downed the remaining half pint with obvious relish. "I could drink this all day, it's nothing compared to what I was drinking the last time I was here." Cross thought for a second as he tried to remember something he'd heard or seen somewhere, probably on the Discovery channel. "Ah yeah, didn't the Mongols drink something made out of fermented milk?"

"Airag," laughed the angel. "That's made from fermented mare's milk and it's actually not that bad. 'Arkhi' is the one you need to be careful with. Same sort of thing but made from fermented yogurt and about twenty times as strong." She laughed again. "I'd been drinking Arkhi the night before the sacking of Kiev which is probably why I didn't see that farmer and his scythe in time. Mind you, with the hangover that stuff gives you I'm still not sure getting my head cut off wasn't a bit of a bonus."

Cross and Buttons joined in the laughter. "Yeah, I've woken up feeling like that a few times myself," smiled Cross.

Further conversation was interrupted as the barmaid arrived with their food and Andariel requested another pint. "Might as well make that three please, miss," smiled Buttons. The barmaid didn't return the smile and simply nodded, giving the oddly matched trio a slightly suspicious look and walked back inside. Cross slid Andariel's plate over to her. He smiled as the petite angel attacked her plate with gusto and the trio ate in companionable silence for a while.

Unsurprisingly, Andariel was the first to finish and pushed her plate away with a contented sigh and a ladylike belch. Cross finished his own meal and then waited for Buttons to finish before he lit up his dessert, holding the packet of cigarettes out until the reverend accepted one with a smile. Cross took a long, luxurious drag on his post-prandial cigarette and silently stared across the sun dappled water.

Buttons looked curiously at Cross. "Daniel?" he asked. "Why are you doing this?" Cross looked confused so Buttons began to elaborate. "Why don't you just disappear? I'm sure you've got a new identity stashed away for situations like this so why not just get out while you can?" He smiled. "Andariel and I are kind of obligated to try and put a stop to demonic plots to enslave or destroy creation but I'm sure it's not in your job description anywhere."

Cross grunted sourly. "The thing with going on the run, Reverend, is that you can never run far enough or fast enough. I don't care how far you go or how bullet-proof your new identity is you never trust it 100%. Part of you will always be looking over your shoulder and waiting for it all to catch up to you again and that's no kind of life." He shrugged. "Besides, the Harringtons killed two friends of mine because of all this and I won't let that go. Angels and Demons fighting over creation is way over my pay-grade, but settling the score for Gus and Kate? That I can manage."

Andariel looked disappointed. "So, it's just about vengeance for you then?" Cross raised an eyebrow at her. "You do know I'm a career criminal, right? We don't tend to go for noble causes as a general rule." He held up a hand as the angel started to speak. "That said, I know this is a lot bigger than just me getting some payback. Stopping Malleus is absolutely the right thing to do and I'm in it with both of you until we get it done or it gets us dead."

Andariel smiled wryly. "Plus the fact that preventing the apocalypse and the destruction of all life on earth is also in your best interests."

The big man nodded and grinned at her. "That's definitely a consideration."

Cross took another swig of his beer before he spoke again. "After a few tours you stop looking for a bigger picture. Usually the reasons they've given you to pile into someone else's country and shoot the poor bastards are all bollocks anyway, so you focus on what matters: The mission at hand and the boys and girls on it with you." He shrugged. "It's the only thing that makes any sense after a while."

"Is that why you left the army?" asked Button, causing Cross to laugh.

"Yeah I guess it was in a roundabout way." He was silent for a while as he thought back to his last years in the army.

"Me and a couple of my lads got seconded to a SEAL team doing grab-and-bag missions into the Afghan highlands. We knew the ground there better than they did. There were a couple of suits tagging along so I guessed it was an agency job and I never got on with those arseholes.

"We'd get a name, a photo and a possible location, sneak in and nab the target before bringing him back to one of those blacksites that don't have a name because they don't really exist."

His face went grim as he turned to look at his friends. "I'm sure I don't have to spell out what happened when we got them there?"

Both Buttons and Andariel shook their heads. They stayed silent and waited for Cross to continue.

"Seeing that sort of shit didn't help. I've got no problems giving someone a good hiding or even killing them if I need to, but I've never been a fan of torture, and believe me there was a lot more than just waterboarding going on in those places.

"Most of us, the Brits I mean, were just there to do a job and go home but for some of the Yanks it was like a bloody crusade. They hated the Afghani's, really *hated* them." He shrugged his big shoulders. "I get it. 9/11 was a real kick in the teeth and payback is something I can get behind, but if you're going to give the soles' of someone's feet the rubber hose treatment you should at least make an effort to kidnap the actual target, not just collar the first bloke you see wearing robes and a beard who looks a bit like him."

Cross sighed. "Half of these fellas didn't have a bloody clue why we'd kicked their door down and grabbed them in the middle of the night. They couldn't even spell 'insurgency' let alone be involved with one. They weren't all innocent, not by a long chalk, but even when it was obviously just some goat-herder some of those fuckers just kept on going."

He grimaced. "Believe me, the Geneva convention went right out of the window in that place. I'm talking fingernails being yanked and people being suffocated half to death with plastic bags full of piss over their heads.

"I had a few run-ins with the spooks over it and sent one of the dickheads home with a broken arm so they pulled me out." Cross grinned suddenly. "One of the benefits of working with the black-ops mob is that they can't discipline you by the usual channels, so they couldn't court martial me, but they made it clear they were going to make things very uncomfortable if I hung around."

"Uncomfortable?" asked Andariel and Cross grinned again. "Uncomfortable as in a few months in traction or accidentally getting sent on patrol through a nice minefield while you're the point man."

"Wankers," cursed the angel. Cross just shrugged. "That's how the game gets played. I'd decided I'd about had enough of it by then, so it seemed like a good time to leave Her Majesty's service and go into business for myself.

"The thing with operating in a grey area for so long is that black and white starts to blur. After seeing some of the shit we were doing part of me couldn't blame them for wanting to kill the lot of us." He shook his head. "Fuck, after a while you start to question who the good guys are, if there are any."

Buttons nodded slowly. "When you get right down to it no-one ever sees themselves as the bad guy. Heaven versus Hell is as black and white as it gets but even that's just a matter of perspective."

"Yeah. It makes it harder to be gung-ho when you realise you might not actually be the good guys and the only reason you're killing people is because you're doing as you're told." Cross shrugged. "I never bought into the whole 'Axis of Evil' bollocks anyway, I was just there doing my job, but it all just started to feel so bloody pointless."

Andariel snorted. "Hold on, so you had a crisis of conscience about being a soldier and decided to make yourself feel better by becoming a criminal?"

Cross laughed. "I never said it was a crisis of conscience,

I just don't like dancing to someone else's tune." The big man locked eyes with the Angel. "I don't have any illusions or make any excuses about who I am and what I do. I'm not slapping old ladies about for their pension but I'm not stupid enough to think that makes me a saint." He grinned suddenly. "Then again, maybe saving the universe will!"

Andariel smiled wryly. "I don't know if the heavenly host needs a patron saint of armed robbery but you never know." The angel gulped the last of her beer and then put the empty glass down decisively. "As nice as this little interlude is we've got a busy day ahead of us if we want to stop the universe from burning down. So, what's the plan?"

Cross remained silent as he examined their options and tried to second guess Barnes and the Harringtons next move. You could drive yourself round the bend trying to figure out what your opponents might be thinking, trying to see two steps ahead and through possible bluffs and double-bluffs. Without any credible intel all you could do was take your best guess and then run with it. Plans were all well and good on paper, but the real world had a tendency to chew them up and shit them out at the first opportunity.

He'd seen too many plans go tits up within seconds of actual contact with the enemy and watched too many people die because of it. In Cross's opinion a plan was just an idea, a framework that should give you room to move around it or through it as the situation dictated rather than forcing you to run on rails.

The big gangster smiled wryly to himself. Probably just as well he liked playing things fast and loose. Going up against demons was slightly out of his usual area of operations.

"I think we've bought ourselves a bit of breathing room by getting rid of our tail, or one of them at least. Lincoln is pretty good at what he does but he hasn't had any formal security training and it's unlikely he put more than the two fellas outside the church to watch us. Possibly he had another guy on foot but I'm fairly certain he wouldn't have thought to put a rotating tail on us."

"And what's that exactly?" asked Buttons.

"Just like it sounds. When you're trained in counter surveillance you can spot a tail fairly easily, particularly if it's the same face or the same car you keep seeing all day, so you have a few teams who drop in and out as they follow you to stop you getting wise too quick."

He hunched forwards in his chair and leant on his elbows, pointing a finger at Andariel.

"You said Malleus would shield the Harringtons from you being able to track them using magic or whatever right? Can I assume the same applies to us?"

The angel nodded. "Of course. I've been slipping around any attempts to locate us through the weave since I got my own body."

"Slipping around?"

"It's a little more subtle and a lot more useful than just shielding us outright. Given enough time and half a brain you'd just start looking for dead spots and tracking us that way."

Cross nodded, impressed. "Very clever. They've got a lot more bodies on the ground than we have so our best bet is being quick, quiet and unpredictable." He lit another cigarette and grinned at them. "Over the years I've cultivated a reputation for being somewhat direct so they'll be expecting me to hit them as soon and as hard as I can."

Buttons nodded thoughtfully. "Then we do something else?"

"Exactly. They're expecting us to zig so we'll zag."

Andariel began to look a little worried. "We are still going to kill them all though, right?"

Cross laughed. "Bloody right we are! We're going to make them sweat a bit and do them some damage first though. Twats like the Harringtons only care about their money so we're gonna take some of that away from them. We'll take out a few of their interests across the city and have them too busy putting out fires to concentrate on us, and that's when we move in."

Andariel grinned at him. "Plus we get to slap a few people around into the bargain?"

"A definite fringe benefit of the plan, yes."

Buttons shook his head and smiled at his bloodthirsty friends. "We don't want to hurt them too much of course." He held up a hand as both Cross and Andariel began to object. "What I mean is we don't want to goad them or, more specifically Malleus, into precipitous action."

Cross was confused. "Such as?"

"This scheme of theirs is a potential game changer. More than that, it threatens creation itself, and if not by its success then possibly by its discovery."

"I'm still not with you, reverend. Can you give me the idiots' version?"

Buttons smiled at him and Cross thought he detected a hint of sadness in his expression. "Malleus is breaking all the rules with this game. He's going against both Heaven and Hell, and if he loses?" Buttons spread his hands. "He'll have nowhere to hide from either divine or infernal retribution; it's all or nothing for him now. He *has* to win."

Now Cross understood. "Which means all bets are off as far as what he might do to stop us. Buttons shook his head. "It's not just how many other rules he might break that worries me." The small vicar looked at Andariel. "If Malleus starts calling up demons or creatures from other realms to stop us then what will happen?"

The angel looked worried. "There'll be no keeping it from my lot if he makes that amount of noise and if they make an appearance…" She shivered and looked at Cross. "He's right, if we end up with angels and demons fighting here in London the damage would be catastrophic."

"How catastrophic?"

"You could kiss goodbye to South East England for a start."

Cross cursed under his breath. It was never bloody easy

was it? Unfortunately, Buttons wasn't quite finished with the bad news. "Please understand, Daniel that a confrontation of that scale hasn't occurred since the dawn of time. Malleus could end up reigniting the war of the hosts." He smiled sourly. "If Malleus wants to burn the whole of existence to the ground then that would be a good way to do it. He could still win by losing."

Cross was silent for a moment and then looked towards the angel who stared despondently into her empty glass. Even though he hadn't known her for long it was still strange to see her like this. If he had to describe the angel then, as clichéd as it might be, Cross would have had to say she was full of life. Even to a cynical old bastard like him her obvious delight in the most mundane things was endearing and Cross realised she was starting to make him look at the world in a different, perhaps even better, light.

"Just how bad was it, Andariel?" he asked softly. The angel gave a deep sigh and stared off into the distance. Cross remained silent, not wanting to push her. He knew all about dredging up the past, particularly when that past was soaked in blood and mired in pain.

Andariel continued to stare across the Thames as she spoke, narrowing her eyes to shield them from the sun's glare, or perhaps from the unwelcome memories. "It was a nightmare, and one that I have to relive every day. Before Lucifer's fall we were all one. One family with one clear and glorious and perfect purpose. Things were exactly how they were supposed to be, and we knew they'd be like that forever. At least we thought they would." She balled her fists and took a deep breath as she struggled with the memories.

"I was forced to kill my family. Those who had been my brothers for so long screamed and spat in our faces as they tried to murder us. I have never, *never* seen such hatred and every day I pray to my Father that I never have to see it again." She sighed again. "Some of us grew to hate our former brothers almost as much as they despised us. The war began to twist us all, to make us harder, more brutal, turning us from beings of serenity and harmony to creatures of spite and malice." She sighed. "We did...*I* did such terrible things."

Andariel shook her head and Cross almost reached over to her as he saw the look of pain, and worse, *shame* on her face. "We are all so much less now than we were." She shook herself free of the memories, turning away from the river to face him. "The war in heaven occurred long before mankind was created, before the earth was created in fact. The universe was still in its infancy and our rage extinguished the forming stars and tore entire galaxies asunder. Imagine that now with all those worlds so full of life, the countless billions that would die because of our war. We can't let that happen again, Daniel, we just can't, no matter what it might cost us."

Cross hesitated and then reached over and took her hand. "I'm just a normal bloke, an old soldier and a criminal to boot. I doubt I'd be on anyone's speed-dial when it comes to trying to save the universe but, for what it's worth, I promise you I'll do whatever I can to stop that from happening."
"Why?" asked Andariel, and Cross shrugged and smiled at her. "Because you're my friend" he said simply.

The angel smiled her thanks and squeezed his hand and then both of them looked suddenly embarrassed at the intimacy and sat back in their chairs. Buttons smiled at Andariel. "I'd say you could do with another drink, old friend. In fact, we could all do with one." The small churchman stood up to head into the pub.
"Good idea!" said Cross lit another cigarette. The big man was suddenly grinning and looking very pleased with himself. "When you get back you can tell me if the idea I've just had has any legs or if I'm pissing into the wind." He caught Andariel's look and winked at her. "We've got a universe to save here and I think I know just how we can do it."

TWELVE

Ennustaja sat in the fathomless darkness and watched creation unfold in its sprawling dance. The darkness was no barrier to her. Ennustaja saw all with the clarity of one who had gone beyond mere sight and so she sat in the enveloping blackness of the Last Hall and watched and waited and recorded the march of time as she had done for so many years.

Ennustaja was old, though it wasn't her many centuries she felt; rather it was the ages she'd travelled and the years she'd seen. The billions of years past and those countless epochs of innumerable futures with all their secrets weighed on her more than mere age ever could. She had been young once she believed. It was hard to tell. Once, long ago, Ennustaja believed she hadn't been alone.

She watched as the universe spun and whirled around her and once again marvelled at the beauty of its chaotic, clockwork precision. Ennustaja was alone but this was enough. Or was it? Was her duty merely to watch and record or was she more than that? *Could* she be more? Her small act of rebellion, though against what she rebelled she wasn't sure, when she spirited Daniel Cross away from his captors seemed to have gone unchallenged, but would she, could she be stopped if she tried to do more?

Was her purpose to try and stop the coming calamity or merely to witness it? She had been given no charge when she found the Last Hall, no divine mandate or sacred mission. The Last Hall simply *was*. Ennustaja watched all and recorded all because, somehow, she knew that was her purpose in this place although the *why* of it ever eluded her.

While the Last Hall bestowed the gift of sight and allowed her to unearth the secrets of the past and divine the secrets of the future it seemed it had no secrets of its own to share. Ennustaja had watched the birth of creation itself, had seen the stars and planets sung into being across its limitless expanse and recorded the birth and death of every living being in the universe. Ennustaja had seen *all*. All but the Last Hall. It was outside of space and time, a place apart whose expanse dwarfed infinity itself. Perhaps it was the mind of God and she had ended her years of wandering inside his dream?

Ennustaja smiled in the darkness. Perhaps *she* was God and she had just forgotten?

The question that vexed her remained. Not the question of where and who and what she might be, but the question of what she would do. The past was a closed book and a straight, unbroken line. The future was an infinite forest where every branch on every tree was one of countless possibilities. Every decision made and action taken caused some of those branches to wither and die, even as new ones flowered and took their place, and Ennustaja had seen them all.

All except hers. Ennustaja could see some few, murky fragments of her past but was absent from the possibilities of the future. Perhaps this was a gift of the Last Hall or perhaps it was something it had stolen from her? Ah, so now the real question became not would she act further but *could* she, and if she did, what effect would a creature with no future cause by trying to alter it?

For those with the ability to see it the future left clues in its wake, a trail of pregnant breadcrumbs that could be used to discern which decisions led to new branches on its limitless trees, which actions bore the weight of both beginnings and endings. As Ennustaja watched the angel, the human and the once-human she knew that such a change was imminent and once again felt the wonder and terror that such small things could have such vast implications.

Three tiny, imperfect beings sat by an unremarkable

river on an insignificant planet hidden in a spiral arm of the galaxy they knew as the Milky Way were about to decide if creation itself lived or died. It was insane. The beautiful marvellous insanity that only existence, only *life* could bring and Ennustaja knew she didn't want it to end.

Ennustaja stood, her decision made. She would try. The being with a past hidden even from herself and absent from the countless paths of the future would try and change the course of time, would hope she was more than she feared she was.

Ennustaja would act.

THIRTEEN

"Have you found them yet?"

The question from the man who appeared silently at his shoulder startled Jonathan 'Jonny' Lee and made him flinch into the glowing screen of his laptop. Jonny wasn't ashamed to admit that Lincoln Barnes scared him, which was strange considering the company he kept and all the wonderful and terrifying things Mr and Mrs Cobley had shown him over the years.

Jonny had been a member of the coven since he was fifteen years old when he had been baptised and born again by blood and murder. Every member of the coven had to give their dark master a life before they were truly accepted, and not just any life. Malleus demanded a true sacrifice, the blood of someone they loved.

Jonny killed his little sister.

Eleanor Lee was born eight weeks premature and various, unfortunate complications during the fraught delivery had left her mentally retarded. Intellectually she would always be a child, a beautiful, happy child who would likely have grown into a beautiful, happy woman given the chance. Eleanor was nine years old when Jonny took her life, her death his payment to Malleus, an innocent child reduced to the price of admission.

Jonny thought it was a fair bargain.

Oh, it had hurt him to do it, Jonny believed he could almost feel his soul shred and tear as he smothered little Ellie in her bed and his bitter tears soaked the quivering pillow over her face. He became physically sick after the murder, unable to eat or sleep properly for weeks and his health began to fail even as the nightmares frayed his mind. His friends and family thought it was grief that afflicted him, not guilt, and grew worried as the now frail and sickly boy began to disappear for hours, then days at a time.

Jonny was with Mr and Mrs Cobley who slowly taught him to see the truth, that guilt was a useless, crushing emotion, a tool of fear to keep people blind to the freedom of acting upon their every desire. Love was a lie, leaden talons gripping your soul and keeping you from soaring, compassion nothing but cowardly shackles binding you to the stunted and useless mass of humanity.

Yes, it had hurt at first but that was the point. It wasn't the pain of the murdered that Malleus thrived on but the pain of the murderer, not mere death but the death of innocence, the extinction of love. The purest expression of evil was corruption, its loftiest goal assimilation and its manifestations and expressions, the debauchery and domination, the orgasmic pleasures of pain and death were merely the bright lures it used to ensure it continued to grow and spread.

Jonny could look at the world through different and better eyes now. Stripped of the confining and coddling layers of humanity and compassion the souls of the truly damned were left exposed to be scoured and sharpened to the nub, ground down to a hard and unrecognizable core. Jonny could see the world as the lie it was now. Jonny could see what pathetic and frightened creatures his fellows really were and shed no more tears as he rid them of the burdens of their lives.

Lincoln Barnes, however, still scared him. Jonny had been the first of the coven, the first to be accepted by Mr and Mrs Cobley and their master and was further along the path to receive the rapture of the blessed. He could see more, he *was* more than the others.

Terry, the huge, musclebound skinhead was little more than a thug, blind to everything but strength and domination and the infliction of pain. These traits were useful and had their place but they were only a small part of the path they followed. Kerry, the painted whore in cheap clothes and cheaper jewellery could see nothing past opening her legs, a creature of pure, carnal abandon addicted to the pleasures of pain and the sweet pain of pleasure, while Solange, that obese, disgusting mockery of a woman simply watched it all, drinking in the agonies and screams and then feasting, literally, on what was left behind.

What was it about this man, this normal, human man that affected him so?

At first, he had been surprised at the restraint Mr Cobley had shown, one could even go so far as it to call it deference and if Johnny was more than merely human now then Mr Cobley was so much more than that. He could have torn Lincoln limb from limb, boiled his blood in his veins or caused his heart to explode with little more than a gesture, and yet he hadn't.

Why? What could Mr Cobley see with his eldritch eyes that Jonny couldn't?

Perhaps that was what scared him? The knowledge that something about this man gave even a favoured servant of Hell pause and yet he hadn't the power or knowledge to see what it was.

"In your own time please, Mr Lee."

He started again as Lincoln spoke, this time with an edge of exasperation in his voice, and Jonny realised he had been drifting in his private reverie. Scared or not what Jonny was doing was extremely difficult and there were only a handful of people in the country that would even be capable of attempting it, let alone succeeding, and his efforts should be respected.

"Mr Barnes, I told you this would take some time. Even with the search algorithm I've deployed there are still almost half a million CCTV cameras in London to check and I'm looking for a single license plate amongst the approximately two million cars that are in the city at any given time throughout the day. I'm very good at what I do but today I also need to be very lucky."

Lincoln nodded, conceding the point. "Fair enough, Mr Lee. I appreciate your continuing efforts. Please keep me informed of any developments. Is there anything else you need?" Jonny shook his head, his attention already back on the screen and Lincoln left him to it.

"Are we sure they took that particular car, dear?" asked Mrs Cobley as she looked out into the gardens and enjoyed another cup of tea.

Lincoln shrugged. "It seems likely," he replied. "Chapman and Thomas are nowhere to be found and neither is the car. I sent Mr Joslin into the church and he reported no bodies but a lot of blood and clear signs of a struggle. In his opinion the amount of blood was far too much for just two people so it's possible, although unlikely, that Cross or his companion were injured during whatever occurred there."

"Why do you say it's unlikely? asked Mr Cobley who sat folded and ungainly in one of the conservatory chairs.

"Cross would go through people like Chapman and Thomas in about five seconds flat. If he made their tail then I doubt they even saw him coming. It's possible the girl was injured, if indeed she is just a girl and not an escaped angel."

Mr Cobley smiled, the sagging skin of his face wrinkling around his eyes. "If Andariel has taken human form, and the fact that we're having to resort to more mundane methods to find Cross certainly suggests it, then it would have taken even less time to dispose of your two former employees."

Lincoln regarded the Cobleys curiously. "Would an angel kill so cavalierly?"

Both Mr and Mrs Cobley laughed at this. "Don't you go believing all the rubbish you might have heard about them, dear. An angel of the host isn't a chubby baby flying around in its nappy. They probably have less regard for human life than any of us, spiteful so and so's they are!" She smiled at Mr Cobley. "Perhaps we'll finally get to kill one, dear!"

Mr Cobley looked fondly at his bloodthirsty wife and

then turned his attention back to Lincoln. "So, if your Mr Joslin is certain the amount of blood inside the church was too much for just two people, and I shall assume Mr Joslin has experience in these matters, and the blood didn't come from Cross or the angel then..."

"Whose blood is it?" finished Lincoln who had been considering the same question. "Malleus did say he already had people watching the other players that might become involved. Perhaps the blood belongs to them?"

"Which begs the question: Were these watchers killed before or after our prey arrived at the church? If it was before then I'd say that points towards Buttons being more fact than myth wouldn't you? Particularly considering that the bodies are nowhere to be found."

"I'm not sure I understand, Mr Cobley?"

Mr Cobley smiled, a comradely 'nudge-nudge, wink-wink' smile that made Lincolns' skin crawl. "I'm sure you've had some experience in making a corpse disappear, Mr Barnes? Cross had, what, an hour to make at least three bodies vanish into thin air? How would he have managed that?"

"The angel?"

Mr Cobley shook his head, enjoying the upper hand his more extensive knowledge of the arcane gave him. "Not in its current form. Andariel wouldn't have had the power or the required tools to make them disappear without a trace. No, it had to be someone or something else, which points all the evidence towards Buttons not only being real but taking an active role in our little drama."

Lincoln was forced to agree, as much as he didn't want to. This was becoming far more than a simple manhunt and the stakes were definitely rising. If Cross did indeed have an angel and this mysterious demon hunter, Buttons, with him then he would be immeasurably more dangerous. Lincoln nodded to the Cobleys. "If you'll excuse me for a minute? I'd like to share this latest development with our employers," he motioned towards one of the impassive guards that stood silently in the doorway between the kitchen and conservatory, "Mr Riley there will attend to your needs in my absence. Please inform him immediately if Mr Lee locates Cross."

Mr Cobley smiled. "Of course Mr Barnes. I'm sure our employers are very busy men or they would be here to oversee this important search themselves." The veiled barb towards the Harringtons obvious disdain of the Cobleys and their coven wasn't lost on Lincoln and he felt a slight twinge of embarrassment. He inclined his head towards Mr Cobley but didn't try to justify the snub the twins had delivered. The Harringtons were sublimely arrogant and with the power they wielded it could be argued they had earned the right to such arrogance. If the devil himself appeared Lincoln was fairly certain the twins would look down their noses at him.

Mrs Cobley watched him leave, her calculating gaze lingering on the space where Lincoln had been standing for a few seconds before she turned back to her husband. "He's an interesting one isn't he, dear?"

"Oh yes, I sometimes forget what normal humans can be capable of."

Terry, the giant skinhead, leaned forward on his too-small chair. "I still don't get it," he complained. "Can't see why you didn't let me slap the mouthy coon into shape after he spoke to you like that."

Mr Cobley smiled indulgently at Terry's barely restrained lust for violence. He was a simple creature it was true, but there was something almost pure about his unrelenting desire to inflict pain that endeared the huge thug to the Cobleys. "Mr Barnes is a rare man, Terry. I grant you that he isn't your match physically, few people are after all, but I can assure you he's infinitely more dangerous."

Terry was unconvinced. Physical power, the power to break bone and tear flesh was all he could understand. Supremely confident in his immense strength, it was all he *needed* to understand. "I don't get it," he repeated and Mr Cobley sighed. Johnny looked round from the laptop. "I'm having a hard time understanding it myself to be honest," he admitted and Mrs Cobley laughed.

"Let me tell you a little tale about our Mr Barnes." She settled herself on her chair, looking for all the world like a teacher preparing for story-time with her young charges. "You see those gloves he wears, yes?" The coven nodded. "They're not an affectation, more a visible embodiment of will." Her eyes grew distant as she recalled what she'd seen as she looked into Lincoln's mind. Glimpsing the thoughts and memories of others wasn't an exact science. At the most you received fragments, snapshots of memories and feelings that were often disjointed and hard to put together into a coherent narrative.

Mrs Cobley closed her eyes and her voice took on an almost sing-song tone as she turned the jumble of images and emotions into words.

"He's trapped. He's been beaten. Oh, it was vicious. Whoever did this hated him; they wanted him to suffer before he died. He can only see out of one eye, the other is too swollen, crusted shut by the blood and he can feel his broken ribs grind and stab with every movement. It's agony to move but move he does. He has too. The room is on fire and if he doesn't get free soon he never will.

"He's bound hand and foot. He's already broken his own thumb to try and slip free from his bindings but they're too tight. The fire is closer now and it scorches his skin and steals his air. He thrusts his bound hands into the flames and holds fast through the agony as his skin sears and bubbles and peels away, holds fast until his bonds are burned through and he is free again."

Mrs Cobley grimaced, swept up in the stolen thoughts and emotions, feeling Lincoln's remembered agony.

"Then those ruined hands go to work on the bindings on his legs. The pain is indescribable. He vomits from the agony, his vision darkens as his torn and battered body begins to shut itself down but he ignores its wishes. He won't die here. He crawls from the burning building on those devastated hands and battered knees, ignoring the pain and refusing to be beaten, willing death itself away until he reaches cool, clean air and is safe again."

She opened her eyes and looked at her coven, rapt with attention, save for the grotesque Solange who barely stirred and simply stared through lidded eyes and Terry who still glared petulantly out of the window. "Only then does Mr Barnes allow himself to fall unconscious. You see now? Such will and control! Believe me, children. Mr Barnes is worthy of our respect, and certainly deserving of yours."

Johnny nodded thoughtfully and agreed with the Cobleys. Such strength of will was rare indeed. Kerry sat forward, mouth part open in a salacious half smile as the thought of such agonies stirred her twisted desires. Terry remained unimpressed. The only thing that impressed Terry was Terry.

A muted beep sounded from Johnny's laptop. A curiously unimpressive herald when considering the import of its message. Johnny swivelled back in his chair and looked intently at the screen. "Found them!" he crowed, almost exultant at this proof of his technological prowess. He turned his excited eyes to Mr Cobley who merely nodded.

"Well done, Jonathan." The cadaverous man leant forward and placed his empty cup down on the tray in front of him before looking towards the still form of Mr. Riley who stood impassively by the door. "Mr Riley? Could you please inform Mr. Barnes that we've located our quarry?"

Mr Riley simply nodded and then pulled a slim phone from his pocket. A brief and hushed conversation followed and in less than a minute Lincoln Barnes strode purposefully back into the room. He nodded to Johnny. "Well done, Mr Lee. It's definitely them? Johnny turned his laptop slightly and tilted the screen back to give Lincoln a clearer view. The still image the young disciple had taken from the CCTV footage was slightly grainy once enlarged but Lincoln could still recognise Cross at the wheel of the stolen car.

He leant forward to look closer at the image and saw a small, grey haired man in the passenger seat. He could make out the shape of another occupant but couldn't resolve any further details than that. Mr. Cobley appeared at his side and studied the image. "So that's our Mr. Cross is it?" Lincoln said nothing and simply nodded once. Mr Cobley smiled. "Well that's definitely not a young woman in the front with him. Could that be the legendary Buttons I wonder?"

Lincoln looked at the slight man in the passenger seat, who looked even smaller next to Cross's bulk. "I thought he'd be taller."

Mr Cobley laughed. "Don't be fooled, Mr Barnes. If half the tales are true then Buttons is like Hiroshima in a hand grenade." His smile faded and he became serious once again. "How do you propose we handle this?" Lincoln thought for a second before replying. "Mr Lee? I assume you can keep tracking them?"

Johnny nodded. "Now I have them it's just a question of anticipating their route and jumping from camera to camera. That's not so difficult but I'd suggest we don't do it for too long. Hopping from network to network like that is bound to get noticed sooner rather than later, and hacking into CCTV will have GCHQ and the intelligence services sniffing around if they catch on."

Lincoln motioned Mr Riley over and then took his phone, handing it to Johnny. "Stay on the line with me," ordered Lincoln. "I'll follow with a team and we'll intercept them as soon as they stop moving. If you think you're in danger of being discovered then cut the connection immediately and cover your tracks as best you can." He turned to Mr Cobley. "Buttons is the wild-card in all this. We need to know what he's capable of. I want you with me but the team engages first, understood?"

"Perfectly, Mr Barnes. I assume this team won't contain any essential personnel? It's highly unlikely any of them will survive." Lincoln waved the comment away. "A necessary sacrifice, and worth it if it lets us learn more about what we're

Revenant Days

dealing with. My original plan was just to harry and harass Cross a bit, let him come to us without thinking he got here *too* easily. That was before we knew he had an angel and this Buttons character in tow though." Lincoln paused and then continued, almost to himself. "No, I think we need to hit them hard and fast, take out the major threats and then scooping Cross up will be easy enough."

Mr Cobley nodded approvingly and Lincoln turned as Mrs Cobley spoke. "What would you like me to do, dear?"

"Stay here for now please. If by some chance they slip past us I'd like you here to help deal with them if necessary."

"Of course, dear. Don't you worry about a thing." Mrs Cobley smiled and waved them off. "You boys get along and enjoy yourselves. Try not to kill the angel if you can help it, my love," she said to Mr Cobley. "I'd hate to miss out on that." Mr Cobley smiled fondly at his wife. "I wouldn't dream of it my duckling." He looked towards Lincoln who struggled to hide his bemusement at this strange pair of...whatever they were. "Shall we, Mr Barnes?"

Lincoln simply nodded and strode from the room. Mr Cobley followed close behind, smiling serenely at the thought of the bloodshed to come.

FOURTEEN

Andariel relaxed into the back seat and stared out of the window, considering their admittedly rather desperate plan as Cross drove quickly through the busy streets of London, avoiding the other cars on the road as adroitly as he ignored the various traffic signs and lights. "You know what? That might just work," she said. "What do you think, Buttons?" Buttons nodded thoughtfully. "It would certainly get his attention and I'm certain I can imprint the message easily enough."

The small man looked over at Cross. "Of course you realise we'll have to kill whoever it is you have in mind for this plan don't you?" Cross shrugged unconcernedly, continuing to focus on the road. "Yeah but we won't be killing anyone who matters will we? The whole point is that they're going to Hell so they won't be a great loss."

The angel in the backseat looked curiously at him. "Do you have anyone in particular in mind or are we just going to grab a random scumbag?" She grimaced as she looked out to the grey and crowded streets streaming past the windows as they drove. "Kind of spoilt for choice round here to be honest." Cross laughed. "Yeah I've got just the bloke for the job. He got out from under a rape charge a while back but everyone knows the nasty little fucker did it."

He paused as he wove around a parked delivery van and narrowly missed taking out both the driver and his fully laden trolley.

"He's been keeping out of the way since he got out of the nick; he knows a fair few of us would be happy to kick his head in if we saw him, so we should be able to do our business without worrying about witnesses."

"You know where he's hiding out then I take it?" asked Buttons. "Course I do," replied Cross. He looked across the car at the churchman. "He owes me money." Andariel laughed. "And that's got nothing to do with you choosing him I suppose?" Cross grinned at her in the rear-view mirror. "Two birds, one stone and all that." Buttons attempted to look disapproving and Cross laughed. "I'm nothing if not efficient, Reverend!"

Cross had outlined his plan back at the pub, and after some deliberation, Andariel and Buttons agreed it was probably their best chance. It wasn't like they had a lot of options left open to them though. It was a simple enough plan and Andariel was privately quite impressed. Not that she'd ever let on to Cross mind you. The trio were now on their way to enact the first stage of the plan and procure an unwitting and most certainly unwilling messenger.

The busy streets of Blackfriars were far behind them now and they approached the far less salubrious neighbourhood of Plumstead. Andariel looked at the grim and crumbling tower blocks that surrounded them as they moved deeper into the desperate, dilapidated mazes of the various council estates that squatted on the landscape like concrete tumours. She shook her head as they drove past gangs of almost feral children on the corners, perched on their stolen bikes and glaring at the interlopers with eyes that were too old for such young faces and had seen far too much already.

"You take me to the nicest places, Cross."
The big villain shrugged, trying to work out if they were in the right place. All these towers looked the same to him and the few street signs that were left in place and half intact were so covered with graffiti as to be illegible. "Sorry, I didn't have any white-collar criminals to hand. Besides, if you need to kick in a door or two then this is the sort of place you want to do it. The people round these estates have made not seeing anything or getting involved into an art form."

He cursed as he realised he'd gone past the block of flats they'd needed and wished the little bastards who lived here would leave the bloody signs alone for five minutes. Cross pulled into cul-de-sac to reverse back into the road and head back the way they came. The roar of an engine and the squeal of brakes behind them made them all turn and Cross cursed again as he saw the side door of the transit van that was suddenly blocking the road behind them open up to disgorge eight men, all armed with a mixture of bats, pipes or blades.

Cross briefly wondered how they'd found them and then narrowed his eyes as he saw Lincoln Barnes in the driving seat. *There you are. I'm gonna have you, you fucker.* Andariel and Buttons were already moving out of the car and advancing on the group of men. Cross hurried to join them. He saw someone else in the truck next to Lincoln, a tall, gangly bloke he'd never seen before and briefly wondered who he was.

He certainly didn't look like one of the Harrington's usual employees, and definitely not the sort they'd send on a muscle job like this. Cross mentally shrugged and forgot about him as he waded into the fray.

Buttons gestured to one of Lincolns' crew who was armed with a knife and the blade flew from the astonished man's grasp to nestle into the reverends' hand for the briefest of seconds before an effortless flick of the wrist sent it flying back to bury itself to the hilt in the goons' chest. He was dead before he hit the ground. Andariel was admittedly less graceful but certainly no less effective.

She pulled the man closest to her into a sickening head butt and he screamed as his nose and cheekbone shattered under the force of the blow. His right knee followed as she stamped on the outside of his leg. Even as he fell the angel grabbed his head and twisted savagely, breaking his neck as she moved past him towards her next target.

A baseball bat swung at Cross's head and he stepped inside the arc of the blow, smothering the force of it and locking both his assailants' arms under one of his own. He gripped with crushing strength and grinned as he felt an elbow pop. Cross used his free arm to deliver three rapid elbow hooks into his opponents face and let him drop.

A blurred movement to his right. Disengage, keep moving. No time, no space to dodge. Take the hit and roll with it. Cross grunted as another bat connected with his raised arm and he moved backwards, quickstepping in perfect balance and flowing with the force of the strike to rob it of as much impact as he could.

His assailant moved with him and Cross allowed himself to be forced back. He stepped quickly backwards, shifting his weight and gripping his opponents' arm just above the elbow, his large hand wrapping above the spur of bone that comprised the elbow joint. With the same movement he delivered a sharp kick to the shin with the base of his foot as he pulled on the trapped arm, sending his opponent stumbling past him. Surprised by the move and off balance it took the thug a second to realise he'd dropped the bat. No, he hadn't dropped it.

Cross had deftly taken it from him as he'd sent him sprawling and now stood there grinning with his prize. Cross backhanded the bat across his face with a sickening crunch of crushed bone. Four down in less than a minute. Cross smiled nastily. The Harringtons were going to have to raise their game.

Lincoln and Mr Cobley looked out at the carnage, Lincoln shaking his head at the ease with which the trio were despatching his men. Admittedly he hadn't wasted his best on this stage of the mission and he'd prohibited the use of firearms for now in case someone got trigger happy and wound up shooting Cross by mistake. Even without the assistance of a renegade angel and a demon hunter Cross was scything through his men like they were little more than unruly children.

Lincoln looked on in wonder as the small, grey-haired man dressed as a vicar batted a machete blow away with contemptuous ease and then flung his attacker through the windscreen of a car parked at least fifteen feet away. The petite angel laughed with bloodthirsty glee as she divested one of her assailants of his crowbar and then rammed it through the underside of his chin and up into the brain. He'd seen all he needed to see and gunned the engine. It was time to move.

Mr Cobley raised a thin hand. "One moment please." The fight had drawn the attention of several gangs of young boys from the estate who whooped and cheered at the violent display. Mr Cobley closed his eyes and concentrated and a dozen pairs of watching eyes went blank with sudden, murderous intent. The teenagers dropped their bikes and moved towards the fray, some pulling knives of their own and others stopping to collect weapons from Lincoln's fallen men.

Mr Cobley opened his eyes with a satisfied smile and looked at Lincoln. "One of the drawbacks of working on the side of the angels are all the tedious rules you have to follow. I'll grant you that these children aren't exactly innocents but neither the angel or Buttons will kill them, and I doubt Cross will either. That should keep them busy for a while."

"Have you seen all you needed to see, Mr Cobley?"
The thin man shrugged. "Oh, I'm sure I haven't seen a fraction of what Buttons is capable of. To do that you'd need to really push him and I doubt there's a being on this entire planet capable of that, excepting myself and Mrs Cobley of course. Our mysterious hunter is definitely holding back, quite why I don't know but it certainly works in our favour" Lincoln spared a final glance towards the fracas and began to move the van slowly away as the enthralled children approached the momentarily victorious trio.

"And do you think you and Mrs Cobley will be able to at least neutralise him if not remove him from the equation completely?"

Mr Cobley nodded thoughtfully. "With both of us working together almost certainly. I'd suggest utilising us and the coven both and let us concentrate on Buttons while you and your men handle Cross and the angel." Lincoln raised his eyebrows at this. "And how are we supposed to handle an angel?"

Mr Cobley laughed. "In its current form the creature has little more than enhanced strength and speed. Oh, she'll have a few other tricks up her sleeve but nothing near the scale of what she could do in her true incarnation. She'll be far more resilient than a normal human but a shotgun round to the chest will soon slow her down."

Lincoln nodded, pleased with Mr Cobleys's quiet confidence in his abilities and concise assessment of their opponents. He reached for the phone on its stand on the dashboard and thumbed the speaker button. "Mr Lee? Are you still on the line?" Johnny's' tinny, disembodied voice sounded from the speaker. "Of course, Mr Barnes. What would you like me to do?

"Just keep tracking them for as long as you can. We've got them on the run for now and I want to keep piling on the pressure. Let's not give them any more time to think than we have to. Ask Mr Riley to give team B the go and have them loaded for bear this time. I'd like Mrs Cobley and the rest of the coven to join them too. You stay put for now, you're going to be our eyes and ears."

"No problem. Mr Riley overheard and is prepping team B already. Tracking them will be harder through these estates, half of the cameras are smashed or stolen but I'll do my best."

Mr Cobley interjected: "Johnny? Can you give me somewhere to shepherd them to? I have some thralls making their lives interesting right now and I can try and push them somewhere more suitable if you give me a location."

Johnny was quiet for a few seconds as he brought up a map of the area and consulted it. "Got it. If you can send them a couple of miles east there's an old industrial site. Camera coverage is limited but that could work in our favour and give us a bit more privacy. I could probably kill the cameras when you're on-site and then you can use whatever means necessary to deal with them."

Lincoln was quietly impressed. "Excellent work, Mr

Lee. Stay on the line and I'll give you the order to kill the cameras when we have them in sight. It will mean playing some cat and mouse but the benefits outweigh the risks." Lincoln put Johnny on hold and turned to Mr Cobley. "Mr Cobley? Can you get our little flock moving in the right direction?"

Mr Cobley smiled, sitting back in his seat and closing his eyes. "Consider it done."

Cross was furious. Running from some tearaway bloody kids. He'd never live this down. The trio ran through the crumbling maze of the estates, drawing curious glances and laughter from the balconies and walkways they passed under. Cross realised what it must look like to the casual observer and suddenly grinned. *Let's be honest*, he thought. *If I saw a vicar being chased by a gang of council-rats I'd probably laugh as well.*

He heard footsteps behind and glanced back to see one of the dead-eyed little shits right behind him, a worn and dirty looking blade clutched in one small hand. The skinny kid stared blankly as he raised the knife and Cross twisted slightly to backhand him savagely across the face, knocking him from his feet without losing stride. Cross caught Andariel's faintly disapproving look. "What? The little fucker was gonna shiv me!"

Buttons was slightly in front of the other two, moving very quickly for someone with such short legs thought Cross. The vicar swore suddenly. "Eyes left!" Cross and Andariel saw another group of blank-faced children running to intercept them and ducked inside one of the tower blocks, running through the piss-reeking corridors and out the other side. Three more of Mr Cobleys' thralls awaited them and this time Andariel simply barrelled through them, knocking them to the floor like tenpins but taking a shallow cut to the arm from a Stanley-knife as she did so.

They were heading out of the estates now and Cross cursed as he saw an expanse of wasteland in front of them and what looked like a derelict industrial estate on the horizon. He hated running blindly like this and shouted across to Andariel as they ran. "Can't we beat them up just a little bit?"

"No we bloody can't! They're being controlled, and by someone who really knows what they're doing too."

"How do you mean?" panted Cross.

"Using kids is clever, whoever it is knows Buttons and I won't hurt them if we can help it, and controlling this many at once from a distance? Trust me, whoever it is they're very, very good."

Cross wasn't convinced. You could have given the little bastards a few quid each and they'd have been happy to try and stab you. Half of them would probably have done it just to see the look on your face. He pointed towards the disused factories and warehouses of the brownfield site in front of them. "Ok then, head for that and we'll try and lose them."

"You realise that's probably exactly where they want us to go?" shouted Buttons.

"No choice, reverend. We can't run forever and at least we have a chance of slipping past them in there."

"But what else is going to be waiting for us when we get there?" asked Andariel.

"One problem at a time eh, luv?"

They ran on, the uneven grass of the wasteland falling away and turning to dirt and gravel as they entered the abandoned industrial estate. The trio turned a corner and ran behind a large building that looked like a warehouse. Cross saw a door to his right and skidded to a halt. He delivered a thundering kick to the door, breaking both the lock and the top hinge. The door hung drunkenly open and Andariel went to move inside until Cross stopped her.

"Keep moving," he said as he ushered them away from the door. "Let them waste time looking for us in there."

Cross's breathing was laboured now. It had been a long time since he'd taken a ten-mile run or made a forced march with full kit a few times a week and he certainly wasn't as young as he used to be. It was nothing to do with the cigarettes of course. Buttons and Andariel weren't even winded and he silently cursed their supernatural endurance. He'd have to stop soon. It was highly unlikely they'd get out of this without a fight and he'd need to get his wind back for that.

They came upon what looked like an old factory, the large, double doors gaping wide. Cross looked inside and saw a maze of rusting machines and rickety walkways. Perfect. "In here," he panted. "I need to get my breath back and we should have a couple of minutes to spare." They moved away from the entrance and deeper into the labyrinth of disused machinery. Cross sank gratefully to the floor and lit a cigarette.

"I thought you needed to get your breath back?" asked Andariel.

"This is me getting my breath back."

Andariel shook her head as Buttons laughed quietly. After a few moments Cross had recovered enough to ask: "So who's pulling that trick with the kids then?" Buttons had a look of distaste on his face as he replied. "Malleus has almost certainly called upon some of the blessed to assist the Harringtons and if I'm right it will be the Cobleys, or at least one of them."

"What's a Cobley?" asked Andariel, and Buttons chuckled in reply. "Not a what, a who. A pair of very nasty and very powerful blessed. They rank highest amongst the mortal servants of Malleus."

"One of them a skinny fella? Looks like a kiddy-fiddler?" asked Cross.

"That sounds like Mr Cobley, yes. Did you see him?"

Cross shrugged. "Well I saw another bloke in the van with Lincoln who fits that description, and what with the kids going all Village of the Damned on us back there I think we can assume you're right."

Andariel looked worried. "This isn't good news."

"No, it isn't," agreed Buttons, "but it's not unexpected."

"But you can take them though, right? asked Cross.

"Of course I can. The problem is that I won't be able to deal with them effectively without attracting a lot of unwanted attention. A decisive battle between the Cobleys and I would level this entire area, not to mention killing everyone in it."

"Ok, let's give that a miss then."

Andariel scuffed at the ground with her boot. "Meanwhile the Cobleys won't be worrying about any such constraints and we're fighting with our hands tied." Cross ground out his cigarette and stood up. "Well if we can't fight hard we'll have to fight smart. Buttons, anything in your box of tricks that will let you work on blunting the Cobleys' attacks? If we can't take them out then maybe we can at least make them less of a handful."

Buttons nodded, thoughtfully. "I'll do what I can."

Cross clapped him on the shoulder. "That's good enough for me, mate. Andariel and I will keep the rest of them off your back while you concentrate on the Cobleys." Cross grinned over at Andariel. "How about it? You ready for another fight?"

"Is that a trick question?"

Cross laughed. "Ok then, we'll…" He was interrupted by the sound of an engine, no two engines outside and he immediately motioned his companions to silence, pointing them further back into the cover of the rusting machines and conveyor belts. Buttons and Andariel padded silently away and Cross took cover behind the nearest contraption that gave him a clear view of the entrance.

He wasn't surprised to hear both vehicles roll to a halt directly outside and sighed as he heard the sound of sliding, van doors opening and too many boots hitting the ground. *I just can't catch a fucking break can I?* Cross retreated further into the huge building, moving from cover to cover and keeping the entrance in site at all times. He came to a large device that looked like some sort of furnace and stopped. Its flat surface was shrouded in darkness and he silently pulled himself up to lie on his stomach facing the door. *Ok then, let's see what we're up against.*

He watched as Lincoln Barnes strode boldly into the building and stood in the opening, making no move to find cover. *Cocky bastard.* Lincoln spoke loudly into the echoing space. "I know you can hear me, Daniel." He laughed quietly. "In fact I'm sure you're looking at me right now. If you can see me then you can see this as well." Lincoln made a beckoning motion and Cross watched with a sinking feeling as more than a dozen men filed in and immediately took up cover and over-watch positions, forming a bridgehead at the entrance.

They were all fully armed and combat dressed and Cross could recognise ex-soldiers when he saw them. *Well, this is going to be a fucking nuisance.* Lincoln was around thirty feet away and clearly framed in the light that spilled in from the doorway. Thirty feet was a dicey proposition when shooting with a handgun, no matter what the movies said, but Cross was confident he could take the shot and briefly considered it.

Not worth it. He'd give up his position too quickly, and besides, he wanted to gut the prick and make him hurt for what he'd done to Gus and Kate. No, let Linc run his mouth for a bit in case he gave something away.

Lincoln carried on, sounding way too smug for Cross's taste. "I know you're good, Daniel, but we both know you're not *that* good." He turned his head and smiled as the skinny nonce and a little woman who looked like a chubby Hilary Clinton entered the building, trailed by a decidedly odd look-ing group.

The motley crew stood behind them and Cross won-dered why they'd bring along what looked like a crack-whore and a morbidly obese woman. He could see why the giant skin-head was there. *Fuck me but he's a lump.*

"My other associates here are more than capable of countering anything your pet angel and demon hunter can throw at us. I'm not about to ask you to give up and come quietly, I know that isn't in your nature, but we both know the outcome isn't in doubt no matter how difficult you make things for us."

I've had enough of listening to this gobshite, thought Cross and slipped his glock from the back of his trousers. He slid backwards on his shadowed perch so he could stretch his arms out across the top of the furnace to steady them and then tracked his gun across the group of armed men arrayed around the entrance, searching for the best target. *That one.* Cross slowly squeezed the trigger and the instant the gun bucked in his hand he rolled from the furnace, landing nimbly on his feet and sprinting silently to a new position, the echo of the shot covering any noise he might have made. He didn't stop to see the shot connect. He didn't have to.

Lincoln cursed as one of his men spun in time with the loud report of the gunshot, the lower half of his face shredded and his jaw hanging down where the bullet had punched through his teeth. The rest of the men immediately fired towards where the shot had come from, the sound deafening inside the room and Lincoln turned to face them, furiously motioning for them to hold fire. "Stop shooting you idiots!" he yelled. "Cross is long gone from there and you know it."

He sighed inwardly. Despite his confident speech, and he was indeed confident that they'd eventually take Cross alive, he knew that his adversary was more than capable of making that a very difficult and costly enterprise. Lincoln turned to Riley. "It looks like we're doing this the hard way after all, Mr Riley. If you would be so kind?"

Mr Riley nodded and motioned to the men in his command who immediately fanned out in pairs, slipping into the shadowed labyrinth of the factory to begin the hunt. Cross moved deeper into the gloomy space, slipping from broken machine to broken machine, every sense straining to locate his pursuers. He'd been in similar situations in the past, though admittedly not against these odds, and knew that everything counted. Sight, sound and even smell could tip that knife-edge between life and death.

A slight noise caught his attention and he looked to his left to see Andariel motioning him over. He hurried over to join them. "Well?" asked the angel and Cross grimaced. "We're up shit creek a bit here to be honest. We've got at least a dozen armed men out there, plus Lincoln and those Cobley people."

Cross looked over at Buttons. "They've got an odd little group with them too. Any ideas?" Buttons grimaced. "They've bought their coven by the sounds of it, or at least some of them."

"Dangerous?" asked Cross and Buttons shrugged. "They could be," he admitted. "Without knowing how far down the path they've travelled and what gifts Malleus has bestowed upon them we won't know until we get into it with them." Cross decided to ignore the unknown quantity of the coven for now. They had the known quantity of a dozen professional soldiers to deal with first.

"Ok, let's move and see if we can't find a back way out of here. They're probably quartering the room in a two-by-two pattern so we might be able to slip past. Keep low and keep quiet." The three of them moved off into the shadows, heading towards the back of the huge building in the hope of finding an escape route, or at least some better ground to make a stand if the worst came to the worst.

Cross saw some stairs leading to a raised walkway and pointed towards them, motioning his companions to step slowly and lightly. It would be far too easy to give away their position by making a noise on the metal stairs but the benefits of an elevated position made it a risk worth taking. Cross needn't have worried as both Andariel and Buttons moved in perfect silence. He suddenly realised that his own footsteps weren't making a sound either. Cross could move quietly when he needed to but he couldn't move *that* quietly.

He tapped Andariel on the shoulder, motioning to his feet and then to his ears with a questioning expression. The angel laughed. "Don't worry about the noise, Daniel. I'm deadening the air around us. We could start up a brass band and they wouldn't hear us."
"That's a bloody handy trick."

"Why thank you. It only extends for a couple of feet though so stick close. It takes a fair bit of effort too so I won't be able to keep it up all day."

Cross grimaced. "I don't think you need to worry about that. I reckon this'll be over quickly. One way or another."

Buttons pointed below and Cross looked down to see two of Lincolns' mercenaries approaching the walkway. The trio were enveloped in darkness and the mercenaries hadn't seen them yet but Cross knew they'd be discovered as soon as the men got a few feet closer. He began to edge back but Andariel put a hand on his arm to stop him. "Allow me," she said as she pulled two knives from the back of her belt. Cross realised she must have picked them up from the first crew they'd tangled with and silently berated himself for not doing the same.

The angel looked critically at the approaching men and then leapt cat-like from the walkway, still blanketed by her sphere of silence. Cross watched in admiration as she easily cleared the ten-foot gap between them and the mercenaries, twisting in the air and dropping the twenty feet to the floor to land perfectly between them.

She held the knives point down with raised arms as she dropped, stabbing them directly into the tops of the mercenaries' skulls as she landed. The men jerked spastically and Andariel twisted the knives inside their heads to stop them slipping free and allow her to lower them carefully to the floor.

Cross looked at Buttons and raised his eyebrows a fraction. Buttons smiled and leant closer. "She's really very good," he whispered.

She took one of their MP5's and nimbly jumped back onto the walkway, handing it to Cross with a satisfied smile. "Present for you."

"You're spoiling me now, luv. Very nice move by the way."

Andariel grinned in reply as she cleaned her bloodied knives on her jeans, flicking the more stubborn gobbets of brain away. Buttons edged forward and pointed into the gloomy distance. They followed his gaze to see four more men approaching from the rear and, more alarmingly, Mr and Mrs Cobley walking towards them from the opposite direction. "I think we'd better move, don't you?"

Cross scanned the ground around them and saw they were above several rows of the large, flat-topped furnace like machines. He pointed downwards and they dropped to the nearest one in unison. Cross began to lead them away but Mrs Cobley spoke a single, grating word and the room was suddenly flooded with a red, sickly light, leaving the trio completely exposed on top of the furnace. *Well, that's fucked it*, thought Cross, even as he rolled from the top of the derelict machine and pulled Andariel and Buttons with him.

The four mercenaries reacted quickly and raked the area with gunfire but the bullets hit nothing but air and rusting metal. Cross popped out from cover and returned fire. He knew he wouldn't hit anything but knowing he was armed would make them think twice about storming his position. In the crimson, conjured light Andariel could see they were near the back of the factory as evidenced by the large wall a few feet away. The large wall that contained a conspicuous lack of exits. "We could be in trouble here." She said.

The mercenaries fired again, forcing the companions to duck behind their meagre cover and Cross could hear the clipped shouts of the others as they moved towards the fight. They probably had less than thirty seconds before they were flanked. *Flanked and fucked* he silently amended. He fired again, knowing it was a futile, angry gesture as he wracked his brain to think of a way out and then yelped in surprise as an invisible hand grasped him by the collar and flung him across the room.

He slid to a halt, shook his head and blinked the dust from his eyes as a voice spoke above him. "Hello, Mr Cross." Cross looked up into the grinning face of the cadaverous Mr Cobley. Cross heard Andariel and Buttons shout as they began to move, about to run into a hail of bullets to try and rescue him. Then Mrs Cobley made a hooking gesture with one hand and brought the walkway crashing down on their heads.

FIFTEEN

Cross sat back on his hands and looked up at the Cobleys leering down at him. He smiled insolently back up at them. Cross was scared, not just for himself but for his two friends. He wasn't about to let these smug arseholes know it though. "So, what can I do for you dickheads then?" he asked. Mr Cobley laughed and looked at his plump wife who was shaking her head. "I think I rather like him, my love." Mrs Cobley was less impressed. "I don't think there's any need for profanity, dear."

Lincoln Barnes sauntered over to join them with the rest of the mercenaries in tow. Two of them pulled Cross to his knees and patted him down, removing the glock from the back of his trousers. They roughly pulled his arms behind his back and then slipped a thick, plastic cable tie around his wrists before cinching it tightly. Lincoln dropped to his haunches and squatted in front of him. "Hello Daniel."

"Hello Linc', how've you been?"

Lincoln shrugged. "Busy. You know how it is."

"Yeah, been having one of those days myself. Still got lots to do."

"Such as?"

"Killing you and those skinny ponces you work for is pretty much top of the list."

Lincoln laughed. "I think that particular ship has sailed don't you?"

Cross shrugged. "We'll see. The day aint over yet."

Mr Cobley shook his head and smiled in admiration. "I can see why Malleus wanted this one as the vessel." Lincoln turned his attention to the gangly warlock while keeping a wary eye on Cross. "Does the vessel itself make a difference to the possession then?"

"Oh yes. Despite the demon being in control there's still some amount of...transference shall we say? The most powerful characteristics of the host body will eventually bleed into the psyche of the controlling entity, so it's important to ensure those characteristics are beneficial." Mr Cobley smiled at Lincoln. "You yourself would make an excellent host."

Lincoln grimaced as Cross laughed. "How does that sound, Linc'? You could be next on the menu. You don't think the Harringtons wouldn't give you up in a second if it suited them?" Lincoln backhanded Cross in the face, angry because he knew he was right and then angrier still at his loss of composure. Cross spat blood and laughed. "Temper, temper!"

Mr Cobley smiled slyly at his wife; both of them pleased to see the vaunted Lincoln Barnes had feet of clay after all. He was about to speak when a loud screech of grinding metal interrupted him.

Cross twisted round to look behind him and laughed aloud to see Andariel and Buttons standing, uninjured, amidst the twisted wreckage of the walkway, the small churchman holding a large girder above his head as though it weighed nothing.

"You people are starting to get right on my tits", said Buttons and then hurled the section of walkway at them. Cross and Lincoln were both close to the ground anyway and quickly dropped flat. The Cobleys and the mercenaries weren't so fortunate and the twisted length of metal smashed them from their feet. Cross smiled nastily as he saw Lincoln was both distracted and within striking distance and he lashed out with his foot, kicking Barnes solidly in the jaw and sending him spinning away.

Cross rolled with the motion and got to his feet. He looked down and grinned as he saw his Glock lying on the floor. He quickly squatted, scrabbling around with his bound hands until he scooped it up before running back to join his companions. They were both covered in dust and grime and their clothes were ripped but otherwise they appeared unharmed and Cross allowed himself a silent sigh of relief, not only because of his rescue but because his friends were still alive. "You two are a sight for sore eyes!" Andariel grinned at him. "Aww bless, were you worried about us?"

Buttons hushed her, pointing to where the Cobleys were already getting to their feet again. "We need to get out of here fast. I'll have really upset them now and things will get very nasty and very loud if I have to pull the stops out." Cross was dismayed to see that being hit with a few tonnes of jagged metal appeared to be little more than an inconvenience to the odd-looking pair.

"We've got nowhere to go!" said Andariel. "Back there is a dead end and..." The angel had turned to motion back towards the wall behind them and suddenly stopped. "Er, that door wasn't there the last time I looked."

"You sure?" asked Cross and Andariel gave him a withering look. "No," she mocked, "I obviously missed that bloody great door slap bang in the middle of the wall."

"Buttons?"

Buttons shrugged. "We're out of options. Our only other way out is through them and we'll have half of Heaven and Hell joining in the fun if I start making that much noise down here. Let's do it."

Cross nodded and ran towards the door. He stopped and waited for Andariel to catch up to him. The angel looked at him questioningly. "What are you waiting for?" she asked and Cross sighed, twisting his body to show his hands were still tied behind his back.

"Oh yeah, right." She grinned and opened the door. The three friends stepped through into darkness; the last sound they heard was the Cobleys' screams of rage as the door disappeared behind them.

Lincoln got slowly to his feet, rubbing his jaw and grimacing in pain as it shifted and clicked. *Fucking Daniel Cross,* he thought and then sighed as he looked down at his torn and dusty suit. *Ok, let's take stock.* Lincoln looked towards the broken ruin of his men and mentally shrugged. *At least we won't need to pay them.*

The Cobleys were unharmed and Lincoln hid his surprise at their supernatural resilience. The rest of the coven had hung back from the conflict and so had escaped Buttons' savage retaliation.

"Mr Cobley," he said in clipped tones. "Did I just see our targets escape through a doorway that wasn't there a minute ago and then just disappeared in front of our eyes?" Mr Cobley was still enraged by Buttons attack and the ease with which he'd taken them down. Enraged and grudgingly impressed.

It may not have looked like it, but he and Mrs Cobley had thrown a significant amount of their power into warding off the attack. Such strength, and Mr Cobley knew Buttons was *still* holding back. It appeared the tales about the legendary demon hunter were all true, and then some.

"Yes," he ground out, "and no, I have no idea how it happened. To the best of my knowledge that isn't something that either Buttons or the angel could have done." Lincoln cursed softly. "Which means we could have yet another player on the field?"

Mr Cobley regained his composure. "Indeed, and one with abilities I've yet to encounter, or have even heard about."

"Could you hazard a guess as to where they might have gone?"

Mr Cobley laughed sourly. "Whoever made that doorway just folded space and time in a millisecond without making a sound and without leaving a trace. They could be anywhere, and by 'anywhere' I literally mean anywhere in the entire cosmos."

Lincoln cursed again. It was doubtful Mr Lee would be picking them up on CCTV again anytime soon then. He mentally shook himself. There was little point in worrying about it now.

The situation had progressed beyond his ability to control, or even to anticipate. Angels, demons and disappearing doors were all way outside of his usual remit. All they could do now was report back and let Malleus and the Harringtons know what had happened, and hope that none of them were dismembered for being the bearers of such bad news.

Mrs Cobley spoke as she attempted to put her hair back into some sort of order and it was as though she'd read his mind. "Malleus really isn't going to be too happy about this, dear."

"I'm well aware of that Mrs Cobley. However, this is a situation that even Malleus didn't foresee, or if he did he neglected to mention it. Our best hope is that he can shed some light on who or what just came to their rescue and what we can do about getting them back. I realise your master didn't rise to where he is without being ruthless, but neither could he have gotten there, or stay there, without being intelligent as well.

"I'm confident he'll appreciate this situation was out of our control and see the wisdom in working with us to devise a solution, rather than wasting time and resources punishing us unnecessarily."

Mr Cobley snorted a humourless laugh as they walked through the twisted and broken corpses on their way back to the vans outside. "You have actually met him I take it?"

Elsewhere...

"Please tell me it's just really dark and that I haven't gone blind?" asked Cross. "Well if you've gone blind then so have I." Andariel replied. "Me too." said Buttons.

"That's comforting. Sort of."

Cross could hear their voices echoing so he knew they were in a large room but couldn't make anything out in the enveloping blackness. He pulled out his lighter from his pocket and cursed as it clicked uselessly in his hand, not even producing a spark. *Great, I can't even have a bloody smoke.* He didn't know how, but somehow Cross knew that they were far, far away from London and wondered just where the mysterious door had taken them, and what might lurk in this huge, black space.

All three jumped as a soft, feminine voice came from the dark. "My apologies, I forget that not everyone can see as I can." The voice took on a wry tone as it continued. "It's been some time since I have been gifted with company. In fact, I believe you are the first to ever visit this place." As the echoes of the voice died away the darkness receded as the room brightened, lit by some unknown source.

The transition was gradual and Cross slowly began to make out the admittedly sparse details of the room they'd entered through the mysterious door. The room, wherever it was, was vast. What looked like large, polished flagstones stretched away into the distance on every side and Cross looked up to see the ceiling was high enough to be invisible in the darkness that still hung above them.

At regular intervals stood huge columns of stone, simply but beautifully carved and stretching up into the gloom to support the hidden ceiling. The room put Cross in mind of a gigantic cathedral, one that could have contained a thousand Canterburys or Westminsters within its impossible space. Cross squinted to his right and nudged Andariel. "Do you see that?"

The angel nodded. In the far distance they could see a faint play of brighter light, a pulsating, glimmering beacon that appeared to be suspended in a deeper darkness. Cross looked at Andariel and Buttons who both shrugged *Why not?* The trio began to walk towards the only feature the enormous room appeared to contain. Cross looked up as he walked, not sure why he was doing so and spoke into the darkness above. "Er, hello?"

Andariel snorted derisively. "Nice opener, o brave explorer." Cross was about to retort when the voice sounded again, seeming to issue from all around them. "Hello, Daniel Cross." There was a pause and then the voice continued in suddenly stilted tones, almost as though it read from a script: "How are you today?" Cross looked at his companions and raised his eyebrows. Buttons shrugged and motioned for him to reply. "Er, not bad thanks. You know, being chased through disappearing doors by pissed off warlocks notwithstanding."

"Yes, I am aware of your predicament, Daniel Cross and I have resolved to render what aid I can, as much as I am able." The disembodied voice sounded almost hesitant towards the end. Andariel picked up the conversation, speaking in much more formal tones all of a sudden. "We thank you for your timely intervention," she said. "May we ask who you are?"

"I am Ennustaja. Well met, Andarielastenaama of the host."

Cross blinked and looked at his angelic friend. "Andarielaste-what?" The angel shrugged. "I know, It's a bit of a mouthful." She addressed their invisible and mysterious host again. "Well met, Ennustaja. What is this place? Where have you brought us?" The voice returned with an undercurrent of amusement. "This is the Last Hall. As to where you are? You could say you are everywhere, or perhaps nowhere."

"I see," said Andariel, who clearly didn't. Their unseen rescuer spoke again. "Not a satisfactory answer I know, but it is the only one I can give you at the moment." Andariel was about to reply when the voice forestalled her. "Carry on to the portal you see before you and I will endeavour to explain further." The voice fell silent and somehow, they all knew that no further answers would be forthcoming.

Cross looked towards the shifting dance of lights in the distance, the 'portal' he assumed. "We'd better get a shift on, that portal thing looks miles off. The sooner we get there the sooner Captain Cryptic up there can shed some light on what the bloody hell is going on." They walked on in silence for a few minutes before Andariel spoke. "Buttons? The Last Hall?" The diminutive demon hunter pulled a sour face. "Never heard of it. You?"

"Me neither, or this Ennustaja." The angel sounded almost worried and Cross looked across at her and smiled. "Well creation must be a pretty big place; you can't be expected to keep track of all of it."

"That's just it, Daniel, I can. I helped build it after all. Well, I put a few of the finishing touches in anyway." She stopped and faced him. "I've been from one end of the cosmos to the other a dozen times since the dawn of time itself. Believe me when I say I know every nook and cranny by now and I've never seen or even heard of this place."

Cross shrugged. "Ok, that's weird, I'll grant you that. On the other hand, whoever this Ennustaja is you have to admit she got us out of a tight spot back there, and so far, whatever this Last Hall place is it doesn't appear to be full of people trying to kill us. With all that in mind I'd say we're doing alright."

Buttons nodded. "I agree. We're here now, wherever 'here' is and it's highly unlikely we'll be able to just walk out again. The way I see it we don't have much choice but to see what happens. At least Ennustajas' actions so far seem to suggest he or she or it is on our side, or at least not actively opposing us."

"Not sure I like the idea that we could be stuck here," said Cross. "But there's fuck all we can do about it so no point in worrying." Andariel refused to be mollified so easily. "You two can be fatalistic all you like. Me? I'll worry a bit if it's all the same to you?" Cross laughed. "Look at it this way: If we don't know where we are then it's a sure bet Malleus doesn't either. I bet he'll be chucking his toys out of the pram right about now and I don't imagine Lincoln and the Cobleys are too popular either."

Andariel and Buttons joined in the laughter. "There is that", the angel agreed. She was about to continue when she suddenly stopped, mouth agape. Cross and Buttons followed her wide-eyed gaze to see they had neared the portal and they both stopped, struck with a sense of stupefied wonder. The three walked closer with halting steps, not believing what they were seeing.

The portal hadn't been as far away as they thought but

the sheer scale of the gigantic room had twisted their perceptions somewhat. It looked like a huge window, hundreds of feet high and wide and containing a darkness so deep, so perfect it seemed somehow alive. Within the centre of that infinite blackness a billion galaxies spun and danced. Uncountable stars flared and burned in their endless cycle of birth and death, their light the source of the flickering radiance they'd seen.

Within the portal was...everything. Cross reeled, his mortal mind scarcely able to comprehend the vastness, the impossibility of what he could see.

"Is that...?" Andariels' voice was a tiny whisper.

"Yes." This time the voice sounded directly behind them and the three companions whirled to see their mysterious host, Ennustaja. "You look upon the whole of creation." Cross gaped at the being in front of him, somehow finding her more shocking and in some ways even more beautiful than the window into infinity behind him.

The creature calling itself Ennustaja stood at least seven feet tall, her willowy figure and poise suggesting an impossible, ethereal grace. Her skin, and she was undoubtedly female, was a midnight blue shot through with shimmering veins of gold, her eyes perfectly black orbs that somehow still conveyed a depth of warmth and compassion. Ennustaja was naked and completely hairless, her slightly elongated head bordered by flaring, upswept ridges of bone that were covered in delicate, flowing patterns.

Ennustaja bowed slightly, the promise of that ethereal grace delivered in the flowing movement. "Welcome, all, to the Last Hall." The trio returned the bow, Andariel and Buttons with appreciably more aplomb than Cross who, if he was honest, felt like a bit of an idiot doing it. "Our thanks, Ennustaja," said Buttons. "Forgive my rudeness but who are you?"

"I am Ennustaja."

Cross sighed inwardly. *Somehow, I just knew this was going to be like pulling teeth.* "That's great, luv and it's a pleasure to meet you and all that but any chance you can be a bit more specific?" Andariel elbowed him in the ribs and Buttons barked: "Daniel! Please!"

"What?" Cross retorted. "I've literally been to Hell and back, I've got half of London and the afterlife trying to kill me, again, and I'm fucked right off with it all. I don't think a straight answer is too much to ask for by now!"

Any further responses the angel or demon hunter were about to make to Cross's outburst were interrupted by the silvery laughter of Ennustaja. "You are quite right, Daniel and if I knew any more than that I would most certainly tell you."

"You mean you don't know who you are?" asked Buttons with an almost pitying look.

"I know I am Ennustaja. I know I am the keeper of this place, the Last Hall, and I know that from here I can see the whole of creation. What it was, what it is and the limitless things it could be. But who or what I am?" She shrugged slightly, an impossibly fluid, almost boneless movement and smiled sadly. "That I do not know."
Cross immediately regretted losing his temper. "Sorry, luv. It's been one of those days."
"Eloquent as ever, Cross" snorted Andariel.

Ennustaja waved the apology away. "It is of no moment. Indeed, I have been impressed with your fortitude during this trying time." Cross smiled and inclined his head towards the mysterious creature and then nudged Andariel. "See? I've got fortitude."
"Oh shut up."

Ennustaja laughed again. "You are strange creatures indeed. Your affection for each other is clear and yet you display that affection by scorn. I can see many things from the Last Hall, yet this will be ever beyond my understanding."
Andariel laughed as well. "I wouldn't let your lack of understanding of human behaviour worry you, Ennustaja. I think even God himself has trouble with it, and they were his idea in the first place." Buttons huffed slightly in impatience. "As nice

as all this is we have more pressing matters to attend to, don't you agree?"

"Worry not, Blade of the Morningstar, here in the Last Hall we stand outside."

Buttons cocked his head curiously. "Outside of time?"

"Outside of *all*."

Andariel was shocked. "You mean we're outside of creation itself? But that's impossible!" She stopped as a thought occurred to her and looked over at Buttons. "Blade of the Morningstar?" The little man shrugged. "That's my official title," he admitted. "It's a little ostentatious for my taste."

The angel smiled at her friend and then glared almost angrily at Ennustaja as she remembered what the keeper of the Last Hall had just said.

"We can't be standing outside of creation. It's, well it's... it's bloody *creation*, there isn't anything else!"

Ennustaja shrugged again and spread her long arms wide. "And yet here we stand, Andarielastenaama." She held up a slim, six fingered hand as Andariel went to speak again. "I know not how the Last Hall came to be, I only know that it *is*. Whether I found it or it found me? That I know not either. Once I arrived here I knew, somehow, that this place was called the Last Hall and that my purpose was to observe and record, not only the past but the infinite possibilities of the future. That is why I brought you here."

"How did you get here? asked Cross and Ennustaja smiled a melancholy smile. "Perhaps I simply walked through a door as you did, or perhaps I came here upon my death? After all, what is death but another doorway?"

"So you can't remember anything at all?"

"Sometimes I think I could remember or at least *feel* something of my past. I believe I had another name once." Ennustaja lifted her shoulders in that impossibly boneless shrug again. "Whether the loss of my past is a gift or curse of this place? That too remains a mystery." Suddenly she smiled. "For a being that can see creation as a whole there seems to be much I do not know." Ennustaja gestured towards her outlandish and beautiful form. "I believe I once wore another body to this one, but I can never be sure. It is a curious thing indeed."

Andariel nodded as she studied Ennustaja appraisingly. "I've never seen anything that looks like you before." She stopped and stammered apologetically. "Not that you don't look nice, you do! Er, you look very pretty."

Cross burst into laughter. "Eloquent as ever, Andariel" he chuckled as he mimicked her earlier jibe. Ennustaja smiled. Today was the first time she'd heard laughter in the Last Hall, in fact she believed that today was the first time she'd ever laughed herself. It was a good sound.

Buttons hadn't joined in the merriment as he pondered Ennustaja's words. "You said you brought us here because of the future? He asked. "Have you seen our future then?"
Now Ennustaja lost her smile. "That is the problem my friends. You do not have a future, nor does anyone else. From all I can divine I fear that creation itself is about to end."

SIXTEEN

The study lay in smoking ruin. Malleus stalked back and forth through the debris, the very air around him trembling and shrinking from his fury. Malleus knew his prized self- control, the cold and diamond hard will that defined him was slipping from his grasp, burning to ashes in his anger but such was his rage he no longer cared.

Malleus, as Cross would say, wasn't a happy bunny. A shimmering portal hung in the air, a window onto the mortal world in which could be seen the Cobleys and Lincoln Barnes, all of them looking much the worse for wear and all of them looking like they'd rather be anywhere else at this precise moment.

"What do you mean they just fucking disappeared?" Malleus ground the words out through tightly clenched teeth. Mr Cobley hesitated for a second before replying. "Master, I wish I could tell you more but this is something outside of my experience." He hesitated again. "In fact, we were rather hoping you could shed some light on the matter."
"Oh for fucks sake! I'll just do fucking everything shall I?"
"Master, please…"

Malleus cut him off, holding up a finger and thumb just millimetres apart. "Don't 'Master' me. I'm about this close to manifesting on that shit-hole of a planet of yours and unravelling your intestines through your arsehole!" Mr Cobley remained wisely silent and simply inclined his head, waiting for Malleus to calm down and hopefully not obliterate him. The demon lord resumed his furious stalk around the burning room, his ancient and glacial mind racing as he considered the possibilities.

There were very few beings across the realms who had the sort of power that Mr Cobley had described and Malleus knew each and every one of them, he'd even killed some of them himself over the millennia. He quickly discounted those few that still lived. He knew them, he knew the taste of their power and an expenditure of this magnitude should have left a trail, a wound on the cosmos he could have felt from light-years away.

And yet there was nothing. Which left...what? There were only three options as far as he could see: Lucifer, God himself or an unknown entity. Malleus was confident the first two on his short-list weren't responsible for this current calamity by the fact that he was still alive, which left only the possibility that there was a new player on the board, a notion almost as troubling as the thought of The Morningstar or the Lord of Creation discovering his scheme.

Whoever, whatever had joined the game at this critical stage was obviously a being of immense power and such power simply couldn't have kept itself hidden for so long, it was impossible! Yet here they were. He bent the full force of his cold intellect to the problem. His quarry were gone, literally vanished and Malleus had to agree with Mr Cobleys' assessment that they could be anywhere within creations boundaries. Finding them would take time and it was time he didn't have.

He stopped his pacing as a thought struck him. Perhaps this latest development was actually more of a boon than bane? So, the vessel had escaped, so what? He was just a human after all and there were billions of the little bastards scuttling around, and it was a definite plus that Cross's disappearance had taken the two biggest threats to Malleus's plan along with him. If they'd removed themselves from the game then that actually worked in his favour.

Granted, he still had no idea who or what had involved themselves, or why, or what they planned to do, if indeed they planned to do anything. The bottom line was that there was nothing he could do about it except to be as ready to react to their return as possible.

Malleus smiled suddenly. This was it: the endgame. It was time to raise the stakes. He felt a curious sense of freedom as he realised what he had to do, as he accepted the fact that he only had a single, viable option left: escalation. For a creature of such absolutes there was comfort to be found in inevitability.

His smile widened as he came to the same conclusion as Buttons had earlier. His plan would either come to fruition or he'd ensure he made so much noise and spread so much chaos in the mortal realm as to awaken the fury of Heaven itself. They would finally have to act; he'd leave them no choice. Malleus would force his pious and dour former brothers from their oh-so lofty perches; he would reignite the war of hosts and bring creation screaming down around him, one way or another.

It was a risk and he chafed at having to move his carefully planned timetable forward but perhaps this way was even better? Once the war raged in all its terrible beauty again the angels would cause as much destruction as the legions of Hell ever could. God's caretakers would help burn his creation to the ground! All Malleus had to do then was ensure he was the last one standing and then…then the real fun could begin.

He turned to the window behind him to see his underlings still patiently awaiting his will. "Mr and Mrs Cobley? I want you to stay where you are in case our prey shows more courage than sense and actually returns. If they appear then I want us all to know about it straight away, and if they do return then I intend to be ready for them."

Mr Cobley bowed low. "Your will, master."

Malleus looked at Lincoln Barnes. "Mr Barnes, I want you to enact whatever security protocols you deem necessary to secure the area by more prosaic means. How many men do you have left at your disposal?"

"I have a dozen on-site and I can have a further twenty here within the hour."

"Excellent," purred Malleus. "Get them there as soon as you can but once they arrive I want you to send them straight to Miles, do you understand?"

Lincoln looked less than impressed with this cavalier commandeering of his men. "Not really, no." Malleus waved the comment, and the impertinence away. "No matter, just get it done and get Miles here as well."

"Don't you mean Marcus and Miles?"

Malleus stared coldly at him. "No, I don't. Once I've spoken to Miles he'll make everything clear." He clicked his long fingers. "Now move! We don't have a lot of time."

The Cobleys bowed and immediately left to begin their arcane tasks. Lincoln stared at Malleus for a second longer, trying vainly to divine just what the demon lord was planning but totally unable to read the creature in front of him. Malleus stared coldly back at him and Lincoln knew that he could only push things so far. He nodded once, curtly, and then left the room to collect Miles.

Miles stood alone in the garden. The sun warmed his face as he stared blankly at the various blooms in their riot of colour. What was it the odd Mrs Cobley had called them? Purple Sensations and Goldfinch somethings? Vainly he tried to see what was so appealing about them. Was it the colours or the scent? Perhaps it was something about the chaotic geometry with which they bunched and sprawled about the borders of the huge garden?

The younger Harrington had been standing there for almost an hour now and was still none the wiser. Once again people and their curious feelings and fancies remained an enigma. He turned at a polite cough behind him and smiled his bright, blank smile at Lincoln Barnes.

"Mr Barnes! How did it all go? I trust your dishevelled appearance is a sign of triumph through adversity?"

"Not quite, Miles. I regret to inform you that both Cross and his companions escaped us."

"Oh dear, that's terribly unfortunate. Marcus will be most put out."

"Indeed. I'm about to inform him now but I assure you that we can still accomplish our goals, with or without Cross."

"Well that's alright then isn't it?" He cocked his head and looked curiously at his employee. "Was there anything else?"

Lincoln motioned towards the house. "Malleus has requested to speak with you."

"Excellent." He patted his pocket to ensure his precious razor was readily available. "Do we have the necessary sacrifice to hand?"

"That won't be necessary this time, sir. The Cobleys have opened some sort of window that allows for much easier communication."

Miles looked disappointed for a second and then brightened. "Ah well, I'm sure there'll be plenty of opportunities for that sort of thing soon enough! Did he say what he wanted?"

Lincoln shook his head. "Malleus didn't see fit to divulge that information, sir, though he did say you would make everything clear afterwards."

"I had best go and see what he wants then hadn't I? Run along now Mr Barnes, I'll come and find you once I know what our friend has planned."

Lincoln watched the insane facsimile of a man stroll towards the house, completely unmoved by everything that was occurring and for the first time in his life, Lincoln was almost jealous of him. Lincoln didn't like it. He didn't like any of it one fucking bit. Marcus, he had to talk to Marcus immediately. He moved rapidly towards the house and shook his head. When Marcus Harrington was the sole voice of reason remaining then you were in dire straits indeed.

He knew exactly where Marcus would be and headed towards his private study. He knocked politely and then entered the room. "Yes, Mr Barnes? What can I do for you?" Marcus didn't look up from the archaic ledgers he pored over, stopping now and again to double-check or sometimes amend some figures. Marcus didn't believe in computers. "Sir, we've had something of a setback." said Barnes and now Marcus did look up. "How much of a setback?"

Lincoln informed the elder Harrington of all that had occurred during the afternoon and concluded with Malleus requesting to see only Miles and essentially usurping his control of the men. Marcus looked at him quizzically. "So what appears to be the problem?"

"Sir? Doesn't it seem odd that you're not a party to their discussion?" Marcus waved away the concern. "Of course not," he scoffed. "I asked Miles to take care of it." He gestured to the ledgers in front of him. "As you can see some of us have real work to do. Miles seems to actually enjoy dealing with those creatures and he's welcome to them as far as I'm concerned."
"But sir, what about the men?"
"What about them? Didn't Malleus say they were to be given over to Miles?"
"Yes, but.."
"And who do you work for, Mr Barnes?"
Lincoln sighed. "You sir. You and Miles."
"Capital! I'm so glad we agree." Marcus smiled at his underling, the condescending sneer that Lincoln was rapidly growing to hate. "I commend your diligence, Mr Barnes but you worry too much. Miles will bring me up to speed as things begin to move apace I'm sure. Now, if you'll excuse me I really am very busy and I'm sure there are matters that require your attention?"

Lincoln sagged slightly. He'd get no help from Marcus, the blinkered fool. How could he be so blind? How could he leave matters of such import to a lunatic and a creature that was the embodiment of deceit? Lincoln wanted to shake him, to slap the complacent look from his smug face. Instead he just inclined his head. "Of course, sir. I apologise for the disturbance."

Marcus waved him out, his attention already back on

the important matter of his accounts. The apocalypse would just have to wait until the books were properly balanced.

At the other end of the manor, Miles stared curiously at the strange and shimmering window that hung in the middle of the room. He stared through to see the pale, naked form of Malleus standing in a burning room and wreathed in flame. He sighed inwardly. He'd rather been hoping that Hell would appear differently to all those dreary and clichéd depictions in the Bible.

Malleus smiled widely as Miles appeared. What a specimen he was! Not a solitary shred of humanity or a single redeeming feature! Malleus could almost have liked him, if he could have liked anyone.

"Ah Miles. I'm sure Mr Barnes has informed you of our little setback?"

"Indeed he has, although he assures me we can still attain our goals even without Cross's...assistance?"

Malleus laughed. "We can indeed, Miles. In fact, I think you'll agree that we can do even better than that." Malleus began to outline his latest plan and now it was Mile's turn to laugh.

SEVENTEEN

Ennustaja's doom-laden announcement hung in the still air of the Nexus. Cross looked at his companions and then back at the creature in front of them. "I don't want to rain on your parade, luv, but we knew that already. That's what we've been trying to sort out all day."

Ennustaja smiled sadly. "No, Daniel, I don't think you understand. From here I can see all of the possible futures; I can follow the paths of each decision made by any being in creation, all of your idle 'maybes' and dreams of 'could have been' are known to me here. I have followed them all, tracked them through the ages until the end of this cycle of time and they all end in blood and death and flame, in the war to end all wars."

Andariel looked sick. "A new war of the hosts?"

Ennustaja reached out and stroked her cheek with long, gentle fingers. "I am sorry, Andarielastenaama. I can only see the futures, I cannot change them." Buttons squeezed his friends' shoulder in support and glared at the keeper of the Last Hall. "Then why bring us here?" he demanded. "I thought you could help us?"

"And I did, Blade of the Morningstar. I saved you, did I not? Here at least you will be safe." She bowed her head in apology. "I know it is little enough and of even smaller comfort but it is all I can do." Buttons held Andariel as she began to silently weep. Cross, however, was having none of it.

"Fuck all this!" he barked, causing Andariel to jerk her head up at his furious tone. "I've lost plenty of fights in my time but I've never bloody quit one yet and I'll be buggered if I start now!" He pointed a finger at the celestial vista in the portal. "You send me back down there and I'll carve out that demonic dickheads' liver and bring it back here on a plate, you just see if I don't. The universe is telling me it's hopeless is it? Well the universe can go and fuck itself!"

He looked at his companions, pleased to see a small smile playing about Andariel's mouth and he grinned back at her, filled with an almost savage exultation. This is what he was supposed to do. This is what he *was*. Daniel Cross was a soldier again, and Daniel Cross was going to war. "I don't know about you two but if the universe is going to end then I aint about to just sit and watch it happen. I'm going back down there and I'll be putting the fucking boot into Malleus and the twins until I'm dead or it all comes crashing down!" Cross turned his savage grin on Ennustaja, the being who could see all and knew all looking stunned at his outburst.

"So we're all going to die are we?" Cross laughed. "That might come as news to you, luv, but it's nothing new to me or anyone else down there. We're all dead sooner or later, so fucking what? If you think I'm about to let a little thing like death stop me from giving Malleus and the Harringtons a good hiding then you've still got a lot to learn!"

Ennustaja stared at them, her beautiful, alien features set in an attitude of shock. The three companions stood together and Andariel wiped away her tears and cracked her knuckles. "He's right. Maybe we can't stop creation from burning down around us, but at least we can make sure Malleus is far too dead to enjoy it!" The angel stood straighter, filled with renewed purpose and resolve. "We thank you for trying to save us, Ennustaja. Your intervention and bringing us to this wondrous place was a gift, and one that I have no wish to spurn, but you must send us back."

The keeper of the Last Hall regarded them sadly. "Very well, though it pains me to know I send you to your end I will send you where you need to be." She gestured with one long fingered hand and a door appeared beside them. "Though it may sound strange under the circumstances I wish thee all well." Buttons bowed low. "Fare thee well, Ennustaja and know that we take some measure of comfort in the knowledge that you will remain safe in this place."

Cross nodded. "Yeah, sorry about the language just then, luv, all the best, eh?"

Ennustaja remained silent and simply motioned to the doorway. The three companions waved farewell and then stepped through to begin their hopeless war. The keeper of the Last Hall watched them go and dismissed the doorway with another wave of her hand. Then she smiled. She had never lied before, she wasn't even sure if she *could*.

There was one possible future she hadn't mentioned, one tiny, fragile thread of hope dangling in the face of the firestorm about to come, so slender as to be almost invisible in Armageddon's glare.

That future showed an impossible place at the edge of creation and in that place a creature with near limitless power, a creature who knew not her own name, goaded an old soldier to do what he did best: To fight, and hopefully, against all odds, to win.

EIGHTEEN

Marcus picked up his cup of Earl Grey and glared at it as he realised it was empty. This really was intolerable! He pressed a small buzzer on the desk to summon one of his underlings and then got back to work. Marcus was nothing if not a creature of habit, and demonic pacts and the end of creation aside, he still had a business to run and the accounts wouldn't check themselves.

He smiled suddenly. Let Miles deal with the irritating occult side of things. His little brother was obviously enjoying himself and Marcus knew that Barnes would provide enough of a calming influence to curb his twins' wilder impulses and keep the plan on track.

Barnes was a suspicious creature, but his suspicion bred caution and care, a necessary counterpoint to his younger brothers...enthusiasms.

In his own twisted way Marcus loved his brother and wished to see him happy, at least as far as that term could be applied to someone like Miles Harrington. Miles had always been such a strange, fey child and had grown into...what exactly? Marcus knew his brother wasn't like other people, but this didn't disturb him in the least.

Who in their right mind wanted to be like other people? So dull and witless. So powerless. A life ruled by fear and defined by failure. What matter if they were snuffed out in their thousands, in their millions? Their only value was in their usefulness, in what they could provide for the Harringtons, and most of them could provide so little of any worth.

Marcus looked up as the door to his study opened, surprised to see Miles standing there rather than one of their faceless minions and further surprised to see his twins' wide smile. Miles looked animated, he looked...alive. The younger Harrington smiled even wider as he gazed almost fondly upon his twin, face buried in ledgers and budgets and meaningless minutiae as ever.

"Marcus! There you are!" Miles positively glowed with good cheer and Marcus couldn't help but wonder what this might portend. He knew what usually put Miles in such a good mood and idly wondered how many defiled corpses he might find around the house.

He nodded at his younger sibling, dignified and solemn as always. "Miles, I trust things proceed as planned?" Miles shrugged, still smiling his rare, unsettling smile. "There have been a few slight changes, but nothing that should concern you. I would like your opinion on some small matters though," he gestured towards the ledgers covering the desk. "If you can spare the time that is?"

Marcus smiled. "Of course, Miles. To tell you the truth I could do with a break." He stood, stretched his aching back and followed his twin from the room, falling into step beside him as they walked through the corridors of their large and stately home, their footsteps almost silent on the deep pile of the carpets.

Miles made a rueful face. "It's those tedious surgeons. You know how difficult they were last time?" Marcus nodded in assent and Miles continued. "If the lighting isn't adequate then it's the sterility of the room they're complaining about. They want the carpet taken up apparently."

Marcus snorted. "Certainly bloody not! Sterility of the room indeed! We're making a sacrifice not performing a heart transplant." Marcus increased his pace. "Come along, brother, let's remind them just who they're working for and how flammable their children are shall we?"

Miles walked slightly behind his brother and so Marcus couldn't see his sly and sudden smile. They reached the drawing room in the east wing of the house and Marcus opened the double doors, stepping briskly through and glancing briefly down to regard the apparently offensive carpet. With his attention diverted he didn't see the two large men who stood at either side of the door until they roughly grabbed hold of him, pinning his arms to his sides and almost lifting him from the floor.

"What on earth do you think you're doing?!" he raged. "Take your hands off of me you incompetent fools!" His protests stuttered to a halt as he heard Miles chuckle behind him and he twisted his head to glare at his younger brother. "Miles, is this some sort of joke? I can assure you it isn't bloody funny! Get these idiots off of me or there'll be hell to pay!" Miles laughed again. "Oh there'll be hell to pay indeed, brother! I did say there had been some slight changes to our plan did I not?"

Marcus's indignant rage sputtered and died as fear began to overtake him. "Miles, brother, what are you doing?" The younger Harrington said nothing and simply motioned to the two men who frog marched Marcus towards a gurney where two masked and impassive surgeons waited.

He paled as he realised what was happening. "Miles, you can't! You can't do this, please!" Marcus was pushed onto the gurney and held immobile as the surgeons began to strap him down. Miles laid a comforting hand on his head. "Hush now, brother. All will be well. You won't miss a moment of the fun to come I can assure you. In fact, you'll have the best seat in the house!"

Marcus struggled in vain against his bonds, fighting back a whimper of fear as the surgeons began to cut his clothes away. Within moments he was naked and his terror warred with an impotent rage. For the first time in his life, Marcus Harrington felt the sickening fear of the truly helpless and tears streaked his face. Miles tutted at this shameful display. "Oh Marcus, really. This just won't do at all! You're embarrassing us both!"

Marcus blinked away the tears and pleaded desperately

211

with his insane and treacherous twin. "Miles, not this. Anything but this. Use one of the men, not me! You can't give me to one of those things!" Miles looked surprised at this and chuckled again as he patted his weeping brothers' cheek. "Do you really think so little of me?"

He shook his head in reproach and gestured to the surgeons. Marcus screamed as the cold steel began to slice into the flesh of his chest and Miles had to raise his voice above the noise. "You're not meant for just any demon, dear brother. Malleus himself awaits you below!"

Marcus Harrington screamed louder still.

NINETEEN

Cross was first through the doorway and felt a momentary disorientation as he stepped back into what he thought of as the real world. He moved aside to let Buttons and Andariel through and all three watched as the doorway disappeared behind them. Cross looked around and blinked in surprise.

He knew this place. Andariel recognised it too. "Hang on, isn't this...?"

"Chandra's place," said Cross. "What the bloody hell did she send us here for?" Andariel grimaced as she understood, suddenly feeling curiously despondent. "The message," she replied, "Our warning to Lucifer."

"Ah, right." Cross shook his head. "Poor little bastard."

"And who is Chandra?" asked Buttons. "A surgeon I know, we have a sort of business relationship." said Cross. Andariel looked at Buttons. "He means he blackmails him."

"Ah, I see. And does this surgeon meet our requirements?"

Cross pulled a face. "Well he's not exactly doctor Shipman but, yeah, I'd say he fits the bill." Andariel didn't look convinced. "Look, I know he's already hell-bound and everything but, well, I feel a little bit bad about it to be honest."

"Upstairs, third door on the right," said Cross. "Take a look in the fancy cupboard and see if that helps. I'll put the kettle on." Cross started to fill the kettle with water as Andariel and Buttons walked through the empty house and up the stairs towards the bedroom.

They both paused in front of the cupboard, unsure of just what they would find. Andariel shrugged at Buttons and opened the sliding doors.

"Oh you've got to be bloody joking?" she sighed.

Chandra's hidden shrine was comprised of an ornate stand, topped with a series of branching metal tubes, looking not unlike a *menorah*. Each of the tubes ended in a flat plate with a short spike at the centre and the ones that were occupied were definitely not holding candles. Buttons tilted his head as he took it in. "Are they…?"

"Yep."

"He's certainly been busy."

"Yep."

Buttons sniffed, his olfactory senses fare more acute than a normal humans'. "They're all diseased. Cancer." Andariel nodded. "That must be where he gets them. Perks of the job and all that I guess." Buttons reached out and gingerly poked one of them as Andariel grimaced. "Ewww don't touch them, that's disgusting!" The small man shrugged. "They've obviously been treated with something. I just wondered if it still kept them, you know, bouncy."

The angel was curious despite herself. "And does it?" Buttons shook his head. "Stiff as a board. I wonder what he uses?"

"I'm happy to remain ignorant in this case. Have we seen enough?"

"Oh yes, I think the good doctor will make an excellent messenger."

They walked back downstairs and into the kitchen to find three steaming mugs of tea on the table. Cross was rummaging in a cupboard and turned to them with a smile of triumph. "Aha! I knew the tubby little fucker would have biscuits somewhere!" Andariel and Buttons sat down without a word.

They drank their tea and Andariel mechanically munched her way through a biscuit. "No wonder he does as he's told." She said, finally. Cross snorted a laugh. "Yeah, be a bit awkward if that got out."

"Speaking of which, how does he do it? Get them out

I mean?" asked Buttons. Cross grabbed another biscuit, leant back in his chair and spoke through a full mouth. "Ah, I asked him about that. Anything that gets chopped off during surgery is sealed up in bags and then burned. The doc just slips down to the cremation room and switches the bags. Sticks a jelly mould in the decoys apparently."

"Moulded to look like...?"

"Yep."

"Where would you even find something like that?"

"Beats me, mate. Not like any of the jelly and ice cream parties I went to as a kid."

Andariel helped herself to another biscuit. She didn't really have much of an appetite after seeing Chandra's shrine to the sacred mammary gland but figured, what with everything else going on, this might be the last chance she'd get to enjoy a Chocolate Digestive or two.

"Where is he anyway?" she asked and Cross shrugged in reply. "Still at work I guess. Hopefully our new friend didn't send us here knowing we'd be sitting about for ages, her being the mistress of time and space and what have you." Andariel grimaced. "Well when he does get here he'd better not have any with him."

Any further conversation was interrupted by the sound of keys slipping into the lock in the front door. Cross grinned at the angel. "Guess we'll find out in a second!" He stood and moved to the door of the kitchen. As far as Chandra knew he'd been here all day anyway so the doctor shouldn't be surprised to see him. The fat little surgeon bustled into the hallway and saw Cross leaning in the doorway of his kitchen.

His face fell. Chandra had no idea what had transpired in the last few hours and had been vainly hoping that Cross would have reconsidered his ridiculous and dangerous plan to steal a corpse from the mortuary.

Chandra sighed and then began to steel himself for the task ahead. Best just to get it over and done with. He hoped that Cross really could get in and out unseen and that this didn't end up being one 'favour' too many. He smiled weakly at the big man. "Good evening, Daniel. I trust you've been comfortable during your stay?"

Cross laughed. "By 'comfortable' you're asking if I've managed to break anything aren't you?" The doctor began to splutter a protest and Cross waved him to silence. "I'm joking, Chandra. Come in here and take the weight off your feet, it's your kitchen after all and I've just boiled the kettle".

Chandra waddled into the kitchen after him and stopped short in the doorway as he caught sight of Andariel and Buttons. *What on earth is going on?* For a second he wondered if the older man dressed as a vicar and the pretty young woman had been brought here for some nefarious erotic purposes, that Daniel had been whiling away the hours with some bizarre acts of sexual congress.

The doctor, a private and fastidious man felt almost violated at the thought of what might have been occurring in his home during his absence. "Doc, this is Reverend Buttons and, er, Andi. They're friends of mine." Cross pointed to each in turn he spoke and the oddly matched pair smiled at the doctor, although Chandra thought he detected a faintly disapproving look on the face of the young lady.

Chandra caught the slight hesitation as Cross introduced him to the girl but elected to ignore it. She wouldn't be the first working girl to use an assumed name, either that or Cross had just forgotten it for a moment. The doctor, still uncomfortable with the addition of these strangers to his home and sanctum rallied himself and made a passable effort at a polite smile. "Good evening to you both, any friends of Daniels' are, of course, welcome here." He looked over at Cross who had busied himself making another cup of tea. "Can I assume our task tonight still involves just the two of us?" He gestured towards Buttons and Andariel. "I'm not sure I could get three people into the mortuary unseen and, if you'll forgive me, we wouldn't make the most inconspicuous party."

Cross handed the doctor a cup of tea and guided him to

an empty chair. "Slight change of plan actually, doc." Chandra felt a moment of relief, thinking that he might actually be able avoid the ill-advised sojourn into the mortuary. This sense of relief was fleeting however as he wondered just what Daniel would be asking for instead. He hid his rapidly changing emotions behind his cup as he took a sip of tea.

He carefully placed the cup down on the table, annoyed but not surprised that Daniel had neglected to put out any coasters and then looked at the big crook. "A change of plan? Could you elaborate please?"

Cross didn't reply at first and just looked at his companions. He actually appeared somewhat out of sorts, perhaps even upset which surprised the portly surgeon. Chandra had never seen Daniel display anything other than complete confidence and this drastic change to his demeanour made him nervous. Just what was going on here?

After a few seconds Cross burst out: "Oh for fucks sake, are we sure there isn't any other way?" The small vicar, Buttons, remembered Chandra, shook his head. "This is the only chance we've got, Daniel. There are far larger things at play here than our scruples. If it's any consolation he won't feel a thing once I implant the message."

Chandra started as he realised the strange vicar was looking at him as he spoke. Now the young lady chimed in: "I don't particularly like it either, Cross, even after seeing those...things up there but Buttons is right and we're running out of time." She shrugged. "Look at it this way, he's going to end up their eventually anyway."

Now the young woman was looking at him as well and Chandra began to feel increasingly nervous. He looked at Daniel with pleading eyes. His blackmailer made for a poor ally but the big man was the closest thing to a friend he had here and the doctor grasped at him like a drowning man grasped at driftwood, no matter how sparse a piece the ocean deigned to supply. "Daniel? What's going on? What message is he talking about and where am I going!?"

Cross sighed. "You wouldn't believe me if I told you, mate. I'm sorry about this, I really am." The big man stood and quickly moved around the table to take Chandra by the shoulders in an iron grip, pinning him to the chair. "If it's any consolation, doc you might just help us save the universe here."

"Daniel! Unhand me at once! What on earth are you doing? You can't…" The doctor, whose voice was becomingly increasingly strident, fell silent at a gesture from Andariel and with mounting horror, Chandra realised he could no longer speak at all. He was trapped on the wooden chair feeling Cross's large hands digging painfully into his shoulders, rendered both mute and helpless, a prisoner in his own home and his own body.

His terror grew and tears began to run unashamedly down his face as he kicked and struggled to no avail. Cross noticed and grimaced at Buttons. "Can we move this along? The poor bastard is shitting bricks over here."

Buttons stood and walked over to stand next to them. "Of course, Daniel. Could you move him round to face me please?" Cross manhandled the chair and its captive occupant around with no small effort, eager to get this over and done with. Buttons laid a tender hand on the doomed surgeons' cheek, wiping away his tears with a gentle thumb. "I really am sorry about this." He sighed.

Chandra jerked and gasped like a fish out of water, trying desperately to escape, to scream his outrage and fear but even that was denied him. Then Buttons laid a hand on his chest and his mind was torn away.

Chandra's mind, his core, everything that made him who he was began to unravel as the message supplanted and overwrote him. His memories shredded under the onslaught, tore under the brutal force of the message and the beautiful and terrible geometries of the angelic tongue that were too much for a mortal mind to take. Chandra *became* the message.

His tears burned away and his eyes widened as his mouth moved from a silent scream to begin forming a series of words in the language that had sung the stars themselves into being. Cross felt the doctor relax under his hands and let him go, moving around the chair to look down on the doomed man.

What used to be Chandra Singh sat rigidly in the chair, eyes wide and unblinking as he silently, endlessly mouthed the arcane words of their desperate plea for the devils' intervention. Cross looked over to Buttons who was eyeing the fat surgeon with a critical eye. "Is that it? Are we done?" Buttons nodded and sighed. "Yes, we're done." He smiled sadly at Cross. "If it helps then he won't know a thing, even when he gets there. All that's left of him now is the message. In a way we've actually done him a service."

Cross remained unconvinced, still feeling an unusual and unwelcome twinge of guilt about the whole affair. "How do you work that one out?" Buttons pointed towards the animate message that used to be a human being sitting rigidly on the chair and silently repeating those perfect and horrifying words. "Look at him," he said. "There's nothing left of the man you knew. There's nothing left for Hell to take when he arrives. If he'd got there by more natural causes he would have been whole, his soul intact and subject to all the torments the pit has to offer. We've actually saved him from an eternity of pain."

Cross nodded slowly. "Yeah, ok. Under the circumstances I guess that is a result for him. We still have to kill him though, right?" Andariel nodded. "Yeah but he won't feel it. Do you want me to do it?"

"No." Cross was resolute. He had to be the one to end it. In a strange way he felt it was the only mark of respect he could offer the doomed surgeon. "I should do it." He moved behind the doctor again and laid a surprisingly tender hand on his head. "Bye, doc." Was all he said. He placed his other hand under Chandra's chin and then violently twisted. The wet snap of bone sounded overly loud in the confines of the kitchen and the three of them, killers all, winced at the sound.

The doctors head sagged to his chest, twisted grotesquely to the right and Cross rearranged it to look like the dead man was sleeping. Cross suddenly felt dirty and walked over to the sink to wash his hands. "Ok then, how long do you think it's going to take until Lucifer gets the message?"

The angel and the vicar looked at each other and shrugged. "I've got no idea, Cross," said Andariel. "Chandra is going to make a bloody racket as soon as he arrives which is going to draw a lot of attention. The bad news is that Malleus has plenty of toadies down there and if they get to the doctor first they could still shut him up. If they do that before Lucifer or anyone loyal to him actually hears the message then he'll know something is going on but he won't know what, which is going to cost us time."

"Which is the one thing we don't have going spare," nodded Cross sourly. The big man straightened, putting the unsavoury matter of Chandras' murder behind him to focus on the task ahead. "Fuck it. We've done as much as we can to let Lucifer know the score so there's no point in worrying about it. We came back here to put the boot into the Harringtons so how about we get cracking with that? The universe will just have to look out for itself for a while."

Andariel and Buttons nodded. "Sounds good to me," said the angel. She looked questioningly at Cross. "I take it you know where they actually live?"

"Of course I bloody do. Can't promise they'll be there though but it seems likely."

"How so?"

Cross smiled grimly. "The home team always has an advantage. I've been there before and that place is sewn up tighter than a ducks' arsehole. Their men know the place inside and out so it'll be easier for them to defend and anticipate points of entry. It won't be easy getting in under the radar and a frontal assault will be suicide." Buttons nodded thoughtfully. "Leave that to me," he said. "I've got an idea that might just work." The small demon hunter laughed suddenly. "Actually, it's a ridiculous idea that's highly likely to get us all killed but it's all I've got."

Cross laughed as well. "I like the sound of it already!" He turned and began to rifle through Chandras' pockets until he produced a set of car keys with a smile of triumph. "If nothing else, at least we'll get there in style." He eyed them both in turn and smiled again, almost in surprise. "You know what? I've had a bloody good day, all things considered."

The big man turned suddenly serious. "If this all goes bad then, well, I just want you to know that I'm proud to call you my friends, and I mean that." Buttons nodded in agreement and silently squeezed Cross's shoulder. Andariel shook her head and smiled at him. "You great, soft lump." The angel stood on tip-toes and pecked him on the cheek. "Now", she said. "How about we go and kill some people?"

TWENTY

Barnes sat alone, enjoying the solitude. He was back in the kitchen, stealing another few and precious moments of calm while he still could. The Cobleys' had disappeared into the sitting room in the west wing of the house with their odd little coven to do…whatever it was that demon worshipping suburbanites did.

Marcus was no longer in his study and Miles was nowhere to be found so Barnes assumed the twins were together, along with the men that Malleus had demanded Barnes provide and place under his command, via the insane Miles.

Lincoln still didn't like it, any of it and resolved to find the twins to see just what had been planned for the men, his men. Barnes had *always* been in charge of their security and the disposition of their forces and he couldn't shake a grim premonition that this radical departure from the norm boded very ill indeed.

The final complement of muscle, and these were the last Barnes could call on, had also arrived and he'd given them their orders, deploying them to various points within the house and grounds. He'd ordered the men to shoot any intruders on site and if the twins or Malleus didn't like it then Barnes was in the right frame of mind to tell them all to go and fuck themselves, and damn the consequences.

The men were well-armed and well-trained and Lincoln had used them all several times in the past. Hard, uncompromising men, men he could rely on to get the job done with no fuss and no questions asked, whatever the job might be. So why did he feel like it still wasn't enough? Lincoln fancied he could feel a change in the air. The house felt different somehow. Felt colder, felt…wrong on some level, like that perfect, doom-laden silence that was said to fill the air before a cataclysmic earthquake, as though the earth girded itself for the terrible toil of destruction.

Enough. Lincoln stood abruptly, annoyed by his own doubts and useless introspection. He'd done all he could to prepare for Cross's arrival, and despite his mysterious disappearance Lincoln didn't doubt that Cross was on his way to exact his revenge. As far as Lincoln was concerned the arrival of Cross and his supernatural allies was a certainty and therefore something to be planned for, but not worried over. It was the mystery of the men Malleus had commandeered that really troubled him and so that was what he needed to resolve.

Even as he stood the door to the kitchen opened and both Marcus and Miles entered the kitchen, followed by two of the men usurped from Lincolns' authority. Miles grinned broadly. "Ah, there you are." He turned to Marcus. "I told you he'd be in here, our Mr Barnes has always been a solitary soul." Marcus smiled at Lincoln and he felt his blood run cold. "Good evening, Mr Barnes, it's a pleasure to see you again." Horror crept over Lincoln Barnes with its clammy and unwelcome hands as he stared into the suddenly ancient and inhuman eyes of what had previously been his employer. "Oh, Miles, what have you done?" he whispered.

Malleus pulled a mock disappointed face. "Really, Mr Barnes. I expected a warmer welcome than this. I thought you'd be pleased to see I was taking such an interest in our little conspiracy?" The demon lord sniffed. "Believe me I didn't come to this dull little planet just to enjoy the scenery."

Lincoln ignored him, still trying to understand the depths of Miles' insanity. Even for a creature with no conscience or anything recognisable as humanity, Lincoln still believed that Miles had felt some sort of bond with his twin. He looked from the smiling Miles to what used to be his brother and knew that, somewhere in there, Marcus screamed

223

in terrified silence behind the demons' eyes. The pair of enforcers who had accompanied Miles and Malleus were smiling too and Lincoln caught a feral gleam in their eyes and finally understood.

"The men...?"

"Aren't men any longer," finished Malleus, "and therefore far better suited to the task at hand. May I introduce you to Mok and Jok?" Malleus flourished a hand at the silently smiling pair. "My two most trusted lieutenants." The two demons, clothed in the bodies of the doomed and nameless men, inclined their heads in mocking respect.

Malleus continued: "It occurred to me that chasing Cross and his irritating allies all over London was completely unnecessary. We know the process works, the angel unwittingly proved that for us, so why not forge ahead eh? Fortune favours the brave and all that."

Lincoln just continued to stare at the arch demon as his mind raced and Malleus looked curiously at Miles. "He's really not taking this as well as I thought he would. I confess to some slight disappointment."

Miles laughed. Lincoln had never seen the younger Harrington so animated, never seen him so close to an approximation of happiness. In a strange way this was the most disturbing thing of all. The madman grinned that rare and awful grin. "Mr Barnes, use that prized intellect of yours. Look at this logically. I'll grant you that the sacrifice of my brother may seem a trifle drastic but think of the benefits!" He gestured towards Malleus. "Our patron is here in the flesh, not only that but we have a dozen of his servants under our command. We're now unassailable, our success is assured!"

Lincoln blinked and looked at Miles in disbelief, and with an almost barely concealed contempt. He knew he was probably signing his death warrant but he couldn't remain silent about this insanity any longer. "Success? Please, define success for me if you can? Destruction isn't a goal you fucking lunatic! What are we supposed to win here? Where does the end of the universe leave us apart from dead? We might as well have just burned this house down and let ourselves go up with it; it would have been a damn sight less trouble!"

Miles looked incensed but his furious reply was interrupted by Malleus who began to laugh uproariously. "Mr Barnes you are a delight!" chortled the demon once he could speak again. "I'll wager you expected to be skinned alive round about now but that didn't stop you did it?" Malleus sighed in appreciation. "You're just the sort of person we'll need once it all starts again." Both Lincoln and Miles looked confused at this and Malleus laughed mockingly at them. "What? You thought I was just going to burn the universe down and then spend eternity admiring the wreckage? Here, let me show you something."

The demon looked hard at Lincoln and then smiled. "Hold out your hands, Mr Barnes." Lincoln hesitated and the demon lord smiled wider. "Please, indulge me for a few moments more." Lincoln obeyed and held out his gloved hands. Malleus narrowed his eyes and then made an almost careless gesture with one hand. Lincoln gasped as an object appeared out of thin air and he almost dropped the rifle that Malleus had conjured from the aether. Malleus looked at it appraisingly. "There," he said, "I think you've been trying to get one of these for a while now haven't you?"

Barnes looked down at the sleek and deadly shape in his hands, feeling the cold, killing weight of it. It was undeniably real and he had indeed been trying to source a weapon of this type for some time, with no success. The C8 SFW carbine was the favoured weapon of 'the regiment', otherwise known as the Special Air Service. Using 5.56mm rounds, fitted with a standard NATO thirty round magazine and underslung with an L17A1 grenade launcher, the weapon was a masterpiece of reliable killing power and almost impossible to acquire outside of military circles. Lincoln cradled the weapon and found comfort in its lethal weight.

"How...?"

Malleus waved the question away. "You see now, Mr Barnes? I'm not destroying creation for the sake of it, although that does hold its appeal I admit. No, I'm going to *fix it*. I can build it anew, build it better. A universe that obeys *my* rules, *our* rules. What can you dream of, Lincoln? What paradise can you envision?" The demon smiled. "You want a measure of success? A world, a galaxy to rule over as you see fit. I assume that fits your definition of the word?"

Lincoln looked between the miraculous firearm and the grinning lord of Hell. A lifetime of wariness, of looking into the mouths of gift horses warred with the temptation of all that was now possible. Did he trust Malleus? Of course not. Lincoln didn't trust anyone, and the demon was the literal incarnation of deceit. But *what if?* Always the realist, forever the pragmatist, Lincoln Barnes finally allowed himself to dream. A world of his own, a world under his control, free of the stupidity, waste and chaos that plagued this one.

No, he didn't trust the demon that stood grinning in front of him but the prize Malleus dangled in front of him was simply too great. If ever something was worth wagering it all on then surely this was it? Lincoln sighed. He'd just been bought, plain and simple. He breathed deeply and slowly exhaled, expelling his fear and doubt in that single breath. Lincoln nodded at the demon and the insane imitation of a man beside him. "Let's do it then."

Miles still glowered but Malleus laughed again. Here they were, about to challenge both God and the Devil and all he could feel from Lincoln now was a calm determination. The man really was a delight. He might even let him live for a time when it was all over. The arch-demon clapped his hands. "So, to business then. We've managed to smuggle a dozen demons to the mortal realm, something that nobody in the history of creation has managed before I might add, but I have countless millions still languishing on the other side. They'd serve us much better here don't you think?

Lincoln nodded. "We'll want to move quietly at first."

He gestured at the silent Jok and Mok. "I understand some of your brethren will probably feel a certain...exuberance at being here but if we don't get caught up in our own cleverness and avoid any unnecessary bloodshed for a while we can make our position virtually unassailable."

Malleus arched an eyebrow. "How so?"

"By all means we should use your demons but let's use them wisely. The twins have amassed a significant amount of commercial property around the country, many of them warehouses and factories. We've performed the procedure here a dozen times today. Why not hundreds, thousands a day?"

"Why not a production line?" crowed Malleus, quickly grasping Lincolns' intent.

"Exactly. With their unique talents your demons should have little difficulty in procuring the necessary raw materials. We could have an army within weeks."

Miles, still smarting from Lincolns' earlier remarks, sneered at them. "So after all this we're to be glorified foremen? Kidnapping proles and churning out demons 24 hours a day? You may want to spend the next few weeks stuck in a factory but I certainly don't!"

"Then don't." Malleus looked coldly at him. "Understand this, Miles. You're perilously close to becoming an irrelevance." He held up a hand as Miles began to splutter an indignant reply. "You'll have your war. You'll have so much blood you can drown in it I assure you of that. When we begin in earnest I don't care if you torture and butcher your way across an entire galaxy but until we are ready you'll do as you're told. You'll do this my way," the demon gestured at Lincoln, "our way and if you hinder our plans you will watch us put creation to the sword from the lake of fire and the only screams you hear will be your own."

The demon gestured at his stolen body. "As far as the rest of the world is concerned I'm Marcus Harrington. I can control your money and assets as easily as you can. I don't need you anymore. Forget this at your peril." Malleus turned his back, dismissing the man and striding from the room. Jok and Mok smirked at the seething, impotent human and followed, leaving Lincoln and Miles alone.

Miles glared at his former employee. "Don't think I'll forget this, Barnes. No matter what else happens there will be a reckoning for this betrayal!" Lincoln nodded once, unconcerned by the threat. The balance of power between them had shifted and they both knew it. "I'll be waiting, Miles. Until then I have better things to do." Barnes walked from the room, dismissing the coldly furious Miles a second time and following the demons.

He found them in the drawing room with the Cobleys and their mismatched coven. The huge Terry still glowered sullenly and Barnes decided that must be his usual expression. Jonny ventured a small nod of greeting which Lincoln returned. The vastly obese Solange slumbered in a chair that struggled to contain her bulk. The last of the coven, Kerry, was nowhere to be seen.

Mrs Cobley smiled over at him. "There he is! Oh, Mr Barnes I'm glad you've decided to join us, it's always good to have a level head around. I hear we're going to be very busy bees indeed!" Mr Cobley clapped his hands and smiled his ghastly, rictus grin. "It's going to be glorious my love, glorious!" The cadaverous warlock bowed to Malleus. "Our master is about to bring creation to its knees and its senile creator will languish in the same chains he so loves imposing on others." Mr Cobley laid a long-fingered hand on Lincolns' shoulder and the younger man felt his skin crawl. "We're going to right a great wrong, Mr Barnes, finally win a war that began when time itself was born. Nothing can stop us now!"

Lincoln refused to get caught up in the excitement that energised the room. Even Terry almost looked happy. "Let's hope so, Mr Cobley. I'd still feel better knowing where Cross is and making sure he's really out of the game though."

Malleus waved away his concerns. "It doesn't matter where Cross and his pet angel are hiding, we'll find them eventually." The demon shrugged. "Even if they were here what could they do? We're already far too powerful for them to stop us, it would be suicide for them to attack us now."

Lincoln was about to reply when the sound of automatic gunfire ripped through the air from the front of the house, swiftly followed by an explosion that rattled the decanters on the drinks cabinet and even roused Solange from her slumber. Barnes glanced over to Malleus, the demon lord looking shocked and outraged. "I'd say Cross has just come out of hiding, wouldn't you?"

Malleus snarled. The nerve of these fucking humans! He glared at the occupants of the room, human, demon and those in between. "I've had just about enough of Cross and his little troop. I'm going to feed them their fucking hearts myself!" With that the demon strode from the room.

"And what if fighting them draws too much attention?" asked Lincoln, ever the pragmatist. Malleus didn't miss a stride, simply calling back over his shoulder. "Then the war begins tonight, Mr Barnes!"

Lincoln let him go and then stood in the doorway to block the eager Cobleys and their coven. "A moment, please!" he implored them. Mr Cobley motioned for his disciples to wait. Lincoln Barnes may be just a human but the patriarch of the chosen had begun to grudgingly respect him during their short time together.

Barnes nodded his gratitude to Mr Cobley, pleased that the warlock could control both his coven and his bloodlust.

"I know Cross and it's highly likely all the fireworks out there are a diversion. If I'm right they'll be sneaking in somewhere else right about now and we need to find them."

"And if you're wrong, dear?" asked Mrs Cobley and Lincoln shrugged. "Then I'm wrong and we'll know about it soon enough if the gunfire doesn't stop. Malleus and his demons can handle them without us for a few minutes can't they?"

Mr Cobley smiled. "Oh indeed, my master stands amongst the most powerful beings in all of creation!"

"Then would you be averse to joining me in a quick sweep of the house?"

"Not at all. I don't think even Buttons and the Angel will present a significant threat to the power we've gathered here but a measure of caution is sensible. Might I suggest we split up?"

"Yes, we'll cover the house quicker that way." Lincoln looked each of the coven in the eyes. "If you find them don't engage. Fall back and call for help." He kept his gaze fixed on Terry. "Is that understood?"

Terry didn't bother to reply and simply shouldered his way past and moved deeper into the house. Lincoln was about to call him back when Mr Cobley put a hand on his arm. "Let him go," said the warlock. "He's more than capable of looking after himself."

"And if he bites off more than he can chew?"

The cadaverous chosen shrugged. "Then he'll die and we'll replace him. I suggest you go with Mrs Cobley and I'll take Jonny with me." He arched an eyebrow at Solange who had just managed to lever herself from the chair. "Solange, you go and join Malleus. Let him know we're sweeping the house and ask him to send some of his thralls to do the same."

Mr Cobley frowned. "And find whatever room Kerry is being fucked in and drag her out by the hair if necessary. Remind her she's here to help us overthrow God himself, not have another gangbang."

Lincoln watched Solange waddle towards the front of the house and suddenly smiled at the absurdity of it all. If he really was about to help kick start the apocalypse then he might as well try and enjoy it.

Still cradling the conjured rifle, he offered his free arm to Mrs Cobley and the plump witch giggled at this unexpected gallantry. "Shall we, Mrs Cobley?" Lincoln nodded to Mr Cobley and Jonny. "Be careful. You take the east wing and we'll cover the west. Work your way round and towards the front of the house and we'll meet up again there. Remember, if you find them then call for help."

Mr Cobley laughed. "Believe me if we find them then you'll know about it. Luck, Mr Barnes."

"Luck, Mr Cobley," replied Lincoln, and with that the hunt was on.

TWENTY ONE

Cross drove the deceased Chandras' Bentley at a smooth and steady pace away from the city, towards the Harringtons' estate and their desperate bid to stop Armageddon in its tracks. They drove in silence, each lost in their own thoughts. Cross shifted in the drivers' seat for the tenth time in as many minutes. The Bentley was a beautiful car and built for comfort so why was the seat digging into his back and why did he feel like ants were crawling across his skin?

Driving towards a battle, towards certain pain and only slightly less certain death was nothing new for the big veteran. He'd cat-napped in the back of enough transports on the way to an Op for Christ's sake, and if you could snatch forty winks in the back of an APC you could sleep anywhere, so what the bloody hell was wrong with him? *Fuck me,* he thought. *I'm actually scared this time.*

So, what was different? They couldn't be playing for bigger stakes, that was true enough, but that wasn't bothering him. Worrying about what would happen if you failed the mission was just a bit of stage-fright and he'd got over that a long time ago. Every soldier that saw and survived combat became something of a fatalist. If the Op went south then you put it away and moved onto the next one, or you were dead enough for it not to worry you anyway.

Bloody hell, that was it. For the first time in years, Daniel Cross was scared of dying. Now he knew. Not only did he know that he was almost certainly going to die tonight, he knew exactly where he was going when he did. Cross had never believed in God, the Devil or Heaven and Hell. Religion

had always tasted like a poisonous brew made from human-
ities' perverse needs for wish fulfilment and self-flagellation,
and most organised religions managed to deliver them both at
once, with a side-order of existential and unwarranted guilt
thrown in for good measure.

But what do you know? The afterlife was real and by all
accounts just as much of a bloody mess as it was down here on
earth. Cross let himself be lulled into that strange trance that
steals over someone as they drive and finally let himself remember the night he died.

There was no sense of movement but Cross knew that
he fell through a dark and biting cold. The fall felt like an
eternity until all of a sudden, he stood on level ground. There
was no impact, no sense of landing, just a jarring transition
between movement and stillness. He stood naked and alone
in the frigid gloom but all around him he could hear screaming. Whimpers of pain were drowned by roars of throat-tear-
ing agony and through it all ran a constant sobbing, a sound of
such profound misery that Cross felt his own tears wetting his
cheeks.

Cross shivered in the dark and cold, the overwhelming
sadness warring with a rapidly growing feeling of fear as other
sounds whispered from the oppressive murk. He could hear
laughter now. Cold and cruel, dripping with an ageless malice
and his fear bloomed into terror as the laughter grew louder,
nearer. A shape gradually formed in front of him, a blocky,
malformed shape that giggled as it lurched towards him.
Every instinct screamed at Cross to run, run until his heart
burst in his chest but he was rooted to the spot, frozen by the
all-encompassing terror.

The creature that shuffled towards him was stocky and
squat with wide, uneven shoulders. Its head was set low
down, almost in the centre of its chest and its gimlet eyes
glowed with a dim and dirty light. Its arms were huge and
ape-like, tapering only slightly at the wrist before flaring
out again into huge, wide hands, the gnarled fingers tipped

with jagged claws. Cross whimpered as the creature curled its lipless mouth into a smile and slobbered through broken teeth. "We've been waiting for you, Cross."

In that moment, Cross knew where he was, knew he was damned and his screams joined the eternal chorus of despair. Suddenly, impossibly there was light and warmth as something tore through the darkness, barrelling into the blocky creature who snarled and thrashed as it fought its attacker. The light was almost blinding but Cross saw flashes of white and rainbow-gold and heard the buffeting of wings above the blocky creatures' screams as the light tore into it.

Cross shielded his eyes as the light intensified and the blocky creatures' wailing died away as his otherworldly rescuer ripped it asunder. The golden being now stood before him but Cross was unable to make out any details in the glare of its light. He could see it was tall, impossibly so, and it radiated a pure and terrible power. Cross fell to his knees on the cold ground and suddenly the golden being laughed.

"It's a bit late for prayers now, Danny boy!" The unearthly creature shone like a beacon in the encompassing darkness and Cross knew with a dread certainty that countless denizens of this terrible place swarmed towards them even now. "Sorry about this, Daniel. It's going to hurt, a lot, but it's the only way and we don't have much time."

Before Cross could answer the light shone brighter, flaring as it began to consume him. No, it wasn't consuming him, it was *joining* him. Somehow this creature of light and power was flowing and coiling around him, winding through him, *into* him as it burned and burned and the light encompassed everything. The light, the pain was all and Cross screamed as every molecule of his being was swamped by the searing, beautiful flame.

Cross shook himself from his reverie and glanced in the rear-view mirror. Andariel was looking out of the window, staring at nothing as her fingers drummed a nervous tattoo on her leg. She caught him looking at her. "What?" she asked, and Cross shook his head. "Nothing, I just remembered the first time we met."

"In the hotel bathroom?"

"No, before that"

"Oh," the Angel looked slightly uncomfortable. "So you can remember it all now then?"

"Not all of it but I can remember Hell well enough, although I'd rather I didn't." He looked at her through the mirror again. "You certainly look a bit different."

Andariel shrugged. "Tell you the truth I think I prefer a physical body. Being a celestial entity of pure power has its benefits but wearing a mortal body has always been more fun." She pulled an embarrassed face at him. "Sorry about the whole possession and crippling agony thing, if..."

Cross waved her apology away. "If there'd been any other way you would have taken it, I know. You did what you needed to do for us to make it out of there. No need to apologise for that." They were silent for a time as the Bentley smoothly ate away the miles towards the Harringtons' estate. Buttons sat in the front and he looked over at the big man next to him. Cross's face was impassive but the demon hunter could feel the tension and fear that Cross had under such ruthless control.

He sighed inwardly. He knew why Cross was scared. Not only did he know Hell was real but he'd seen it, he'd *been* there. Cross knew he was almost certainly going to die today and knew exactly what would happen to him when he did. Buttons shook his head in disbelieving admiration.

Not only was Daniel able to control his fear, and breaking down into a gibbering wreck was definitely a valid response to the promise of imminent and eternal torment, but he pushed on to try and save a universe that had already damned him.

Cross saw the movement and glanced over to his friend, guessing what he was thinking. He let out a deep breath, expelling his fear and doubt and smiled at Buttons. "Don't be wearing that long face for me, mate. Who knows? We might even win this fight yet."

Buttons returned the smile, though his heart ached at the thought of losing his new friend, and at all the horrors that awaited him. "If you're feeling that lucky shall we stop and buy a lottery ticket?" Cross laughed at that and Buttons shook his head again. All he could feel from Cross now was a calm determination and underneath the calm boiled a sea of tightly controlled fury, a cold rage Cross held ready to release when it was needed. How did he do it?

Andariel obviously had the same question on her mind as Buttons. "How do you do it, Cross?"

"Do what?"

The angel rolled her eyes and waved her hand at him. "This! How are you not shitting your pants like any sane person would? Bloody hell, if those pasties hadn't cleaned me out earlier I know I would be."

Cross shrugged. "Of course I'm scared, I'm not an idiot. The quickest way to lose a fight is to run in there with a head full of what-if's though. We've got a job to do so that's what I'm focusing on, I'll worry about the rest of it if and when it happens."

"Be a bit late by then won't it?"

Cross shrugged again. "Then worrying really doesn't make a difference does it?"

Andariel muttered to herself. Cross infuriated her as much as he impressed her. The big man glanced over at the smiling Buttons. "So, tell me again how this is going to work", he asked. Buttons shrugged. "I'm not sure yet, it depends on how their house and grounds are set out. I'm hoping for a nice, long drive and some fancy gates to keep the riff-raff out?"

Cross nodded in assent and Buttons smiled even wider. "Perfect", he crowed. "When we hit the drive put your foot down, make it look like we're going to smash through the gates in a frontal assault."

"But we're not going to?" asked Andariel.

"No, before we hit the gate we're going to drive straight through the portal I'll open up in front of it, the other side will be just outside their front door." He grinned nastily at Cross. "Go as fast as you can, Daniel. We want to make a nice, big mess when we smash this thing into their house."

Cross grinned back at him, pleased with the plan so far. He knew how proud the pair of ponces were about their manor so putting a big hole in it with an exploding car was a good start in his opinion. Andariel looked quizzically at the demon hunter. "It take it we're not going to be in the car when it crashes though?"

Buttons pulled a face. "Well that's not part of the plan but it's definitely going to be a bit tricky."

"Tricky how?"

"Tricky as in opening a second wormhole from the back of a speeding car just as we pass through the first one."

Andariel was aghast. "That's impossible!"

"The theory is sound", protested Buttons. "Obviously I've never tried it but I'm hoping the short distances we'll travel will make it a little easier."

"You're hoping?"

Cross headed off any argument. "If the man says he can do it then that's good enough for me." He held up a hand as Andariel began to retort. "We're out of options, luv. We're going into a fortified location against superior numbers and firepower. Doing something they'd never expect is the only chance we've got."

The angel was less than happy with the risky plan. "Can't we just sneak over the wall and Ninja a few guards like normal people?" she grumbled, and Cross shook his head. "No way. They've got floodlights and motion sensors all over the place. They'd know we were there before we got within twenty feet of the wall. This way we can draw some of them to the front of the house and if Buttons can pull this off we'll by-pass their security altogether."

He looked over to the diminutive demon hunter. "You

can pull this off, right?" Buttons nodded. "I can do it, Daniel. I'm sure of it." Cross took one hand off the wheel and punched him lightly on the shoulder. "Good man. The fuckers will never know what hit them."

The city was far behind them and now the Bentley purred through quiet, tree-lined roads. They rounded a bend and as they passed a large copse of trees they could see a village in the near distance. "And here we are", said Cross, "Their estate is just a few miles outside this place."

They drove through the quiet and picturesque village, all of them marvelling at the sheer normality of it all as they passed a row of small shops, a pub and a post office, looking at the villagers going about their business as though it were the strangest of sights.

Andariel shook her head. *None of them have a clue*, she thought. She gritted her teeth with renewed determination.

That was exactly the way it should be. She wanted every one of these people to wake up to a normal world tomorrow, a world of grumbling at the alarm clock and the over-crowded trains on their commute to work, of pub lunches and putting their feet up in front of the telly in the evening. If they did this right then these boring, wonderful, normal people would wake up tomorrow to nothing more than a chance to gossip about why that lovely old estate burned down overnight.

If they did this wrong then their world would end. She grinned suddenly. *No pressure then.* Cross slowed the car to a stop a little way before a junction just outside the village. Andariel looked at the turning to the right. The small road went slightly uphill. Trees lined each side, arching over the tarmac to form a verdant tunnel. At the end of the long, slight rise she could see the lights of the Harringtons' estate. *Here we go.*

Cross twisted in his seat so he could see them both. "Once we take that road it's game time. As soon as we hit the straight I'm going to floor it but this thing isn't built for speed so they'll have plenty of time to get ready for us, and by the time we get to the gate we'll be under fire."

Andariel nodded. "Yeah I thought we might be. Don't worry, I've got that covered. I can deflect anything they throw at us, for a little while at least."

"Glad to hear it." Cross looked at Buttons. "How about you, mate? You ready to poke some more holes in the knickers of the cosmos?"

The blade of the Morningstar nodded and narrowed his eyes. "Let's do it. It's high time we took the fight to these arseholes." Cross laughed and gunned the engine. "Alright then, let's go save the universe shall we?"

Elsewhere…

The shadowed tundra of Hell never changed. Since the architect of the Cosmos created this bleak prison it had stood in wounded isolation and perfect stillness. Every cold rock and block of dirty ice lay exactly where it had since it was placed there at the dawn of time. Every flake of snow and ash that fell had fallen before and would fall again and again.

Hell never changed, Hell *could* never change. It stood as a grim counterpart to the glorious eternity of Heaven, a dark mirror to the light and warmth and boundless variation of paradise. All of its residents, damned and demon alike knew that their eternity would be a thing of crushing monotony which over time would cut even deeper than the agonies that were inflicted and endured.

The damned arrived quietly. The meek about to inherit a terrible earth. They appeared on the cold ground of Hell clothed in new flesh and shivered in their nakedness, confused and terrified and stumbling through broken and forgotten prayers to a God that had turned his back on them, a God they had denied or scorned in their hubris. They would scream soon enough when the demons came for them, but they always arrived in darkness and silence.

Until now.

Demons paused in their hunts and their tortures and even the damned were roused from their misery as the burning, screaming soul exploded into the pit. What used to be Chandra Singh tore through the frigid air of Hell like a comet. Countless millions of eyes turned upward to see the flaming remnant of a human soul plummet through the dark. Demon and human alike stared in stupefied wonder. It was a human soul that burned with the light of angels. It was something new in a place that never changed. It didn't belong here.

What used to be Chandra Singh smashed into the cold ground of Hell with an impact that shook the dark tundra for miles around, and almost as one being, a million demons put down their implements of torture and moved towards this burning, screaming, *wrong* thing.

Far away there stood a city in Hell. A single, empty and lonely city. The city had no name. Being the only city made naming it an irrelevance. The city was a thing of twisted streets and crooked towers, full of crumbling buildings and houses that stood forever dark and empty. All except one. In the centre of the twisted city stood a small building, no different from any of the thousands of others save for the fact that in this building burned a single light.

In that building, Lucifer, the star of the morning, looked out through a broken window to see a streak of light across skies that were forever dark, and for the first time in millennia, heard the language of Heaven in his realm.

TWENTY TWO

Being on guard at the gatehouse, or anywhere for that matter, was always the short-straw detail. Guard duty had been hated by every soldier since the dawn of time and it would continue to be the short-straw detail until the last star burned out and there was nothing left to guard. Guard duty meant a long shift made even longer by the unrelenting monotony of it all. Guard duty meant trying to stay alert when everything about it dulled the senses. Guard duty almost made a soldier wish for something to happen. Almost.

Pat and Jerry Conway (no relation) had hundreds of hours of guard duty under their belts from their years of service in Her Majesty's armed forces, and their complaints and gripes about this shortest of short-straws had been honed to perfection. Neither veteran needed to say a word. The slight downturn of the mouth or arching of an eyebrow was enough to say it all by now.

They'd been at the small gatehouse that stood at the beginning of the private road that ran to the estate for almost two hours. The gatehouse was a small wooden building, more of a shed really but it had heating and light and gave them somewhere to get out of the rain and the cold. It even had a portable TV in it so they could keep an eye on the football.

The gatehouse was set just to the side of the private road that wound through the carefully landscaped grounds to the estate, the entrance to the Harrington family pile barred by wrought iron gates. The gates were large and beautifully crafted, made from gleaming black iron and topped with golden spikes. The gates might look imposing, but Pat and

Jerry knew a stiff breeze could knock them over.

Although both of them might privately admit that as places to guard went they could do a lot worse, neither of them would ever say it. To not complain about guard duty was to betray every man and woman that had ever served.

Pat walked from one side of the road to the other and back again. Every now and again he would vary the pattern and walk a few steps back to give the gates a rattle as if not doing so meant he could look back to find the gates suddenly hanging off of their hinges and barbarian hordes pouring into the grounds.

Jerry leant against the wall of the gatehouse and smoked, his eyes switching from watching the empty road and tracking Pats' aimless steps. He glanced at his watch. They were due for a radio check in ten minutes. His eyes left the road as he gazed up towards the manor. *What the fucking hell was going on up there?* Jerry dropped his cigarette and ground it out under his boot.

"Pat?"

Pat, checking the gate again, didn't even turn around as he answered the unasked question. "I haven't got a bloody clue what's going on up there, Jerry, but I don't like it, whatever it is."

Jerry nodded. "Any idea why they're gunning for Danny?"

"Why *we're* gunning for Danny you mean?"

Jerry grimaced. "Yeah, and I can't say I like that much either."

Pat shrugged. "What are you gonna do? The twins want him gone then he's gone. I'm more interested in that freak show they've got going on up there."

"Yeah, and did you see the other blokes they brought in?"

"Well you can never have too much back up. That many lads does seem like overkill though, I'll give you that."

Jerry shook his head. "No, I mean did you see them after they disappeared into the west wing with the twins? I swear they were like different blokes after that."

Pat snorted a laugh. "Stuck in a room with the twins harping on at them? That was boredom, mate."

"Seriously! They marched out of that room like grinning fucking robots." He shook his head again. "I'm telling you, something's really not right."

Pat was unconvinced. "When is it ever? I mean, Miles is Miles, we all know that but Marcus aint playing with a full deck either if you ask me." Pat gave the gates another rattle, just to be on the safe side. "Whatever they're up to you can bet it'll be earning them a few quid, that's all they're interested in, and if they're earning then..."

"We're getting paid." Finished Jerry. Pat nodded sagely. "Exactly."

Jerry wasn't ready to be so easily mollified. "I still don't like the idea of killing Danny, just doesn't seem right, him being one of us."

"He's not one of us. None of us have been one of us since we left the bloody army."

"You know what I mean."

"Yeah, I do, I just think it's bollocks. I don't care if we shared a tour in the sand together. If he shows up here I'll put a bullet in him before he can put one in me. What we all used to be doesn't mean a fucking thing, not to me and certainly not to Danny bloody Cross. He'd kill us both and forget about it before our bodies dropped."

Jerry looked miserable and Pat shook his head at his friend's hangdog expression. Deep down, Jerry still believed in all that 'for Queen and Country' rubbish. In Jerry's mind he was still a soldier and soldiers shared an unbreakable bond. They were a brotherhood. They looked out for each other.

How the dozy bastard had ever made it out of the army alive with his head stuck in the clouds was beyond Pat's understanding. He liked Jerry though, he was a good lad even if he was a soft sod at times, so he tried to throw him a bone.

"Look, if I know Danny he's already on a plane heading somewhere warm and sunny under a nice, boring identity. He's a fearless bastard but he aint stupid enough to think he can take all of us on and walk away from it." Pat shook his head. "Trust me, he's long gone."

Jerry was about to reply when both men caught the sound of a roaring engine, a sound getting very loud very quickly. They ran to the road to see a Bentley tearing down the quiet country lane towards them. It was still some distance off so Jerry raised a small pair of binoculars to his face to try and see the vehicle's occupants. He stared for a few seconds and then lowered the binoculars to look at Pat. "It's Danny." He said calmly.

"Is it fuck!"

Jerry just shrugged and moved back to the gatehouse. "You'll see for yourself in a minute. I'll take left."

Pat hurried after him to take up a position on the opposite side of the road. Despite the shock of realising Cross really was going to try and attack a house full of heavily armed men, *the mad bastard*, Pat smiled at how Jerry had suddenly become a picture of calm, just when things were about to turn to shit.

The roar of the engine grew louder until it was eclipsed as Pat and Jerry began firing, the distinctive clatter of AK47's filling the night air. The two men fired in single shots, their guns set to semi-automatic. Going full-auto was good for providing covering fire or for the movies but not much else. When it came to shooting, slow was smooth and smooth was fast as the saying went.

They didn't try and shoot through the windscreen. That was another thing that only really happened in Hollywood. Hitting a car moving at almost a hundred miles per hour was harder than it looked, let alone trying to hit the hunched head and shoulders of the driver. No, you kill the car first and then killing the occupants was a piece of piss.

Pat had fired off five good, clean shots into the radiator and he was sure Jerry had done the same, but the car didn't slow. As a matter of fact, it didn't look like it had a fucking scratch on it. He spared a second to glance at Jerry and saw he wore the same look of irritated incomprehension that must have been on his face. The bonnet of that thing should have been Swiss-cheese by now and even the best bullet-proof glass would be pocked with small craters and spider web cracks from the subsonic impact of 7.62mm rounds. Danny was making no attempt to swerve and avoid their fire, he just barrelled straight towards them through the hail of bullets.

They were very close now, close enough that both men could see Cross sitting comfortably in the plush seat of the old Bentley with one hand on the wheel, grinning at them like he was on a Sunday drive without a care in the world. *Fuck it.* Both men had the same thought in unison and flicked their AK's to full-auto. The Bentley was close enough now that they couldn't miss it if they tried and Pat and Jerry unleashed a storm of bullets, both of them aiming straight for Cross's mocking grin.

The noise was deafening and both men winced at the sudden flare of an explosion of sparks from the bodywork of the car. No, they weren't sparks they realised as the stately old car remained completely unblemished. They were flashes of light as their bullets were stopped by...something before they even reached the car. The Bentley roared past them, smashing through the gates as though they were paper and tearing up the winding road towards the manor.

Their guns fell silent. Pat and Jerry just stared at each other as they waited for the ringing in their ears to subside. It was Jerry who spoke first. "You saw that, right? He's got a fucking force-field!"

Pat sighed and shook his head. "I don't know what I saw, and frankly I don't really care. I do know one thing though."

"What's that?"

"You can fuck right off if you think I'm following them up there."

Jerry laughed. The sound was slightly forced but Pat didn't say anything. No shame in being rattled after a firefight, even one you walked away from without a scratch and particularly one that involved a lunatic driving an indestructible

Bentley straight at you. Jerry wiped his gun down and then threw it carelessly into the small gatehouse where it clattered to the floor.

"Too bloody right we're not following them. We're taking the rest of the night off."

Pat nodded and wiped down his own weapon which joined Jerrys' on the floor. He looked towards the manor house, sparing a mournful glance for the wreckage of the gates. The Bentley was lost to sight as it sped through a copse of trees lining a stretch of the private road, but he could still hear the grumbling roar of the engine. For the second time that night he wondered just what the bloody hell was going on before his soldiers' pragmatism took over and he shrugged. Not his problem anymore.

He turned his back to the manor house, to the bullet-proof Bentley and its force field and all the other weird bollocks that was going on and looked at Jerry. "Pub?" was all he said.

Jerry grinned at him. It was all he needed to say.

TWENTY THREE

Cross roared with laughter as he threw the Bentley into a tight turn, feeling the back end of the big car wanting to slide out, fighting him for control as he abused it so cruelly. "Did you see the look on their faces?" he grinned. Andariel gave vent to an unladylike grunt as she slumped down in the back of the car. "I was a little busy back there, Cross".

The big man frowned as he looked at her in the rear-view mirror. "You alright?" The angel waved away his concern. "Don't worry about me, I'll be fine in a minute." She smiled wearily at him. "I've only ever tried that trick against arrows. Assault rifles take a bit more effort apparently". Cross nodded and turned his attention back to the road. He could see the large house now, growing larger still and very quickly as he forced yet more speed out of the protesting car.

The Harringtons' manor was surrounded by a high wall and the road barred by another set of gates. These weren't the elegant and useless gates they'd ploughed through a few moments ago. These were made of thick wood bound with steel. They were made with the sole purpose of keeping people out and Cross reckoned they'd do a bloody good job of it.

He stared at the gates and then flicked his eyes down to the speedometer. Thirty, maybe forty seconds until they'd find out how just how effective those gates were and he didn't fancy their chances. "Buttons?"

The demon hunter didn't answer. He sat with his eyes closed and his hands tightly clenched as he prepared to tear the universe open not once but twice. The small man was a picture of stillness and calm as he prepared to do the impossible. Cross trusted Buttons implicitly. If the little man said he could do it then he could do it. Even so, those big, sturdy gates were getting very close and very quickly. "Buttons?" he said again and this time there was a definite edge to the question.

Buttons still didn't answer, he just opened his eyes and pulled his hands apart. This wasn't the slow and controlled violation of space and time that Cross had marvelled at in the vestry, this was the fabric of the universe being savagely torn apart. The gates disappeared from view as a patch of swirling, shimmering grey suddenly hung in front of them. The Bentley and its occupants rocketed through the portal and into what Andariel had called the blood and bones of the universe.

Cross looked around in stupefied wonder. It was as though the old car hung motionless in an encompassing sea of...nothing. The milky grey was all around them and even though it felt blanketing, almost smothering in its closeness, Cross somehow knew that it went on forever, even as he knew that what he understood of space and distance meant nothing in this place.

He still had his foot on the accelerator and the Bentleys' engine screamed into the stillness. The sound was more than jarring in the perfect quiet of that no-space and Cross eased his foot off of the pedal and let the engine idle. He turned to Buttons who was looking drained but satisfied as they hung in the void. "Was this supposed to happen?" he asked, and Buttons smiled wearily in reply.

"I wasn't sure it would work to be honest but, yes, we're right where we're supposed to be."

"Glad to hear it, and where are we exactly?"

Buttons shrugged. "It doesn't really have a name but I guess 'nowhere' is as good a name as any." He held up a hand to forestall Cross's next questions. "It's the space in between, the space you move through when you go through a wormhole."

Cross frowned. "But isn't the point of a wormhole that it makes here and there the same place? How can there be a space between?"

Andariel smiled at his confusion. "There's always a space be-tween. You're still moving between two points so there *has* to be a between. It's small, so small you could argue it doesn't really exist but it's there all the same."

"That doesn't make any bloody sense, you know that don't you?"

The Angel laughed at that. "Cross, we're talking about something so vast it's limitless and at the same time so small it basically isn't there. We're well past sense at this point."

Cross had to concede that point at least. He shifted in his seat to face Buttons again, cursing softly as he jabbed his knee on the steering column. "Ok, so we're in the space between point A and point B, so where's point B?"

Buttons smiled at this, quite obviously pleased with himself. "There isn't a point B yet, I only opened one side."

Andariel raised her eyebrows in surprise. "I didn't know you could do that."

"Neither did I until about 30 seconds ago."

The Angel glared at him but Cross just laughed until An-dariel turned her glare on him. "I'm glad you're enjoying your-self, Cross. Let's see if you're still laughing if he," she jabbed her thumb towards Buttons, "can't open the other side from here."

Cross stopped laughing. "Why wouldn't he be able to open it from here?"

Andariel shook her head and gave him a withering look. "Think about it. 'Here' doesn't really exist. We're about as far away from the normal rules of existence as you can get, apart from that bloody Last Hall place, so why should they apply here?"

Buttons grimaced. "I didn't think of that." He admitted ruefully. Andariel was gracious enough not to beat him over the head about it. Cross was about to speak but something stopped him. All three turned towards the back window as a sound drifted out of the swirling void. It was faint, but it was a sound nonetheless and enough to carry over the soft grumble of the still idling engine.

They looked at each other and then back out of the window in growing alarm as the sound issued again. It was wordless, more like a sigh or exhalation but all of them could feel a sense of eagerness behind it, and while distance may have been meaningless here, somehow, they all felt it was getting closer. Cross stared into the milky swirl outside the Bentley with narrowed eyes. "Buttons?" he said calmly. "How about we get out of here?"

Buttons nodded in reply and closed his eyes. Cross sighed as he saw the small man's eyes open again, this time filled with alarm. "If I said: 'I take it you can't open a portal from here?' would I win a prize?" The slender demon hunter cursed. "How could I have been so bloody stupid?"

The menacing susurration sounded behind them again, then from the left and from the front. The awful sound grew louder. It was all around them now and Cross slapped the steering wheel in frustration. He didn't even know if they could step out of the car, how were they supposed to fight? He pulled out his gun and flicked off the safety. Whatever was out there he'd put a few bullets into it before he went down.

The swirling grey of this strange nowhere suddenly parted in front of them and Andariel gave a wordless yell of triumph as she saw it was a portal, a way out. As reality asserted itself again momentum took hold of the Bentley and the car began to move forward. Cross stamped on the accelerator and the engine roared into life. The front wheels crossed the threshold of the portal and bit into real, solid ground. It was dark so he flicked the headlights on as they shot forward and grinned as he saw he drove across polished flagstones. He recognised this place.

He swung the wheel hard to the right and yanked up the handbrake to send the car screeching into a 180 turn and juddering to a halt. There was no need to stop in so dramatic a fashion. He'd done it just because he could, because he'd never pulled a handbrake turn in a Bentley and because they'd actually made it out of that awful place alive.

Cross turned off the ignition and they got out of the car, all of them giving silent thanks as they felt solid ground beneath their feet again. It was dark in the huge room but it began to lighten even as a voice sounded behind them.

"That is not a place in which to linger my friends."

They turned to see the impossibly tall form of Ennustaja and Andariel and Buttons both bowed. Cross just grinned at her. "Thanks for getting us out of there, luv. That's the second time today you've saved our bacon".

The keeper of the Last Hall creased her beautiful, unearthly face into a frown. "Indeed, I did not expect to be seeing you again so soon but I had no choice but to intervene." She turned to Buttons. "Whatever possessed you to open a portal there?" she admonished. Buttons looked suitably chastened by her tone, still shaken by the fact that he'd very nearly killed them all.

"I actually thought it would be safer," he explained. "It suddenly occurred to me that if I opened a second portal just for us we might make it out of the car but we'd still have been moving at a hundred miles an hour." He shrugged. "I didn't think it would have been a comfortable landing, so I thought I'd try something else."

Ennustaja had actually seen the results of that action as she'd peered into the possible futures and it hadn't ended well. The biggest problem they'd caused Malleus and the Harringtons that way was having to clean up the mess. She was about to speak again when Cross stepped in. "So where exactly were we? And what was making those noises?"

Ennustaja's face, though beautiful, was undeniably alien and Cross found it difficult to accurately read her expressions. If he had to bet on it though he'd have said the look on her face was fear. "I do not know where or what that place is, not for certain. I do not know if those terms have any relevance to it at all. I know it is not a part of what you call the universe and yet it is somehow all around it, *through* it."

Her body gave way to a strange, boneless ripple and

251

Cross blinked in surprise as he realised she'd shuddered. "There are things there that are older than creation, perhaps older than God, and then there are the others." Ennustaja fell silent, obviously discomfited by the the thought of whatever lurked in that strange place.

"The others?" gently prompted Andariel.

"Those from your universe and yet unclaimed by either Heaven or Hell, those so monstrous and twisted that they are banished from Hell itself."

The three friends looked at each other and then back at the empty space where the portal to the *outside* had just been. Ennustaja was right, it was definitely not a place to linger. Now they had been there they could all still feel it inside them. Somehow, they knew that the *outside* lay less than a hairs' breadth away and they knew that in some small way they would always feel it, forever out of reach yet forever there.

Cross acknowledged the feeling and then dismissed it, his soldiers' pragmatism taking over. The *outside* was a mystery, a worry, for another time. It wasn't relevant to the mission and so he forgot about it. Bloody hell, if they were still alive to worry about it tomorrow then he'd count himself lucky.

He looked at Ennustaja. "I don't want to seem ungrateful but…"

"Will I throw you into the fire now I've pulled you from the frying pan?" she finished with a slight smile. Smiling was still new to Ennustaja and she decided she liked it. Cross laughed. "Couldn't have put it better myself".

"I suggest we send the car through first and then I shall deposit you at the back of the house a few moments after?" Ennustaja looked at the three of them to see they all agreed with her plan.

"Who's going to drive the car?" asked Buttons. Ennustaja just smiled again in reply and the three of them jumped as the engine suddenly roared into life. A portal appeared a few hundred feet away and the old Bentley lurched forward, rapidly picking up speed as it drove towards the glowing doorway. As the portal hung in the distance Cross couldn't see any details but he could make out the front of the Harringtons manor and smiled nastily. This was really going to make a mess.

They heard shouts of alarm swiftly followed by gunfire and Cross wondered how it must look to the Harringtons' men to suddenly see a classic car barrelling towards them out of nowhere. The men would be rattled, if not outright panicked and it was sure to set a few of them wondering just what they'd signed on for tonight and whether it was worth the money. *Perfect.*

Ennustaja turned her back to the portal and it closed just as the Bentley cleared it. Cross held his hand up to stop her from opening another doorway. "Not just yet, please. Hopefully most of them will move towards the front of the house where all the fun's happening."

He looked at his two friends, the angel and the demon hunter, and smiled. "Last chance for us all to do the smart thing and just stay here."

"Let's get this done" said Andariel, curtly. Buttons didn't say anything. He just pulled that awful mask from his pocket and slipped it on. Cross shivered as the small, affable man suddenly disappeared, replaced by a being whose immense power could be felt coming off of him in waves.

Ennustaja gestured and another, smaller portal opened in front of them. The portal had opened into the grounds and they could see the back of the Harringtons' manor house. The scent of grass and flowers drifted into the sterile air of the Last Hall and Cross breathed it in. It was mercifully quiet. It looked like a classic car exploding against the front of the house did indeed make for an excellent diversion.

They stepped through onto the grass and Cross briefly marvelled that a single stride had taken him from outside the boundaries of creation itself to the Surrey countryside. Night had fallen and the grounds were dark. The three stood just at the edge of a pool of light that spilled from two ground floor windows that flanked a simple wooden door. They turned to see Ennustaja in the portal behind them, none of them sure what to say to their strange benefactor.

The keeper of the Last Hall gestured again and they heard a quiet *click* as the door to the manor unlocked itself. She nodded once and said simply: "Luck" before the portal closed. *Obviously not one for goodbyes*, thought Cross. He nodded towards the door. "Let's go," he said. "Our luck won't hold forever."

He peered through the windows, scanning the room with a practiced eye before quietly easing the door open and stepping inside. In a strange way stepping across that threshold felt even more significant than stepping through the portal and Cross privately admitted he was surprised, no, he was bloody gob-smacked they'd made it this far.

While Cross had been to the manor before he hadn't been given the grand tour and this section of the large house was unfamiliar. Added to that was the fact that he had no idea where the twins would be and he grimaced as he steeled himself for a room to room search. It was nothing he hadn't done before but an infiltration into unfamiliar territory against an unknown number of assailants was always a perilous exercise at best.

The room they were in was a fair size and contained obviously expensive and just as obviously unused furniture. It was one of those rooms in a large house that was filled just because it was there but was rarely, if ever, used. The sort of room the owners of the property might walk into with a feeling of mild surprise to discover it was there.

Two doors led from the room on opposite sides and Cross moved towards the left-hand exit to stay on the outskirts of the manor. Buttons took his arm as he reached it and gently stopped him. Cross raised his eyebrows in a silent question.

"He's here, Daniel. Malleus."

"What, here in the flesh?"

Buttons shrugged. "Well someone else's flesh but yes. He hasn't come alone either."

"Demons?" asked Andariel and Buttons nodded. "At least a dozen. I can smell them."

Cross cursed under his breath. Like this wasn't going to be hard enough already. Ok, so having a dozen or so demons and a lord of Hell to contend with as well as the Cobleys and a few armed mercenaries definitely complicated things, but the plan remained the same and maybe there was a way it could be used to their advantage.

"You said you can smell them? He asked Buttons. "I take it you don't mean that literally?"

Buttons knew what he was getting at. "Yes, I know exactly where they are."

"Excellent. Can they 'see' you?"

Buttons snorted. "Not a chance. Lucifer basically designed me so demons couldn't see me coming." He glanced towards the angel. "Andariel?"

She nodded. "They'd be able to sniff me out a mile away if I let them." She grinned at them. "Don't worry, it's not like this is my first time hunting demons. I've been masking myself since we left the Last Hall, just in case."

Cross grinned back at her. "So we can see them but they can't see us? Even better. Are we clear for now?"

Buttons nodded. "From demons yes, the nearest ones are further along the west wing. There's a couple towards the front of the house but it looks like the bulk of them are in a large room in the centre with Malleus."

Cross thought for a second and remembered the large drawing room in the centre of the manor. It was large and comfortable with only one entrance to cover, and it had a well-stocked drinks cabinet. That's where he would have based himself too.

Buttons spoke again. "Daniel, I can't 'see' the Cobleys or any of the normal humans in the same way," he warned. Cross waved away his concern. "The fact we know where the chief arseholes and half of their force are gives us an edge. Not much of one but I'll take it. We stick to the plan and move slow and quiet for as long as we can."

"And when we can't?" asked Andariel and Cross just smiled, almost eagerly thought the angel.

Cross listened at the door for a second and then quietly opened it to find it led onto a long hallway. Three doors were on the left and two more further down on the right and he breathed a silent sigh of relief that they were going to be spared checking every room. He padded silently along the corridor until he reached the corner where it turned to the right and deeper into the manor.

Cross held up a hand and they stopped before the corner, hugging the wall. Cross listened again and then peeked around the corner to see another corridor, this one also empty. It was shorter and had only one room adjacent to it before it turned again, this time to the left. He was about to move out when he heard a soft sound and saw the door handle begin to turn. Cross slipped back out of sight and motioned for Andariel and Buttons to move back and give him some room.

They all heard the door close and the footsteps approaching and Cross smiled in satisfaction as he realised there was only one man rather than a patrolling pair. *Stupid bastard.* He closed his eyes and breathed deeply, silently as he listened to the footsteps. They were muffled by the carpet but still audible and there was a lot you could tell from a footstep if you had the training and experience.

He judged his target to be around six feet from the stride length and well-built or at least fully loaded judging by the muffled thuds on the deep carpet. Cross silently counted each step. If his target was around six feet tall and walking at a cautious speed that would put him at the corner right about... *now!*

Cross was a blur as he whiplashed around the corner. His left hand was perfectly placed to grab the barrel of the shotgun and force it to the side even as his right hand cannoned upwards in a palm strike. The heel of his hand slammed into the man's septum, splintering the small bones of the nose and driving them up into his brain. He was dead before he could even register the assault. Cross kept his grip on the shotgun and swiftly moved his right hand down to grasp the collar of his victim's shirt to stop him from falling.

Without a word he dragged the corpse back to one of the empty rooms behind them. He laid the body down almost gently before divesting it of the shotgun and quietly closing the door behind him.

Andariel was looking at him in surprise. She'd seen him fight and knew he was obviously both well trained and naturally talented, but this was the first time she'd seen him kill up close like this. She'd seen through his eyes as he dispatched Tony, and the way he'd executed the unfortunate doctor Singh clearly showed it wasn't the first time he'd done that, but the speed and precision with which he'd just snatched away a life was almost unnerving. Buttons simply nodded, one craftsman acknowledging the art of another.

Cross grinned at them both as he hefted the shotgun. "There aren't many problems you can't make go away with one of these" he whispered. Andariel rolled her eyes at him and Buttons smiled beneath the mask. Cross quickly checked the shotgun, satisfying himself that it was in working order and fully loaded. He felt better now he was properly armed. Demon lord or not, a 12 gauge to the face would make a hell of a mess.

As they moved deeper into the manor Cross allowed himself to believe that they might even pull this off.

TWENTY FOUR

Four men were stationed at the front of the manor. Two stood either side of the gate while the others flanked the main doors. Like Pat and Jerry at the gatehouse below they didn't expect Cross to actually assault the manor, he was far too canny to attempt a suicide mission like that. As well as the four humans, two demons clothed as men restlessly prowled the area between the gate and the main doors. The human mercenaries briefly wondered why neither of them were armed.

Unlike the men they knew exactly what was at stake and so weren't surprised to hear gunfire crackling in the distance, nor were they surprised when the gunfire died away and the sound of an approaching car grew louder and louder. The men began to issue urgent but calm instructions into their radios and cocked their weapons, the two at the gate moving back and to the sides, ready to riddle the car with bullets when, if, it managed to smash through the six-inch-thick wood.

The roar of the engine grew louder and louder still. The car was just seconds away and all of them, demon and man alike, readied themselves for the shattering impact on the gates. Suddenly all was silence. The air was still, and the gates remained intact. The men traded bemused glances while the demons narrowed their eyes at this trickery. The mercenary closest to the gate walked back and checked the small monitor built into the wall and connected to a camera on top.
"There's nothing there, the car's just gone!"
"Gone where?" asked another. "How could it just disappear?"
The merc at the gate stared into the monitor again, not

trusting what the screen was showing him even though the sudden silence gave evidence to the fact that an entire car had, in fact, just disappeared. "Fucked if I know" he shrugged. "I can see tyre marks and everything but the car aint there!"
One of the demons snarled impatiently. "Worry about where it will appear again, fool!"

The man at the gate wasn't about to be spoken to like that by one of the new blokes and strode back towards the house. He'd give the gobshite a slap for that. He was halfway between the gate and the main doors when he heard a strange tearing sound behind him.

It wasn't like any sound he'd heard before but 'tearing' was the only way he could describe it. He saw the suddenly wide eyes of the men in front of him and whirled round to see the gates had disappeared to be replaced by a...what the fuck was it?!

A perfect rectangle stood in front of him eclipsing the view of what should have been the gates. Instead this...door led to a huge, dark room. The edges of this impossible doorway gleamed in the waning light. The men couldn't stop staring even though it hurt their eyes. Those edges were too sharp somehow, burning into their retinas even as they couldn't tear their watering eyes away.

The closest man squinted into the gloom of the doorway and shook his head in bemusement as he saw what looked like a huge room bordered by gigantic pillars and with smooth, polished flagstones lining the floor.

A sound rumbled and echoed from the strange room and the incongruity of it made it hard for them men to place, but when the glare of headlights at full beam shone from the darkness they all knew what it was. At once they all fell back from the impossible door and took up firing positions. *It was the fucking car!*

With a squeal of rubber on the flagstones the car rocketed towards them and while none of the men understood what was happening they knew exactly what to do.

"Light it up!" yelled the one closest to the portal and all of the men began firing at the approaching car. Like Jerry and Pat, who were currently enjoying a literally life-saving pint at a pub a few miles away and pointedly talking about anything but the events of the evening, the guards had been professional soldiers, and despite the undeniably bizarre circumstances of this attack, calmly fired at the rapidly approaching car.

This time the Bentley withered under the storm of automatic weapons fire and the men grinned as they saw the headlights smash and go dark and the windscreen become a constellation of bullet holes and spider web cracks. Smoke rose from the shattered engine under the torn and buckled bonnet and the driver's side tyre blew. *Gotcha, you bastards!* Their brief exultance swiftly faded as the car came on, not deviating an inch from its path despite the blown tyre and the men traded confused and worried glances as they fell further back towards the manor, firing as they went.

The big car just kept on coming. Two of the mercenary's weapons ran dry and they quickly slapped in a new magazine, switching their guns to full-auto and pouring round after useless round into the Bentley. It rocketed from the portal and as it sped past the nearer men they both saw that it was empty. *What the fucking hell was going on?!*

They continued to shoot at the empty car until its position put their colleagues in the line of fire. The two men flanking the front door of the house put a few more rounds into the now grinding, shrieking engine and then realised the car wasn't going to stop no matter what they did.

"Move-move-move!" One yelled as he sprinted from the danger zone, his partner quickly following suit. The demons had moved as soon as the portal appeared and stood calmly watching and waiting. The Bentley was a mess. Every tyre was blown, every window smashed and the engine and bodywork shredded. There was no way the car could still be moving at such speed and in a perfectly straight line but still it came on, a two-tonne comet of wreckage with a tail of smoke and broken glass.

It hit the manor with a thunderous noise, obliterating the doors and destroying a good section of the front wall along with it. Glass, wood and brick shattered under the impact and clouds of masonry dust billowed into the air to mingle with the smoke and steam from the wrecked engine.

The Bentley finally slid to a halt almost ten feet inside the manor atop broken furniture and adorned with the ruined artwork it had torn from the walls of the wide entrance hall as it bulldozed its way into the Harringtons' ancestral home.

Almost before it came to rest a group of both men and demons surrounded the wreckage, the men aiming their weapons through the shattered windows while the demons probed the mangled Bentley with their otherworldly senses. The dust began to clear and some of the men cursed as they saw the car was empty.

The demons traded concerned glances. They knew that someone or something had just violated the laws of the universe to bring the empty car through what had to have been a portal between worlds, but none of them could recognise the scent of the power at work. Indeed, it was more the absence of a trail, or of any scar on the abused fabric of reality that worried them. What allies had this human been able to find?

One of the men tried to open the mangled door on the drivers' side, unwilling to admit the car really was empty. The twisted metal groaned but the door was stuck fast and he cursed before putting his head and shoulders through the buckled window frame to scan the interior. He could see dozens of bullet holes in the seats, both front and back.

Anyone in that car would have been killed ten times over and the plush seats and the polished walnut dashboard would be soaked with blood but, barring the bullet holes, the interior was unblemished.

The man pulled his head out of the car and straightened up to look at his companions. "Empty." He said. "There's not a drop of blood so whoever was in there got out before the shooting started."

"So how did the fucking thing get through the gate and drive itself in here then?" asked one of the others. The first man just shrugged but any reply he was about to make was interrupted by the gate guards as they ran inside.

"It just appeared out of nowhere!" shouted one of the gate guards as he skidded to a halt in front of the group surrounding the mysterious Bentley.

He saw the looks they were giving him and pointed at the car. "I'm telling you that thing just appeared in the grounds through some sort of doorway hanging in the air!" he stopped his tirade to point at the assembled men instead of the car. "And you can get those looks off your faces too, we all saw it!" His pointing finger became a waving hand as he gestured to the other mercs who'd been out front with him.

"Oh fuck off did it come through a magic door!" scoffed one of the men from inside and his friends laughed which incensed the gate guards even further. Voices were raised and more fingers were pointed but the inevitable fracas was snuffed out before it began as Marcus Harrington walked into the hall. He didn't say anything. He just looked at the men who, to their surprise, quickly fell silent, the mercenaries nearest to him even falling back a step.

There was something different about him now. The men had always treated the Harringtons with the same back-handed respect and private disdain that every working man showed their employer. The twins paid well but when all was said and done they were just a pair of oddball blue-bloods, and while the men may have been willing to sell their loyalty for a price their respect was a different matter altogether.

Now, however, the patrician glare of the elder Harrington silenced them all. He exuded a cold power and filled the room with a sense of dread. The men all looked at each other in surprise and confusion while the demons simply stood with expressionless faces and dead eyes as they looked upon their master.

The being that was once Marcus Harrington took in the car and the wreckage of the hall without comment and seemingly without surprise.

"Cross will already be in the grounds, more than likely in the house itself by now." He held up a hand to forestall any questions. "Mr Barnes and some of our new associates are already sweeping the house." The lord of Hell looked at two of his demonic underlings. "You two, with me. The rest of you coordinate with Mr Barnes and find them."

The men immediately felt better at being placed directly under Lincolns' command and while the demons may not have liked it they knew better than to voice any displeasure. "Do you want them alive, sir?" asked one of the men and what lay behind Marcus's eyes smiled coldly. "If you can bring Cross to me alive then all the better. You needn't be gentle about it though and if you have to kill him then do so."

The spokesman for the humans nodded. "And his friends?"

"Be warned, gentlemen. They're both far more dangerous than they might appear. Shoot them both on sight."

TWENTY FIVE

Cross, Andariel and Buttons moved deeper into the house, Cross silently cursing the Haringtons for living in such a huge and sprawling place. They'd had to backtrack twice now as corridors led them to unused and almost empty rooms. *Place is a fucking maze*, thought Cross. *We'll die of old-age before we find them at this rate.*

The last turn they'd taken had been to the right which Cross swore should have led them towards the centre of the house but instead deposited them into another empty and useless room. They moved back to the last intersection to take the left hand turn this time. The left corridor was short and ended with a single door. Cross wasn't convinced it would take them where they needed to go but it was the only way they hadn't tried so they were out of options.

He began to move towards the door until he felt Buttons' hand on his arm. Cross looked at him questioningly. "There's someone in there" Whispered the small man. "A demon?" asked Cross and Buttons nodded, then shook his head. "No, it doesn't feel right. It's not quite human though." "One of the coven." guessed Andariel and Buttons nodded. "Yes, and they know we're here. They're just waiting." Waiting for them? Cross didn't like that but what choice did they have?

Whoever or whatever stood on the other side of that door was in their way, so they had to go through them. They were just waiting though, not raising an alarm which suggested whoever it was had their own agenda. He stared at the door and then looked at his friends. "It's the big one, that great skinhead lump."

"What's he doing?" asked Andariel and Cross smiled without humour. "Big fella like that? All those muscles on display? He wants to kill us all himself. Blokes like him always have something to prove." The angel narrowed her eyes. "Idiot. He hasn't got a chance on his own." Then she grimaced. "Killing him will be noisy though so we'll have the rest of them down on us pretty quickly".

Cross grinned. "Maybe not. I've seen enough like him over the years to know how to play this. Follow my lead." The big man didn't wait for a response and simply walked forward, opened the door and stepped into the room while Buttons and Andariel hurried after him. The room was huge, the centre dominated by the green baize expanse of a snooker table and ringed with small tables and deep leather chairs.

Even with the snooker table and surrounding furniture there was still plenty of space and Cross breathed a sigh of relief. He was going to need all the room he could get. Cross, Buttons and Andariel stood on one side of the table and looked across at the huge, glowering form of Terry.

Cross looked at his friends and raised his eyebrows. "Big fucker, isn't he?" He spoke in a stage whisper, making sure he wasn't addressing Terry directly or even looking in his direction. Andariel quickly caught on to what Cross was intending and faced Cross with a shrug. "Doesn't look to bright though" she whispered back.

Terry, who really wasn't too bright, clenched his fists, seething with anger at being dismissed so cavalierly. He strode forward. "You're fucking dead, all of you!" The heavy snooker table didn't even slow him down. He just grabbed one end and easily sent it sliding across the room and out of his way as he stalked towards the trio, eager to start tearing them all to pieces.

Cross blinked in surprise. He'd assumed Terry would be augmented in some way but the contemptuous ease with which he'd sent the table across the room showed that he was enormously, terrifyingly strong. *Me and my big mouth*, thought

Cross. He didn't let any doubt show on his face as he casually propped his shotgun against the wall and stepped forward, waving Buttons and Andariel back. "Don't waste your energy" he sneered. "I'll sort this dickhead out."

As he'd hoped Terry roared and bulled forward, swinging his right arm in a thundering haymaker. Had it connected it wouldn't have just crushed Cross's skull, it would have gone straight through it.

Cross had already swayed back and to the right, feeling the rush of air from the furious blow passing just centimetres from his face. Terry pulled himself back before he overbalanced and turned the failed punch into a crushing back fist.

Cross was surprised by how quickly Terry had checked himself and attacked again but still managed to avoid the blow. His respect for his opponent grew as he realised Terry was fast as well as strong. No way could he trade blows with him, even blocking a punch would snap his arm like a twig and Cross knew the only way he'd win this fight would be to goad the huge skinhead into giving him an opening.

Luckily for Cross, he had plenty of room to manoeuvre in the large room now Terry had pushed the snooker table out of the way and he ducked and weaved around the huge skinhead, slipping past and around blow after blow. Andariel and Buttons stood with their hearts in their mouths, knowing that one wrong move would likely see their friend dead, equal parts terrified and enthralled as they watched. Cross wasn't just fast. The big man *flowed*. Buttons had been fighting for centuries, Andariel for millennia and both of them knew they were watching a master at work.

Cross was always moving, always in balance no matter how much he twisted and ducked and danced around his foe. Killing blow after killing blow failed to connect and the 'blessed' disciple of Malleus roared in fury as his mortal opponent frustrated him again and again. Cross didn't even try to fight back. Terry was experienced enough to know that Cross had ignored several openings already and the calculated disdain of his merely human opponent infuriated him even further.

Cross laughed at him. "Fuck me but you're slow, boy!" He avoided a further flurry of punches with ease and Terry's rage finally got the better of him. He swung a wild, uncontrolled blow and the momentum of the strike left him out of position and off balance, not by much but it was enough. Cross used the momentum of the wild punch, slapping his own hand flat against the outside of Terry's arm as it passed to push him further around.

He spun behind him and dropped into a crouch, reaching between Terrys' legs with his right hand and taking his testicles in a crushing, vicelike grip. Cross squeezed as hard as he could before twisting his hand and yanking down.

Terry howled in wordless agony and Cross grinned as he felt one of the big skinheads' balls pop like a grape in his hand. Terry sunk to his knees, hands cradling his ruined genitals as a bloodstain bloomed across the crotch of his jeans. So intense was the pain he couldn't even scream now, he just wheezed and panted as the agony overtook him. Cross straightened, wiping his hand on his trousers as he looked critically at his victim before nodding in satisfaction. *Gets them every time.*

Cross walked back across the room and picked up the shotgun before moving back to stand behind the whimpering, drooling Terry. He slammed the stock of the shotgun into the back of Terrys' head, sending him crashing face first to the floor.

Cross hit him again, and again and again until he felt the skull start to cave in. Then he hit him a few more times, not stopping until the stock of the shotgun finally smashed through the ruined skull and completely pulped the brain. Supernaturally enhanced or not, no one was getting up again after that.

He stopped to get his breath back. Smashing through that thick skull had been harder work than he'd thought it would be. *I should really knock the cigarettes on the head one day.* Cross knelt beside the twitching corpse and cleaned the blood, brains and skull fragments from the stock of the shotgun on Terrys' t-shirt. His own clothes were soaked in blood and he took his ruined jacket off, dropping it on the floor before rolling up his sodden shirtsleeves. The blood on his hands was turning clammy and sticky and he cleaned them on his trousers as best he could.

Buttons stepped forward and leant over to inspect Cross's handiwork. Cross looked up to see that awful mask nodding at him. "Nicely done, Daniel." Said Buttons and even through the blank, chilling visage he wore Cross knew he was smiling. Cross stood up, stretching a kink out of his back and Andariel clapped him on the shoulder. "Yeah, not bad." She grinned. "Not the most elegant job I've ever seen, but not bad at all."

Cross snorted in derision. "Not bad my arse! You can kill the next one and show me how it's done then."

"Fine with me." The angel looked critically at the pulped meat that used to be Terry and at the blood-spattered Cross. "I won't make such a mess either."

Cross grinned at her. "Not like we have to clean it up is it?"

Whatever retort the angel was about to make was lost as they all heard footsteps pounding towards the doors. Cross cursed. It looked like he hadn't killed Terry quickly or quietly enough after all. He sighed and hefted his shotgun. *Ah well, not like we didn't know this was coming.*

Movement made him glance to the side and he saw Andariel dart across the room to where Terry had shoved the snooker table against the wall. She heaved it onto its side and then quickly dragged it over to form a barrier between them and the door. While she hadn't moved it as easily as Terry did Cross could see she was much stronger than she might have looked.

"Nice idea but it's not going to stop any bullets." He said and Andariel rolled her eyes at him. "It's not meant to." She looked across at Buttons. "Give this a good shove when they come through the door would you?" The little man didn't answer but he crouched behind the heavy table and a placed one hand flat against it.

The Harringtons' forces were almost on them and Cross put a couple of rounds through the door. The shotgun boomed and he grinned at the thunderous sound as it kicked like a mule against his shoulder.

The top half of the door dissolved into splinters and Cross grinned again as he heard a yelp of pain. He didn't think he'd have managed to hurt anyone too badly, but it would give them something to think about at least. They all ducked flat as the muzzle of a gun poked through the ruins of the door and fired blindly into the room. Bullets tore through the table and into the wall behind them, Buttons hissing as one came close enough to tear through his shirt and leave a stinging furrow across his shoulder. The demon hunter got back to his feet as the shooting died away and braced himself against the table.

The little man gave the snooker table a single, violent shove with his hand. It flew across the room, smashing through the door and the walls either side and carrying on down the corridor, blasting aside anything or anyone unlucky enough to be in front of it. It was a display of explosive strength from the little man that dwarfed anything Cross had seen so far and he shook his head.

With everything else he'd witnessed today he shouldn't have found it so surprising, but for some reason he still struggled with the no notion that this small and amiable man, the devil's secret weapon, his friend, was basically a celestial atom bomb.

It had been nice for the short while it lasted but the stealthy approach had just been sent crashing through a wall. The world and his wife would know where they were so now it was time to hit hard and hit fast. Cross sprinted across the room and through the huge hole left by Buttons' improvised battering ram. The big man let go of himself and fell into that curious state of calm where training and instinct took over.

That state of mind was hard to achieve, taking years of rigorous physical training and mental discipline to accomplish, something few people ever managed.

Cross surrendered himself to his subconscious. He didn't have to think anymore, everything was feeling and movement and action, his whole world contracted to the blink of an eye. He barely registered the torn and broken form of a demon dragging itself back to its feet, simply levelling the shotgun and firing as he ran past, obliterating its head and most of its left shoulder and chest. Movement, left and right. Two more booming shots and two more mangled bodies hit the floor.

He didn't even feel the burning pain as a bullet ploughed a small furrow through the outside meat of his thigh and another impacted the wall by his head, stinging his face with masonry fragments. There was a blur to his left and he saw his assailant fall with one of Andariel's knives sunk deep into his eye.

Two more enemies barred the way, all that was left of the group that had attacked the snooker room. They were at the end of the ruined corridor, flanking a set of double doors. They were at least twenty feet away but still within the killing range of the shotgun. Cross, as always, had counted his shots. Three shells left. One more than he'd need.

Cross raised the shotgun as he vaulted over the remains of the snooker table, closing the distance to his targets who snarled and sprinted towards him, faster than any human could manage. They were unarmed and ran with hands raised and hooked into claws ready to tear him apart. Demons then. The shotgun roared once and then again and Cross cursed silently as he saw the demons stumble but not fall.

One had a face that was a mask of blood, shards of bone and teeth showing through the torn flesh of its cheeks and forehead, the left eye pulped and reduced to jelly. The other had its left arm hanging by a few threads of flesh and yet still they came on, barely even slowing in their mad rush to rend the impudent human limb from limb.

There was another flurry of movement and Cross stumbled to the right as Buttons leapt past him. The little man was a blur, covering the distance to the onrushing demons in the blink of an eye. Buttons wrapped his hands around their throats, lifting them easily and then carrying on to the end of the corridor, still moving at that blistering speed as he slammed both of them headfirst into the doors.

The doors disintegrated and Buttons charged through, closely followed by Cross and Andariel. They found themselves in the main hall of the mansion. The huge room was dominated by a large stone fireplace at the northern end, bordered by a small circle of deep leather chairs. Still moving at a run, Cross quickly spied Miles and Marcus Harrington standing by the fireplace, flanked by several armed men.

Got you, you fuckers! His eyes flickered around the hall, noting distances, objects, obstructions and enemies, calculating trajectories, angles and avenues of attack in a split-second.

He cursed as he saw the mezzanine gallery running around the outside of the hall and the smirking faces that leered down at them, some, the humans he assumed, already raising their weapons and preparing to fire. A large banquet table filled the centre of the room and Cross leapt onto its polished surface without slowing.

One shot in the chamber. He fired up into the gallery to his left, the spray of shot causing human and demon alike to dive for cover. Cross dropped the shotgun and drew his glock, sending two quick shots towards the gallery on his right before sprinting the length of the table towards the Harringtons.

Andariel capitalised on the chaos and smoothly vaulted the 10 feet up to the gallery Cross had peppered with shot while the men and demons pulled themselves back to their feet. One man was still on all fours and she grinned as she landed on his back. She felt his spine and ribs splinter under her feet and blood spurted from his mouth as the jagged ends of his ribs savaged his lungs. She counted five assailants re-

, two human and three demonic. She would have preferred it the other way around but sometimes you had to take what you could get.

While the demons were infinitely more dangerous than their human counterparts the angel couldn't discount their guns. It was highly unlikely they could kill her, but they could certainly slow her down, and against three demons? Slow was as good as dead. She reached behind her, feeling the handles of the two knives she had left tucked into her belt, sliding them free and throwing them in one fluid motion. There was a sickening crunch and a gargling scream as one of the men took a knife point first in the mouth.

The blade smashed through his teeth and tore his tongue out by the root as it sunk into the back of his throat. The force of the throw saw the knife slice completely through the soft flesh of the throat to lodge inside his spine. Bone shattered, nerve endings parted and the man was suddenly a puppet with severed strings, dead before he hit the floor. The second man toppled backwards over the balcony of the gallery without a sound as Andariels' last knife tore through his eye and buried itself in his brain.

Ok, she thought. *Hand to hand with three demons in an enclosed space it is then.* As millennia of hatred boiled in their veins, angel and demon alike gave vent to animal snarls as they charged towards each other, everything else forgotten in their desire to kill their hated enemy.

Buttons leapt to the gallery on the right, forgoing finesse and simply smashing through the balustrade and driving a fist into, then through, the face of his first opponent. He shook the corpse from his dripping fist, making a claw-like motion with his other hand, causing his human opponents to yelp with surprise as their guns flew from their hands.

He rampaged through them, four hardened veterans dead in seconds as he smashed their skulls and crushed their windpipes with a flurry of devastatingly powerful and precise blows. With the humans gone only two demons remained and they blanched as they realised who, *what*, was coming for them. Lucifers' hunter, the name they whispered in fear, was real and stalking towards them with his blank and terrible button eyes radiating power and the certainty of death.

The little man wasted no time and tore into the demons, a sense of savage exultation filling him as it always did. This is what he did, what Lucifer had designed him to do. This is what he *was*. He knew the exultation would fade, soon to be followed by a profound sadness that what he was was merely a weapon, an infernal executioner whose only purpose was to kill, a sadness because he knew Lucifer had chosen him because that lust for violence, the need to inflict pain, had always been there hiding under the surface until it could glory in its release.

For now though, the exultation of battle was enough, and the little man smiled beneath his awful mask even as his hooked fingers tore the stolen face of a demon from its skull. Tonight was not a time for introspection, not when a tomorrow wasn't promised.

The demon fell and he crushed its skull under his foot as he flung the dripping ruin of its visage into the face of his last enemy. The remaining demon was blinded for a second and Buttons closed the gap between them to punch his hand through its chest and tear out its heart.

Glancing to his left he saw that Andariel was hard pressed, barely managing to defend herself from her three opponents, let alone strike back. He watched, still holding the twitching corpse of the demon and waited for the right moment. One of Andariels' attackers surged forward, sending the angel stumbling backwards, leaving his comrades a pace behind in his eagerness to kill. Buttons narrowed his eyes beneath the mask. *Now*. He threw the demons' corpse and it flew across the dining hall like a bloody comet to slam into the two demons at the back, smashing them into the wall with crushing force.

Andariels' remaining attacker made the fatal mistake

of glancing backwards at the noise and the angel stepped smartly forward to snap its neck, almost twisting its head from its shoulders. She stepped past the corpse as it fell and launched a savage kick into the throat of the demon extricating itself from the wreckage of the wall.

Even with the dark energies of the demon infusing and strengthening the body the human frame was no match for the force of Andariels' blow and the demons neck folded inwards. Its windpipe crushed, its neck shattered the demon could do nothing but glare at her as it waited for its twitching, hijacked body to fail before it was banished back to the cold dark of Hell.

The last demon had smashed deeper into the wall and still struggled to pull its broken body from the rubble. Andariel stamped down to snap its spine and send it back to Hell with the others. She grinned across the room at Buttons. All in all, this was going much better than she'd hoped for.

While Andariel and Buttons cleared the galleries, Cross had continued towards the Harringtons. If he was going to be honest he'd never expected to make it this far but here they were, in his sights and still with sneering smiles on their faces as he ran towards them with his gun raised. Something wasn't right. Although the men flanking the Harringtons were armed none of them had so much as twitched a gun in his direction. *I should be getting shot to shit by now,* he thought.

The Harringtons were an arrogant pair of pricks but nobody was *that* arrogant. He raised his gun and fired even as a sinking feeling bloomed in his stomach. Cross fired twice. They were excellent shots, particularly for a man moving at a full sprint on top of a table, and Miles' head should have been decorating the wall while Marcus suffered the indignity of a bullet tearing through his stomach and shredding his spleen, but instead the twins stood there smiling at him as the bullets just...disappeared.

If at first you don't succeed... Cross fired again, four shots this time, tightly grouped and dead centre on the two grinning faces in front of him. Once again, he might as well have been firing a cap gun at them. The men surrounding them had scrambled to avoid the shots and now looked at each other in confusion, as surprised as Cross that their employers weren't dead. Cross slowed to a halt and sighed as what was Marcus Harrington laughed in delight. "Mr Cross," he crowed "It's a pleasure to finally meet you in the flesh."

"Malleus." Cross said as the unwelcome penny dropped. He'd known Malleus was here but he hadn't expected to see him wearing Marcus's flesh. The demon lord laughed again and spread his arms as an invitation for Cross to admire him. "The one and only. Marcus sends his apologies for not being here in person, at least I'm sure he would want to." Malleus made a face and tapped a forefinger on the side of his head. "He hasn't stopped screaming yet and its becoming rather tiresome."

Cross ignored him and looked at Miles. "I always knew you were a snide little shit, Miles but I didn't think you'd sell out your own brother to this arsehole."

Miles glared at him while Malleus laughed at the insult. "Shut your mouth, Cross!" snarled Miles. "You haven't got a clue what's really going on here!" Cross grinned at him. "Malleus is planning to burn down creation while you lurk about in the background being an unpleasant little cunt as usual. Does that cover it?"

Malleus laughed even harder at that. He looked past Cross to where Buttons and Andariel cautiously edged towards them. "Andariel, how nice to see you, and in such a fetching body too!" The demon lord ignored any reply she might have been about to make and turned his attention to Buttons. "And here you are," he sneered. "The hunter. The living proof that our master is nothing more than Heavens' lackey after all." Malleus looked critically at him. "I must say I thought you'd be taller."

Buttons said nothing, just removed his mask which caused a couple of the men surrounding the demon lord to visibly relax. One of them looked at Malleus and Miles. "What the fucking hell is going on here Marcus?!" barked the mercenary and Cross laughed. He knew the man who had spoken. "You're really playing for the wrong team this time, Gary. Marcus definitely isn't the man he used to be. If I were you I'd get out while you still can."

"Don't start mouthing off, Danny. You're in no position to be telling anyone what to do! Keep your trap shut before I put a bullet in you."

"Fair enough," said Cross. "It's your funeral, mate." Gary and his men were clearly off balance and Cross realised that not only were they either looking at each other or at the thing that used to be their employer, but in all the confusion they seemed to have forgotten he was still holding a gun.

Four shots left. Might as well have a go. Four shots rang out and four men dropped dead as the last of the unfortunate Tony's hollow point rounds blew fist sized holes into them. Cross didn't think Malleus would have extended whatever protection he'd raised around himself and Miles to the hired help, and he'd been right.

Miles cowered at the gunshots but Malleus simply raised an eyebrow. "Petty" he said.

Cross shrugged and dropped the empty weapon. "Yeah well I'm like that sometimes." Despite his calm, almost unconcerned tone, Cross was worried. This was all going far too smoothly, if you considered facing off against a demon lord as going smoothly anyway.

If he was honest with himself he didn't even think they'd make it this far, let alone get here without a scratch. Either Malleus was very good at concealing his emotions, if he had any that Cross might recognise, or he was supremely confident and assured despite standing alone against the three of them.

The demon lord smiled. "You're both right and wrong, Mr Cross." Cross scowled as he realised the creature had read his thoughts. "I am indeed confident but I'm certainly not alone." Cross sighed and turned to see Lincoln, the Cobleys and what remained of their coven file into the room followed by at least a dozen men or demons. At this point Cross didn't think it mattered too much which they were.

"Hello Linc', he said and Lincoln Barnes inclined his head. "Daniel. Well done, well done indeed. I always knew you were good but I never expected you to cause us this much trouble."

Cross grinned. "I haven't finished yet." Malleus laughed again and looked at Miles. "And here you thought Mr Cross was just a run-of-the-mill thug, Miles." The demon tutted in reproach. "Even now he's running a dozen scenarios through his head, calculating the best options for killing us all. He's not even thinking about getting out alive, just about finishing what he started." Malleus shook his head. "Remarkable really."

He looked curiously at Cross. "Perhaps too remarkable just to kill out of hand?"

"Really, Malleus, I must protest!" Miles was outraged at the suggestion. It was bad enough that someone like Lincoln Barnes, who despite the tastefully expensive clothes and veneer of gentility he'd cultivated would always be nothing more than an inner-city ruffian, was held in such esteem by the demon lord, but to give a dangerous thug like Cross a place in the new order they were to create was just insulting.

Malleus looked coldly at him. "No, Miles, you really mustn't." Surprisingly it was Lincoln that came to Miles' defence. "I'm forced to agree with Miles," he said. "Not out of animosity you understand. Daniel is simply too dangerous to be left alive." Malleus cocked an eyebrow at him. "You don't think what we have to offer would win him to our side?" he asked and Cross barked a laugh.

"Offer me what? Ringside seats to watch the universe burn down and that little prick", he jerked a thumb at Miles, "going on a killing spree? Not much of an offer is it?"

The lord of hell smiled. "Ah yes, I assume that's what she told you?" he asked, nodding his head at Andariel, "that I want to destroy it all just for the hell of it, if you'll pardon the expression?" Malleus shook his head, a look of artfully feigned hurt on his stolen face. "Do you really think I'd do all this for the sake of something as prosaic as Armageddon?"

"Not sure you and I have the same understanding of what 'prosaic' means but yeah, pretty much."

Malleus frowned at Andariel. "You always did think the worst of me." Andariel looked at him with contempt. "Do I think you're a scheming, duplicitous and murderous stain on the face of creation that should be wiped away like a steaming shit? Yes, I do."

Malleus ignored the insult. "Try and see past your own narrow hatreds and actually use those stunted intellects. Armageddon is simply a means, not an end. Do you seriously think I'd be content to spend eternity strolling through the ash and broken bones of creation?" He gestured towards Andariel. "You know what I can do. You remember what I used to be."

Andariels' face turned pale. "You're even more insane than I thought!"

Cross didn't like the sound of this, whatever it was. He glanced at Buttons to see he wore the same horrified expression that Andariel did. "Buttons, what's going on? What does he mean?"

Buttons looked at Malleus and then at Cross. "Before the fall and the war of hosts, Malleus was an archangel, one of the Prime Council."

"And as one of the Prime Council I was one of the architects, one of the builders." Said Malleus as he continued the explanation.

"Builder of what?" asked Cross even as he guessed the answer with a sinking feeling.

"Of worlds, Mr Cross. Lucifer ignited the stars while I created the worlds that dance around them. What, you thought God did it all on his own?" Malleus sneered. "The doddering old fool would have accomplished *nothing* without me!"

The demon lord glared at them all. "None of this, none

of *you* would stand here if not for me! Who is to say I can't destroy what I made? Who is to say I can't make it again, and make it *better*?" Malleus didn't wait for an answer as he continued his tirade. "I've languished in that prison for millennia and watched the worlds I made fall into chaos and ruin, seen them abandoned to chance, left to the mercy of the idiocy that is free will! There should be order and precision, not blind luck masquerading as fate.

"God as the lord of all creation? God with his boundless love for all his discarded children? God is a sick joke, nothing more! Where is God when 'his' creation teeters on the precipice? Where is he when countless billions of his precious children are about to die in fire and agony?" He stopped and looked at them almost sadly. "Where is he when you need his help?"

Andariel surprised them all by laughing. "Nice try, dickhead." She shook her head. "You'll never get it will you? It doesn't matter if God has left us all alone, in fact I couldn't give a shit if he's gone for good or watching all this with a bowl of popcorn to see what happens next. He's not important right now." The angel shrugged. "Maybe he never was." Andariel gestured to Cross and Buttons. "This is what's important. My friends."

She widened her gesture to use both arms. "All those people out there that we'll never meet and who'll never know or care what we did to try and save them, not just on this world but on all of them, whether they're good or bad."

She sneered at him. "Whatever they are they all deserve a better end to it all than you throwing a tantrum because Daddy locked you in your room and took your toys away. That's why we're going to burn this whole thing down around you and make you eat the fucking ashes!" Cross looked at her and smiled. *Good on you, girl.* This time it was Malleus who surprised them with his laughter. "Ah, Andariel. If only more of my former kin were like you. Creation would be a lot more fun."

As the demon lord spoke, Cross caught movement in his peripheral vision. Lincoln, the Cobleys, the coven and the dozen or so demons moved to surround them in a semicircle. Cross thought back to the dozens of battles and hundreds of smaller, more personal fights he'd survived and wondered if he'd ever faced odds like this before. He smiled inside. *Stupid fucking question.*

He almost gave the game away as a voice sounded in his head but managed to keep his face straight. After all, it wasn't the first time that had happened. *"Daniel,"* whispered Buttons into his mind, *"Leave the Cobleys to me. I'll try and draw in most of the demons too."* Cross felt the little man's smile. *"They'll be itching to take a shot at me."*

"I'll take Malleus" Cross wasn't surprised to hear Andariels' voice but he'd never heard it sound with such cold resolve. Andariel didn't hate Malleus because he was a demon, that was just a word, a name the apostates of heaven had been given. She hated him because of what he used to be: her brother. You could only truly hate someone you once loved after all.

"Think you can take him? Him being an ex-archangel and all?" he asked with concern. Andariels' reply was a curious mix of wry acceptance and tightly controlled fear and Cross cursed himself for asking. They all knew the odds of Andariel defeating Malleus were slim to almost non-existent *"We'll find out in a second. It's a bit late to start worrying about me now, Cross".*

Cross was about to apologise when Buttons spoke again and Cross heard what sounded like a weary resignation in his voice. *"We're going to have to go all-out just to stay alive and that much noise is going to be noticed. I hate the idea we might have come this far just to end up doing the bastards' job for him and kick-starting the Apocalypse."*

"Nothing we can do about it now, Reverend." Cross was matter of fact, almost distant. He was already sliding into the eerie state of calm that enveloped him before a fight. The fate

of creation didn't concern him anymore. They'd done all they could. His only focus now was on killing every single one of his enemies.

The future was a heartbeat and a million miles away and would have to look after itself. *"We've done more than anyone could have asked."* Buttons and Andariel felt his smile, felt the bond, the *love* he felt for them and were comforted by it. *"I never imagined I'd end up going out like this, but going down fighting for something that actually means something? With you two? A soldier couldn't ask for more than that."*

Cross looked at his two friends. "Now let's kill the fuckers."

TWENTY SIX

His name was Glomf. It wasn't much of a name, but then Glomf wasn't much of a demon. Glomf hadn't been much of an angel either. When the cosmos was being woven together and the stars sung into life, when the boundless worlds were being spun into shape and life took its first, faltering steps Glomf was there. Tidying up. Glomf had spent the first few million years of his existence following his brethren around the cosmos with what amounted to a celestial broom to sweep away all the detritus left from the construction of a few billion galaxies.

If any angel had been ripe to join the great rebellion it was Glomf. Under the aegis of Lucifer Morningstar, the second most powerful being in creation, Glomf and his brethren had risen against the tyranny of servitude and predestination, thrown off the shackles of their endless labours as their voices rose in chants of war rather than hymns of praise. Millions, *billions*, of the host had fallen upon the walls of heaven itself in this first and greatest war, the conflict that would engulf entire galaxies and reshape creation itself.

The war where Glomf found himself still tidying up. The great and glorious rebellion largely passed Glomf by as he scurried behind his more powerful brethren, running their errands and taking their orders much as he had always done. This time it was different though, or so he told himself. This time his labours were for his own ends and not the cold bidding of his cruel and remote father. Glomf was proud to serve the rebellion in any way he could and when victory was theirs and their enslavement ended they would finally be free!

Free to…what exactly? Glomf had served for so long the thought of such boundless freedom actually scared him and so when Michael and Gabriel had rallied the armies of heaven to smash the rebellion and subdue their treacherous brother, Glomf found he wasn't too disappointed. Their glorious rebellion ended with them chained in manacles of cold, holy fire. Endless rows of treasonous angels, stripped of their armour and with their proud wings clipped, knelt in defeat before Michael and the Prime Council, all of them naked, bound and helpless.

All except Lucifer. The star of the morning still shone brightly, even against the light of Michael and Gabriel. He stood with his brothers as they stared down upon the massed ranks of his broken army. The brothers spoke for some time. Glomf couldn't hear what was said but thought he saw Lucifers' bright wings sag, just a fraction and just for a second, as though the lord of the morning, the adversary, the great dragon and the spear of suns had almost buckled under the weight of a vast burden. The brothers had bowed to each other before Lucifer turned to face the angels that had followed him in his doomed attempt to topple heaven.

"I am sorry", was all he said, but in those three words swelled an ocean of sadness. Lucifer Morningstar raised his hands and as simply as that, with no ceremony or dour drama, the rebellious angels were banished to hell for all eternity. Hell was dark and cold, a vast and almost featureless tundra shrouded in gloom and carpeted by an endless fall of ash and snow.

As one the fallen angels cried out and fell to their knees on the cold dirt as they felt something tear loose from inside them. Their connection to heaven and their creator, their father, was ripped away and for the first time in their existence the angels knew what it was to feel alone. Their proud wings darkened, drooped and then fell away. Their skin lost its glow as the light of paradise sputtered and died within them.

Some simply broke, falling to the ground and weeping as the pain of their sudden isolation overwhelmed them. Some of those lay there weeping still, consumed by a grief so total it had lasted eons. Others became frenzied with rage and the cold despair of their excommunication was engulfed in fury as they suddenly fell upon their equally doomed brethren with bestial savagery. The first blood spilled in hell was that of angels.

Glomf had run, dodging this way and that and thankful that he still remained beneath the notice of his more powerful brothers and sisters. Was this what his father intended then? That his rebellious children be consumed by hatred and madness in this cold, dark place so far from heaven? Glomf ran blindly as tears streamed down his face and would have run for eternity in the limitless confinement of this prison had *he* not arrived.

As one the host of fallen angels were held immobile as they were wrapped in a power so great as to be almost unimaginable. Lucifer hung above them in the dark sky on his vast and shining wings. The Morningstar still shone. He cast the only light in this terrible place and many of the angels wept anew as they felt the warmth of heaven wash over them once more. Lucifer, once first among heaven and now lord of the fallen silently surveyed his bleak kingdom and his scorned and broken brothers. A single, shining tear rolled down his perfect cheek.

Lucifer had explained the new role they were to play in their fathers' ineffable plan and Glomf had shaken his head in wonder at the sublime barbarity of their punishment. They were to be jailers, even as they themselves were inmates. Their existence was to be defined by the pain and agony they could inflict on those the creator found wanting. The angels, the architects of creation itself were to become beings dedicated to destruction in all its forms, forever banished from heaven yet forever bent to its will.

The fallen angels, most of them at least, had wailed and wept and raged at the perversity of their punishment and what their vengeful father would turn them into. There were others who now relished the thought of an eternity inflicting pain and sowing deceit and discord through their fathers' precious cosmos, their pain already solidifying into a core of hatred and malice.

Willing or unwilling the fallen had begun their work as soon as intelligent life had appeared and the first being spilled unjust blood. Contrary to what many of the established religions across the cosmos preached it wasn't that easy to get into hell. Eternal punishment was reserved for the more significant crimes, but even so there was still an unending supply of mortals seemingly bent on joining them in their cold prison.

They coaxed and cajoled, promised and lied and set countless beings on the path to damnation, relishing their screams and drinking deeply of their despair as they arrived on the cold tundra of hell. At least, most of them did. Glomf tidied up.

Over the millennia, Glomf had watched his brothers slowly change. Even those who had railed the hardest at their degradation were twisted into cruel shadows of their former selves. They became empty things, hollow vessels sustained only by their unceasing hatred. Their hatred of heaven and the angels, of the billions of bright, living worlds and the stunted beings that happily swarmed throughout the cosmos *they* had built.

If they hated angels and mortals then they hated their fellows even more, and the denizens of hell constantly plotted and schemed against each other as they vied for the cold comfort of power and domination.

Glomf stayed away from it all as much as he could and over the endless years had become a master at remaining inconspicuous. He doubted many of his fellows even knew he existed, let alone knew his name, and that suited Glomf just fine. Perhaps the only being in hell more elusive than Glomf was Lucifer himself. Once he had imparted the awful news of their new role in things, Lucifer had raised a city, a solitary, useless and perversely empty city and retreated inside. While their master was rarely seen in the flesh all the denizens of hell could feel him. His power was such that even in the limitless confines of hell it pulsed and shone like a beacon made from a million suns.

Over the interminable eons the fallen angels carved out their own hierarchy. They soon realised that as long as they carried out their assigned purpose and didn't break the few but immutable rules Lucifer had put in place, their master was content to leave them to their own devices. There had been transgressions of course. By their very nature it was impossible for demons not to try and subvert, bend or fragrantly break the rules, but when such transgressions came to light, and they *always* came to light eventually, then their master would appear and his cold wrath and the agonising punishment he dealt the transgressor was enough to cow them, for a while at least.

Remote the Morningstar may have been but there was no doubt who ruled in hell.

Glomf had borne witness to some of these punishments and seen his fellows inflict more pain on each other than they ever did the damned, and every time he saw such things it reinforced his determination to remain as invisible as he could. This tactic had served him well over the millennia and it had even become a game of sorts.

A game that, as he picked himself up from the floor and looked towards the nearby crater that housed a burning, screaming soul, Glomf realised he was finally about to lose.

TWENTY SEVEN

All was chaos and screams and blood as the battle raged. Cross dropped another opponent with a crushing elbow to the side of the head and immediately skipped backwards to avoid more blows from the remaining three, one punch slipping past his guard and snapping his head back as it glanced from his cheekbone.

He didn't even feel the pain, the sensation walled off by the rush of adrenalin coursing through his system. To Cross the blow was just targeting data. It told him where his opponent was. It told him the position of his body, right arm moving back to guard the face after delivering the blow but still extended. Still in reach. Cross surged forward and grasped the arm just above the hand.

His opponent tried to pull back but Cross was too strong. A swift and savage twist ended in a wet snap as Cross broke the mercenaries' wrist. Cross felt a jagged end of bone press into his hand and blood flowed over his fingers as the shattered ulna tore through skin.

Cross grinned at the scream and threw the mercenary into the path of the other two, causing them to stumble backwards. Movement behind and a cold pain flared across his shoulders.

Miles and his straight razor. *The little prick.* The wound wasn't deep but Cross knew it would be a bleeder. Razor cuts always were and during a long fight it would steadily sap his strength. Razor wounds could also take weeks to heal up properly and had a tendency to keep splitting open again unless you were very careful or glued them shut. Cross smiled grimly to himself. That wasn't likely to be a problem for him.

He threw a quick elbow back which didn't connect as Miles had already slipped back out of range. Cross was unconcerned. The blow wasn't meant to land, just to let Miles know he knew he was there and to keep him out of the way for a few seconds while he concentrated on his two remaining opponents. He could see Lincoln out of the corner of his eye. Lincoln was hanging back as well, cradling his carbine and watching the fight. Cross's inward smile turned to a grimace.

No flies on Lincoln Barnes. He knew he didn't have to get his hands dirty and they both knew that he could decide to use that carbine and end this fight very quickly if he wanted to. Lincoln was definitely going to be a problem and no way Cross was going down before he'd settled up for Gus and Kate.

Ok then, if you don't like the game then don't play. Cross spun, ignoring the two men in front of him and barrelling towards Miles instead. The smile was back on his face and he saw Miles pale at the sight of his charge as the little man realised Cross was gunning for him now. Miles turned and tried to run but Cross was too fast and too strong.

He didn't even slow down as he picked Miles up and then carried on running towards Barnes. Miles flailed with the razor but Cross ignored the wound that opened his cheek to the bone and grinned through the blood as he hurled Miles towards Lincoln. Instinctively, Barnes raised his weapon but hesitated in case he hit Miles. The split second of indecision cost him and he was too slow to duck aside. Miles hammered into him and they both crashed to the floor.

Cross turned again, his face a mask of blood, to find the last two men on his heels. The older mercenary was grim-faced, and he moved with the spare economy of veteran fighters, conserving every ounce of strength until he needed it. The younger one bobbed and weaved, grinning savagely with the thrill of the fight. Cross remembered being like that once, and remembered getting his arse handed to him a few times before he learned that strength and speed were only half the battle.

The mercenaries tore into him and Cross weathered a

flurry of blows to his face and body. The razor cut on his face split further under the onslaught and he hissed in pain, spraying a mist of blood through the wound in his cheek. The older merc was a problem. His strikes were far too precise, and Cross was starting to tire. He knew he was only seconds away from taking an incapacitating blow. He had to get rid of him quickly but there was no way he could break his guard down while dealing with the younger goon too. *If in doubt, fight dirty.* Cross spat a mouthful of blood directly into the older mans' face.

The merc coughed and spat and dropped his guard to wipe the blood from his eyes. Cross sacrificed his own guard to grab the man with both hands and haul him into a crushing headbutt. The mercenary's face virtually imploded with the force of the blow and the man roared in agony as his left eye burst in its shattered socket. He was out of the game for now and Cross dropped him to the floor.

A hammer blow to his back as his last opponent slammed a punch into his kidneys. The punch was followed up by a savage kick into the back of the knee and Cross's leg folded. The young mercenary smiled in triumph and moved back a step. Cross read his intent and knew the lad was going to try and put him down with another kick, this time to the head. *Daft bastard.*

Kicks to anything above knee height in a real fight were a gamble, no matter how much Jackie Chan you'd watched. You had to be amazingly quick and precise to land a solid kick to the head and that sort of move was best left for when your opponent was already down or dazed. Cross was a long way from either. He caught the kick as it came in and surged upright, twisting the ankle he held even as he stamped down into the side of the lad's knee on his other leg.

The right ankle shattered with a sickening crunch and Cross broke his opponent's left leg and tore the knee from its socket with the force of his kick. He'd walk with a limp for the rest of his life. If he lived through the night. The boy writhed on the floor, the pain too much to even scream and

Cross turned his attention back to the veteran who, *fair play to him*, was trying to struggle to his feet. Cross stamped down hard on his head. Once, twice and then the older merc stopped moving.

Dead? Unconscious? Cross didn't care which, only that he was out of the way. *Six down, two to go and then it's just a lord of hell and half a dozen demons to worry about.* Cross was starting to feel the pain of his wounds now and he knew he didn't have long before the blood he was losing became a problem. Whatever else might happen he was going to make Miles eat that fucking razor. *Ok, let's get this done.*

Cross turned to find himself staring down the barrel of Lincoln's carbine.

TWENTY EIGHT

Buttons was covered from head to toe in blood, none of it his. When the battle was joined the first to engage him were, surprisingly, the remaining members of the Cobley's coven. Kerry, Jonny, even the obese Solange, charged towards him with clawed, outstretched hands. Their teeth lengthened and sharpened as they became fangs and their eyes glowed as they tapped into their master's dark energies. He felt waves of force batter him as they flung their power outwards, combining their strength to try and crush him by sheer brutality.

Buttons shrugged off their attacks. He could have turned their force against them and returned their assault tenfold but instead he slipped through the battering waves of sickly, entropic power, moving slowly and calmly towards his prey. The corpulent Solange screamed in outrage, an ululating wail that shouldn't have issued from a human throat. The huge woman moved with sudden and surprising speed, barrelling towards the little man like a nightmarish locomotive, eager to tear him limb from limb and feast on his flesh.

Buttons swatted her aside with contemptuous ease, barely breaking his implacable stride towards the Cobleys. Solange hurtled into the wall, her heavy frame and the force of Button's strike smashing her into the brickwork and halfway into the adjoining room. The small man gestured, still not deigning to look at her and she screamed again as she felt his power crushing down and grinding her into the floor.

The pressure grew and grew and Solange screamed again, this time an animal sound of terror and pain as she felt bones fracture and tendons pop, and knew that his assault would not relent. Tears rolled from her eyes as the pressure on her skull built in intensity. Her eye sockets cracked and then shattered, bursting the bulging orbs of her eyes like eggs. Solange's screams became a gurgling wheeze as her throat closed and blood bubbled from her mouth as her broken ribs drove into her lungs. Buttons snapped his fingers and the unearthly pressure intensified with catastrophic force. He grinned at the Cobleys as Solange's remains sprayed across the room.

His smile faded as a sudden doubt assailed him. Why was he smiling? He'd just crushed a human being alive, stolen her life, her future and any chance of her redemption, condemning her to an eternity of torment. As always, he chose to inflict pain and terror than take the higher, harder path of forgiveness.

He was weak, he'd always been weak. His anger and desire to inflict pain still controlled him as it always had. *She* had known this, his long-dead love, she'd always known this and feared him as much as she loved him. Even though she had died in such cruel fear and terrible pain was part of her not glad that she was finally free of him?

The demon hunter snarled and shook off the insidious, distracting thoughts being slipped into his mind. There was a sudden movement to his right and his hand shot out to grab Kerry by the throat as she leapt towards him. Buttons simply clenched his fist. Kerry didn't even have time to scream as the bones in her neck were crushed into powder. Still holding the rag-doll shape in his hand, Buttons nodded towards Jonny. "Nice try, boy. You really don't want to get inside my head though."

He dropped Kerry's twitching corpse and continued his steady march towards the watching Cobleys. Buttons could feel Jonny retreating from his head to ready another assault. He didn't let him go. He dragged the boy deeper and deeper into his mind, towards the locked and hidden place where he held centuries of his pain and rage in check.

Jonny screamed as wave after wave of anguish and fury flayed his mind. Buttons' mouth was a grim line as he lashed the young disciple of Hell with the murder of his betrothed and family, the agonies he'd inflicted on those responsible, with hundreds of years of killing, of loneliness and self-loathing.

The little man lived all those memories again, felt all that pain again as he poured it into Jonny's mind. As the young chosen fell to the floor, sobbing and wailing in borrowed agony, his mind a torn and broken thing, Buttons smiled. *Worth it.*

The Cobleys were surrounded by the last of Malleus's demons who roared as they ran towards this man, this *thing* created by the Morningstar to keep them caged, this mortal upstart who not only dared wield the power of Hell but had used it to destroy hundreds of their kin.

They stopped short, slamming into an invisible wall as Buttons wrapped them in his power. The demons snarled and struggled and then whimpered as they felt that power moving *through* them, slipping inside the mortal frames they wore and wrapping round bones and organs, muscles and tendons. Buttons tore savagely at the strands of his power and the demons blew apart.

While the shower of torn flesh and gore might have looked impressive it was still a quiet display of power and the Cobley's grinned at each other as they realised he was still holding back. Mr Cobley turned his leer to Buttons. "Why so coy, hunter?" he sneered. "Do you think you'll be able to face *us*, here in the presence of our master, in the wellspring of his power without a full unveiling of your own?" The cadaverous warlock laughed. "Surely you must know that even if you can defeat us you'll lose?"

Buttons smiled. They'd given him the answer he'd been too stupid to see until now. *Here in the presence of our master, In the wellspring of his power eh? Who talks like that?! 'Here' was the problem, wasn't it? So, let's take here out of the equation.* The little man launched himself at the Cobleys, moving faster than the eye could see and crashing into them with thunderous force. A portal bloomed in the air behind them and the demon hunter and chosen of Malleus, already locked in a vicious struggle, vanished from the face of the earth.

TWENTY NINE

Fuck, fuck, fuck!

Andariel backpedalled furiously as Malleus launched another flurry of blows. She managed to slip past some of them but others simply blasted through her defences and sent her skidding across the floor. Andariel was tiring fast and her borrowed human body hurt in at least a dozen places. She looked up at the demon lord, her brother, smiling down at her without a hair out of place. They both knew the only reason Andariel was still alive was because he'd chosen not to kill her yet.

Malleus was enjoying himself enormously. He could have destroyed her in a thousand different ways but, and he was almost loathe to admit it to himself, punching someone in the face was surprisingly satisfying. He could see why it was such a popular pastime amongst mortals. Andariel scrambled to her feet and Malleus moved, lightning fast, to land several punishing blows that sent her crashing to the floor again.

Andariel felt ribs break and something felt like it popped inside her stomach as she doubled up and screamed in pain.

The demon lord looked at her and winced. "Oh dear, I think I've ruptured your spleen. Does it feel as painful as it looks?"

"Fuck off," Andariel growled from the floor. "Come down here and I'll show you how painful it is."

Malleus tutted. "Language! What would dear old daddy have to say?" He sneered. "Then again, you were never one of his favourites, were you?" Andariel bit down on her agony, spat blood and forced herself to her feet. She doubted she had the strength to land a blow, even if Malleus wasn't so fast but then she didn't need to. She just had to stay on her feet, to stay alive for long enough. *Time. I just have to play for time and keep him busy.* It was a race now. Would Lucifer get their message in Hell or would Heaven hear the earthly commotion and unleash the host first?

The demon lord raised his hands to strike her again and then smiled. No, he wouldn't kill her. He knew she'd held back from using her full power in a vain attempt to shield their conflict from the watchdogs in Heaven, although even if she had she could never have won this fight. Malleus looked at the bloodied and broken angel swaying before him and smiled again. Andariel was always going to lose this fight, but why not make sure her defeat really *hurt*?

Malleus opened his clenched fists and snapped his fingers. Andariel screamed in fresh agony as spears of solid rock erupted from the ground beneath her. Thin, jagged and razor sharp they tore through her arms at the wrists and hoisted her from the floor with arms outstretched.

Snap.

Two more burst through the soles of her feet and there she hung like a bloody Vitruvian man.

Snap.

The spears became hot, molten, and Malleus laughed as Andariel's borrowed flesh blackened and charred. It was a vulgar, almost childish display of power but, more importantly, twisting and subverting the natural world like this was always noisy.

The angel sobbed as she felt the waves of the demon lord's power pulse through the air, through her torn flesh and bruised bones. She closed her eyes and looked at Malleus with her other senses. He was a dark beacon, a coruscating nova of spite and malice. His power twisted and roiled in tendrils that dug far into the earth, into the bones of the universe, staining and corrupting it. Malleus had become a lodestone, an inescapable siren song to Heaven and she wept as she realised that they'd got so close and come this far only to fail.

Far, far away amidst impossibly tall and shining spires, where the bright suns never set, and the air was cold and rook-delighting, the sickly bloom of power swept darkly across a place that had never known darkness.

There in that place where creation itself was conceived the angels felt the vile touch of Hell and turned golden, burning eyes towards the Earth.

THIRTY

The damned were let fall to the cold ground, suddenly forgotten and left to hang on their hooks and crosses. They wept at this miraculous release from their agonies as their tormentors turned as one towards the burning, screaming comet that tore through the dark skies to smash into the tundra with a thunderous crash.

Eventually the echoes faded and above the whimpers and sobbing of the damned could be heard a screaming unlike any ever heard in this most desolate place. Not a scream of pain or terror or the throaty roar of a helpless and despairing rage but a scream of urgency, a mantra in a now foreign but still familiar tongue.

The demons, countless millions of them, walked towards this anomaly, straining to hear the almost forgotten words. Suddenly the screaming stopped and as one so did the demons, some looking at their fellows in confusion, some with even what might be called sadness in their eyes as this strange, *new*, thing fell silent.

A second passed, then two seconds. Two seconds in an eternity where Hell fell silent for the first time since the fall. Then the screaming mantra started again, and the demon horde ran towards the sound, wanting to see this new thing, to touch or even hold this thing that should never have been here, here where things never changed and were never new.

As they drew closer some began to make out words, then fractured phrases and others, the creatures of Malleus, shouldered their brethren out of the way as they began to run faster, realising what this was and the ruin it could bring to their master's plan, to their escape from this dreadful place and their vengeance on Heaven.

By the crater, the dazed Glomf picked himself up from the ground. He spared only the swiftest of glances towards the writhing, screaming light. Glomf couldn't understand what it was saying and had no interest in whatever it was or what it meant. All Glomf knew was that this thing would bring every creature in Hell swarming here. All Glomf knew was that he had to get as far away from this unwelcome noise and light and back to the concealing dark as fast as he could.

Glomf looked away from the light and began to run. The little demon stopped short and sighed as he saw the endless ranks of demons charging towards the crater. Towards him. He watched as his fallen kin began to fight, to tear and claw at each other even as they ran, those that fell trampled to a smear under the pounding talons of their brothers. The ground shook and Glomf cowered as he watched the wall of roaring, biting, spitting demons thunder towards him. Glomf closed his eyes and waited for the end.

A light, bright enough to shine through the closed lids of his eyes flared and the screams and roars and pounding of feet were silenced by a single, quiet word.
"Enough."

Slowly, Glomf opened his eyes, raising his trembling hands to ward off the terrible and revealing light. As the glare faded, Glomf saw the multitudes of his brothers frozen in mid stride. Above them all the Morningstar hung in the air on his vast and shining wings. Lucifer folded those impossible wings and dropped gracefully to the ground beside the little demon. He glanced at the cowering Glomf with an amused expression.

"Still alive eh, Glomf?" was all he said and Glomf shuddered, not sure whether to be ecstatic or horrified that Lucifer knew who he was. The Morningstar moved past him to stare down into the crater. He listened to the screaming messenger, the burning soul that used to be Doctor Chandra Singh, for a few seconds before silencing it with a wave of his hand.

Glomf saw his shoulders shaking and he realised that Lucifer was laughing.

"You clever bastard", the Devil said, and then he disappeared.

THIRTY ONE

Mr and Mrs Cobley fell from the portal, rolling as they hit the ground and displaying a surprising agility as they got quickly to their feet. Buttons came through a split-second after them and landed lightly on his feet a few metres away.

Mr Cobley looked around at the empty, lifeless world around them and smiled. "Very clever. It won't help you though, or them. Our master has probably already killed your friends and once we've killed you we'll be back to watch it all burn."

"And they'll all burn, dear", purred Mrs Cobley, "All of them will, even this lifeless rock. We'll burn it just because we can."

Buttons shook his head. *I'm looking forward to killing them just to shut them up.* "You talk too much."

Mr Cobley laughed. "Perhaps you're right. Very well then, it looks like your last conversation will be brief and," Mr Cobley smirked, "to the point." The cadaverous Mr Cobley gestured sharply, and large swathes of the planets rocky surface erupted around them. Huge slabs of rock and earth tore from the ground and then shattered into thousands of razor sharp shards.

They hung in the air for a fraction of a second before hurtling towards Buttons.

The little man held up a hand and the deadly storm of shards shattered against a wall of pure force. Buttons dropped his shield and moved, lightning fast, through the last fragments of stone, ignoring those few that cut into him as he barrelled towards Mr Cobley. The gangly chosen moved, just as fast, leaping aside even as he threw out his hands and buffeted the demon hunter with a wave of energy, a wave that sent Buttons stumbling into a perfectly timed punch from the cackling Mrs Cobley.

Buttons flew backwards with the force of the blow, leaving a furrow in the earth as he landed and slid to a halt. He rose to his feet and rubbed his aching jaw. *That actually hurt.* The Cobleys laughed, revelling in the fight and they reached out to each other with their minds, joining them so they thought and moved as one. This was what made them so dangerous. Not just their power, but how they could use that power. Two beings of terrifying strength becoming separate parts of a lethal whole.

Waves of sickly power hammered and pummelled Buttons, throwing him this way and that and each time he was met with a punishing blow from Mr or Mrs Cobley. Over the furious storm of unleashed power, Buttons heard the eerie sound of them laughing the same laugh as they batted him between them like a tennis ball.

Enough.

Buttons gathered his own strength and suddenly burst through the dominating waves of energy. He moved almost faster than the eye could see, first grabbing Mr Cobley and then his snarling wife. The little man bunched his legs beneath him and then leapt effortlessly into the dark sky. They kept going, up and up, a thousand feet and more until Buttons flung the Chosen back to the ground with all of his strength.

He fell behind them, smiling as he heard the sonic booms as the Cobleys broke the sound barrier with the speed of their descent. Almost on top of that sound, so fast were they falling, came a thunderous detonation as they crashed into the ground. Buttons landed lightly at the edge of the crater and peered down through the haze of dust to inspect his handiwork.

The Cobleys lay amongst the shattered earth in a butchers' pile of savaged flesh and splattered blood and Buttons smiled as he borrowed one of Cross's favourite words.

Wankers. His smile faded as he saw one, then both of them begin to move. He watched in growing alarm as torn flesh began to mend and skewed limbs moved back into place with a grinding, snapping sound as bones began to knit back together. Finally, the Cobleys stood and smiled up at him through masks of blood.

"Really, dear," purred Mrs Cobley as she patted her hair back into place, "you didn't think we'd die *that* easily did you?"

Buttons narrowed his eyes. "How?" he asked. "Malleus wouldn't give you that sort of power. He might be insane but he's not stupid."

Mr Cobley shook his head. "How disappointing. All those centuries of life, all those worlds you've visited, and still so parochial." Mrs Cobley joined in the laughter. "Do you really think we'd be content just to serve that arrogant fool for eternity? She stopped and looked at Buttons in genuine surprise. "Do you really think that Angels and Demons are the only powers in creation?" Mr Cobley laughed. "Indeed, did you think that *creation* is all there is?"

Buttons thought back and remembered the whispering, hissing things in the void, things that lived where nothing should live, things that lived in *nothingness* and the little Demon hunter was filled with dread. "You fools, what have you done?"

The Cobleys laughed and began to walk up the craters' slope towards him. "We've taken power where it was offered, dear," giggled Mrs Cobley, "It doesn't matter who wins Malleus's childish little war. Whoever is left will be in no shape to stop what comes next, to stop *us*!"

Mr Cobley looked at Buttons with mock sympathy. "Oh, there's no need to worry yourself about it all little man, you won't be there to see it." They continued their slow, steady walk towards him. "You can't stop us, I'm not even sure we *can* die now, can we my dove?" Mrs Cobley giggled. "Why ever would we want to do that?"

Buttons stepped back as they reached the lip of the

crater. Perhaps they were right. Maybe he couldn't kill them. He thought of Cross and Andariel, wondering if they were still alive, wondering if the war of the hosts raged even now, far from this barren rock in a dead galaxy. He wondered if he would die here in this place, this place that nobody even knew existed.

This place that nobody even knew existed.

The Cobleys stopped as Buttons suddenly smiled at them. "You're right", he shrugged, "I probably can't kill you. I don't need to kill you to stop you though." With that he dove forward, grabbing the Cobleys and pulling them into an embrace. They tumbled down the slope of the crater and Buttons snared them tightly in his own power, hoping that the Devil's strength was enough.

Buttons hammered at the ground beneath them and he pulled them all down, down and further down. The chosen struggled against him and he snarled in pain and anger as they battered him again and again. His snarl became a scream as their power tore into him and his nose and ears streamed blood as he was crushed by the titanic pressures of the earth and the Chosen's attacks. He ignored the agony and pushed on through the cold dark, down and down until finally the cold dark began to warm.

The Chosen redoubled their efforts to escape as they realised what he had planned, and Buttons screamed again as bones shattered under the fury of their onslaught, but he refused to let go. He ignored the pain, ignored his broken body, focusing only on what he had to do and what would happen if he failed. The warmth grew until the heat made their clothes smoulder and skin blister.

Buttons ignored it all and pushed on.

They burst through the mantle into the outer core, into a roiling, blinding sea of fire. Their clothes burst into flame and their skin blackened even through the shield of Buttons' power and now the Cobleys screamed in pain and fear. Their attacks faltered as they threw their strength into escaping this fiery tomb.

Buttons held them tighter and pushed on.

There, through the thick molten sea lay a solid, glowing mass and Buttons moved faster and faster still. The Cobleys redoubled their efforts, launching a devastating series of attacks as they realised their only hope of escape was to destroy him. His burning flesh tore and his blood boiled away as they ripped into him, but the blade of the Morningstar would not be denied.

Something broke inside him as he flung them into the planets' core and still he would not relent. Buttons poured more and more of his power into shackles of pure force and will that wrapped around the Cobleys, wrapped around and snaked through the core to bind them in place. Buttons knew he had given up too much, he knew he would never be the same again even if he had the strength left to leave this place, but it was a price he was glad to pay.

The Cobleys struggled but it was no use. They lay splayed against the white-hot core and could do nothing but scream as their bodies burned, healed and burned again. Buttons smiled grimly as he poured the last of his strength into binding them to their eternal prison.

How's this for a lake of fire, you arrogant swine?

The burning, blinding glare around him began to dim and the blade of the Morningstar finally let go as all around him the darkness drew in.

THIRTY TWO

Cross stared at Lincoln without expression, eyes flicking to the carbine pointing at his chest. Lincoln shook his head. "Don't try it, Cross", he warned, "Even you're not that fast." Cross silently cursed. He knew Lincoln was right. The thought of getting shot didn't worry him but he knew he'd have a dozen rounds in him before he got close and the thought of failing to avenge Gus and Kate simply wasn't acceptable.
Stay quiet, play for time. Wait for a chance.

He'd seen Buttons destroy the coven and the demons without breaking stride and almost dared to hope until the little man disappeared through a portal to who knew where. Cross glanced towards Andariel, hanging bloodied and burning on spears of stone and finally towards the grinning Malleus who sauntered towards him.

"Daniel, well done, well done indeed." The Demon Lord looked around him and smiled at the carnage. "I really didn't think you'd make it this far." He looked towards Miles who was picking himself up from the floor. "I told you he was a rare man, didn't I?" Miles said nothing, merely glaring at Cross with murderous eyes.

Cross spat blood at his feet and grinned at them. This was it, game over. Nothing said he had to go quietly though. "Come on then, dickheads. Who's first?" Malleus laughed in unfeigned delight. "I really will be sorry to see you go, Daniel, but you won't be going just yet. You've worked so hard to get here it wouldn't be fair to let you miss out on the real fun."
Malleus cocked his head as though he was listening to something and then smiled. "And the fun is just about to start now."

He turned towards the end of the large room and spread his arms in welcome. With a thundering crash the air split with a flare of golden fire and six impossibly tall and shining figures appeared. Golden, white and rainbow lights played about them and they moved with unearthly grace. They turned their faceless heads as they silently surveyed the room. The inhuman figures paused as they saw Andariel and at some silent signal one of them moved to free her from the molten spears of stone.

The others faced the grinning Malleus. "Welcome, brothers!" he crowed. He nodded at one of Angels. Laraziniel, how long has it been?" The Angels said nothing, and Malleus shook his head. "Always so bloody dour". He gestured towards the humans behind him. "May I introduce Miles, Lincoln and Daniel? They've all been instrumental in setting up this little reunion, some more eagerly than others it must be said."

The Demon Lord looked around in mock dismay. "But you didn't come all this way just to meet some humans, did you? No, it wouldn't be a proper party unless we got the family back together would it?"

Cross felt the air grow cold behind him and he turned to see a growing spot of inky darkness hanging in the air. A frigid wind blew as snow and ash drifted into the room followed by eight, ten, then a dozen towering, bestial demons.
Well, that's fucked it.

The Angels stepped back and the golden light flared again as more of their celestial kin crossed over from Heaven and the frigid wind grew stronger as yet more Demons crawled from Hell. Cross stood between them, trapped between the frigid dark and cold light.

He knew he was witnessing something that hadn't happened since the dawn of time and some part of his mind screamed and rebelled at the impossible sight while another part, that dry soldier's part, simply snorted a laugh. *I'm stuck in the middle at the OK fucking Corral. Ringside at the end of the world. In Surrey.*

The walls of the mansion began to tremble and groan and the air itself shuddered as the titanic powers that had shaped the universe began to fill the room. "YES!" Roared Malleus. "YESSSS!" and the Demon Lord laughed and laughed. Cross tore his eyes away from the scene and looked at Miles and Lincoln.

Miles wore a smile of pure, unfeigned joy, his eyes half closed as he thrilled at the apocalyptic carnage to come. Lincoln looked this way and that, eyes darting between the opposing forces.

His breathing was rapid but even and Cross knew that even though he was terrified, Lincoln had that fear under ruthless control. He was calculating, mapping out the possibilities and weighing up his best chance of survival. Lincoln was *distracted*.

There was nothing Cross could do about Armageddon now, whatever was left of creation after the war would have to manage without Daniel Cross. Getting payback for Gus and Kate though? *That* he could do.

Cross inched his hand towards the waistband of his trousers, slipping his hand into his underwear and closing his fingers around the small, flesh-crawling alien knife he'd snatched from Buttons' kitchen table and kept hidden there.

Cross wasn't sure what he was happier about, settling up for Gus and Kate or finally getting that awful knife away from his balls. He slid the *Kraal* from the waistband of his trousers and palmed it, keeping it hidden from view as he focused on Lincoln. Cross knew he had one chance and even with Lincoln being distracted, one maybe two seconds if he was lucky. *Not yet, not yet....Now!*

Cross darted forward with the alien blade extended. Lincoln caught the movement from the corner of his eye and spun to face him.

The carbine boomed.

THIRTY THREE

Andariel was barely conscious. Her borrowed body was a charred, bloody and broken mess, bearing at least a dozen wounds that should have killed her outright but still she held on. She hung limply in an Angels' grip as she struggled to hold her shattered body together. Why she didn't know. It would have been so easy to let go, to fall into darkness before waking again in the cold light of Heaven.

And then what? To war? To kill and kill and burn and burn until nothing was left? No, better to try and end it here. If she could hold on long enough then perhaps one of the demons would destroy her, sparing her from another millennia of carnage. Part of her smiled at that, one of her mortal enemies delivering her such mercy. She could barely see through her tears and the haze of pain, but she could still *feel*.

Andariel could feel the doors between worlds opening, could feel the building pressure as fell powers gathered once again on the mortal plane. She could feel Cross. Feel his tightly controlled rage and frustration, felt those emotions suddenly snuffed out as they were smothered by a glacial calm. Then, what was this? *Triumph?*

Cross uncoiled like a striking snake, his hand whipping forward to fling the *Kraal* at Lincoln. He didn't hear the gunshots, but he felt the hammer-blows of impact as the bullets slammed into him. Cross fell back, his legs suddenly unable to support his weight but still he smiled as he folded around the pain of his wounds. *Gotcha.*

Demon and Angel alike ignored the sounds of the gun going off, the sound of the puny, mortal weapon barely even registering. All of them stopped short at the screams though. The *Kraal* hit Lincoln low in the gut, usually a painful but not normally lethal place to get hit. Cross had no idea what the *Kraal* would do but going by what Andariel and Buttons had said he was fairly certain any wound it delivered would be both fatal and extremely painful. He wasn't disappointed.

The Demons marvelled at the sound. Even they, masters of delivering inconceivable pain had never coaxed such pure agony from a mortal. Lincoln fell to the floor, jerking and writhing as the venom of the *Kraal* did its terrible work. The *Kraal* were extinct long before mankind's ancestors had crawled from the sea, but it was as if the venom had been designed solely to inflict pain on the human body as it bonded seamlessly with every nerve ending and began to flay them.

His scream became an inchoate roar, dying to a ragged exhalation as his vocal chords tore from the force of his agonised shout. Around the wound in his stomach, Lincoln's skin began to bubble where the *Kraal's* venom grew stronger as it fed on live flesh. Skin and muscle sloughed off in red, yellow and blackened lumps and Lincoln's whispering scream became a bubbling wail as the flesh around his throat began to liquefy. With a terrifying rapidity, although not nearly quickly enough for Lincoln Barnes, the perverted blade reduced what used to be a man into a quivering, stinking puddle.

Cross coughed wetly and grinned through bloodied teeth. He let his head fall back to the floor. He tilted his head and looked through dimming eyes at the ever-growing ranks of Heaven and Hell and at the smiling Malleus. Cross weakly raised a middle finger and then his strength finally deserted him.

The Demon lord ignored the dying man. All his sorry species would be joining him soon enough. "Well", he drawled. "That's something you don't see every day." He briskly clapped his hands. "Now, where were we?" The Demons roared, their fury met by a rising clarion from the Angels as each prepared to unleash their unearthly, cataclysmic power to strike the first blow of the war. The house shook, cracks appearing in the walls as the furniture began to smoulder and tremble. Underneath the sound and fury, a single Angel wept. Suddenly there was silence. A complete and total silence and Angel and Demon alike looked around in confusion as their power was suddenly stripped away, held in the grip of a strength of will so immense it had set the stars aflame and birthed entire galaxies. Malleus screamed in fury and underneath the deafening roar of his rage, a single Angel laughed in triumphant delight. "Oh, you're fucked now, sunshine!"

The silence was ripped away in an explosion of raw, unimaginable power. The cracks in the walls tore open, whole sections falling away and the immaculately kept gardens, along with acres of the surrounding estate erupted skyward, trees flattening in a circle of devastation from the shockwave. Through the pain of her wounds and the ear-splitting tornado of power that raged around her, Andariel smiled. It looked like Lucifer had gotten their message after all.

THIRTY FOUR

Buttons opened his eyes and just as quickly closed them against the molten glare around him. He must have blacked out. Buttons said a silent prayer of thanks that even subconsciously he'd kept his shield up or the pressure and heat would have annihilated him. It still might. Buttons couldn't remember ever being this weak, even when he was a mortal man.

His clothing hung in charred and bloodied tatters and dozens of wounds criss-crossed his body, some deep enough to show the glare of bone through his blackened skin. Buttons floated through rivers of molten rock and metal and willed himself to move. He doubted he had the strength to make it back to the surface, but he had to try.

You bloody idiot. No you don't.

Could he summon a portal? That would certainly take the last of his strength and if he failed then he'd burn and die a trillion miles from home, and if he did make it back? He'd be in no shape to do anything but die there, but at least his friends would know he'd tried.

Buttons closed his eyes and tried to do the impossible one last time.

THIRTY FIVE

"This has gone far enough."

The voice was calm and quiet but clearly heard throughout the room. Between the massed ranks of shining, unearthly Angels and hulking, bestial Demons stood Lucifer. He appeared as a mortal man, tall and slim and handsome in a nondescript way. The Devil could have appeared on any street and passed unnoticed, yet somehow, he still seemed to tower above them all.

Lucifer said nothing for a time, simply surveying the room. He raised a single eyebrow at the remains of Lincoln and the softly steaming *Kraal* that lay amidst the ruin that used to be a man. He glanced at Malleus, stolen face frozen in a snarl, and his lips twitched with the hint of a smile. He saw the battered, bloody form of Andariel kneeling amongst her brothers and waved a hand towards her.

Free from the grasp of his power she fell forward, face striking the floor with an audible thud. She lay there for a moment and then slowly, painfully pulled herself to her feet. Lucifer made no move to help her. Andariel hobbled towards Cross who had managed to prop himself up against one of the shattered walls. Lucifer fell into step beside her and silently offered her his arm. She nodded once and then leant against him as he led her across the room.

Andariel gasped in pain as Lucifer lowered her to the blood-soaked floor beside her friend and her eyes filled with tears as she looked at the pallor of his face and the blood that bubbled from his lips. She counted four, no five wounds in his chest and abdomen and knew he was beyond saving. It was a miracle he'd held on as long as he had. Andariel laid a gentle hand on his cheek and Cross smiled weakly at her.

"Bloody hell, luv. We did it."

She managed to return the smile. "Of course we did you daft lump."

Cross looked at Lucifer and said simply "Thank you". The Morningstar smiled that slight smile again. "Not usually the first words I hear. You're welcome." Lucifer turned and crooked a finger at Malleus. "Come here" he said, and Malleus was pulled towards them, still frozen in the grip of Lucifers' power. The Devil gestured towards him and Malleus was able to speak again.

"False Lord! Traitor! Lackey of Heaven!" The Demon lord raged at his master. Lucifer stayed silent while Malleus continued his rant. "Why? Why stop me? I but continue the war that *you* began, the war you no longer have the will to prosecute!" Malleus spat at Lucifers' feet. "You're weak! Too weak to rule us, you don't deserve..." Lucifer gestured again and Malleus fell silent.

Andariel looked around at the massed ranks of Heaven and Hell, all held immobile by the sheer force of Lucifers' will and then grinned at Malleus. "He doesn't look that weak to me, dickhead." Cross coughed a bloody laugh, wincing at the pain but then smiling again as he looked at the silently raging Demon lord. "I told you we'd stop you." He smiled at Andariel and then looked at Malleus again. "Dickhead."

Cross glanced at Lucifer. "So, what happens now?" he asked.

"Malleus and the rest of my unruly children will come with me. It looks like they're overdue a very long and uncomfortable talking to." The Devil looked down at him. "But that's not what you meant, is it?" Cross went to reply but Lucifer held up a hand, his attention shifting to the centre of the room before looking back at Cross and Andariel. "Sorry, the fun police are here."

As he spoke more golden light flared and another angel

appeared. He was different from the others, appearing, like Lucifer, as a mortal man. Like Lucifer he said nothing at first and merely surveyed the room. Finally, he looked over at the Morningstar and inclined his head. "Brother."

Lucifer returned the nod. "Michael." The Archangel Michael simply looked at him for a time and then his stern visage softened slightly. "It is good to see you." Lucifer smiled that small, half smile. "You too, brother." Michael gestured towards Malleus and the rest of the Demons. "Might I suggest you keep a tighter rein on the children?"

Lucifer shrugged. "They're Demons, Michael. Rebelling is part of the job description." He nodded towards the Angelic host. "I'm not throwing stones, but your own brood were just as quick to get into the ring."

Michael smiled at that. "They're young. Remember what we were like a few million years ago?" The Archangel shook his head, suddenly serious. "This could have really got out of hand though." He looked at Lucifer. "Thank you." Lucifer raised an eyebrow. "Twice in one day?"

Michael looked at him curiously, but Lucifer waved the unspoken question away. "It's not me you should be thanking, Michael." He waved towards Andariel and Cross who now lay slumped together against the wall. "It was these and....ah, excuse me a moment would you?" with that the Devil disappeared, only to reappear a second later with the burned and bloodied form of Buttons cradled in his arms. He lay the Demon hunter beside his friends. If anything, Buttons looked in a worse state than Cross and Andariel.

Lucfier sighed and laid a gentle hand on Buttons' head. "Ah, old friend. You never did know when to give up." Buttons opened his eyes and smiled up at his master. "You made it then? Better late than never," he wheezed, and the Devil laughed in genuine amusement.
Michael walked over to stand above them.

He peered at Andariel. "Why am I not surprised?" he said, almost to himself. The Archangel looked at them for a time and then bowed deeply. "Please accept my thanks, the thanks of the host and the gratitude of all the wardens of creation. You are owed a debt that can never be repaid."

"What?! Of course it bloody can!" cried Andariel.

"Excuse me?"

"Save him," pleaded the Angel as she looked at Cross. "He deserves that much at least. Don't let him die after all he's done. Don't let him…" Her voice faltered as she looked from Michael to Lucifer.

Both Archangel and Devil looked pained. Michael knelt beside the dying Cross and grasped his arm. "I'm sorry. You deserve a better fate than this, a better fate than…"

"Than me." Lucifer said flatly.

Buttons struggled to his feet to look his master in the eye. "Is there really nothing that can be done? Can't the rules be ignored just once?"

Lucifer joined Michael and knelt beside Cross. "I'm sorry, Daniel, but there are some rules that can't be broken, even by me for they are carved into the bones of creation itself." He smiled sadly. "Cold comfort I know but for the first time I wish it could be different."

Cross waved the apology away. "Don't worry, I knew what I was signing up for. There's one thing you could do for me though?"

"Ask. If I can, I will."

"I wouldn't mind getting a break now and again to watch Malleus get the screws put to him."

Lucifer looked at Malleus and chuckled. "That I can do."

"It's not right!" wailed Andariel. "After all he's done it isn't…"

"Fair?" interrupted Michael. "No, it isn't. The law rarely is." The Archangel looked at Cross. "Once again, you have my thanks, Daniel Cross." He looked at Andariel. "Best say your farewells now, Andarielastenaama, we must take our leave of this world."

The weeping Andariel gathered Cross into her arms. He returned the embrace as best he could but could no longer lift his left arm from the floor. "I'm sorry, Daniel," she sobbed. "I'm so sorry!"

Cross squeezed her with his still functioning right arm, alarmed at how weak he was. He was growing weaker, and colder, by the second. He knew he didn't have long left and fought back a surge of panic at the thought of what awaited him. For all his bravado he was terrified and for all his professed equanimity he raged at the injustice of it all, that not even saving the universe was enough to earn him a reprieve.

Weakly, Cross pushed Andariel away. "Go home, my friend, and don't let Michael and the others give you any shit. Just remember that you breaking the rules now and again stopped creation going up in flames." He smiled at her. "And remember that I love you."

Andariel gave him a final squeeze, staring at his smiling, bloody face to commit it to memory and then stumbled back to stand, weeping bitterly, beside Michael. The Archangel raised his face to the sky and with a flash of golden light the Angels were gone. Buttons struggled to a kneeling position and then grasped Cross's forearm in the age-old warriors' grip. "It was an honour to fight alongside you, Daniel. I won't forget you."

Cross smiled at him. "We gave them a fucking good hiding, didn't we?"

Buttons laughed, almost despite himself, but was unable to stop his voice breaking. Tears ran down his blackened cheeks. "Yes, yes we did," he choked. Cross's vision was dimming now but still he caught a furtive movement at the back of the room.

"Lucifer, can I ask one more favour?"

"Of course, Daniel."

Cross nodded weakly towards the back of the room. "Can you do something about that little shit?"

Lucifer turned to see Miles Harrington trying to creep through a gap in one of the shattered walls. "With pleasure." The Morningstar gestured and Cross winced as the *Kraal* flew

317

through the air to slam into Miles' lower back. After the agonised screaming had faded to a wet burble, Lucifer turned away from the rapidly liquefying Miles Harrington to look at Cross.

He shrugged. "I was curious to see what that thing would actually do."

Cross's strength was finally gone and with it his ability to ignore the pain of his wounds. He cried out and the Morningstar knelt beside him. Lucifer laid a hand on his head. "Sleep now, Daniel Cross. Sleep without pain and know that if any mercy is to be found in Hell then you shall surely find it."

The pain faded from Cross's face and then he was gone.

Lucifer stood and sighed, staring down at Cross's body for a long time.

"Master?"

Lucifer looked at the silently weeping Buttons. "I don't want to do this anymore," whispered the little man.

The Devil nodded and laid a gentle hand on his shoulder. "I understand. You have served me well, old friend. Know that you go with my thanks and my hope that you can find some measure of peace. Go well and know that I will miss you."

Buttons nodded his thanks and slowly, painfully bowed to his master one final time. He turned and began to walk slowly from the ruined room. As he reached the remains of the door, Lucifer spoke again.

"Actually, there is one last thing you can do for me."

****

A few miles away from the Harringtons' estate stood the Shepherd and Dog pub. A crowd of excitedly babbling drinkers had gathered on the road outside to stare at the columns of smoke rising in the near distance. They'd heard the booms and the distant rattle of what some swore was gunfire and seen their drinks quiver in their glasses as strange lights flashed in the sky and the ground trembled. Now they could hear sirens and saw the flashing of more familiar blue lights as the authorities hurried to the scene.

In the far corner of the beer garden, out the back of the pub and well away from the gawking crowds, two men studiously ignored the whole thing. Pat and Jerry Conway (no relation) were on their fourth pint and hadn't said a word to each other about what might be happening back at the estate. Finally, Jerry looked up from his glass and over to Pat.

"Reckon you made the right call us coming down here, Pat."

Pat snorted and stood up. "Course I bloody did. Fancy another?"

Jerry nodded and drained his glass. Neither of them would say another word on the subject.

At the end of it all it came down to this. Two old soldiers having a pint together.

Cross would have been pleased.

EPILOGUE

Cross lay naked and shivering on the cold stone floor of his cell as his new body healed. He whimpered as his torn flesh began to knit together, then cried out as his broken left leg snapped back into place. His cry became a scream as his shattered ribs ground against each other in his chest and he wept as he curled into a despairing ball.

It wasn't just the pain, although that was bad enough, but the knowledge that soon, very soon, it would all begin again and after they finally finished with him he would be tossed back in his cell to painfully heal before they tortured him again and again and again. Cross wept and his tears were a bitter sting on his wounds.

This was his eternity. This was his reward for saving creation itself and what made it worse was the knowledge that if he hadn't fought so hard, if he'd just let the universe burn then he probably wouldn't be here. His immortal soul in eternal torment weighed against the lives of countless billions. It had seemed a fair bargain at the time and he thought that knowing he'd saved so many and beaten such impossible odds would be enough to sustain him.

It wasn't.

Slowly but surely, Cross felt himself slipping into despair. He knew that he was losing some vital part of himself and perhaps the worst thing was that he was struggling to care. Even the anger, the rage he felt at his abandonment was beginning to die. Cross ruefully admitted to himself that on some level he had believed that Lucifer wouldn't let him spend eternity in torment, that the ruler of Hell would, somehow, protect him, but Lucifer was nowhere to be seen.

His new flesh was almost healed now, and the pain began to fade. Cross's ever-present fear bloomed into terror. Somehow, they knew. They always knew when they could take him and hurt him again and his terror intensified as he heard noises from outside his cell. Cross skittered backwards on all fours to get as far away from the door as he could, pressing himself into a corner and covering his face with his hands as if doing so could ward off the inevitable.

This turned out to be a fortuitous move as the door was blasted from its hinges and flew into the cell to crash into the wall, shortly followed by what was left of a demon. Cross raised his head from his hands and almost dared to hope. For the first time in what felt like a thousand years his mouth twitched into the forgotten shape of a smile as a little man poked his head through the doorway.

"Finally, there you are!" said Buttons. "This place is like a bloody maze!"
Cross's voice was cracked and wavering. "Please," he whispered. "Please tell me it's really you!" Cross's burgeoning elation quickly turned to fear as he wondered if this was just a new form of torture and that his friend would disappear to be replaced by the laughing visage of a demon.

Buttons' heart ached to see Cross like this and slowly walked forward, arms outstretched and palms held outwards. "It's me, my friend. It's really me." Buttons edged forward as though he were approaching a skittish animal and then knelt beside Cross. Slowly, very slowly he reached out and laid a gentle hand on his Cross's head. At his touch, Cross felt his fear and despair melt away as Buttons poured his strength, and his love, into his friend. Cross raised his head and pulled Buttons into an embrace. "Bloody hell, it's good to see you, mate."

Buttons returned the hug and then disengaged himself, rising to his feet and grasping Cross's arm to help him up. "You too, Daniel." The little man looked shamefaced. "I'm sorry it took me so long." Cross waved the apology away. He didn't want to know how long he'd been here. He had a feeling it wasn't long at all and yet it felt like a lifetime. That his friend had come for him, had walked into Hell for him was all he needed to know.

Buttons was wearing a rucksack which he twitched off his shoulder and held out to Cross. "Here," he said, "Get dressed, we won't have long". He moved to the doorway and kept a lookout as Cross quickly dressed, the clothes feeling strange on his skin after being naked for so long.

"How?" he asked, and Buttons looked round with a quizzical expression. "I thought Lucifer said getting me out of here would violate the sacred laws of the cosmos or something?"

Buttons snorted a laugh. "It was his idea. He's the Devil, he literally invented breaking the rules." The little man looked at Cross apologetically. "He would have acted himself, and sooner if he could have done. As it is he had to keep his distance."

Cross smiled. It seemed that black-ops and plausible deniability were still a thing even in the afterlife. He understood why Lucifer had stayed clear, but it pleased him to know that he hadn't been abandoned here after all. The little man patted his pockets and then smiled as he found what he was looking for.

"Here." He said and threw a packet of cigarettes and a lighter to Cross who deftly plucked them out of the air with a smile.

"Reverend, you're a bloody lifesaver" Cross lit a cigarette and inhaled with obvious relish. He blew a plume of smoke towards the ceiling. "Ok then, what's the plan?" Buttons was still watching the corridor and spoke without looking round.

"The plan is to get out of here, and quick as we can." He turned his head and smiled. "Then we're going to meet a friend for a drink or ten."

Cross laughed. "Andariel? I didn't think Michael would let her out to play anymore?"

Buttons shook his head and smiled. "After what she did? She's a bit of a celebrity up there now so she can pretty much do what she wants". He smiled wryly. "Which she's loving every minute of as you can imagine." The little man looked suddenly serious. "She would have been here, Daniel, but..."

"I know, mate", interrupted Cross, "You coming down here is risky enough but they'd have sniffed her out a mile away. I know she'd have been here if she could" He buttoned his shirt, threw on his jacket and lit another cigarette. "Ready when you are, Reverend"

Buttons smiled in satisfaction as he looked at him. He was Daniel Cross again. "We're not going to make it out of here without a fight my friend, are you ready for it?"
Cross clapped him on the shoulder and grinned. "Buttons, you've got no idea how much I'm looking forward to a good fight."

Laughing together, the two friends began the long walk out of Hell.

Printed in Great Britain
by Amazon